The Thicket

Also by Joe R. Lansdale

Edge of Dark Water
Leather Maiden
Lost Echoes
Sunset and Sawdust
The Bottoms
A Fine Dark Line
Freezer Burn

The Hap and Leonard Series
Devil Red
Vanilla Ride
Captain Outrageous
Rumble Tumble
Bad Chili
The Two-Bear Mambo
Mucho Mojo
Savage Season

JOE R. LANSDALE

The Thicket

MULHOLLAND
BOOKS
HODDER

First published in Great Britain in 2013 by Mulholland Books
An imprint of Hodder & Stoughton
An Hachette UK company

1

A CIP catalogue record for this title is available from the British Library

Trade Paperback ISBN 978 1 444 73691 5
eBook ISBN 978 1 444 73690 8

Printed and bound by CPI Group (UK) Ltd, Croydon, CR0 4YY

Hodder & Stoughton policy is to use papers that are natural, renewable and recyclable products and made from wood grown in sustainable forests. The logging and manufacturing processes are expected to conform to the environmental regulations of the country of origin.

Hodder & Stoughton Ltd
338 Euston Road
London NW1 3BH

For Terrill Lee Lankford

We remember our lives as if they were fables.

Anonymous

THE THICKET

1

I didn't suspect the day Grandfather came out and got me and my sister, Lula, and hauled us off toward the ferry that I'd soon end up with worse things happening than had already come upon us or that I'd take up with a gun-shooting dwarf, the son of a slave, and a big angry hog, let alone find true love and kill someone, but that's exactly how it was.

It was the pox got it all started. It had run through the country like a runaway mule and had been especially unkind to the close-by town of Hinge Gate. It showed up there as a bumpy, oozing death, and killed so many it was called an epidemic. Two of the ones that died were our ma and pa, and neither of them had ever been sick a day in their lives. I, on the other hand, was sickly all my early life up until the time I got my health, and Lula had been kind of scrawny her whole time, but neither of us took it. I was by this time a healthy sixteen-year-old, and she was fourteen and right on the verge of her bloom. That ole pox passed us by as if it was blind in one eye. It crept up on Ma and Pa, fevered them up, covered them in blisters, and made it so when they tried to breathe it sounded like a busted squeeze box. The worse thing was, we had to sit and watch them die, and there wasn't a damn thing we could do about it. We couldn't even touch them for fear of coming down with it.

Pox ran all through the town like it was looking for money. Dead people were piled up outside houses, loaded in wagons, buried quickly. In some cases they were burnt when nobody knew who they were, as there were folks who traveled through town and got it and died without leaving information on their names or where they'd been going. Sheriff Gaston finally had to put signs out on the roads coming in that said nobody could leave and spread it, and nobody could come in for fear of getting it.

There was people who burnt smoke pots around their houses and inside, thinking that would keep the pox out, but that didn't help—it just made it smoky and caused the ones who had it to have a harder time breathing than before.

We lived out on the edge of town, and I always figured it was the tinker who brought it around, carried it to our place like it was one of the wares in his wagon. I think when my pa shook hands with him and bought a skillet that was the end of it. He and Ma came down with it right away, though that tinker didn't have a spot of it on him that I could see.

Right away I rode into town on the mule and fetched the doctor. He came out, seen right off saving them was like trying to bring to life an oil painting. Wasn't a thing he could do, though he gave them a couple pills to take just so as to look like he was trying. A few days later Ma and Pa got real bad, and I rode into town to see I could get the doctor back out. Doctor had died himself of it, and was already buried, and someone had left a burning smoke pot on his grave. I knew that because I seen it out there in the cemetery when I was riding in, and then seen it again going out, knowing then whose grave it was. I guess someone thought that smoke would keep it from spreading from the dead body. Hard to know what people were really thinking, because that pox had not only killed a good bunch of folks, it had scared the living and taken their reason, and mine wasn't all that good, either.

When I got back home Ma and Pa were both dead, and there was Lula out in the yard crying, a strangled chicken still flopping in one hand because she was setting about making dinner, even with them dead in the house. Me and Lula had been living out under a tree to stay out of the way of getting the pox, and we cooked out there and ate out there. Grandpa would come in and check on Ma and Pa cause he couldn't catch it. He'd had it and lived through it when he was younger, and he couldn't get it anymore. He caught it way up among the Cheyenne near the Wind River Range, which was nowhere close to where we were in East Texas. He got it the same way the Cheyenne did—some infected blankets given to them by white folks as a kind of joke. He was a missionary and had lived up there with them. Both he and Grandma had it and lived, and then some years later Grandma was run over by a frightened cow near Gilmer, Texas, while she was trying to calm it down for milking. The pox couldn't kill her, but a cow that didn't want to be milked had.

I barely remember Grandma. I guess I must have been about five when that cow done her in. Lula was three years old. Grandpa, according to family story, shot the cow and ate it. I guess he considered that was getting even, having a steak made of the murderer. I never heard him speak sadly of the death of Grandma or the cow, but he and Grandma seemed to have gotten along fine, and up until that day neither he nor the cow had experienced a minute's trouble, I've been told.

On the day Ma and Pa died, I went in and looked at them, but I didn't stand too close and I didn't touch nothing. They looked horrible, all pocked over and bloody where they had scratched and those little odd blisters with the dents in the middle had broken open and bled. I rode our tired old mule over to Grandpa, who lived down from us a little ways, and he put on his dusty suit coat and hat and rode back beside me, driving his wagon. He brought with him some sacks of lime he had for his garden and a couple of pine boxes he had already built, being pretty certain what was coming. He had also packed some bags and put them in the wagon, too, but at the time I didn't know what that was about and was too stunned to ask. If a pig had flown by with a deck of cards in its teeth it wouldn't have fazed me.

Me and Grandpa dug graves for Ma and Pa. Because Grandpa couldn't get the pox, he rolled them onto fresh sheets, dragged them out of the house, lifted them into those coffins, and poured lime on them. I helped him lower the coffins down in the holes with rope. He said when we were covering them up he felt the lime would hold back the disease so it wouldn't spread from their bodies and give it to others. I don't know. I figure six feet of dirt helped quite a bit.

We got them buried and he preached some words over them with the Bible in his hand, but I couldn't tell you what section he preached from. I was too stunned to tell, and Lula looked as if her mind had gone to a place no one could find; she hadn't said anything since I found her with the dead chicken, which we had ended up tossing in a ditch. When he finished up with the preaching, he set fire to the house and put us in the wagon and started us out, my old mule tied on a rope line behind the wagon.

"Where are we going?" I said, looking back at our blazing home. It was all I knew to say. Lula was all huddled up and not talking at all. Anyone didn't know her they'd have thought she was a pretty mute.

"Well, Jack," Grandpa said without so much as looking over his shoulder, "we're not going back to that burning house, that's for sure. You're going on up to Kansas to stay with your Aunt Tessle."

"I don't even know I've met her," Lula said, this being something that brought her out of her stupor and gave her a tongue. She said it so suddenly and unexpectedly I hopped a little, and I think Grandpa did, too.

"I barely remember her," I said.

"Be that as it is, you're going to live with her," Grandpa said. "She don't know it yet, but I figured it might be best not to give her time to recollect on it. We'll spring a surprise on her. And considering I'm planning on staying as well, though I'll come a little later, so as not to overwhelm the situation, it'll be a surprise. Never cared for Tessle, actually, as she always seemed to be Mama's favorite, but tragedy makes strange bedfellows."

"You sure that's the best way?" I said. "Just showing up?"

"It might not be the best way," he said, "but it'll be our way. I'll tell you two another thing. I saw this coming, and I've sold off all my livestock except these two mules, and you have your pa's mule, and you now have contracts for both pieces of land, your father's and mine. They're in the bank at Sylvester. I didn't put them in your hometown bank because I figured with all the pox going on, there was just too much confusion. I have set it all up with a lawyer named Cowton Little. He's to sell the property for a fair price, when you're ready, and give you two the money, minus his commission, of course. I have no idea how long this will take, but mine is prime real estate when the town grows out, and it will. Your folks' land is good land, too, soon as the pox passes, and there's no consideration on how they died, it, too, will be prime. You understanding all this?"

We both said we understood, though Lula seemed to have drifted away again, like a balloon. She was flighty enough under normal circumstances, always wondering about the shape of clouds and asking about why things were green or some such and never taking "God made it that way" as an answer. She was always looking for some greater truth, like there was one. Grandpa used to say she always had to figure that if there was a hole in the ground something was in it, and for a reason, and it had a history, even if she couldn't see it. She never could accept a hole might be empty and if something was in it, it might not have thought on why or how it got there at all. "Beware a woman that wants reasons for everything," he said.

Grandpa reached inside his suit coat and pulled out a paper, said, "This here is all the paperwork you'll need on the matter of the property. I go up to Kansas I won't be coming back, and you might not, either, but you can do your dealings with the lawyer by mail, you need to."

I took the papers he gave me, folded them up, and stuck them down deep into the pocket of my overalls.

"You mind those papers, now," Grandpa said.

"I will," I said.

"They're in both your names, but if one of you was to get killed or die, then it'll go to the other. You both get killed, well, I guess if I'm still alive it will go back to me, and if we're all dead, I guess Tessle owns everything, though I thought about giving it to one of the churches in town, but they're all Baptist and they're going to hell. I thought maybe I could start a Methodist church on my land, but that ain't gonna happen now. Even if I wasn't leaving, I haven't got the energy for it. I left you as the executor, though, Jack. Lula gets a piece of any part or all of the land you sell, but it's yours to make the deal because you're the oldest and a man, or will be one."

Now, it may seem I was taking all this damn well, the death of my parents, but I assure you I was not. I had sort of seen it coming for a few days, and there had been so much death about I guess I had embraced the whole thing better than I might had I just got up and found them dead without any sign of sickness. We had even laid aside clothes early on and kept them at Grandpa's, just in case they didn't pull through. They were something that might be clean of the pox and out of the house. I realized now those clean clothes were still in those bags he had packed for us, along with other things we might need. He had just rolled them up in the sheets and put them down. That sounds cold, but Grandpa was a practical man.

Still, down deep in my bones—and I'm sure it was the same with Lula and even Grandpa, for that matter—I was trying to get my heart and head wrapped around the idea that they had been taken so brutally and so quickly from us. It was like I was too dry to cry. I wanted to but couldn't. Lula was the same way. That's how we Parkers were. We took what came the way it came. Least it was that way on the surface. You scratched us a little, though, you could find some jelly there pretty quick. We were the kind that found it hard to cry, but once we got started you best be ready for high water and the loading of animals two by two.

So there we sat in that butt-rattling wagon, as stunned as if a stone had been dropped on our heads. Pa's mule was tied to the rear of it. Lula was in the wagon bed, and I was up beside Grandpa, him clucking to his mules and being rather pleasant with them, which was different from what I was used to. Pa always cussed them and called them names and such. He didn't mean nothing by it. He was good to those mules. That kind of talk was just his way, and the mules understood it and dismissed it, being a whole lot smarter than horses. Two horses put together haven't got the brains of one old mule, and bad language can make them nervous.

"Way I figure it," Grandpa said, "I can leave out for a few days to get you to the train over at Tyler, and then you can go on up to Kansas. I'll give you some directions on how to find Tessle, but it wouldn't hurt when you got there if you asked about for her house, cause I don't remember where she lives all that well. I can come on by wagon, as there's some places I want to see along the way. I figure this is my last trip anywhere. Besides, I don't want to buy three tickets."

I was surprised he wanted to buy two. Daddy always said Grandpa was so tight that when he blinked the skin on his pecker rolled back. Grandma was always wanting some little thing or another, Mother said, and he wouldn't want to buy it. He kept everything he had up to snuff so not much needed replacing; he had tools he had bought used that looked better than new ones cause of the way he kept them. He figured you wanted to buy something, if you couldn't use it for something practical or eat it, then you didn't need it. And that included new sun hats and dresses Grandma wanted. I guess with Ma and Pa dead, and him realizing he might have to put up with us all the way to Kansas, maybe it was worth two train tickets just to have peace and quiet and the pleasure of his own company.

"Don't you think you ought to write her a letter?" I said, still thinking on Tessle. "Let her know we're coming?"

"By the time I write and mail it and it gets there, you two could have the pox. No, sir. You and your sister are leaving out of here today."

"Yes, sir," I said.

"They were just fine a few days back," Lula said. It had popped out of her like a seed squeezed from a pomegranate.

"That's how it works," Grandpa said. Sitting by him on the wagon seat, I felt him tremble a bit, which was the only sign he'd given yet that the whole thing had got to him in any way. I reckon a man who has buried a number of children, preached some funerals, butchered animals for food, seen death among the Cheyenne, and survived the pox gets a bit firm in his thinking about dying; and then there's that whole thing about Grandma being killed by a cow. He was a religious man and always had the view he'd see everybody again in heaven. It was a firm and solid thing with him, and it comforted him under all circumstances, and he had taught me that was the way to deal with the world, and to not go and think too much on my own, cause it might lead to other ideas that might be right but unpleasant.

As we went, I saw the sky was darkening up more in the northwest, and the smell of rain was on the air, sweet and dirty, like a damp dog. When we got to the Sabine River the sky was furious black, and the bridge for the crossing was burnt out. There were just a few timbers on both sides of the water, and they were charred and broken down. It wasn't a wide expanse of river, but it was broad enough and deep enough a bridge was normally needed, except in a really dry season.

There was a shallow crossing about five miles down, but that wouldn't be necessary, because now there was a ferry that came across in place of the bridge. We could see it on the other side. It was a pretty wide ferry and could hold a good bit of horses and such, and the man who was managing it was a big, hatless, redheaded fellow, like me. He was waiting for a wagon pulled by two big white horses to roll off the ferry, and when that was done he closed up the gate, started pulling on one of the ropes that was hooked to a trolley rig, and began drawing the ferry back across.

The ferry was new, built as of recent, and the ferryman was having a hard time of it. There was something about his motions that made me think he was new to the process, as if it were a recent trade he had taken up. We waited on him to get to our side, and when he did, he threw a kind of wooden brake on the rope and let down the hatch on our bank of the river. He stepped out on solid ground in a manner that made him look as if he were standing on peg legs, which was for me another clue to his newness to the profession. Grandpa gave me the lines, got off the wagon, and walked over to him. I could hear them talking.

"What happened to the bridge?" Grandpa said.

"Burnt down," said the ferryman.

"I can see that. When?"

"Oh, a month ago thereabouts."

"How?"

"Caught on fire."

"I know it caught on fire, but how did it catch on fire?"

"I can't say."

"Is someone going to build it back?"

"I ain't," said the ferryman.

"Guess not. How much?"

"Two bits."

Grandpa stared at the ferryman as if he had just asked him if he'd like a stick in the eye. "Two bits? You are surely exaggerating."

"Nope," said the ferryman. "Don't think so. If exaggerating means I might be saying a price I don't mean, I ain't doing that, not even a little bit."

"That's highway robbery," Grandpa said.

"No, sir. That's the fee to cross this river on my brand-new ferry," said the ferryman, scratching at his red hair. "You don't want to pay, you can go on up five miles and cross in the shallows. But you do that, you got a rough patch before you can get on a trail that will then lead to the road, say, a mile or so later. It would be a tough go for a wagon."

"I need to get across now," Grandpa said. "Not five miles from now."

"Well, then you're going to need to pay two bits, now, aren't you? You could maybe swim the horses across, but it's too deep for a wagon, and to float it, you'd have to cut trees and tie them to the sides, and that would take more time and effort than you might want to do with. Besides, I bet you ain't got an ax, and I don't loan any. So now that leaves you with the other choices, going that five miles to the shallows or turning around." The ferryman held out his hand.

Grandpa pushed his hat up on his head, letting his wild gray hair escape. "Very well, but I do it under protest, and with the warning to you that God does not like a thief."

"It's the toll—nothing thieving about it. It's just more than you want to pay, and God ain't needing to cross the river. You are. Now, you want on or don't you?"

Grandpa dug in his pocket like he was reaching down in some dark mine for the last piece of coal left in the world, and pulled out his hand with two bits in it, slapped it on the ferryman's palm, and came back to the wagon. He appeared more upset about that toll than he was about putting his son and daughter-in-law in the ground earlier that day.

He climbed up on the wagon and sat there for a moment, looked up at the sky. "I reckon we could go five miles, but that storm looks to be coming quick, so I gave him his overpriced fee, and I'll let him live in God's judgment."

"Yes, sir," I said.

"I think he burnt that bridge to build that ferry," Grandpa said as he looked down at the ferryman. "He looks to me like a man who would do that, don't you think? Not a God-fearing man at all."

"I don't know, sir," I said. "If you say so."

"I say so, but we need to cross. And when we get on the ferry, mind the ferryman and keep your distance. I think he has a head full of lice."

Grandpa clucked up the mules and started guiding the wagon toward the ferry. While he had been sitting there, contemplating, a big man on a sorrel horse had ridden up and got on the ferry. We could hear him discussing the fee with the ferryman. He seemed to come to the conclusion it was worth it a lot sooner than Grandpa had, and by the time we got down there, I could see that across the field, coming down the trail where there were still trees on either side, were two men on horses. Rain-cloud shadows lay over them like dirty moss. It looked like the ferry was going to be filled tight with folks and horses and our wagon.

Grandpa's mules were tied to a railing up front, and the wagon wheels at the back were scotched with blocks so they wouldn't roll. My old riding mule, Bessie, stayed tied to the rear of the wagon, and me and Lula stood near her—but not too near, as she had a habit of kicking out sideways like a cow, trying to clip you a good one if she felt you were too close to her rear end. I'm not sure what she thought might be going on back there, what plan we might have, but I want to note quickly that we were not Bessie's first owners.

The big man on the horse had dismounted, and he took his sorrel up front and tied it alongside one of our wagon mules. He came by us and looked at Lula, said, "Aren't you the prettiest thing?"

I haven't spoken on how Lula looked, really, and I guess I should now. She was tall and lean and redheaded, with her hair streaming out from under a pretty blue travel bonnet with a false yellow flower sewn on one side of it. She had a silver star on a chain around her neck. I had bought that for her in town in the General Store. There were other gewgaws there, but they were silver flowers and little hearts, and I reckon they would have suited her fine, but just the year before she had pulled me outside the house and pointed up at the night sky and said, "See that star there, Jack? I'm claiming that as mine." That made about as much sense as polka music to me, maybe less, but I remembered it, and when I was in town one day and had a bit of money, I bought it for her. She never took it off. I was proud to have given it to her, and I liked the way the light caught it and made it wink around her neck. She had on a light blue dress with yellow trim to match that flower, and she wore high-topped laced boots, black and shiny as axle grease. It was clothes that Grandpa had taken out of the house early on, before they got tainted with the pox. Dressed like she was, she looked like both a young woman and a child. She was pretty as a picture, but the way that man said it bothered me. Maybe it was the way he smiled and the way his eyes ran up and down her; nothing you could lay a hand on or put a word to, but something that made me keep an eye on him nonetheless.

Lula just said, "Thank you," and ducked her head modest-like.

The man said, "That ain't a bad looking set of mules, neither," which to my mind sort of put some dirt in his earlier remarks.

I don't think Grandpa heard all this. He was still fussy and talking to the ferryman, seeing if he could get back part of his money.

When that didn't happen, Grandpa said, "Well, then, what are we waiting for?"

"On those two men on horseback," the ferryman said.

"How about you take us across, then come back for them?"

"It's work for nothing," said the ferryman, scratching his red head, then looking at his fingernail to see if he had captured anything of interest.

"We paid our two bits," Grandpa said. "We should go across. Besides, two more, that would be a tight load on this craft."

The big man said, "Those are friends of mine, and we can all wait."

"We don't have to," Grandpa said.

"No," said the man. "But we will."

"I think we should," said the ferryman. "I think we should."

Now, let me explain something. Grandpa was a large man. He may have been around seventy, but he was still commanding, with a big shock of gray hair that was once red, and it surrounded his head like a lion's mane. He had a thick beard the color of dirty cotton, and that made him look even more like a lion, even when he was wearing a hat. He had a face that was always flushed. He looked as if he were about to boil over all the time. He called it his Irish skin. He was wide-shouldered and strong-looking, having done hard work all his life. And then there was that air about him of I-know-how-the-horse-ate-the-apple, this being due not only to his size and experience but his true and abiding belief that God was on his side and probably didn't care as much for anyone else. This was a sentiment I figured came from having been a preacher and feeling that he had been handed special knowledge about life, and that when he got to heaven he'd be singing hymns with God personally, maybe the two of them leaning together with smiles on their faces, passing some tasteful joke between them—meaning, of course, it wouldn't have anything to do with women or the outhouse.

But for all his size and bluster, when Grandpa looked at the big man who had rode in on the sorrel horse, he went quiet as a mouse tiptoeing on a soft blanket. He had seen something there that didn't set right with him, same as I had. Grandpa could be silent a lot of the time, but when he was anxious to get on his way, or was in a spin about money, he could be talkative and angry, way he had been earlier. Looking at that other fellow took it right out of him, sent him into a stone silence. I could see why. The man was big as Grandpa, easily half his age, and he had a face that looked to have been shaped with a rock and a stick wielded by an angry circus monkey. He was scarred up and his nose was bent and one of his eyes had a lid that drooped over it about halfway, so that his peeper seemed sneaky all the time. I was pretty sure that at some point someone had tried to cut his throat, cause he had a scar across it, jagged in spots. When he spoke, it sounded like he was trying to gargle with a mouthful of tacks. He was wearing an old derby hat, and though he could have done without it, it had a long white feather in it. His black suit was expensive-looking and new, but the way it fit, it was like the clothes were borrowed. To button that coat someone would have had to have let about ten pounds of air out of him and pulled it together on both sides with a team of mules.

Grandpa made a noise in his throat, which was about as far as he went to disagreeing with the big man, rested his hand on the wagon, and looked out at the water as if expecting Jesus to come walking up on it. The air had gotten that heavy feel it gets when a storm is coming, and the sky was as dark as a drunkard's dream. The man with the derby said to Grandpa, "You're a man used to getting your way, aren't you?"

Grandpa turned and looked at him. I think at this point he wanted to let it go, but that Parker pride was there. "I am a man that thinks everyone should act promptly and get things done, even if it's burying kin. Just today I buried my son and daughter-in-law."

"I suppose you believe your misery makes you special and that I should care about it," said the man with the derby.

"No," said Grandpa. "I don't. I am just stating a fact in answer to your question."

"I didn't ask you if you buried anyone. I said you were a man who was used to getting his way."

"I guess burying them was on my mind, so I spoke of it."

"Why don't you just keep your views about things to yourself?" said the big man. "Cause just this morning I was at a funeral myself. Rode up on it when it was finishing up and everyone was going off, and the grave diggers, couple of niggers, were going to cover up the hole. I pulled my gun"—here he shoved back his coat and touched the yellowed, bone-butt of a revolver that was turned backwards in a holster with the tips of his fingers—"and had them stop what they was about to do, work that coffin out of the hole, and bust it open. Sure enough, man had on a good suit, better than the clothes I was wearing, so I had them niggers take off his duds and I gave them mine to put on him. No one will be the wiser, and I got a good suit of clothes that would have rotted in the ground, and them niggers got to live."

"Why are you telling us this?" Grandpa said.

"Cause I want you to know what kind of man you're dealing with."

"A grave robber? You're proud of that? I'm not dealing with you at all, mister."

"Thing is, you old fart, I just don't like you. I don't like the way you look. I don't like the way you talk."

"There's nowhere to go with this conversation," Grandpa said. "There's nothing for me to say to an admitted grave robber but that you'll pay for that transgression."

"Guess you're talking about God," said the man.

"I reckon I am," Grandpa said.

"I think you're the kind of sniveling coward that will tell the authorities on me, that's what I think you are. I don't think you'd wait for God to do anything. I think you'd tell the law on me."

"You don't want things told on you, then you shouldn't tell them on yourself," Grandpa said.

"That right?" said the big man. It was pretty clear he was spoiling for a fight.

I think Grandpa could sense this was turning raw, so he said, "Look here, that's your business. I don't like the idea of it none, but that's your business. Just keep me out of it."

"I think you're just saying that," said the big man. "I think you're a talker, and no sooner than we get to the other side you'll tell some law what I told you."

Grandpa didn't respond. He turned sideways on the man, leaned on the wagon, and looked out at the river. He put his right hand in his coat pocket and left it there. I knew he kept an old two-shot derringer in that pocket and that he was actually watching things carefully, ready to pull it if need be. I had seen him draw it once, on a threatening drunk in town, some two, maybe three years back, and that draw had been sufficient enough to sober that bully up and send him running off down the street. So I knew Grandpa was at the ready, but I could also see that the hand that hung free was trembling slightly. That was probably more out of anger than fear, though it occurred to me that he might have bit off more than he could chew, knew it, and was trying to ride things out. I also knew, as that man had said, that when we got to the other side, Grandpa would report to the law about the grave-robbing incident. Course, it might not be a true story, might be a blowhard moment from the big man to get Grandpa's goat, but the way that suit fit I didn't think so. I felt he was speaking honest and proud of it, like he had performed a special job of wardrobe shopping.

I turned to watch those two other men come riding up because I could hear their horses, even though the wind was rising and there was starting to be some rain with it, and it was getting stronger by the moment. I looked back at the river, saw the rain coming through the trees, shooting drops into the water, and then the drops turned fierce and the river began to roll a little and the ferry commenced to bob. The men rode up and I got a good look at them. One was a short, fat man with a plug hat and a lot of facial hair that seemed to dip back into his mouth on account of him missing teeth. His eyes looked like a couple of black berries buried in his head. The other man was a tall, broad-shouldered colored man, built blocky, like bricks and sound mortar. He wore a big sombrero with dirty cotton balls on strings that dangled off the brim. He might not have been younger than the fat man, but maybe just looked that way because he had all his teeth. Those choppers were white and firm in his head, and he was smiling like something amused him. Both of them wore clothes that had the look of having been rolled in a pig sty and given to a goat to piss on. I could smell them strong-like because the wind was up and the rain was stirring their stink. Both of them were wearing their guns out in the open. The colored man had his hickory-handled pistol in a holster, old-style, like in the Western dime novels, and the fat man had one of the newer automatic pistols stuck in his belt, pushed out by his belly.

The two men brought their horses on board, and when they did the ferry dropped down a might, making everything heavier all of a sudden. Water splashed up over the sides of the ferry, and it rocked.

"You ought to have those men wait on this side till you take us over," Grandpa said. "They're too much weight."

"They don't have to wait anywhere," said the big man. "They're just fine."

"I think it's all right," said the ferryman, looking out at the river and the rain, but from the looks of him, I could tell he wasn't all that certain. I had come to believe, like Grandpa, that he was indeed new to such matters as river crossing and maybe even common sense, but even so, I still thought things were going to turn out all right. This was when I had a more sunny personality and was optimistic.

The fat man looked at me and laughed. He said, "Mr. Ferry Fella, is this your son?" Meaning me, of course. His voice sounded strange because his mouth was loose and his words were gummy.

"Ain't never seen him before," said the ferryman, glancing at me.

"Like you, he's got that fiery hair," said the fat man. "You two ought to get some hats and cover that up. You know what they say. I'd rather be dead than red on the head." The fat man chuckled slightly, swiveled, and looked at Lula, who was starting to shake, either from rain or fear or both. The fat man opened his mouth to smile, but without teeth, it was like a hole had opened in the earth. "Course now, there are some exceptions to that."

"Take the ferry out," said the big man.

"I'm telling you, there's too much weight," said Grandpa.

"You think there's too much weight," said the big man, "you can push that wagon backwards, the mules with it, and get off right now."

"I've had about enough of you," Grandpa said.

"Have you, now?" said the big man, and he pulled back his coat to show Grandpa his revolver again.

"I've seen it already," Grandpa said.

"Then you ought to take mind of it," said the big man.

"You're tough with a gun," said Grandpa, acting innocent, even though I knew he was holding that derringer in his pocket.

"Well, now," said the big man. "I can do what I need to do without a gun. Fatty." Fatty—the fat man, of course—came over, and the big man gave him his gun. Fatty stepped back and leaned against the wagon with the gun in his hand and looked at Lula like a dog about to lick a greasy pan. Lula had her arms pushed across her chest, keeping them under the big wide sunbonnet like it was an umbrella. This was a waste of time, because the rain had washed her hat down on all sides, dampening her hair until it was like strands of blood flowing along her cheeks and shoulders.

"Gentlemen," said the ferryman. "Let's forget our differences."

"You shut up," said the big man. "Fact is, you can start this ferry across. This ain't gonna take me long."

"Yes, sir," said the ferryman, and he closed up the ramp and started working the winch. He even tried whistling, maybe thinking he'd lighten the mood, but that didn't stick, and he quit after a few notes.

That's when the big man took a wild swing at Grandpa. Grandpa ducked. He was quick and easy about it, and when he bobbed up, he shot out his left hand and busted the big man in the face. It was a good lick. Blood ran from the man's nose, across his mouth and chin, and was washed away by the rain.

"Why, you old bastard," the big man said, touching his nose. "You got more than just hot air in you, don't you?"

"You can find out," Grandpa said, shuffling his feet, smiling.

"I think you broke my goddamn nose," said the big man.

"Come on and let's see if I can straighten it out some," Grandpa said.

By this time we were out on the river, and the ferryman was desperately working the crank and pulley, water sloshing over the sides. Fatty and the colored man watched all this with amused interest. Lula hadn't said a word, but it was clear from the look on her face she was trying to wish us to the other side and on our way.

The big man came again, and Grandpa, like he was a dancer, slipped another wild punch, stepped inside, hit him with a jab again, crossed with a right, bobbed low, and gave the big man a left to the ribs then a right uppercut to the chin that put him on his ass. It happened quick as a snake strike.

Just as quick, the rain turned cold as a well digger's ass, and the river was washing up over the sides of the ferry more than ever. It got the big man wet and soaked his grave-robbed suit.

"I hope I'm giving you a bit of a challenge," said Grandpa, looking down at the big man. "It's been kind of a trying day, and I could be off my feed some."

"You old fuck," said the big man. He came to his feet, stumbled back a step, said, "Fatty."

Fatty immediately tossed him the revolver.

"You skunk," Grandpa said, and pulled the derringer out of his pocket and pulled the trigger. The derringer popped, and the big man's left shoulder jerked back, but only slightly. The big man lifted the revolver and fired. The shot hit Grandpa so hard it knocked him on his butt. The ferry swayed. Water tumbled up over the sides of it and rolled onto Grandpa, who was sitting up, a hand clutched to his bleeding middle.

"Grandpa," Lula screamed, then ran over and helped hold him up.

The big man, leaking blood from his shoulder, leveled the pistol at him.

I said, "You done done it to him. He's got good. Leave him be."

"I'm gonna pop you, too," he said, glaring at me. "And then I'm thinking me and the boys are going to court your sister for a while, though we're going to go straight to the marriage bed without benefit of flowers and preacher."

That's when Grandpa shot him again with the derringer. The shot sounded like someone snapping their fingers. The bullet hit the big man in the thigh and made him drop to one knee. "Goddamn it," said the big man. "You bit me again with that thing."

Fatty and the colored man lunged forward at Grandpa, but at that moment Grandpa went limp, done for, held up only by Lula. Then there was a popping noise as the ferry rope began to fray. If that weren't enough, there came a howling sound, like a wolf with its paw in a trap. It was the wind lifting the river into a water devil, blowing down the big middle of the Sabine, causing the water to swirl and heave, tearing trees apart on both banks. Then it smacked the ferry. The rope finished coming apart, and we all went flying.

Last thing I remember seeing before I hit the water was my mule flying overhead like it had sprouted wings and had decided to go on ahead without us.

2

Swirling down under the water, I thought I was done for. All manner of things were bumping into me, and I was starting to black out, then the river brought me up. I gasped for air so hard I felt as if my lungs would blow out of my chest. I went down a time or two more, and finally I found myself, through no work of my own, lying on the bank of the river. Or halfway lying on it. My legs were still in the water, but the rest of me was kind of tucked back in a hollow in the bank.

I saw the water tornado then, a little thing, but fierce as a wildcat, spin by me in a dark twist of wind and river and wagon parts. It lifted my legs some, like it might yank me after it, but I was able to grab some roots sticking out from the bank and cling to them. My body was floated up and sucked at, but I held onto those thick roots, and then the water devil passed and I was dropped. I scrambled to peek around the edge of my den, saw that twister tearing across the river, veering, making landfall, spitting pieces of trees in all directions. It made with a last howl, as if injured, and died out quick as it had come, collapsed into the woods with a rattle of leaves and limbs and a swirl of mud and water.

I touched my head. It was bleeding some, but considering what had just happened, it was nothing at all. I worked my way out of the den and crawled onto the shoreline. I had to crawl. I couldn't stand up. I felt weak as a newborn kitten. I sat down on the bank and looked out at the river. It was still raining, but not hard.

Wagon parts and ferry parts were washing by, and with them I saw the body of the ferryman. He was facedown in the churning water, his right arm bent behind his back in a way you can't make it go when it fits correctly in the shoulder socket. His hand was twisted up, too, and his fingers were wiggling, as if he were lifting them off his back in a friendly little wave; it wasn't him moving them, though, it was the water. The river churned him on and under and out of view. I tried to get up, but had to sit down again. The sky seemed to be on the bottom, the land on top.

That's when I felt hands on my shoulders, looked up to see a man and a young woman beside me. It was the man had his hands on me. He was a thin fellow with a big hat that near swallowed his head. He couldn't have looked any sillier if he'd been wearing a bucket on his noggin. He said, "You all right there, boy?"

"I been better," I said.

"I hear that," he said. "I seen it all happen. Me and Matilda."

"That's right," the woman said. "We seen it."

Like him, she was soaked. She was bareheaded and dark-haired and had a long face with a chin that carried extra room on it. If she had been an ounce thinner and her clothes more worn, I could have seen her backbone and maybe the countryside beyond it.

"It just blowed that whole damn thing away," said the man.

"Did anyone make it?" I said.

"I don't know who died," said the man. "But there were three men and a girl and some horses got to the other side. A fat fellow and a big man rode on one horse, and a nigger and a girl on another. I don't think she was happy to go with them."

"Did you see an old man's body anywhere?"

"Nope," said the man. "We didn't. There's a big sorrel horse in a tree over there, though." He pointed. I looked in that direction and could see one horse leg hanging out of a shattered elm on the bank of the river.

"That's why they're riding double," I said. It wasn't exactly a revelation, but that's what came out of my mouth.

"Reckon that's right," he said.

"You see any mules?" I asked.

"When they were on the ferry," he said, "and then a little bit in the river. One was flying through the air and the other two was in the water. I ain't seen them since. They was there, then they wasn't. I figure they're down there with the catfish, or maybe the way that wind was blowing you'll find one up your ass later."

The woman snickered like a horse, and the man liked that she did. He laughed a little. I wasn't up for a lot of humor myself.

"Did you know any of them people got to the other side?" Matilda asked.

"I knew my sister, Lula, and my grandpa. He was shot. He was dead before the water devil hit. Those men took my sister. I got to get her back."

"By the time you swim the river, get to the other side, go after them on foot, they'll be farther ahead of you than you can catch up. That water is still rough, too. I don't think a gator could swim it right now. You'll be better off to see some law on this matter. Can you get to your feet?"

I found that with his help I could, but once there I was wobbly.

"We ought to be taking you somewhere," said the man. "Me and the wife come down to try out the new ferry, go over to the other side for a picnic, just for the hell of it, you know. We was watching from the hill. Planned to catch a ride across when that ferry fella got through hauling you folks over, and then we seen that twister."

"I ain't never seen a twister before," said Matilda. "On land or water."

"I've seen three or four," said the man, "but never a little one like that, and running right down the river. That was something, all right. I heard some niggers talking once about a thing like that, a twister in the river, but I thought it was just nigger talk."

"It just didn't seem real," Matilda said.

"It was pretty real," I said.

The man patted my shoulder.

There wasn't any use trying to go into Hinge Gate for the law, because the pox was running through the town and there were armed guards at both ends of it. I thought for a moment, said, "If I could get you to take me into Sylvester, I'd appreciate it. I know it isn't the nearest town, but it's not quarantined like Hinge Gate. I'd give you money, but I haven't got any."

"That ain't no problem," said the man, showing me a big row of horse teeth. "Sylvester ain't but a few miles. It ain't a problem at all. Hell, boy, we come from Sylvester. What's your name?"

"Jack," I said.

"Mine's Tom," he said.

Their wagon was parked up on the hill. It had a cover over it, like a covered wagon of old. I could see it from where I sat, looking over my shoulder. They helped me up, one at either side of me, and guided me to the wagon. When we got there, they lowered down the back end and had me sit on it. They broke out some sandwiches and some warm tea in a big fruit jar, insisted I ought to eat and drink. It's the way we Southerners do things. A tragedy happens, first thing you need to do is eat and have some tea or coffee.

It did help, though. When I had some of my strength back, if not all my piss and vinegar, I asked them to get me into Sylvester so I could speak to the sheriff. I wanted to look for Grandpa, too, but knew that bullet had done him in before the storm. I was sick about his body washed away somewhere, but with Lula kidnapped time was wasting, so I had to make the choice, and I made it for the living.

They rode me to town, dropped me off at the sheriff's office. It was clear as we came in that there had been some doings, because the town was like someone had turned a box of cats upside down and let them loose. People were moving about quickly, and there was activity at the bank. Across the street from it, I saw the law office of that fellow Cowton Little that Grandpa had told me about; his name and business were stenciled across the window glass clearly in white paint. But I couldn't get my mind on that, outside of touching my overalls pocket to feel the damp deed inside of it. There was just too much to draw my attention, like the wagon pulled up in front of the bank, and there was a pair of boots sticking out of the back end of it, and whoever belonged to those boots, the rest of him was covered up with a stained tarpaulin. The street was splotched over and wet in spots. There were dark pools of what looked to be blood turning black on the boardwalk in front of the bank. Down from that a few paces was a dead horse. Right by the door to the bank was a plank that had been leaned against the wall. There was a dead fellow propped on the plank, and a man in the street had a Kodak camera set up, one of them kind with an accordion eye on it. He was taking the man's picture. Even from a distance, I could see that dead fellow was all shot up. Part of his head was missing, though curiously he still had on a kind of shallow-brimmed hat; it was lifted up a little on one side, and that was the side where his head was gone, along with an ear. His clothes were ripped up and stiff with dried blood. Nails were driven on either side of his head, and a rope was fastened to the nails and passed under his chin; that's what was holding him up. They had folded one of his arms across his chest and had put a pistol in his hand to make him look ready for action. What he looked was dead.

"Damn, now," Tom said. "There has been some messy activity here of a sorts."

I was curious, of course, but my mind was more overwhelmed with my own worries. I thanked Tom and Matilda and started into the sheriff's office as they rattled away in their wagon. The door was wide open. There was a fellow not much older than me standing behind a desk, emptying things out of a drawer, tossing them on the desktop. There was a jail cell at the back, and there was a thick blond man in it. He was sitting on a bunk and had a rag tied around his head; it was leaked through with blood. He had one leg in splints and his face was black and blue all over, as if he were a spotted hound.

I said to the man emptying the drawer, "I'm looking for the sheriff."

"Don't shut the door," he said. "I don't want nobody to think I've barricaded it."

I wasn't sure what he was talking about, and I didn't ask him to explain. Instead, I came up to the desk and asked about the sheriff again.

"You'll find him under a tarp in the back of that wagon parked across the street."

"Who are you?"

"Deputy," said the man. "Or was. I'm clearing out, taking what's mine, and some of what's the sheriff's. He won't care. He ain't got no kin and wasn't well liked."

I looked at what he was placing on the desk. It was little knickknacks and pieces of junk, except for a couple of badges and a ring of keys. I said, "Since you're the deputy, I'm here to report a crime. And I'm going to need you to throw together a posse pretty quick."

He lifted his head and looked at me. "You are, are you? Well, I'm quitting, and in about five or ten minutes there's going to be folks coming through that door with a rope, looking for these here keys, and that fellow there"—he nodded at the blond—"is going to end up at the end of that rope with his tongue hanging out, his pants full of shit."

"You don't know that," said the man in the jail.

"About the shit in your pants, the tongue hanging out, or the part about the rope?" the deputy said.

"Either part of it," said the man.

"I had a cousin hung himself over a girl split with him and married a carpenter," the deputy said. "The rope killed him and the rest come naturally."

"You're supposed to protect me," said the man.

The deputy poked a badge on the desk with a finger, said to the blond, "Fellow wearing a badge is. But that ain't me anymore. I figure I don't want to get shot by the likes of you, or get shot protecting you. No, sir. I am plumb out of the deputy business. I'm thinking of learning barbering."

"But what about me?" said the blond, sounding like a child who had missed his turn. "You can't just leave me here and let them get me."

"Your situation might have been different had you not decided to rob the bank and kill the sheriff," the former deputy said, closing the desk drawer. "You think on that?"

"I wasn't the one shot the sheriff," said the man in the jail.

"Well, I'll let you and the townfolks sort that out," the former deputy said.

"Why me?" he said. "Them others got off all right. They rode right off. But I got nabbed."

The former deputy reached a hat off a peg on the wall behind him, scraped most of the stuff on the desktop into it, and left the keys and badge there. He placed the hat on the table and looked at the blond.

"Your horse was slow and took a bullet, and that's the end of that story. But you ain't the only one with bad luck. There's at least one more of you didn't make it, and his mortal body, what's left of it, is out there on a board, and you'll see him shortly on the other side. When you do, tell him Deke said hey and thanks for being a lousy shot, or I'd be out there in that wagon next to Sheriff Gaston."

"I ain't never had a stroke of luck in all my days," said the man. "And this just caps it off. I was born with bad luck. Some people have it, and I'm one of them."

"Well," said the man who had identified himself as Deke, "one thing is for sure, this ain't your day."

"I got to have some law," I said. "My grandfather was murdered by a man with a scarred throat, and my sister was kidnapped by him and two other men, one colored, and one a fat fellow."

"That would be Cut Throat Bill, Nigger Pete, and Fatty Worth. Them's the ones, along with the man on the board out there, and this desperado, that robbed the bank, killed the sheriff, and took a shot at me. One that come close enough it caused me to know I had to change professions."

About that time the doorway filled with a passel of men. One of them, who looked angrier than the rest, was wearing a small-brimmed black hat and was all dressed up like he was about to go to church. He said, "Ain't no use in trying to stop us, Deke. We got our mind set."

"I have removed myself from law enforcement," said Deke. He poked the keys on the desk. "One of them go to the cell. You can sort it out."

Deke picked up the hat full of little items and headed for the door, and the men standing in it let him pass. They looked at me, but no one said a thing to me. The man who looked as if he were ready for church came and swiped the key off the desk and walked over to the cell. It happened quick after that. The blond man started yelling, got up and stood on top of the bunk, like if he was higher up they couldn't get him; he managed that with the splint on his leg and without having any real trouble about it. He was so scared he might have been able to walk up the wall wearing it. He prayed loudly to Jesus to save him. Jesus didn't show, and considering what that fellow had been a part of I couldn't blame him. They had that cell open and grabbed him quicker than you could say, "The barn's on fire and my baby's in it."

"Oh, God," the man yelled as they hauled him out. "Have mercy on Bobby O'Dell's soul. My mama never raised me this way, and I regret the day I went wrong."

"I bet you do," said one of the men.

They dragged him out in the street, him bouncing along on that splinted leg, grimacing. I followed, managed to worm my way through the crowd until I was up front. I yelled at the struggling man. "Where's that Cut Throat fellow going? One you was with."

The man didn't pay me any attention, as his mind was preoccupied with the fact he was about to be hung up like laundry to dry. They half tugged, half carried him toward an electric light pole at the edge of the street. There were little metal bars sticking out from the pole, making a kind of ladder. Using them to climb, a little man with a coiled rope over his shoulder scuttled up that pole like a squirrel. He flicked the rope over one of the metal bars at the top of the pole and dropped it down. It was snatched up by a fellow on the ground, and a loop was made quick and fastened around Bobby O'Dell's neck.

"It's too long," someone in the crowd yelled up, and the little man, clinging to the top of the post like a dry leaf on an oak, readjusted it till everyone was happy except the man whose neck the loop was around. The man in church clothes come up with a strip of leather to tie Bobby O'Dell's hands behind his back, and when Bobby complained it hurt, someone yelled out, "That's all right. It ain't gonna bother you for long."

I had gotten pushed back in the crowd, and now I fought

my way forward again, worked at it until I was at the front, right beside the condemned man. Fear had turned him near gray as ash, and his eyes were big and dark and weaving from side to side like a drunk trying to figure his direction home. His face was slack, but his words came out clear. "I guess I ain't got no way out of this. I want everyone to know this ain't my mother's fault."

"Fuck your old mother," said the man who had commented previously on the short time Bobby O'Dell would have to wear his bonds.

"Now, you didn't have to say that," said Bobby. "That wasn't necessary."

"Hell it wasn't," said the man in the crowd.

About that time another man lurched out of the mob and hit the condemned man a good one on the side of the head with his fist. The blow knocked Bobby to the ground. He was quickly pulled up and held upright by so many men he seemed to float to a standing position.

A big man took hold of the end of the rope that was draped over the metal peg and pulled on it. This tightened the rope on Bobby's neck and lifted him to his tiptoes.

"This isn't how it's done," said Bobby, bleeding from under the rag around his head. "You don't hang a man proper this way. Where's my trial?"

"This is it," said the big man holding the rope.

"You ain't hanging me. You're gonna strangle me."

"Now you got it," said the big man, and then several men took hold of part of the rope, and they began to pull, backing up as they did. Up went Bobby O'Dell.

He wasn't pulled more than about a foot off the ground before the men wrapped their end of the rope around the pole and tied it off. When they did, the rope slipped a little and the man was lowered until his toes nearly touched the ground. He kicked furiously, trying to stretch his feet far enough to take hold, but that wasn't happening. He kicked so hard one of his boots came off and flew into the crowd and hit a young boy in the chest.

The boy ran forward, said, "You seen that? He kicked at me."

He ran over and hit Bobby then, a weak blow that caught the strangling man in the chest. Next moment, the boy scampered off, because Bobby really did try and kick him this time, and for a man hanging by a rope and being strangled slowly, it was a ferocious kick, and a part of me sort of wished he'd connected.

As Bobby spun around and around like a piñata, men came forward, almost in turn, and hit him. Some were throwing dirt clods out of the street, and harsh language was applied in near-ceaseless intervals. The hanging man's tongue was sticking so far out of his mouth he could almost lick himself under his chin. After a moment, he did a kind of shimmy, like a snake wiggling through a tight space, and went still. They kept hitting him.

"Ain't hanging him enough?" I yelled out.

"It wasn't your money, I figure," said the church-suit man, then someone clipped me one in the back of the head. Next thing I remember I was tasting dirt and trying to see, but all I saw were some boots coming my way, then I didn't see nothing for a while except memories of Grandpa being shot and that damn storm.

When I woke up it was near dark, and I was still lying in the street. There was something wet poking at me, and when I was able to get my thoughts and sight together, I seen it was a big black boar hog with stains of white fur at his belly. I shot up to a sitting position, and the hog edged closer. It was a big hog, had to have topped out around six hundred pounds, and with tusks as long and sturdy as the business end of a pickax. One eye appeared to hang lower than the other, as if it might be thinking of going someplace without the rest of the hog. The critter's breath was a mixture of corn and cow shit, which is what was on its snout, and now on my face.

"Don't move fast again," said a voice. "He don't much like surprises. He might decide to eat your face off."

I turned my head slowly and saw a colored man standing behind me with a corncob pipe in his mouth. He was lighting it up by striking a lucifer on his greasy pants. He had the handle of a shovel poked under his armpit, and the shovel itself was touching the street, and he was leaning on it. He was bigger than Cut Throat had been—solid and thick, with legs and arms like tree trunks. The flame of the match looked like a firefly cupped in his black palm. He had a lot of nice teeth, and he used them to clench his pipe tight when he lit it. His face looked smooth as silk and dark as long-boiled coffee.

"You know this hog?" I said, inching back from it.

"Quite well," he said, shaking out the match. "Me and him had been until lately sharing a small stretch of living quarters out the back of Rutledge's farm. I worked there, and he followed me around. I found him when he was a wild piglet. Bunch of dogs was trying to tear him apart. He was trying to fight them, and him about the size of a rat stuffed with cabbage. I ran them dogs off, took him home with me, and was going to raise him up and eat him. But me and him mostly got along, so I let him stay around. Now and again we have a row, but on the whole we do all right together. He's smarter than any dog."

"I'm glad you and him are happy," I said. "Can you get your hog to stand back a bit?"

"He ain't mine," said the colored man. "I said he stays with me. Now and again I get the feeling he knows I considered eating him once, knows if things turned one way or the other I might yet. I think he feels pretty much the same about me."

Now that I was up I realized I was hearing a thudding sound. I looked toward where that sound was coming from, and there was that boy the dead man tried to kick. He had a stick and was hitting the hanging man with it. He wasn't in any hurry about it. He took his time cocking the stick and swinging it, but he was hitting solid, and it sounded loud and made me hurt a little. Bobby O'Dell was good and dead, of course, and was plastered with dirt from clods that had been thrown, and his face had dark marks all over it, like he'd been lying facedown on a flapjack griddle.

"You stop that," I said to the boy. "He's already dead."

"Then he won't mind much," said the colored man.

"It ain't right," I said.

"Lot of things ain't right," said the colored man. He smoked his pipe and watched the boy work with his stick. He said to him: "All right, now, that's enough, I reckon."

The boy didn't stop.

The colored man picked up a pretty nice-sized rock from the road and slung it whistling through the air. It caught the kid just above the ear and knocked him down, causing him to fling his stick away. The colored man went back to smoking his pipe. The boy got up slowly with his hands under him, then pushed up on his knees and shook his head.

The colored man picked up another rock. The boy turned and looked at him.

"You didn't have no cause for that," said the boy.

"You about to get another one, you don't get on up and out of here," said the colored man. "I'll sic that hog on you."

The kid got to his feet quickly and ran off, but he ran with a slight lean toward the side where the rock hit him. The hog ran after him a piece, then came snorting back our way as if he were laughing.

"That was a pretty good lick you put on that kid," I said.

"Which is it, then?" said the colored man, dropping the rock. "You worried about the dead or the living?"

"I'm worried about my sister," I said. "She's been kidnapped, and my grandpa has been murdered."

"Say they have?" said the colored man. "Well, I guess you tried the law yonder?"

"Deputy has quit, and the sheriff's dead."

I looked down the street, saw the wagon with the sheriff's body in it was gone, and so was the man on the board, along with the dead horse.

"Sheriff was brave," said the colored man. "I seen it all from the corner of the General Store there. I was coming up the alley from behind it when it all come down like a hailstorm. I think them robbers thought they had it made easy. They didn't. There was lots of shooting. But the ones got away took the money with them. They split up there at the end of the street, to meet up somewhere else, I figure."

"The river and the ferry," I said.

"Oh, you mean that rig that pulls across the Sabine. That son of a bitch owns it burnt the bridge to have that ferry."

"It didn't do him any good," I said. "The ferry got hit

by a water twister right after Grandpa got shot. I was near drowned, and them others were the ones got away with robbing the bank. They took my sister with them."

"That ain't good for her," said the colored man. "Not with one of them being Cut Throat Bill. And I think there was Nigger Pete with them. They been in the papers, mostly robbing banks up north. They got prices on their heads, considerable ones. Papers say Bill rode with Frank and Jesse James when he was just a kid. He liked the work and has been out doing it for near thirty years or so, off and on, between that and other mischief. I don't know nothing about the fat one. There was some dime novels about Cut Throat Bill, though they made him out a hero and such. There ain't no heroes."

"Fatty is all the name I know," I said. "That's what they called him. Deputy, or former deputy, seemed to know who he was. Not that it mattered. He's quit and gone on to hunt out another career, possibly barbering."

"Well, that barbering is a pretty steady job, cause there's plenty like a neat haircut and a shave they don't have to do themselves," said the colored man.

I tried to get up, but my legs weren't ready, and I had to sit back down. It was then that a bunch of dirt fell off me and I knew I had been hit with a mess of dirt clods while I was out, not to mention that I ached all over from having been kicked and whopped on. I figured that kid had been at me with that stick a little.

"Only good thing come of this is that ferry is gone," said the colored man. "I don't like to pay for crossing a river when there was a perfectly good bridge there. Though you got to give him credit for coming up with that ferry idea. I might have done it had I thought of it."

"I got to go find my sister," I said. "I got to get some law some kind of way."

"Good luck to you, kid," said the colored man. "Ain't no law wants any part of that bunch. Not after what happened here. Sheriff was brave, and what it got him was a final ride in the back of a wagon with a tarp slung over him. The deputy, soon as the shooting started and a bullet whizzed in his direction, he run off like a rabbit. If he'd have run any faster, he'd have run out of his clothes."

"He was telling me he had a kind of revelation that the law wasn't his kind of work," I said.

"I bet he did tell you that," said the colored man.

I tried to get up again, and this time the colored man grabbed me under the arm and helped me to my feet.

"You might get a Texas Ranger involved," he said. "They are some bad men. But by the time you find one of them, your sister could be on the dark side of things, and there ain't no certainty about them Rangers."

"What else is there?"

"You could hire a bounty hunter or a tracker."

"Do you know one?"

"Well, I've done the work. I'm part white, part nigger, and part Comanche injun, and I'm the part of that last part that knows how to track. I was taught by my mother and some of her people. They could find a fart under a stone at the bottom of a lake. I'm not that good, actually, but I'll do. I mean, I'm pretty damn good. So I could find him, but I wouldn't do it without Shorty going with me, and I don't know he would. Neither of us would go without being paid. And we can take the hog, too. He helps track. Well, not really, but I'm used to his company. But I got to have enough to make it worth my salt and bacon. I'm going to chance ending up like the sheriff, I got to get paid for my work, and more than he did."

"Therein is the grit in the lard," I said. "I haven't got any serious money."

"How much you have that ain't serious?" he said.

And then an idea hit me. I dug in my overalls for those papers Grandpa had given me. They were still wet while the rest of me was dry, so I was careful pulling them out. They had been folded, and were on good solid paper, and had survived the damp well. I said, "When these dry, they are papers that say I own land. And if you and this Shorty fellow will help me find my sister and get her back, and avenge the death of my grandpa by bringing those men in that are responsible, I will sign them over to you. You can sell them or do as you like after that."

"That's owner kind of land?"

"I own it, I sign it over to you and Shorty, you'll own it. And the man that's got the right to do that is right here in town. But there ain't no need for me to sign anything unless I get my sister back. You do that, then these papers and the land is yours to do as you would."

"How much land?"

"It's two places," I said. "One is a hundred acres, my grandpa's old place, and one is twenty-five, my folks' place, but it's on good farmland. Grandpa's isn't as good."

"Farmland is what you make of it," said the colored man. "You got to know the right way to break down animal manure, and I do. I had some land of my own I could grow corn so high you'd have to be a bird to see over it. I was doing that for Old Man Rutledge, but he died and his wife didn't like me. Her family, the Cox family, used to own my people, and when the change come the old man could stand it, but she couldn't. She didn't like having to pay me in crop and some wages for what they used to get for free from my folks. I was looking for some new work when I come into town and these fellows and his friends robbed the bank. I thought I could get a job burying them. I've done that off and on for years, since I wasn't making all that much on the farm. Oh, I left now and then to track and do sundry work, like digging graves. Usually pays a quarter apiece for burying; least it does for me. I've done it quite a few times. White man digs a grave, it's fifty cents a corpse. Like the way he digs it is different and better than the one I dig for a quarter."

I decided not to mention that my parents had died of the pox and that they were buried in coffins full of lime, as I figured that might possibly bring down the property value. I said, "Then you'll do it?"

"That depends on if we can get Shorty to sign up. He'll do it, I'll do it. But I got to have someone like him at my back. And my guess is all those men, especially Cut Throat Bill, have prices on their heads. Me and Shorty could make quite a collection if this comes out right. If it don't, well, we could get ourselves killed, and you, too. And you look green enough they might even kill you twice."

"You get my sister back and help me catch those men that killed Grandpa, see they get justice, I'll sign both properties over to you. Then, like you said, there's the possibility of rewards for those skunks."

He rubbed his chin. "We'll need some supplies, but I reckon to have any we'll have to steal it."

"Wait a minute," I said. "I don't want to get in the wrong life myself, end up hanging beside Bobby there. I won't steal. That's not how us Parkers do things."

"So far the way you Parkers do things is you get yourself killed and kidnapped and knocked out in the street. You are not off to a good beginning, young man."

"I won't steal," I said. "I can't. My grandpa was a preacher, and he would roll over in his grave if he had one. Only he's somewhere in the Sabine River or washed up along its banks. I get sick thinking he's stuck to some root down under and catfish are at him."

"Tell you what," said the colored man. "Let's go see Shorty, see what he thinks, and we can see about supplies from there. He might not go. We'll see him first. You say your name is Parker?"

"Jack Parker."

"Mine's Eustace Cox, and I think we might be cousins of a sorts."

"How's that?" I said.

"You sound a little offended that you might be part darky. Well, rest assured, white boy, it's me that's part of you. Cox family married in the Parker family, and one of them Cox boys, some forty-five years back, made me with my mother—against her will, I might add—and she was colored and Comanche, and so here I am. So we could be relatives."

"I don't care one way or the other," I said. "I just want to rescue my sister, and time's wasting."

"Not me been lying out here in the dirt, cuz," he said. "But it's near night now, so ain't much you can do. We can get over to see Shorty maybe, talk to him. I'll have an answer for you then. If we can't help you, then you're on your own, cause I got no other suggestions. Like I said, I got to have the right man riding with me, and no offense, you're just barely grown."

"Nineteen," I said.

"You're lying," he said.

"Well, I might be closer to seventeen," I said, still stretching the blanket.

"In my day that was grown and then some, but not now," he said. "You are green behind the ears, and pretty much green all over. Actually, you're more pink in spots. You got the sunburn on the back of your neck from lying out here in the street. That's gonna smart some come morning, if not sooner. Let's go see if we can find Shorty. But first, I got to bury this one. I already tucked the other one away at the cemetery."

"The one on the board?"

"That would be him. Now I got to get this one. I'm going to have to cut him down and drag him, because I don't have a horse."

I won't lie to you. I was horrified at the thought, and even more horrified when he gave me the shovel to hold, put his pipe away, pulled out a big knife, and reached up on his tiptoes to cut the rope high. When he did, he let the man fall, got hold of the nub of rope, and started dragging him down the street with that big old hog trotting after him. After a moment he and the hog paused, and both looked back at me. Eustace said, "You coming?"

Carrying the shovel, I went after them.

Eustace dragged the body through an alley and out back of the town buildings, over some rough ground toward a line of trees that was on a hill above Sylvester. This was quite a trip we took, and the body of Bobby O'Dell kept turning over and over, and by the time we got to the trees, what was left of his face didn't look so good. I won't talk about what happened to his eyes during this event.

Finally we come to the trees, and Eustace dragged the body some more through the tree line, then there was another hill, and up on that hill were some crosses. No tombstones—all crosses, simple things made from cheap lumber. By this time the sun had gone down and I was seeing all this by moonlight, but it was a half-moon and bright enough. It gave those crosses a kind of glow.

There was a freshly covered grave there—the one he had referred to, of course—and he let go of the rope and started digging next to it. The hog sat down on the ground and watched, as if taking note of the proper way to get the job done. In no time at all Eustace had broke the red dirt down to about three feet deep and six foot wide. He gave me the shovel then. I took to digging. Eustace sat on the ground with his back against a cross and gave me instructions. I dug for a long time. Eustace didn't offer to spell me, and of course the hog was out of the mix, being more of a spectator.

Eustace said, "This here is where they bury colored, paupers, and outlaws. I done got my money for this, which is a good thing. Sometimes the grave's dug, town council don't want to pay. They done me that way once—for the good, white people's graveyard—and I dug up that old woman and her child and took them over and laid them on the mayor's doorstep. Since they had died in a fire, they didn't look so good. They had to pay me what they owed me, and they done it quick, and they had to pay me more for burying them again. They could have got somebody else, but they knew I'd be mad about it. You don't want me mad. You especially don't want me drunk and mad, which is why I don't drink. There's a demon in the bottle when I do, and the town knows it, and the nigger haters have tried to settle me down, but they got settled, so they live with me. That whiskey, it'll make me do wrong. One sip I'm happy, two I'm mad, and three I'm crazy. Maybe it's the Indian blood I got, or maybe it's just me."

I had almost quit listening at this point. I was still thinking about what he had told me about the woman and child. I said, "You dug up a woman and her child?"

"Took them right out of the coffins. They were dead, so it didn't matter none to them. I needed that fifty cents, and when it was all said and done I made a dollar. By the way, I ain't sharing the grave money with you just because you're digging. Consider this like a down payment on me hunting down those fellows that's got your sister. Tell you what. You stay here and pat that grave down some more, and I'll go borrow a horse, pick you up when I got it."

I didn't like the sound of that, but I had a feeling that there was only so much I could worry about at this point, though I might could make a mention of Jesus to him at some point and see if he'd come around to a better way of thinking. Eustace and the hog went off about their mission, leaving me to finish the work.

I trembled when I thought again of Lula. We had always got along fine, and I had even stooped to playing dolls and tea parties with her, though I had never even known anyone of my acquaintance to have an actual tea party. She was a good girl, and we were good friends for a brother and a sister. Though when I was younger, I do remember chasing her more than once with a frog to scare her, or with a sticker-burr switch. She was a good runner. What I remembered most about her was how strange she could be, studying on things and considering on matters of no interest to anyone else. Like how could a hummingbird fly backwards and a chicken that had wings couldn't do any real flying at all. It didn't seem a deliberation of prominence to me. She was always coming out with that kind of thing, and I was always telling her if God wanted us to know the answers to such, he'd have written it down. One time she looked at me when I said that, and said, "You're telling me God wrote the Bible with his own hand, and in English? And knowing all things, he has no word on the hummingbird and the chicken?"

I had never thought on such a thing for a moment, and before I could say as such, she had already moved on to some other contemplation that most likely had no explanation, either.

I patted the grave down some more, then got bored and leaned on the shovel. Then I got tired and sat down. The sunburn on the back of my neck had started to sting, but there wasn't a thing I could do for it but bear it. About the time I began to think I'd been hornswoggled into digging a grave for nothing, I saw Eustace riding up the shadow-covered hill on a horse, the hog trotting behind him. There was a bridle and reins on the horse, but no saddle.

When he got up by me, I saw he had an automatic pistol stuck in his belt. It was the same sort Fatty had. He said, "We better get on our way."

He held out his hand and I took it. He swung me up on the back of the horse. We went away at a trot, the hog running along beside us, hardly blowing any air at all.

It wasn't an easy ride, bareback like that, and I nearly bounced off several times. I had to put my arms around Eustace to stay hung on. This was a bit troublesome for me, as at the time I felt I was a grown enough man that I ought not have to cling to him like a child waiting for a nipple. But that was the size of it, and I put it on to wear, so to speak. Hog, as the porker was called, made his way easily and quickly, and I was surprised at how fast he could go.

The moon was high by the time we came to where we were going, which was on the other side of the river. We crossed at a narrow spot, but the water was high from the rain the day before and was still rolling fast, if not exactly raging.

The water washed over the belly of the horse, then its sides, and up over our knees as we rode across. Once, we hit a sinkhole and the water came up to the critter's neck and we got a good drenching. I was nearly washed off the horse. Finally we made it to the other side and rode up a high, slanting portion of the bank. I really had to hold on for dear life, but eventually we made the lip and Hog paused there to shake like a dog.

Eustace turned the horse down what was more of a rabbit path. After we had gone that way awhile and the night air had begun to dry us some, everything opened up. There was a grassy hill, and on the hill I spied something I couldn't quite make out. As we rode up, the moonlight fell down on it like a splash of buttermilk. I saw it was a telescope mounted on the hill, pointing up at the stars, and there was a child looking through it. And as we topped the hill, I could see beyond him a house and corral and a small barn, all of it nicely laid out.

Closer yet, I realized that the child was not a child at all but a man, a dwarf.

3

My first view of Shorty was on that hill under the moonlight. He noticed us long before we came up, but when he saw us good he turned back to the telescope and continued peering through it.

Eustace reined in the horse. Hog sat on his haunches, lifted a back leg, and snapped at his ear with his hoof like a dog with a paw.

I slid off the horse, my butt numb as my legs. Eustace dropped down and held the horse by the reins. He said by way of greeting to the dwarf, "You up for hunting down some folks and maybe killing them? Rescuing this boy's sister?"

The dwarf pulled his eye from the telescope and studied Eustace. "Does it involve money, as I am about to a spot where I need some more?"

"It's got some twists in the road, but it could be about some money," Eustace said.

"A maybe job," the dwarf said. "I do not know. That is somehow not as enticing as a solid offer."

"It sounds all right," Eustace said. "Ain't nothing without a chance in it, is there?"

"Some things have fewer chances," the dwarf said.

"Why don't we go on to your place, have some coffee, and talk on it?" Eustace said.

"Time's wasting," I said. "Every minute things could be worse for Lula."

"Lula?" the dwarf said.

"My sister," I said.

"I see. Well, sir, she is not my sister, and until I know the ends and outs of this enterprise, you cannot consider me bound for action."

"Come on, then," said Eustace. "Let's go palaver."

"I see you have both crossed the river," said the dwarf.

"Yes," Eustace said. "But we're drying out good."

By this time I was much agitated, as my grandfather used to say, but it also occurred to me that his agitation might well have led to his death as much as a bullet did, so I pulled my feelings up tight and followed the dwarf toward his house, Eustace leading the stolen horse and Hog trotting along with us.

It was odd to watch the dwarf walk, for his movements were somewhere between that of a grown man and that of a child. His head seemed large and heavy on his shoulders, which were broad for a man his size. He was hatless, and in the night his hair looked dark, black, even. I had noticed a bit of a shadow on his face from unshaven whiskers, yet there was about Shorty a kind of delicateness of habit, like a man who belonged in better surroundings. I don't know how else to describe it other than that, but that was my first impression. Like he was visiting royalty shrunk down to size and quite angry about it.

When we got to his shack, he went inside and after caring for the horses, we went with him, Hog included. It was clean, if simple and small. It was two rooms. I could see from where we stood through an open doorway to another room, where there was a small bed in a simple wooden frame. On the other side of the room where we stood there were stacked books and papers and magazines. Shorty lit some kerosene lanterns and pretty soon it was yellow inside and I got my first real good look at him. He was indeed dark-headed and had an evening shadow of black whiskers. His eyes were blue or green—the light was not bright enough for me to be certain, though later I would determine they were gray. He was dark-skinned from working outside, and behind what at first seemed a delicate face were hard-edged bones that poked at his cheeks and punched out his chin. He was a handsome dwarf, and had he been six foot tall he would have undoubtedly been what they call a ladies' man.

He had a wooden step in front of the cast-iron stove, and he poked some wood in the burner and lit a fire. He poured water from a bucket into a pot, got coffee into it, and set it on the fire hole to boil. He seated himself in a chair at the table in the middle of the room. It was the only chair. It was a low table, and me and Eustace, without discussing it, sat cross-legged on the floor, which put us at about the same height as Shorty. We looked across the table at him. Hog laid up in the open doorway, his head and shoulders in the shack, the rest of him hanging out in the yard.

Shorty said, "I have to be out and about and maybe hunt down and kill someone, I need to know the entire enterprise."

"Are you sure you're up to it?" I said. "I was expecting someone else."

"A taller man, perhaps?" said Shorty.

"I won't lie. Yeah, someone with some height and weight."

"Gunpowder and shot come in all manner of containments, but all of them are powder and shot, and some of the small ones are tightly packed and have a considerable punch. Consider me a tightly packed package."

I had my doubts, but I was desperate. I laid out all that had happened, about my dead and river-claimed grandpa, my kidnapped sister, and the papers I had that showed ownership of property. To make that more certain, I pulled those papers out—now dry, as they had not gotten seriously dampened by the river—and folded them open carefully on the table for them to gander on. While they were doing that, I reminded Shorty of the bank robbery and how it was the same bunch of scoundrels. I told him of the rewards that would be on the heads of Cut Throat Bill, Nigger Pete, and Fatty and tried to be eloquent and persuasive in my telling.

"I got a thought," said Eustace, "and it's this. There might be a whole passel of them bad men lumped up together. More than was in town. Would be my guess they all have a price on their heads."

"You are saying it might well be a bonanza," said the dwarf.

"I reckon I am," Eustace said.

The dwarf leaned back and considered. "It has its merits." The dwarf got up and found a cigar in a box he pulled from a cabinet. He took out one of the cigars. It was a big cigar. He put it in his mouth, moved the coffeepot, bent over the stove, and poked his face toward the fire. Red shadows flared across his skin, and then he pulled back, puffing the cigar. He replaced the coffeepot and went back to his little chair, blowing clouds of reeking blue cigar smoke into the air.

"What we need to do is get going," I said. "She's been gone now near a day, and they could be miles away."

"Oh, they are," Shorty said. "They are many miles away, but my guess is they have stopped with the night."

"You don't know that," I said.

"You are correct," he said. "I do not. They could well be traveling by night, but I think it is best we do not. We cannot easily find their track by night, but tomorrow when there is light we can, and we can proceed at a rapid pace."

"I could just go on ahead, and you two can do without the reward," I said.

"You could do that," said the dwarf. "And you are welcome to proceed. But if we should decide to follow tomorrow, we would catch up with you posthaste, and perhaps find you with a broken leg, having stepped into a rabbit hole or drowned in the river if you got off course. All this being a slow go, by the way, if you are without a horse, which you would be, as I have no intention of loaning you one."

"Eustace stole the one he got," I said. "I could take it."

"Now, didn't you tell me you didn't want no part of thievery?" said Eustace. "Now you're talking like a common horse thief."

"I've reached a point of extreme anxiousness," I said.

"Say you have?" Eustace said, and laughed at me.

"You cannot have the horse," Shorty said. "If you want us to go after these men and rescue your sister, we will be about it at first light and on horseback."

"Eustace said he was a good tracker, and could track a fart under a rock in a river, or something like that."

"No," Eustace said. "I said my mother's people could, least the Indian side of her. I said I wasn't near that good."

"But you're good?" I said. "Right?"

"Yep," Eustace said.

"Listen here, son," Shorty said. "Eustace is not as good as he thinks. He is nowhere as good as he brags. He cannot track at night, or in a rainstorm, or after too many days when it has grown cold. His mother and his mother's people could. It is not something that runs in the blood. It is taught, and he learned something of it."

"I do all right," Eustace said.

"Yes, you do all right," Shorty said. "I remember once when you and I tracked a renegade Indian for four days, only to discover we were following an old white man riding on a donkey. With all due respect, Eustace, you can track, but you need daylight and some luck, and you are often wrong."

Eustace made a grunting noise, and I felt my heart sink a little.

"Am I right?" Shorty said to him.

"I do all right," Eustace said again.

"Of course you do," said Shorty. "You do all right, but that is not in the mother-lode vein of amazing. We can start here just before daylight, get to the spot where it all happened, see what sign is left. Let me tell you something, though, boy. Your sister, if she is with those hard men, she may already have given up her flower, if you know what I mean."

"I do," I said, having trouble saying it. "And I've thought about that."

And I had, and the thought of it made me sick.

"Our job is to rescue her, kill the hell out of the men who stole her, and collect a reward," Shorty said. "Am I right?"

I said, "I would guess that the rewards from the law are dead or alive, so it might not be necessary to kill anyone. My reward for you is the land, if you get my sister back."

Shorty and Eustace looked at me as if I had just dropped my pants and taken a big dump right there in the room.

"Might not be necessary to kill no one?" Eustace said. "You had a drink or two I don't know about?"

"I'm just saying killing may not be necessary," I said.

"Meaning you do not have the stomach for it?" Shorty said.

"Meaning it might not be necessary if we can bring them to trial," I said.

"Town will give them the same trial they gave that one you seen hanging on the light pole," Eustace said.

"We perhaps can try some other town," I said.

"Each town has its own jurisdiction," said Shorty. "They will end up back at Sylvester, where the bank was robbed. It does not make sense to not kill them when we will take them to Sylvester in the long run, and they will dispatch them there, trial or no trial. We do the job up front, we save everyone some time and worry. The kidnappers know this, and when we find them they will use the time they are being carried back to the law as a possibility of escape. I do not want to fret with that. If they are dead, they cannot escape. This, sir, is a fact."

"I don't want to kill people if we don't have to," I said.

Shorty leaned back, clasped his hands together, and laid them on his chest. He looked up at the ceiling. "Well, there might be an option," Shorty said. "And we can consider that."

He looked at Eustace. Eustace said, "All right, we'll put that thinking in our thinking pipe and smoke it."

I didn't think he or Shorty sounded particularly sincere, and the whole thing made me feel weak. I wanted my sister back. I wanted justice. But I didn't want anyone to be killed.

I decided to say no more on the matter and cross that bridge when we got to it.

"We need a grubstake," Eustace said.

"Where did you borrow this horse you have?" Shorty asked Eustace.

"Sylvester. Where the bank robbery was."

"All right, then," Shorty said. "I have horses we can ride, and we can sell the borrowed one along the way, provided a buyer presents himself. And I believe I can put together enough supplies for us until that time and perhaps beyond."

"You're going to sell a borrowed horse?" I asked.

"Well," Shorty said. "I believe we will. Yes."

"My shotgun here?" Eustace asked.

"Did you leave it here?" Shorty asked.

"You know I did."

"Then it is still here, Eustace. Did you think perhaps it had taken legs of its own and gone a-gallivanting?"

"I reckon not, but I thought you could have swapped or sold it."

"You know why I keep it here," Shorty said. "I would not sell or swap it, and you know that."

Eustace nodded. "Times got hard, I would."

"It is in the back room, if you have a mind to take it. It is back there along with your bag of shot and some of the makings for more, if you believe you will need it."

"I'm hoping that's enough," Eustace said. "If I can get them fellas to covey together, I can bring down a whole mess of them firing but one barrel."

We had coffee and some cold cornbread that was in the bread box, and then Eustace went to the back and to bed, making a pallet on the floor with some of Shorty's blankets. That left the bed for Shorty. Shorty gave me a blanket, and that left the floor in the smaller front room for me and Hog.

I was still not certain about Shorty as a manhunter. I began to suspect I might be in for a switch-around, these two killing me for my land papers, though I doubted they would be able to pass my signature. However, it wouldn't take much in the way of torture to get me to sign it repeatedly and sing a little song as I did. I had no false ideas about how tough I was. I only wanted to find my sister and get even with those villains who had killed my grandpa. For me, them paying their dues in prison was enough of a debt.

I folded up the land papers, put them back in my pocket, and slept on the floor of the main room, under the dwarf's low table, on a blanket that smelled like dried sweat. During the night Hog crawled up with me, and I had his foul breath to deal with, which was a little like wrestling the ghost of a billy goat, prone as they were to stick their heads between their legs and piss on their beards. I tried to say my prayers, but they felt hollow, unlike when I was at home and my family was in the house with me and everything was in order. Prayers seemed fine then, but right now I felt empty. I asked the Lord to forgive my lapse of conviction, and figured that under the circumstances he would. I tried to get some rest, but I didn't sleep much, just a nod here and there that made me feel worse than trying to stay awake.

Finally I got up and lit a lamp, wandered around the room, and looked at the books Shorty had. There were all manner, but a large batch of them were travel books, including some by Mark Twain, one of which, *The Innocents Abroad,* I had read myself. I looked through some more books, found that many of them had marked maps and marked passages, sentences underlined with a fountain pen. They were mostly about exotic places, many of which I had never heard of. I read a little of this and that, but under the circumstances none of it could hold my interest. I put out the lamp, left Hog snoring, crept outside, and got some air, which was rich and sticky, like a sweaty horse shank, full of the sounds of cicadas and crickets and more than a few bleating frogs.

While I was standing there in the night, I glanced up at the hill and saw Shorty was back up there looking through the telescope. I thought he was in the back room asleep, and even though I had been mostly awake I hadn't heard him walk by and leave the house. The air was full of fireflies, and they flittered about him like fairies, kind of made a halo above him with their little yellow lights.

I strolled up on his lookout, but went wide and tried to come up behind him. I'm not sure why I did that, but I did. When I finally got up the hill, being stealthy as I went, and was right on him, he said, "You walk like a goddamn buffalo. If I had time, we would work on that."

"I thought I was pretty quiet," I said, coming on ahead until I stood beside him. He hadn't removed his eye from the telescope.

"For a buffalo you are most delicate," he said.

"Do you really plan to help me?" I said. "I am dead serious, you know."

"I do, but I think you are asking another question. Do you doubt me because I am small? That was your earliest indication, something you said when we first met."

"I don't know," I said. "Right now, I don't know how I feel about a lot of things. I'm sort of worked over, to tell the truth, and I got a sunburn on the back of my neck on top of it all. And yeah, perhaps I am worried that you being a midget could make it a difficult task. There you have it. You asked, and there you have it."

"It is better when people are straightforward about what they think of me. It is the lying and the dodging and the shifty-eyed looks that annoy me. I came to a comfortable conclusion with myself some time ago. Well, should say I have come to a more comfortable conclusion. I will not say it is complete and something I can nestle down into like a feather pillow, but I have made my bed a lot better to lie in than it once was by learning to accept what I cannot change. Mostly I think my size is other people's problem, not mine, though an easier way for me to get on a horse could be devised. So you have your doubts about me. Any other questions?"

"Can Eustace actually track them?"

"He can. And he is better than I let on, but you cannot let Eustace think too much of himself, because he becomes too confident, and, oddly, that leads to the bottle, and he cannot handle the bottle. Boredom is not good for him, either. He gets crazy when he has drink. That's why I keep his shotgun here. It is why he is best without too much money on hand, and why he often leaves part of his money with me. None of which I have now. A coin for him is like a snake in the pocket. He cannot wait to rid himself of it, where I, on the other hand, am tight with a nickel."

"You keep his gun so he won't sell it for liquor?"

"So he will not shoot anyone and everything in sight. His skin color affords a large number of angry opportunities, and Eustace does not cotton well to someone treating him poorly because of it. He has his color, and I have my size, and that is our connection. We both wear albatrosses. But if you are wondering if we can do the job, I assure you we can, though in the end I do not promise it will not become messy. Messy is the nature of the business, child."

"I am sixteen," I said.

"Good for you," he said. "May you make seventeen."

He said all this without so much as removing his eye from the telescope. Then he did, and said, "Like to take a look? Just put your eye to it, and leave your hands away from it so as not to destroy my setting. I have it lined up just right."

I went over and took a look. What I saw was a lot of moon. There were shadows on the moon. I said, "What are the shadows?"

"Craters. Mountains, perhaps. I read a story in a magazine of recent, or recent to me. A man in Hinge Gate, at the general store, used to save magazines for me that did not sell. He gave them to me. In that one story I read, a man goes to Mars by just holding out his arms and wishing he were there. He went, and he saw a strange world with strange beings and monsters. I really enjoyed that story, and standing here one night, with Mars, not the moon, in my scope, I considered doing the same. Then it occurred to me, what if it worked and I went? It would be worse than here, all those monsters he wrote about, and me out there on Mars, and it being dry and no trees. I liked reading it, but decided I would not like living it after all, having enough problems without compounding them with Martians. Besides, I have long ago given up on wishes. Perhaps there is something out there on those worlds. Something like us, or something better. I dream sometimes of a world not where I am the height of others but where everyone is my height. But that is a dream, not a wish. I know better. Wishes do not come true, and there is no such thing as true love and a happy hunting ground when we cash in our chips."

"I don't know. I believe that," I said, standing back from the telescope. "About true love, anyway. I think it exists, and there's someone for everyone, and you just got to wait till they come along."

"That so?"

"My folks were much in love."

"Were?"

"They died."

"How did they die?"

"There was an illness, and it got them both," I said, being careful not to describe their death too clearly, for fear Shorty might think I was carrying smallpox around with me, ready to cough it on him. "That's why Lula and I were with our grandpa, heading toward Kansas."

"And he left you all that farmland to sell?"

"He did. He didn't plan on coming back home."

"He was correct in that assumption."

"I guess he was," I said.

"Your folks got along, but that does not determine in my mind true love, or love at first sight, or someone waiting in the wings for you. Here I am, high in my forty years, and I have yet to find a woman with long legs who is ready to let a dwarf nestle between them on a regular basis unless she is paid for the service. So true love? I do not think so. There can be a getting used to, I believe, and some might call that love, but I do not believe in love at first sight, or the ordained love that I have read of in books. You might make something called love between the two of you, like creating a stew, but I do not accept that love is lying in wait for you, except in your mind. Lust at first sight, or availability that might become love, but nothing ordained."

"Seems like a sad way to be," I said. "Just figuring everything is by accident, or of your own making, and there is no divine plan."

"That is what you call it? A divine plan?" Shorty shook his head. "As for it being sad, well, that is the nature of man, I believe. As for sad about there not being true love and not thinking it is all preordained, quite the contrary. It avoids a lot of disappointment and false expectations."

"I believe God has plans for all of us," I said.

"Set plans?"

"Yes."

"Predestination?"

"Yes."

"So the tornado coming along and sinking the ferry, your grandfather shot and killed, your sister nabbed and taken away, and you nearly drowned are all part of his plan?"

"I believe so."

"Then why worry about your sister? If it is part of his plan, then it does not matter how much you worry or concern yourself, because it is all going to come out a certain way anyway."

"Grandpa was not a worrier," I said. "I am. He trusted in God. He trusted in his plan."

"And God pulled a good one on him, did he not?"

"There is a reason."

"Unknown to us, of course."

"Someday, perhaps, in heaven."

"If you are in town, and there are horses running down the streets, coming from both directions, fast, do you look both ways before you cross the street?"

"Of course."

"Then you do not have the faith you claim," he said. "If it is all preordained, then you will be hit or not hit by those horses no matter which direction you glance, because it is all laid out."

"It is common sense," I said.

"Not if you believe as you do."

This was making my head hurt, and it reminded me of the sort of confusing questions Lula asked. I decided to abandon the talk by going silent.

Shorty put his eye back to the telescope. "Do you know how I became interested in the stars and the moon and the planets?"

I didn't really care, but since I was looking for his help, I decided to at least feign a bit of interest. "No," I said. "How?"

He turned from the scope and looked at me.

"A book by a man named Lowell. He wrote about Mars, about the canals he thinks are there, and if you look through the telescope—though the one I have is not truly sufficient to the task—you can certainly understand why he might think such a thing. Then the story I read that I mentioned, admittedly fiction, expounded on that, and excited my imagination. I had to save quite a bit from my dealings here and there to afford to send off for this telescope."

"Was it worth it?"

"I believe so. Yes."

While we were having this talk, all I could really think about was my sis out there in the wilds with those horrible men, one of them the murderer of our grandfather, and all of them bank robbers and killers and no telling what all. I kept wanting to bring that up, but I knew it was no use. We were not leaving tonight. I knew, too, from a reason standpoint, Shorty and Eustace most likely knew what they were talking about as far as catching sight of any sign.

"You are wishing none of what has happened to you had happened," said Shorty. "And you are wishing that your sister will escape, and that she and you will meet up and things will be as they were. Well, she might escape. It could happen, but through no wish of your own—through luck and circumstance, perhaps good planning on her part, initiative taken. Is she a good planner, a good thinker?"

"Not really, no," I said.

"There you have it. What you have to harden yourself to is us finding her and getting her back, and knowing things will not be as they were but as you make them. And we may not get her back. Though I can guarantee within reason we will find her if she is alive, and possibly if she is dead, and we will find them as well and take care of your business and seal our agreement. But once again, things may not be so happy when it is all over."

"I understand that," I said.

"Maybe you do, but youth can confuse you. Let me tell you a little something about why I do not believe in wishes. I was born to a man who named me Reginald Jones. I thought for a long time I would grow to be a normal height and be a son he could treasure. But I did not grow to a normal height. He called me his goddamn midget. My mother loved me and called me Reggie. She died when I was nine. My father put me to work at that age, and I do mean work. He was a harsh man. When I was ten he rented me out like a mule to a cotton farmer. On the way to work one morning, riding a paint pony called Old Charlie, I fell off and burst my eardrum. It was a terrific fall. I could hardly stand upright, and all the world seemed to tilt. I rode home, my ears bleeding. My father took a quirt and whipped me with it until I bled so bad the blood came through the back of my shirt. I climbed back on the horse, went to the cotton field, and put in a full day's work. That is how it was for me. Hard work, and there were few considerations. A year later my father told me we were going to the circus. I cannot explain the sort of excitement I felt, as it was not only the fact that I was a child and we were talking about the circus, which at that time was mysterious to me, but also that my father had made the plans and had included me to be with him. We did in fact go, but he left without me. I stayed. He sold me to the circus, and for not much money. Can you imagine? I was not the Reginald he had expected, and with my loving mother gone, he couldn't abide me and sold me like a household trinket. I was kept there like a wild beast, at the mercy of the owner. Let me tell you, in short order I decided the circus was nowhere as fun as I had anticipated. Not by a long shot."

"I'm sorry," I said.

Shorty sat down on the ground, and I did the same.

"No use to be sorry," he said. "It is what it is, and if you look at it at a proper angle there is a humor in it. It gave me my philosophy in life: trust no one completely. I have made some exceptions. I trust Eustace mostly, though when he drinks, he cannot be trusted by man or beast. Even Hog hides then, and Hog is fearless. I trust the sun to rise and the sun to set, though I know one day it will do these things without me, and I find that peculiar to think about. Do you?"

"Haven't never given it consideration," I said.

"Not a man of deep thoughts, huh?"

"I don't actually know," I said.

"You have not given your consideration much consideration," Shorty said, and gave out with a laugh that sounded a little like a bark. "When I was in the circus, a man named Walter the Midget taught me to think about such things. I do not know if I should be glad of it or if it would have been better to have been bathed in the shadow of ignorance. He once said those who refuse to consider what they do are cloaked in the shadow of stupidity, but they enjoy the shade. It is cool and comfortable there. He and the circus were my teachers. I do not say this expecting to be considered wise, but to suggest that most of us merely travel through life without much thought—or perhaps we consider some silly promised land where we will go when we die, knowing in our heart it is only one of those wishes I spoke of but trying to convince ourselves of its authenticity because we are afraid of the void."

"As I said, I believe God watches over us."

"If he is up there, he has certainly looked the other way during the course of my life. To begin with, he started me out with a handicap, or at least what others would think of as being one."

"He gave you a challenge."

"I did not want a challenge," he said. "I wanted to be tall. But what I got was Walter the Midget, the other midgets, and the circus. But Walter, he was educated, and he educated me with Shakespeare, Dante, Homer, books of poetry and philosophy, and his practical experience. He taught me how to be a clown as well, to make people laugh at my smallness. I have since then had very little to laugh about, and have been uninterested in making others laugh.

"Walter the Midget gave me the only true education I ever received. But the circus, I hated it there. I hated the people we worked for, if you can call what we did honest work. One time, a lion being whipped and poked with a chair, killed and ate part of the ringmaster right in front of a large audience, who did not leave during the event but acted offended at the same time they watched the lion have his dinner. It was for us, the midget clowns, a red-letter day, and we drank to it. We were sadder when they killed the lion. He had only done what most of us wanted to do, and that was kill one of the tall people. It was a good moment in a not-so-good life.

"Then one day there came an accident, and the main tent caught on fire. I am uncertain as to what started the fire. Some moron with a cigar or a cigarette flipped it against the outside tent wall, perhaps—I have no real idea. But you see, the tents were coated with oil and resin and wax to resist the rain, and they did do that most faithfully, but they were also death traps in a fire. When the fire spread to the top of the tent and jumped to the other tents, that hot burning residue that was created by the mixture of oil and wax dripped down and scalded animals and men and women and children alike. The tent collapsed in a hellish inferno. Being small, we clowns made our nimble exit easily beneath the bleachers, though I do bear a scar from the hot mess on my left shoulder. Anyway, to shorten it all—which, if you think about it, is what could be called a pun—both Walter and I made our exit through a rent in the tent and were gone. We were out in the world. I think the other midget clowns stayed with the circus or were perhaps consumed by fire. I never knew. Walter and I had had our fill, however, and made our path from town to town. We found that by performing some of the acts we had learned in the circus, mostly comedies that relied on our size for a laugh, we could pick up enough money to eat. The very thing that had made us miserable now made us able to fend for ourselves, though we often stayed in stables or outside, even in the rain.

"I believe it was cold weather and rain that led to Walter's coughing demise. The repeated exposure to bad weather gave him a terrible cold that turned into something worse. He died in a cemetery, of all places, under a tree. I had no idea what to do with him, so I left him there, went into a livery that night, and stole a shovel. I went back and buried him in a grave that already existed, on top of some soldier who had died in the Civil War. I felt Walter had fought a war of his own and deserved something of that nature, and, to be even more honest, the ground was softer there and not infested with roots. So to the best of my knowledge, there still lies Walter, with a soldier's corpse beneath him, and I moved on."

"You know," I said, "I think I will go down and get some sleep."

"You listen to me. I am leading up to a moment. So I went on then, and I came across none other than Buffalo Bill's Wild West show. It was on its last legs, and would soon become part of another show. Bill was mostly a sad old drunk by then, using bird shot in his pistols instead of bullets so he had better ability to shoot his tossed-in-the-air targets. But I was there when Annie Oakley was there, and let me tell you, she was a vision. Delicate and sweet, and to the best of my experience the finest rifle and pistol shot alive. When she dies I do not expect anyone to surpass her, though there was a great shot by

Billy Dixon with a Sharps rifle just under a mile that knocked a Comanche warrior off his horse and killed him."

"No one can shoot someone from a mile away," I said.

"Dixon did. That shot saved a whole passel of buffalo hunters out West Texas direction, at a place called Adobe Walls. He went on to win the Medal of Honor. One of the few civilians ever to receive it. But I was saying about Annie Oakley—and I will say, too, that this was before I knew true love was a crock. For when I saw her, I was instantly in love. It came on me like a fire, hotter than that circus tent had been. I felt this way even though she was married, and it was my view then, in my ignorance, that my true love would be her true love, that it would be requited. But it was not. She took to me, all right, though not in that way, and in time my ardor faded from lack of having the flames fanned, and I became her friend. Though between you and me, I still wanted to bend her over a stool and fuck her like a savage, but that was not to be.

"She taught me to shoot the rifle and the pistol, and, as I said, she is the finest shot ever. Perhaps Billy Dixon is second. However, I am no slouch. I can do what needs to be done when it comes to a gun, and old Sitting Bull, who was there briefly at the Wild West show, taught me how to use a knife. There is not much to it, actually. You just have to move fast, poke and slash where a fellow bleeds the most, and hope the other guy is unarmed. Sitting Bull said the best way is just to sneak up on someone and get them when they are not looking, and that is a fighting philosophy I have held to ever since. In a number of narrow situations, it has served me well. It served me when I helped track down the last of the Apaches, being the youngest and shortest scout the army ever hired. I got the job due to a recommendation from Buffalo Bill and

Annie Oakley. Later, I hired on to the Pinkertons and helped them break some strikes, shooting and killing a few folks in the process."

"What did you have against them?" I said. "Were they desperadoes?"

"I had about a dollar day against them," he said. "I am trying to make a point here, and I am going about it carefully so that you understand what kind of man I am. So again, let us return to our matter at hand. I am up for the job. Eustace and I are the men for the job, even if we stumble a bit now and then, as men will do. But I want that to be clear. I do not know you yet. I may never care to really know you, as there is a short list of people I care about. Fact is, it includes only Eustace, and though he is not a people, I care about Hog, though with less affection, not because of him being an animal but because of his unpredictable nature. Considering Eustace has made some unexpected moves, that is saying something. For me, if not for others, Eustace is predictable enough if whiskey is kept from him. But I have veered from my point, which perhaps I have belabored too long. I tell you all this to say simply that I do not know you. If you lie to me about that land, your ownership, just so you can rescue your kidnapped sister, I will not make an exception to a rule I have for myself about being cheated or led into something that will not pay me money when money has been promised. I will kill you deader than a rabid dog and leave you lying in a ditch beside the road. Do we understand one another?"

I was taken aback and tongue-tied.

He repeated himself. "Do we understand one another?"

I gathered up the words in my head and put them in my mouth. "We do," I said.

"Good. Now, I suggest you go to bed. First light is always nearer than you think, and we will actually rise before that, leave the moment the sky breaks bright."

I stood up, a little shaky from the threat. I said, "I don't intend to cheat anyone, you angry little asshole."

The dwarf smiled. "Good for you. See that you do not. And when you go into the house, be careful not to wake Eustace, as he does not like that kind of surprise, and it might be best not to startle Hog, either. The two of them are similar in personality, though Hog is a little less friendly at times, and, as I said, even more unpredictable."

I went down the hill and started to go in the house but didn't. I went on down a ways and thought seriously about walking away, trying to find a path to a road and march back into Sylvester. I felt if I left then, I might be in Sylvester by midmorning, and perhaps I could make new arrangements for Lula's rescue, something that didn't involve Eustace, the dwarf, and a belligerent pig. But I only walked awhile before I came to a clearing. I heard the running water of a creek and then saw it in the moonlight. I went toward the water. I was at the mouth of its source, a little spring. I sat down by it, cupped some water in my hand, and drank it, and then I burst out crying. I mean I let go. I told you how we Parkers are, and how we're just fine in grim circumstances, or seem to be, but when it comes upon us, when we can figure on something bad long enough, we get crying fits. And that's what I got. I let loose and had to put a hand over my mouth to keep from howling. I hoped I was far enough away that that goddamn dwarf wouldn't have the satisfaction of hearing me cry. Right then I wished that he had been killed in that circus fire, burnt up and trampled by an angry elephant, or beaten to death by monkeys with sticks. Then I tried to get those thoughts out of my head, realizing how unchristian they were.

As for Eustace, I had no particular feelings of goodwill for him, either. Not for a man who would dig up a burnt-up woman and her child and lay them on a doorstep for money. I probably felt the best feelings for Hog because we had shared a bed without incident, though the night was not yet over.

When I quit crying, and it took a while, I washed my face in the spring, then went back up the hill and into the house. I got back under the table, careful not to startle Hog. I found him a willing bed partner, albeit one of a strong aroma. He lifted his head slightly, scooted his back against me, and made a snorting noise before dropping his head back down on the floor. In a moment, I could hear the beast snoring, sound asleep.

Me, I couldn't get what the dwarf had told me out of my mind, and wanted to be sure that there would be no misunderstandings on his part or mine that might lead to me lying in a ditch like a rabid dog, and no one left to rescue Lula. I lay there and thought about all that had happened. I remembered how Grandpa had fought Cut Throat Bill and would have whipped him solid had he not gone for a gun. I remembered that mule flying over me, and somehow, the way I saw it in my troubled head, I was on that mule's back, and it had wings, and my sister was sitting behind me, her arms around my waist, and we were flying rapidly up and away, into a sky blue as a Swede's eye.

Eustace toed me awake with his work boot, and when I got up it startled Hog, who nearly knocked the table over getting to his feet. Hog was pressed up against me, his mouth open, his teeth showing nasty and yellow, his breath strong enough to tie knots in my eyebrows. He was making a wheezing sound that made me nervous.

I said, "Eustace, can you call him off?"

"Ah," Eustace said. "He ain't mad. He just didn't like I had to wake you two. He likes to think he's on the job all the time, and mostly is, but he was dozing good there. Actually, I think he likes you. Little later, you two sleep together enough, he might want some of your ass."

We went outside. It was still dark, and there remained a few stars and the half-moon. I looked up the hill, but the telescope and the dwarf were gone. A moment later Shorty came around the side of the house leading three horses. Eustace already had the borrowed horse out in the yard, holding him by the reins. I could see the automatic in his belt, winking in the moonlight. He also had on a vest with a thick pad on the right shoulder. I had no idea what that was about.

Saddles were lying across the three horses' backs over saddle blankets, but weren't fastened down. On the backs of the saddles were bedrolls, and the saddlebags bulged with possibles. The borrowed horse, whose reins Eustace held, still didn't have a saddle, as he was to be sold when a buyer turned up. The reins, in fact, were now a long rope, which acted as a lead.

Shorty handed me the reins to one of the riding horses, said, "You ride this one. But you have to fasten on the saddle. You know how to do it right? Watch that he does not blow up on you, making his belly bigger, then when you get on, he will let out his air and dump you."

"I do know what I'm doing," I said. "I was born on a farm and have ridden horses same as you and everyone else."

"That does not mean anything," he said. "Lots of people born on farms do not do it right. They do it to get by."

"You don't worry about me," I said, still angry from the night before. "You just do your part."

"Then go at it," he said, and walked inside the house. I went about the business of putting the saddle on right and tightening the belt and such. The horse tried to blow his belly up on me, as Shorty said he would, but I knew how to work around that. When Shorty came out he had a big-barreled two-shoot gun with him and a couple of crunched-up wide-brimmed hats and a good-sized bag. He gave the shotgun to Eustace, then gave him the bag and said, "There are your loads."

"You are a fine little white man and a gentleman," said Eustace.

"No insults are required," said Shorty. Then he turned to me, handed me one of the hats, plastered the other on his head. "We will need hats for the weather. The heat. You can have one of mine. It is not much account anyway."

I took the hat and put it on. It rested large on my head. It was my ears that kept it from falling over my eyes. I was glad to have it, though, because the back of my neck still ached with sunburn, and I didn't want to burn it further.

I glanced at the horse Shorty was planning to ride, saw that a rifle butt was sticking out of a sheath on the side, and there was a kind of rope ladder that hung down from the saddle horn.

I said, "I'm going to need a gun."

"Well, I got that Sharps and a pistol, and I intend to carry them both," Shorty said. "And I have a derringer in my boot. If we don't find you a gun before we need one, I'll give you that one."

"A derringer?" I said. "Grandpa already shot Cut Throat Bill twice with one, and it didn't kill him."

Shorty laughed. "He shot him? Priceless. You said he whipped him, but he shot him? That is something. I will say this, your grandpa had sand in him, and plenty of it. A derringer is mostly for real close work, and you have to pick your targets. It can kill you dead as a stick of dynamite, but you have to hit someone right for it to do it."

"That's what I mean," I said. "I'm not that good a shot. I can hit something if it's nailed down and I'm standing on top of it, but I'm no sharpshooter. I should use Eustace's shotgun."

They both laughed. "This here four-gauge," Eustace said, "would do you more harm than it would them."

"Four-gauge?"

"There aren't many of them, and I had this one special made," Eustace said. "I can cut down a field of hay with this thing, and maybe stack it."

"I need something to fight with," I said.

"Then perhaps you should cut yourself a sturdy stick," Shorty said. He went to his front door and closed it, then pulled a padlock the size of my elbow out of his coat pocket, for now he was wearing a light jacket, which, considering the heat even at early morning, he didn't really need. He clicked the padlock into place, said, "That should keep honest people out."

Shorty used the ladder to help him climb on the horse, then pulled the ladder up and put the last loop of it over his saddle horn. He tongue-clicked to his horse. We started out with it still night, us riding and Hog trotting along like he was out to see the scenery and maybe write some kind of travelogue on it; he kept turning his head and looking up, as if he were amazed at the lightening of the sky. We hadn't gone hardly any distance at all when the moon began to look like a pat of butter melting in an iron skillet, and the stars got hard to see. Then there was pink light crawling through the dark, and a blue sky crept in. By the time we got down to the river, being on the side where Cut Throat and his gang would have made their escape, the sun was up, and the river smelled of fish and rot. In the morning light the land and trees and the surface of the river were the color of fresh blood.

4

We rode alongside the river until we came to where the ferry would have docked had it made it across. Eustace got down off his horse, started looking about for sign, Hog looking with him.

I said to Eustace, "Can Hog follow sign?"

"He ain't a hound dog," Eustace said. "He probably could, but if he did, he wouldn't tell us about it. I think he just likes to look busy so we'll maybe think he's in the know."

While Eustace looked about, Shorty pulled a cigar from inside his coat pocket and put it in his mouth. He produced a match and lit it, licked his left thumb and forefinger, pinched the match head dead with his wet fingers, and tossed it onto the riverbank. He puffed a bit, looked at me, said, "Did you hear a wolf howling and caterwauling down by the spring last night?"

I knew he had heard me after all, so I didn't answer him. Eustace said, "I did. I thought it sounded more like someone crying. Maybe a girl, or a little child that wanted some titty milk."

He and Shorty looked at one another and snickered.

"That's very nice of you two," I said. "I was worried about my sister."

"Worrying will not find her," Shorty said.

"I got something here," Eustace said, breaking the direction of our conversation, and I was glad for it. "Two horses carrying two riders. They went off that way. One of them is bleeding."

"Maybe they went that way, and maybe they did not," said Shorty. "I remember the time we tracked an old man on a donkey."

"They did go this way, smart-ass," Eustace said. "I can follow this sign as it stands, plain and simple."

"Maybe you can, and maybe you cannot," Shorty said. "Or maybe you can until whoever is bleeding runs out of blood, my sweet Gretel."

"What?" Eustace said.

"It is a fairy tale," Shorty said. "And I have made you a character in it."

"You can go fuck your little short self with your little short dick in your fairy tail," Eustace said, then got on his horse. "This way."

Shorty looked at me with a grin, said, "I may be short, but the appendage to which he refers is not. Sometimes in the night, I mistake it for a full-grown water moccasin and try to choke it to death."

"That is no concern of mine," I said.

"Eustace there thinks when I say 'tale,' I am saying 'tail,' as in a tail you wag, and that I am referring somehow to a fairy, one of those little winged creatures, so he thinks I have made him a character inside a fairy's tail. How would anyone ever arrive at such a notion?"

"I have no idea, and I don't care," I said.

"It is because he does not know fairy tales," said Shorty.

"I said I didn't care."

"I do, for after all, I am a dwarf, and they seem to appear frequently in those stories. And speaking of that, I always thought if I were a dwarf in the story about Snow White, I would have worked seriously on dipping my wick in that bitch."

I rode on ahead of him, not only because I was finding him somewhat offensive but also because, like Eustace, I wasn't entirely sure what he was talking about. When I got up beside Eustace, he said, "Howdy, cousin."

"He's crazy," I said.

"Don't I know it?" Eustace said. "But there ain't no man, taller or bigger, I'd rather have at my back."

We traveled along a trail bathed in birdsong, mosquitoes, and blood drops, riding into the thick woods for a long distance. Eustace, now in the fore, was leaning out from his horse, studying the ground. Shorty came along behind us, leading the borrowed horse, as they called it. Hog trotted with us, occasionally disappearing into the woods, only to burst out of it at unexpected moments like a cannon shot.

Eventually, Eustace reined up and we all came to a halt. Eustace hopped off his horse, stood holding the reins and looking about.

"There was some kind of dustup here," he said, pushing his hat back on his head.

"A falling-out among thieves, perhaps?" Shorty said.

"I don't think so," Eustace said, wrapping the reins of his horse around a bush, then walking off into where the growth was thickest.

"You found something?" I asked.

"Got to shit," he said from within the brush.

He was gone for a while, and when he came out, Shorty said, "You did not wipe your ass on poison ivy like you did that time in Arkansas, did you?"

"Nope," Eustace said. "But I found something in there that tells me they have another horse."

"It is probably a note containing that information," Shorty said, looking at me, chomping on his cigar. "As that would be Eustace's best way of finding anything of complex origins."

Eustace grunted, went back into the brush.

We got off our horses, Shorty using his rope ladder, and tagged after Eustace. Hog, who had been wandering ahead of us by some distance, returned and trailed us into the undergrowth.

"You don't want to step over there," Eustace said when we were in the thicket. "That's where I left a little something. But if you look in that ditch next to where that honeysuckle is growing, you'll find what I'm talking about."

We looked, noticing pretty quick as we went that what we were smelling wasn't honeysuckle. There was a boy lying down in the ditch. He was about twelve, I figured, and he wasn't taking a nap. His throat was cut so wide and long it looked as if he had a second mouth. There were ants on him. His eyes were wide open—or what was left of them was, as the ants, and probably birds, had been at him for a time. He didn't have a shirt on, or shoes. Hog got down in the ditch, bit at the kid's hair, tearing it loose.

"Get away from there," I said.

Hog ignored me. I started to kick at him, but Eustace said, "I wouldn't do that you want to keep that leg."

I didn't.

"Hog," Eustace said. "Get out."

Hog got out, went crunching and smashing through the brush, as if throwing a tantrum.

Eustace said, "I could see out there on the trail that they came by another horse, and when I come in here to drop my apples, I found him. They robbed him of his ride, killed him, and left him. They probably took the shirt to bind those wounds you said your grandpa gave Cut Throat with his derringer. The shoes may have been for one of them lost theirs in the river. Maybe they just wanted an extra pair of shoes. No telling."

"All right," Shorty said. "That means they have found another horse to aid them in their escape, which means that, not having to ride double, they can continue wherever they are going more swiftly. And I would say that Cut Throat Bill himself has been at work. Word is, due to his having had his throat slit once, it is his favorite method of operation when it comes to dispatching someone."

Eustace and Shorty started walking out of the brush toward the trail. I said, "We can't just leave him here."

"I do not want to," Shorty said, "but we are losing time. Your sister is in need of rescue now. We do not need distractions."

Shorty could see I was having a hard time accepting this. He said, "Here, now, this is what we will do." He pulled a big knife from under his coat, slashed a hickory by the trail several times with it, and put it back. "We will have to let him remain in the ditch, but when we finish with our duty, we can let someone know he is here, and they can reunite his bones with his family."

"Which is what I figure will be left," Eustace said.

"That's unchristian," I said.

"You know where I stand on those matters," Shorty said.

"I am mostly Christian," Eustace said, "but I think it would be more Christian to help your sister out. That boy ain't going to need no helping. And we ain't got no shovel, and he ain't paying us anything, either."

I remembered then that burying was in fact part of Eustace's profession, and he had been known to dig up the dead when not paid properly, so appealing to his Christian learning wasn't going to have much impact. I looked at Shorty. Nope. Nothing there. He was smoking his cigar and swatting at a bug. I was beginning to fear the men I had fallen in with. It was as if I had gone to visit Lot in Sodom and Gomorrah and had encountered the men who wanted to bugger the angels. I wanted to be holy, but there didn't seem a way I could show it. Unlike in the sermons I'd heard, where the righteous fellow laid out his views on matters and the unwashed suddenly came clean, cleanliness of that sort was not in the making.

I decided I had no choice but to go on with things, but I will tell you quite sincerely that my guts ached and I felt as if Jesus had laid a disapproving hand on my shoulder. In fact, its warm presence was with me for a while, until later in the day I discovered I had been messed on by a bird.

The trail went along easy for some time, then, with me still brooding on matters, we came to where it forked. Eustace said, "Y'all wait here."

He rode off and we waited. Shorty's face was scrunched up, his lips pursed, his eyes narrowed.

"What's wrong?" I said.

"I think he lost the trail a ways back," Shorty said, pausing to relight his cigar. "I could tell the way he hesitated, and began searching around. It was easy to see he was hoping spoor of some manner would present itself. I think it did not. I believe the bleeder has stopped bleeding and is less easy to follow. You, too, would notice these things if you paid less attention to what is said and more attention to what is in fact true instead of what you prefer to be true. Suppose you are in a tough situation, and a man is smiling at you, and he is telling you something you want to hear, but his hand is reaching inside his coat, or behind something, or is resting on anything that might be used as a weapon. Well, watch his true action, not his false mannerisms. One can be faked, the other cannot."

"Isn't a mannerism and an action the same?" I said.

Shorty snorted as if he were trying to blow out a cantankerous booger. "Hardly. A mannerism is how you work your mouth and eyes, the way you try to sound when you talk. You saw something in my face then that concerned you, but you had to ask me what it was I was thinking. An action is what you actually do. It is not what you say, it is what you do. That is true in all matters of importance. You have to be cautious when you are in this line of work. It helps as well if you are good at it. Eustace, when it comes to tracking, is very much hit or miss. Currently, I believe he is in the miss position."

"That can't be good," I said.

"Of course not," Shorty said. "I told you he is not the master trailsman he pretends to be. His mother and her people were so good he cannot quite accept it. He seems to think it should be an innate quality, not one that is obtained through teachings from skilled trackers as well as from one's personal observations."

"He said he was taught."

"Yes, but he thinks you are born with certain attributes, like tracking and cooking skills. He claims both and has neither in abundance, though he can follow a trail sometimes and well enough, if it has not rained or the trail is not too cold. I should also add that Eustace is dogged in his own sometimes distracted way, and will eventually return to the snoop and manage to sniff something out, even if it is only squirrel shit in the pines or an old man riding a donkey instead of a deadly outlaw on a horse."

None of this sounded particularly encouraging.

"His cooking," Shorty said, "is fair to middling. He can heat beans, which is no great feat. However, he can fry you up some nasty pork with a gravy straight from the ass of the devil."

We sat there on our horses for what seemed a long time, and then I realized we were missing one of our companions. I said to Shorty, "Where's Hog?"

"He will find us," Shorty said, puffing his cigar. "You want the truth, I believe he has gone back to examine that boy's body."

"You mean eat it?" I said.

"That could be the case," he said. "We can hope he does not scatter the bones too far, so that those markings I made will still be of use to the family."

He sounded about as sincere as a lawyer whose client was holding a smoking gun.

By this point I felt as if I had fallen off the face of the earth and right down into hell, where I'd been led by these fellows with their stories—all this shiny business about what they could do and so on. Grandpa once told me that man lusted after silliness, women, shiny things like silver and gold, and all manner of big, bright lies. He warned me that you have to be careful of such things, because a sparkle isn't always a traveling light or a reward. It can be misleading. He said everything sparkles in hell.

About that time, Eustace came riding back, his head held down a little more than usual. When he got up to us, he reined in, dismounted, and said, "Here's what we got. Where the trail splits, well, I think some of them went off in the woods there, maybe cause they thought it was about time to throw anyone might be following off their scent, and one man went down this other trail for his own reasons."

"Toward No Enterprise?" Shorty said.

"That's the look of it," Eustace said.

"Does the man that went toward town have my sister?" I asked.

"No," Eustace said. "That man is riding single. She would still be riding double with one of them. They wouldn't have given her the spare horse. You said the men were also riding double, so it stands to reason one of them would end up with the horse. Which means she's with them that made their own trail through the woods."

"Then that's the way we should go," I said.

Eustace didn't say anything, but he had a look on his face like a blind man wishing he could see.

"Ah," Shorty said, leaning back in his saddle. "I can tell you right now we have a problem."

"Here he goes," Eustace said, kicking the dirt.

"Eustace has lost their trail in the trees, and the only trail he has is the one that goes right down the center of that little wagon road toward No Enterprise. Am I correct in this assumption, Eustace?"

"I guess you have assumpted right," Eustace said.

"Can't you find the sign to go after the others?"

"Maybe," Eustace said. "The woods break up in there a piece, and there's flat rock for a long ways, and a few straggling trees. It's not normal for around here. I'm not used to it."

"He means he cannot track over flat rock very well," Shorty said.

"Then what use are you?" I said. I think if I had a gun right then I would have used it on one or the other of them. Certainly I would have shot Eustace, and might have at least managed to wing the dwarf.

"Thing is," said Eustace, "we know one of them is going down the wagon road, and we can follow that. We find him, we got a good chance of knowing where the others went."

"Why would he go off like that?" I said. "Is he setting a trap?"

"I doubt that is his reasoning," Shorty said. "We have come too late for them to be on to us, to know we are following. He has broken off just in case someone is in pursuit, but he certainly would have no idea that we are. If I have read between the lines of the newspaper accounts of Cut Throat's robberies, there is seldom anyone brave enough to follow them for long. If the rabbit is running, the hound pursues, but if the rabbit pauses, and in fact turns out to be a wolf instead of a rabbit, then the pursuers lose interest. Or, to be more precise, townsfolk are brave in a cluster and in their own surroundings, but ultimately they do not want to be led out into deep water, so to speak, and drowned for some bank money, even if part of it is theirs."

"While we're chasing this clown . . ." and then I paused, remembering Shorty's previous profession, and looked at him. "No disrespect, but the ones that have Lula are heading into the woods, and will soon have her carried away, and maybe never to be found. So why would we follow this other fellow? It doesn't make sense."

"We would be wise to find the person who would most likely know where they are going," Shorty said. "And that would be the man who has ridden away on his lonesome. One is easier to handle than several. It would not surprise me to discover that he has gone to No Enterprise for supplies. Sending one man would be smarter than all of them going. But his intent for riding into No Enterprise is not a matter of concern; catching up with him is."

"And what if he isn't going into No Enterprise?" I said.

"Then that will be a new concern," Shorty said.

"Horse he's riding, one they took off that kid?" Eustace said. "It's got a nick in its shoe. I can follow the track clear, and when we catch up with him we can talk to him, see what he knows."

"You can't figure out how to track the others?" I said.

"I might could glance about and poke around till some sign showed up," Eustace said. "That could come quick or not at all. And if it rains, or there's lots of horses and wagons come this way, the tracks we got and know belong to one of them fellas could get lost. We could end up with nothing in our sack. A bird in hand is better than two in the bush."

I sat on the horse, bewildered.

Shorty said, "This is not like a Nick Carter story, son. We

do not always find a red feather in a cow plop that shows us the way. Mostly we stumble along until we find them. And if we only get one of them, which we have an opportunity to do, we pistol-whip the shit out of him until he reveals to us what we want to know. Which in this case would be where they have taken your sister."

I nodded, feeling numb all over. I had been raised to live and let live, to forgive and forget, but I couldn't forget. There was a burning part of me that wanted a gun in my hand. Not just for protection, but to kill. That scared me. It made me feel as if I was no different than one of Cut Throat's gang—a package of sweaty flesh full of bile for blood, dynamite for bones, and horse manure for brains. I thought about how my father would only give me four shells for squirrel hunting so I wouldn't chase the urge to shoot at will. "A gun is a tool," he used to say. "And you don't need to get so you don't want to stop pulling the trigger."

The situation left to us was to follow the boy's horse—the one that had been stolen—and even as we discussed it we were riding in that direction, our minds actually made up. Eustace, watching the trail, rode ahead of me and Shorty. As he went, Hog came out of the woods and ran alongside Eustace's horse as if he had been there all along and didn't want Eustace to know he had been wandering. I speculated on the possibility that he had in fact eaten that poor boy, or at least part of him. It was a horrible thing to think about, that boy's flesh bouncing around inside Hog's belly.

"My guess is our bad man is surely going into No Enterprise and will not veer," Shorty said. "He has some bank money, and most likely will want to spend some of it on drink and a woman and whatever is provided in the way of entertainment.

I have been to No Enterprise on many occasions myself, and know that for such a small place it is quite lively and deadly, which is another reason he chose it. It does not cater to the less-than-bold, and it is not a town full of idle talkers, even if they suspect you have killed a pack of women and diddled a sheep on the steps of the Baptist church. They pretty much keep it to themselves and consider it your business, as long as the women are not theirs. Or the sheep."

"What if the bandits have all the supplies they need?" I said. "Why would he leave the others? Maybe he's split with them over something, and doesn't know where they're going."

"Perhaps that is the case, but perhaps he is the one who was shot—Cut Throat Bill—and he needs medical attention. I doubt it, however, because Cut Throat has survived this long by not being overly foolish, and in spite of what I said there might be a limitation to what one could expect in the way of protection in No Enterprise if there is money involved. As you said, there is a price on his head, and of course, there is the bank money itself. You do not know how much was actually taken, do you?"

"No," I said. "I haven't got any idea at all."

"I have made very little of it, but Cut Throat Bill is known to me by newspaper accounts, and I confess to having read a couple of dime novels about his exploits—not that I believe any of them. It is said that he likes to cut throats, though, and time has proven him clever, or he would have been dead or captured long ago."

A new thought struck me about the money as Shorty talked. What if it was the bank money itself Shorty and Eustace were after? That would make me and Lula both expendable. But if that were the case, they wouldn't need me at all.

They could have killed me early on. Or ignored, or lost me, and gone after the loot for themselves. They hadn't. When I came to that somewhat satisfying conclusion, it was a comfort, at least for a few moments.

"Cut Throat Bill is pretty smart for one of his profession," Shorty said. "Most of them are not. Jesse James was, at least until Northfield. The Daltons were a mixed batch, and mostly lucky. Cut Throat Bill sees the angles. I read in the papers of one shootout in Missouri where he shot several children in the legs so that the town's attention would be drawn there while he and his gang made their escape. I think had he killed those children, folks would have gone after him outright, but he made it so they had to save them, get them to a doctor. It worked. There was considerable anger over the episode, but by the time they were ready to give chase, he was long gone. And he knows how to lose trackers, especially one like Eustace."

"Keep it up," Eustace called back to us.

"I think what we have here is one of the solos going his own way. Cut Throat Bill is unlikely to be anything more than a general leader with a team that does what they please when the job is done. Besides, this will give us a chance not only to catch up to one of them, but we can sell the borrowed horse to get a solid grubstake."

By this time I had been beset with fresh misery. My butt ached, and my thighs were raw from riding. Eventually the trail widened and emptied out of the woods. On either side of the road, trees had been sawed and chopped and made a mess of. Stumps had been blown out of the ground with dynamite, or dug out, piled up, and burnt. The recent rain had washed through it all and carried off the good topsoil, put a lot of it in a ditch beside the road and the rest of it in the road itself.

"Dumb sons a bitches," said Eustace, who had slowed down so that we were all riding together now, Hog having fallen behind a ways. "They've wrecked good farmland and a woodlot. They've cut the trees clear instead of cutting it in such a way that it could be plowed and they'd have a back line of trees to hold the dirt. Without the trees there's just runoff and the soil that went with it."

"I was just thinking that," I said, feeling this might be a good time to bring back up the reward they were working for. "Pa's farm, the one you'll get when this job is done, has soil as fine as what washed away here. Better, actually—darker and deeper, fattened and richened with wood ash and chicken manure. It has terraces to hold the water in, to keep it from washing all the topsoil off. You get the job done, you'll have it, or you can sell it for a better price than any farm in the county, the whole of Texas."

"So you have been everywhere," Shorty said, "and know the quality of the soil here and abroad?"

"Leave him alone, Shorty," Eustace said. "He's speaking big. I know what he means. If the dirt's half that good, I can raise my elephant-eye corn."

"I bet I am the only one among us who has actually seen an elephant," Shorty said. "And certainly the only one to ride one."

"They're tall, though, aren't they?" Eustace said.

"They are," Shorty said.

"Then it don't matter if I've seen one or not, does it?"

"You have a legitimate point," Shorty said.

The slaughtered woods and butchered soil went on for some space, and as we got close to town there were shacks thrown up alongside the road, made more by hope and lean than nail and level. In the distance, far out to the right, I could see a wooden tower. It was wide at the bottom and thin at the top and made up of what appeared to be broad slats of wood. It was like a dead tree without leaves.

"What in Sam Hill is that?" I said.

"You are country, are you not?" Shorty said. "That, Jack, is an oil well tower. I think it is dead, or drilled a dry hole. But all the same, oil is the future, not farmland. Mark my words."

"Yeah," Eustace said. "I'll make that note. That stuff is just messing up the land, oozing out all over. That damn tower will end up forgotten, if it ain't already. Wait and see. In fact, here's one of the reasons you can count on it being forgotten."

Eustace pointed.

Bouncing down the road toward us was a horseless machine. I had seen a few, but they never ceased to amaze me. It hummed and banged along on its little tires, causing the horses to startle. As the machine drew close, we split and let it pass between us. A man was driving and had a woman sitting beside him. They were dressed up, him with a derby, her with a sunbonnet. There was a picnic basket between them. The man tipped his derby as they rattled past. The couple looked well fed and remarkably content.

"That is the future," said Shorty, watching it cough along. "It runs on oil products, and soon those devices will be the way people get about. Not as a lark. Not as a short-lived inclination but as the future."

"I hate them things," Eustace said. "I thought about shooting it. Those damn things will never catch on, and there will go your so-called oil products beyond lighting a lamp."

Shorty laughed. "You, Eustace, are wrong. We use oil for all manner of things. There will come a time when men no longer travel by horse but by those oil-fueled carriages. Mark my words."

"I'll do that," Eustace said. "I'll make me a note of it."

We continued past more shacks, another gap of mauled countryside, a couple more of those oil towers, a large acreage of cotton, and then the first of the town's buildings, which was as big as a barn and painted the color of spring grass.

"That there is the opry house," Eustace said. "They had some blind colored singers there once, five of them, every one of them dead in the eyes but with voices like goddamn angels. I heard about it, come over to see them, thinking it was for colored, but it wasn't. It was for white folks to listen to. They wouldn't let colored in, and they had colored singing. Later that night, them five did a show in the niggertown section, too. I got to see that. They were damn good. Like doves and canaries, they were. Except they were as black as wet crows, blacker than me."

"Angels or birds?" Shorty said. "Which was it?"

"Both," Eustace said.

"I saw a singing group called the Marx Brothers in that place once," Shorty said. "On the upper floor, a year or so back, and they were not good. I would much rather have heard the colored boys singing in niggertown, or perhaps a dog howling with a chicken bone in its throat. Listening to them caused me considerable pain, though they told a few jokes and I thought those were quite entertaining."

More buildings followed on each side of the street. They didn't look nearly as sophisticated as those in Sylvester, but they were larger than those in Hinge Gate and brighter in color than anywhere else I had been. The town, however, looked to have been laid out by one of those blind singers.

It was as if everyone got together and decided on a different color for the buildings just so nothing would be anything alike. Actually, I have exaggerated the variety of color. There was green and blue and red, and everything else was some darker or lighter shade of those, except for one building that was two-story, blue at the bottom, red at the top, buttercup yellow on the windowsills and the gallery railing. A door on the upper floor was also buttercup yellow, and the knob had been painted bright blue, like a giant robin's egg.

As we passed that building, Shorty said, "That is one of the biggest and best whorehouses in East Texas. They call it a club for cattlemen. But you do not have to know one end of a cow from the other to enter, though you should know which end is up on a woman. I have been known to be accepted into the arms of ecstasy there, my money being larger than my size. Though after both myself and my money are spent, suddenly I grow smaller and considerably less attractive."

"Hog," Eustace said, "you best run off now. Hunt some acorns or such."

Hog grunted as if in reply and drifted off into the woods.

I said, "Does he really understand you?"

"I don't know," Eustace said. "For all I know he's messing with me. Maybe he ain't hunting acorns at all. Maybe he's hunting for a girl pig or making plans for your grandpa's land. He might not want to farm with me at all. He might want to throw in with Shorty and buy an oil well."

"Hog is a lot like his daddy," Shorty said, nodding at Eustace. "Unpredictable. Yet I would welcome him into the oil business with me in a heartbeat. I have seen how fast and deep he can dig with that snout. I think he might find oil sooner than a rig and drill."

The town had a smell about it. Not like Sylvester or Hinge Gate, but a floating stink of raw sewage and horse manure, of which there was plenty of both in the streets, running in rivulets, stacked in piles. In Hinge Gate and Sylvester there were people whose job it was to shovel it up, and there were honey wagons to take out the human sewage. Here, there were outhouses back of places, but the drops were not too deep and you could see streams of offal oozing out from beneath them toward the street with nothing but a now-and-then board crossing over the rot. We rode along next to one of those ditches, and in one I saw a bird of some sort drowned there. He looked tarred and, of course, feathered.

The streets themselves were wet and rough. They had all manner of pocks and holes in them, and there were ragged boards stretched over the street in places to make a path from one boardwalk to the next. On the right, we passed a gap in some buildings, and there were a bunch of men and young boys, a few girls, gathered in a circle. We could hear a terrible squawking that was almost as loud as the men cheering and yelling.

Shorty took off in that direction right away. I rode after him with Eustace. Eustace said, "Now, this ain't in our plan, but I can guarantee we're about to take detour from it."

I wasn't sure what that meant, but by this time I had dismounted with Eustace and Shorty and realized what was going on. A chicken fight. Men had made a circle around two red roosters and were betting on the winner. A chicken fight is nasty business, and I hadn't never seen but the natural ones, where roosters will take to one another on the yard. This is why some folks will say they're not doing anything they wouldn't do naturally, but if they're not forced, and they have the opportunity, one of them will usually break and things will be all right. And it is a fight of their choosing, not that of some man with a dollar to bet.

This way—when they were fought for money—one of the roosters, maybe both, were not going to be all right, because little metal claws had been made for their feet and fastened there. When they jumped and swiped at each other, it was like a razor fight between men. The ground where the roosters fought had been made dry with sand and raked over, but now it was wet with hot rooster blood, and the smell of it gave me a taste in my mouth like biting into copper.

Shorty pushed through the circle and yelled, "Better make clear, or you will catch a bullet."

One man on the far side said, "What's that midget saying?"

By that time, "that midget" had drawn a little .38 belly gun out from under that coat he had on, which I guess explained why he wore it even though the weather wasn't suitable. He pointed it at the man who had spoken with a sure hand. The man made a run for it. That side of the circle broke as well, making a wave to the left and right, creating a gap like the parting of the Red Sea.

One of the roosters was breathing heavy, and its head was hanging with exhaustion. The other one was moving in for the kill. Shorty said, "Kill them and eat them or leave them alone," and he fired, two quick snaps, taking those roosters' heads off cleaner than you could have done with a hatchet and them with their necks stretched out on a chopping block. One of the headless roosters fell over and kicked, the other started running around in circles, flapping its wings, as if it might find its head, put it on, and take off to parts unknown. It did that for what seemed a long time before falling over, shaking once, and finishing out its string with a last long squirt of blood from its neck.

"You bunch of goddamn cowards," Shorty said.

The crowd had mostly gone away, but there were still some that remained. One of them, a large man, said, "That big one was my rooster. You owe me for him, you little sawed-off piece of shit."

Shorty didn't look up. He put the pistol under his coat, picked up the man's rooster, pulled out his big knife, and cut off one of its feet. When he did, that metal spur sparkled in the sunlight. He turned toward the man, said, "I advise you to be careful what manner of speech you direct to me."

"Where did you learn to talk?" said the man. "In some foreign country? Talk American, for God's sake. We had a bet going, and my rooster was winning. You haven't got any right to wreck our fun and cost me money."

"Call that fun?" Shorty said.

"I do," said the man, and no sooner were the words out of his mouth than Shorty leaped, put his foot on the man's knee, grabbed his shirt with one hand, and, holding the rooster spur in the other, brought the metal blade across the man's cheek, cutting a red river in his skin.

"Hell," the man said, trying to push Shorty off. "Hell, now." But it was like trying to pull a raccoon out of a tree by the tail. It wasn't happening. Shorty was all over that big man, up one side and down the other, slashing with that razor-tipped chicken foot.

The man started yelling for us to get our midget off of him. Eustace handed me the reins of the horses and the rope to the borrowed horse, ran over, and clutched Shorty around the waist. He yanked him back from the man, set him down on the ground, and placed his hand on top of his head to weight him down. Shorty tried to get up and plow ahead, but Eustace's hand covered the entire top of his noggin, crushing Shorty's hat. Shorty twisted beneath Eustace's hand, cussing and waving the rooster foot at the big man like it was some kind of witch's charm.

By this time the man Shorty had been working over with the rooster foot had fallen on his knees and was bleeding quite smart, as he was cut from head to belly button, his clothes hanging in rags where the blade on the rooster's foot had done its work.

"There is some fun for you," Shorty said as Eustace pulled him back by the collar.

"You better keep that little crazy bastard off of me," said the man, "or I'll—"

"You'll do what?" Eustace said. "You get on up and out of here or I'll let him go."

The man got on up and out of there as suggested and ran away fast. It was then that I noticed everyone that had been left in that circle had disappeared like the morning dew. All that was left was us and those two dead roosters.

"That is no way to treat a bird," Shorty said, and his little shoulders sagged.

Eustace was soothing him with a repetition of "Now, now, now, Shorty. It's all done up now. I tell you what I'm going to do, I'm going to let you go, and you don't have no cause to do nothing else now. Everybody's done run off."

"Do not treat me like a child, Eustace," Shorty said.

"Course not, Shorty. I wouldn't do that."

Eustace let go of Shorty's collar. Shorty shook a little, as if trying to settle back properly inside his coat.

"I'm going to stuff these here chickens in my saddlebag," Eustace said, "and fix them up for our dinner in a bit. Ain't no use for them to go to waste, being as how they're dead."

"Damn them and their so-called sport," Shorty said.

Shorty marched over to where I was holding the horses, grabbed the reins to his, started leading it back into the street. Eustace came over, shaking the blood out of the chickens as best he could, then put them inside one of his saddlebags.

"That ain't even him mad," Eustace said. "He's just irritated. It's real irritated, but it ain't mad yet."

I wasn't exactly sure what to make of what had just happened. A man who would leave a boy dead in a ditch but fight a man twice his size with a bladed rooster foot for mistreating a rooster wasn't a man I could wrap my feelings around, not even a little bit.

It was decided that since I was the only one who had seen the men on the ferry, and that only Cut Throat Bill had a mark they could identify, it would be best if I wandered about to see if I could locate the lowlife who had taken the dead kid's horse. I was to take note of him, come and find Shorty or Eustace so that they could take care of the problem. I was told that under no circumstances was I to try and take on the man myself, and that what we needed from him was information as to the whereabouts of the others, not a killing; least not right up front. That was all right with me. Bad as I wanted to avenge my sister, I wanted more to find her, and frankly had no desire to kill a man, only to have him captured and jailed. They were speaking a language I wanted to hear.

While I looked around, it was their plan to go to the livery, sell the borrowed horse, and buy us a grubstake. It was also their plan to grain and water and rest the horses, and maybe ask if a man had come in on a horse with a bad shoe.

It wasn't a plan up there with Napoleon's, but it's what we had. Before I left out, Eustace came and stood by me as Shorty moved toward the livery with the horses.

"Here's that money I got for digging those graves, cousin," he said. "I want you to hold it for me so I don't get the need to spend it on liquor. I spend it on a piece of ass back there in niggertown, that's all right, but I'm afraid one might lead to the other, and I don't want to get myself going in the wrong direction, considering what we got ahead of us."

"Just don't drink," I said.

"I don't have money, I won't," he said, and he closed my fingers around his four bits. "You want to buy some ass, they got it cheap over at the whorehouse there, and you might find your man inside, too."

"I don't think I want to do that," I said. "I mean, I want to find the man, but I'm not interested in the other."

"You do what you want, but you either spend it or hang onto it. I get in a town like this, start looking around, next thing I know I got me a jar of lightning and I'm putting it in my belly. But it don't stay there. It goes straight to my head, sparking and hissing and making me wild."

"All right," I said. "I'll take the money."

Eustace nodded, followed Shorty to the livery.

I poked the four bits in my overall pocket, went wandering about. I first went to one of the three saloons, but didn't see anyone there I recognized from the ferry. One thing Shorty and Eustace hadn't mentioned was that since I knew the robber, he would know me. Maybe with my hat on, my red hair would be mostly covered, though it still leaked over my ears and hung down the back of my collar. If he spotted me right off, he might take flight, or might decide to kill me. With this in mind, nervous as a long-tailed cat in a room full of rocking chairs, I went about the saloon but didn't find my man. I felt strange being there, as I had never been inside a saloon before. I had the feeling everyone knew it and was watching me, which, of course, was unlikely.

I left out and looked in the other two saloons, but still didn't see anyone I recognized. I saw a fistfight in an alley between two big men, and one man finally knocked the other one down and was kicking him when I went on by. I came to where the bright buildings ended and saw above them on the hill a different batch that were whitewashed and simple-built. There was beyond that a few houses with white fences around them, flowers in the yard, struggling against the heat, as by this time of day it had warmed up considerable. I also saw in the distance a cotton gin and wagons of cotton being brought to it. The air was starting to fill with the lint of cotton from the gin, and in the sunlight the lint was yellow, not white, and I could smell it being ginned.

Further up the street, I saw the sheriff's office. It was located between the brightly colored buildings and the whitewashed ones. Up the hill, in the less brightly painted part of town, was where the more orderly citizens lived, perhaps with families and jobs. I thought then of going to see the sheriff, but hesitated. If I let him know the bank robber was in town, he might think I had come to kill him and would want to pull me off the search. I figured it might be best if I found the man first and then told the sheriff. I stood there looking at the sheriff's office for a long time, thinking not only about that but also about the boy in the ditch. At some point, I had to let the sheriff know about the kid with the cut throat and give some idea as to the body's location. Maybe the boy's family could be found. But not right then.

I turned around and started walking back into the brightly painted section of town. When I got to the whorehouse there wasn't a lot of activity, but the main door was open, and there was a closed screen door behind it. I looked through the screen. There was a man sitting in a chair in the hallway facing the door, and he had an old .410 lever-action shotgun across his knees. I had only seen a gun like that once. Pa had one when I was younger, and he had swapped it for something with the same peddler who had most likely carried the pox to him.

I took off my hat and went in, the screen squeaking like a nervous bird. It was exactly the kind of place Grandpa would have hated. The man with the shotgun looked at me, said, "They're mostly sleeping, except for Jimmie Sue."

My plan had been to come in and look about, hope to spot someone from the ferry, but now that I was inside I realized just how stupid that idea was. If the man were here he would probably have taken a room with one of the whores. I considered coming back at night, when there might be more activity, but I feared I could miss my man, as he could move on. I decided to think on it.

I said, "You know what? I'm going to think about it and come back later. I'm not sure I have enough money."

The man with the shotgun eyed me like I was the pox myself. "Think about it?" he said. "You either want pussy or you don't."

"A man can change his mind," I said.

"I wouldn't change my mind," he said.

"I guess that's where me and you differ," I said. Then I heard the stairs creak and saw a woman in her bloomers coming down the stairs. The only time I'd ever seen such a thing before was in the Sears, Roebuck catalog, which I would look through before tearing a page loose to use to wipe in the outhouse, and though I had thought some of those women looked pretty good in that catalog, this was an altogether different thing, and better.

She had hair dark as Eustace's skin. It fell all the way down to her shoulders. Even from a distance I could tell her eyes were greener than the outside walls of the opry house, and it was also clear she had some very nice structure beneath those underclothes. She didn't look any older than me.

"Ain't you the redhead?" she said, as if I might not have noted it yet.

"Ma'am," I said, and since I had my hat off, I kind of nodded.

"Ma'am?" she said. "Now, ain't that cute? And all mannered, like a real gentleman."

"I seen him," said the man with the shotgun. "And right off I thought, now ain't he cute and redheaded and all. I want to fuck him myself."

"Oh, shut up, Steve," she said.

He laughed a little.

I said, "I was just about to leave."

"You ain't even got here good yet," she said. "You ain't even all the way inside the door."

I stepped forward a little.

"Would you like a nice ride?" she said. "It being a hot and miserable day."

I just stood there.

Steve said, "She don't mean a pony ride, son, and you don't need to have brought a saddle."

"I know that," I said.

"Do you, now?" he said. "You look to me like a man that's mostly worked his knob with his fist."

I gave him a hard look.

"That part about it being hot and miserable ain't that big a calling card," Jimmie Sue said. "But if you're going to be hot, you might as well be hot and bothered and end up with your ashes hauled and me with four bits in my poke."

"Four bits?" I said.

"You got four bits, don't you?" said Steve. "You ain't, then we can end this pleasant conversation now. You can put your hat on your cute little red head and go."

"I've got four bits," I said, determined not to be made a low dog by Steve and his shotgun.

"Well, come on up," Jimmie Sue said. She turned and started up the stairs.

I considered for a moment, and then followed. Steve said, "Don't fall off, Red, or get bucked. You got to really get your spurs latched into that one."

"Ignore him," she said as we went up the stairs. "He's an asshole."

At the top of the stairs was a long hallway, and there were doors along it, and outside the doors were men's boots. As I followed Jimmie Sue, the floor creaked and groaned. No one stuck their heads out of the doors, and I hitched along to where Jimmie Sue went through an open door. I went inside and stood by it.

"You can close it," she said, "unless you like other people to watch. There's some that do."

I closed the door. I said, "First off, I'm going to give you the four bits. Eustace's four bits. But it ain't like you think."

"Eustace? Is your name Eustace?"

"No. That's the man who gave me the four bits."

"Is he coming here, too?" she asked.

"No."

"That's good, because I don't do two men for four bits. You'd both need four bits apiece, and if me and you and Eustace all get in bed at the same time, it's extra."

"Forget Eustace," I said. "I got off on a different train track there. What I mean—"

"You are red as fire," she said. "You're all blushed, and you got cotton lint stuck to your face. That is so cute."

"I don't mean to be cute," I said.

"That's what makes it so cute. You ain't never had any pussy, have you?"

"I'm not here to discuss that," I said.

"There's no discussing to do," she said, and started taking her clothes off.

"You don't have to do that."

"If you want you a little, I do. You see, the hole is under the clothes."

I could feel myself blushing. It was like hot water was rising up from inside me, boiling to the top of my head. Before I could say anything more, she had shucked her drawers and was standing there in her birthday suit. It was the first time I had ever seen a woman naked. My heart soared like a hawk. She looked so natural there, her small, round breasts riding high and the dark patch between her legs. All I could say was, "I'm actually looking for someone."

"I'm the only one awake. You got someone else in mind, you're shit out of luck."

"It's not that."

She studied me, tilted her head, said, "And I don't reckon you ever been here before to have someone in mind. You are a virgin, aren't you?"

"That's not important," I said.

"Then you are one," she said. "You might as well be waving a flag that says you are. I can tell. Come here, honey."

I didn't move.

She came over to me. She said, "I've taken a bath. There ain't any other men on me or anything of theirs in me."

"God, I hope not," I said.

She took my hand. "Come here to bed."

"I just want to talk, ask some questions."

"I'll teach you whatever you need to know. It ain't like there's a line of customers around the block, so I got time."

"I want to know about a man," I said.

She paused and let go of my hand. "You like men?" she said.

I had to figure on that a moment. "No. I'm looking for someone I think might be staying here."

"Well, who is it?"

"I don't know exactly."

"You are perplexing, Red."

"I don't mean to be. I'm looking for someone who was involved in killing my grandfather and stole my sister."

"So you don't want me?"

I wanted to say no right out, but the word wouldn't form in my mouth. Instead I said, "I didn't say that. I mean, it's natural, I guess."

"It sure is. Can I see the four bits?"

I dug the four bits out of my pocket and opened my hand and showed it to her. "There it is," I said. "And if you can help me find who I'm looking for, it's yours."

She ran a hand over my face. "You are so damn cute. I was going to leave this life, it would be for someone like you. I can tell you're kind, too."

"How can you tell that?" I said.

"In this job you get so you can tell a lot of things," she said. "You get so you can read people pretty quick. Men especially. Come here, honey. Let's go over here and lay on the bed, and then I'll see I can straighten things out. I'll go ahead and take the four bits now."

I don't even know exactly how it happened, but pretty soon I was naked and in bed with her, and she said, "I like that you've got red hair down there," and then she started teaching me some things.

I caught on right away. When we were done, I was weak with delight. Some of the sin Grandpa warned me about had got hold of me, and hadn't been near as unpleasant, disappointing, and soul-sapping as he had described it.

I lay there wishing for another four bits. It took me longer than it should have for me to realize why I was really there and that time was wasting, but before I could do anything about it, sin got hold of me again in the name of a free one, as she called it, and I did the deed once more. It was long and sweet, and the warm wind through the window fluttered the curtains and the bedsprings squeaked like mice and the cotton lint drifted in and settled over everything, including our sweaty bodies. Jimmie Sue moaned in a way that didn't make me think she was wounded, and being a fellow who cared about his money, I thought: I am actually only paying two bits apiece here, and it's Eustace's money, and this way he will not be driven to drink. The last part was something I was proud of. I was protecting Eustace from himself.

"By the way," she said, snuggling up to me when we were finished, "what's your name?"

"Jack Parker," I said.

She said, "Parker. I know some Parkers."

"I doubt there's a connection," I said. "It's a common name."

"You ain't any kin to Old Caleb Parker, are you?"

"That's my grandfather," I said, surprised she might know of him.

"Why, that old fart," she said. "You and him are kin. Now, that's a coincidence."

"How's that?" I said.

"Why, now I've diddled you both."

5

I started questioning her like she was on trial. She told me about Grandpa, and she described him right, said he liked to leave his union suit on and just unbutton the fly. She said, "If I'd known he was religious, I wouldn't have told on him. Religious people like to keep this part of their life quiet, that and their drinking. Way I figure it, Jesus forgives, so why not enjoy yourself? He'll understand."

"I don't know it works exactly that way," I said.

"Well, it ought to," she said.

I was stunned to find out Grandfather and I had shared more than the hole in the outhouse and the water dipper at the well. It was like finding out your face belonged to someone else. But I couldn't dwell on it.

"I'm really here to find my sister," I said.

"You could have fooled me," she said. "Does she work here?"

"Nothing like that," I said. "She's a decent girl."

Soon as I said it, I wished the words had not come out of my mouth. I could feel Jimmie Sue tense beside me. "Ain't that something?" she said. "You rode me like I was the Rock Island Line, and now you want to say I ain't decent."

"I didn't mean it like that."

"I think you did."

"All right," I said. "I did. But I was wrong. I shouldn't have said that."

"I let you have it twice," she said.

"And I'm grateful."

"You ain't going to be like your grandpa, now, are you? Make me kneel by the bed and say a prayer and promise how I'm going to give up the life, and then him tell me he'll see me next month on the first Tuesday?"

"He came that often?"

"When his wife was alive he came to see the other girls, or so they've told me. I don't know how long ago that was, but I was told when she died he came here more often, and . . . if you don't mind me asking, how did she die?"

"She got run over by a cow," I said.

Jimmie Sue almost spit. "A cow? She got run over by a goddamn cow? I ain't never heard of that. Now, that is some shit, that is. A fucking cow."

"Happens more than you might think," I said. "Out in the country."

"Well, I'll be goddamn. A cow. It must have took some work to make a cow mad. It wasn't a bull?"

"It was a milk cow," I said.

"That is something," she said. "Sorry. But that is just funny, that's what that is. He never said a thing about it. I guess that isn't something you go around spouting. My wife got murdered by a milk cow. Was the cow armed?"

"It's not that funny," I said.

"It's kind of funny," she said, and laughed a lot to prove it. When she laughed she looked even better, her teeth all firm and white and shiny, her face damp with sweat, her grass-green eyes so wide and deep I wanted to fall into them.

When she got hold of herself, she said, "About your grandfather. When I went to work here six months ago, he came to see me more than any once a month on Tuesday. He always says that, about being here once a month on Tuesday, because he likes to go to prayer meeting or some such thing on Wednesday, but he's been coming to see me twice a month easy. How is the old prayer-spouting bastard?"

"Dead," I said.

She sat up in bed. "Oh, I am sorry."

"That's all right."

"A cow didn't get him, did it?"

I looked at her.

"Sorry," she said. "That wasn't very nice. I just couldn't resist. Was it a goat? Or a sheep, maybe?"

"That's enough of that."

"Sorry," she said.

"I'm out to avenge him, actually. Well, I don't really want to hurt anyone. I want to see them that killed him locked up. Mostly, though, I just want my sister back," and then, without even knowing I was going to do it, I told her everything that had happened, and in a pretty detailed way, and when I was finished, I knew why it was supposed to be that generals and kings talked to their mistresses too much. Diddling, as she called it, makes you weak in both legs and mind.

"The one you said was fat, and missing some teeth," Jimmie Sue said. "That's Fatty."

"Yeah, that's what they called him," I said.

"He was here last night, and still might be. I've seen him two or three times before, though he ain't never been with me. I know it's not good business sense, but there's some so ugly or smelly I try to draw the line, as long as there's someone else willing to take them on. And he's got a cousin here who will."

"A cousin?"

"Way Katy looks at it, it's her business to take care of men, and he's one, and they ain't close cousins or nothing. Cousins marry all the time."

"Not in my family," I said, then I was up and pulling on my clothes. "So he's here?"

"I don't know if he's left or not," she said. Her face turned sour, or as sour as that sweet face could look. "Now I see what it was you really wanted. I misunderstood and have led you off your mission."

"To be honest, I think what I got was what I really wanted," I said.

"That's kind of sweet."

"I just didn't know I wanted it."

"It's like finding out about chocolate cake. Once you've had it, from then on you crave it. Look, I can point Fatty out to you, but keep me out of it." And then I could clearly see a thought land on her head, surely as if it were an eagle. "No. Better yet, Red, take me with you."

"Why would I do that?"

"We can do what we were doing here for free if I go with you. I'm a good traveling companion. I've learned a lot of jokes working here. Don't ask me to cook none, though. I can't boil water without setting it on fire."

"You can't set boiling water on fire if you wanted to," I said.

"That's one of my jokes."

"It isn't a good one. It doesn't make any sense."

"You can damn sure boil it down until the pan catches on fire," she said. "I've seen me do it."

"You really want to run away with me?" I said.

"I want to get away from Steve," she said. "He told me this was a fun life, but it ain't. There's some perks. There's that whole thing about the place here having electric lights and a gas burner for cooking, but like I said, I don't cook very well. And we got shitters inside. They're down the hall in a room right here in the house. You can do your business in them and pull a chain and water will wash the mess away. Only place in town that's got indoor shitters is this whorehouse. I like that plenty, cause you don't have to go outside in the night and worry about some bug or snake crawling up your bare ass in the outdoor convenience. But as I was saying, this ain't no fun life. That was a goddamn lie Steve told me. He found me at the train station in Austin when I got off. I had run away from home because Mama wanted me to be a goddamn seamstress like her, and I didn't want to spend a life with needle pricks in my thumb. I wish now I was back there wearing a thimble. Course, I wrote her once and she wrote me back, but there wasn't any invitation back home. She said not to write her anymore. And Steve, he said he loved me, and he'd take me away to better things, and the next thing I knew I'm here flat-backing, and this ain't better than nothing except for what I was saying about gas and electricity and the shitter. And now and again there's a man who is not bad to do it with."

"You've enjoyed it with other men?" I said.

"You think I been just living here waiting on you, Red?"

"I guess not," I said, but my confidence was a bit stepped on. I was thinking I had been so good with her my first time out she was ready to quit the whoring business and go off with me. But she mainly just wanted to quit the whoring business.

"I just met you, and now you want me to be the love of your life?" she said.

"No, but—"

"Listen here," she said. "I like you. I do. But all I'm asking is you get me by Steve and out of here, and I'll try to show you the fat man if he's here. I'll go with you for a while, and you can have all of me you want, except if I'm having a mood. I can get out of a bad mood if I'm getting paid, but if I'm not being paid, and it's one of those dark times, I'm not as friendly as I ought to be. I thought I'd warn you ahead of time."

I was discovering that Jimmie Sue was quite the chatterbox. I decided to get right to the point, or at least the point I was now the most concerned with.

"Won't Steve shoot me if I try and take you away?"

"He will, and several times if he catches us," she said. "He thinks he owns all of us, like we're sheep or something. Some of the other girls, they're all right with that. But me, I want to leave. I can do it, now that I've got someone to help me."

"I didn't agree to that," I said.

"But you want to, don't you?"

"I suppose," I said. "But I don't like that part about getting shot."

"Then there it is. You're going to help me, and we're going to try and make sure you don't get shot."

"Try?"

"You think life ain't got a risk or two, hon?"

"Yeah, but this is one I don't have to take."

"But you will, won't you?"

I didn't say anything, but she acted as if I agreed. When she was dressed, she picked up a little handbag that had a drawstring, put the four bits I had given her into it, and looped the bag over her wrist. She said, "Way we can tell if he's still here is his boots."

"Steve?" I said.

"No, hon. Fatty."

Out in the hallway I looked both ways and saw the boots. I didn't know one pair of boots from the other. But Jimmie Sue did. She pointed. "That's his, the ones with the silver toes. He's got them that way to kick people. He brags about it to some of the girls, how's he's kicked men in the knees and balls. Katy, his cousin, she thinks it's funny."

"I haven't met her," I said. "But I can tell you right now, hers is not an opinion I would hold highly on anything, especially family relations. You're sure those are his boots?"

"Pretty sure."

"How can you be completely sure?"

She crept down the hall and picked up the boots and held them head height, whispered to me. "Look, you see they got little blades under the toes."

I went over and looked. There were indeed little blades that fit right under the toes and stuck out about an inch.

"It's him, then?" I said.

"It is," she said. We crept back down the hall and stood in front of her room. "If you break in the room and shoot him, that'll cause a ruckus, and we won't be going anywhere. So you want me to go with you, it'll have to be another plan."

"I need information from him," I said. "We intend to interrogate him."

"Interrogate him?" she said. "That sounds like something I do in the bedroom."

"According to Shorty, it means we'll pistol-whip the shit out of him until he talks. Those are his words."

"Why didn't you just say so, Red? I know what that means."

I was thinking about a lot of things all of a sudden. Fatty, of course, and Grandpa, who had been a danged liar and a cheater on Grandma, before and after the cow incident. And from the way it sounded, them cow hooves hadn't long been on Grandma's head and her in the ground when he was here doing what he had been doing all along, only more regular.

If those thoughts weren't bad enough, now I had Jimmie Sue to worry about, and pretty soon I'd have to explain her to Shorty and Eustace. I was also thinking about that boy lying in a ditch, and of course my sister out there in the wilds of somewhere, and here I was wasting time with a whore and not hating it too much. I was, in fact, wrapped up in a kind of cloud, having finally experienced what I'd heard men talk about. From my point of view, they hadn't been exaggerating.

Back in Jimmie Sue's room, we got the sheets and tore them and tied them together, making knots that could be grabbed on to. We fastened the sheets to the bedstead on one end and dropped the other end out the window. It was two stories down. The sheet rope wasn't as long as we had hoped. I used my pocketknife to cut up a blanket, and we worked that in with the sheet. Now we had something that would almost reach the ground, leaving Jimmie Sue with only a short drop.

Plan was she'd go out that way and I'd go out the way I came, another satisfied customer. I helped Jimmie Sue out the window, and, clutching the sheet-and-blanket rope we had made, she started down. She was about halfway there when a knot slipped and she fell the rest of the way. It wasn't a terrible drop, but she landed hard, on her butt, let out with a charge of air that at that moment seemed loud enough to be heard at the other end of town and maybe on up at the cotton gin.

She glanced up, gulped in some air, and got up. She waved me on.

I went out then, down the stairs, started out the door. I waved at Steve and his shotgun. He didn't wave back. He just glared at me. I thought if I were him I would consider that sort of attitude bad for business. I went on out.

Outside, I moved carefully but briskly to the rear of the whorehouse, met Jimmie Sue coming around the corner.

"You okay?" I said.

"I think my ass is flat," she said. "Can't you tie a goddamn knot?"

"I did the best I could," I said. "Way I remember it, it wasn't me tied all the knots."

"I can tie a knot," she said. "I bet you a dollar to a bull's nuts it was you who tied the knot that slipped."

"It doesn't matter now," I said.

We went wide of the place, behind a couple of buildings, and came up behind the livery, where Shorty and Eustace were to sell the borrowed horse and have our mounts fed, watered, and rested.

We went around to the front of the livery and were about to go in so I could ask if the liveryman might know where Shorty and Eustace were, when I saw them coming toward us, Eustace with a tow sack slung over his shoulder, carrying the four-gauge in his other hand. Shorty seemed to bounce as he walked. Hog was with them, having reappeared from wherever he had been visiting. Even from a distance he looked a mess, with all manner of mud and greenery twisted up in his short, bristly hair.

"They have a hog with them," she said.

"Noticed that, did you?"

"Why is a hog with them?"

"He's a friend of Eustace's," I said.

"A friend."

"Yep."

"My God, that porker looks wild."

"He is said to be," I said.

As they got within earshot, Eustace said, "Is that your sister?"

"If I am," Jimmie Sue said, "then we are going to be in deep trouble with the law and a whole bunch of preachers."

"She's not," I said. "She told me where Fatty is."

"So he's the one that come here," Eustace said.

We were all standing in front of the livery now, grouped up. "How did you come by her and that information?" Shorty asked.

"We met at the whorehouse," Jimmie Sue said, watching Hog as she talked. "He's helping me run away."

"I suppose you work there," Shorty said.

"I have decided to remove myself from the work," she said. "It has long hours, can be smelly, and is short on any kind of benefits, outside of an indoor toilet and electric lights." She stared at Shorty. "Aren't you precious?"

"You think so?" Shorty said. "If you believe that, maybe you could return yourself to your previous business for five minutes up in the hayloft. I have four bits."

"No," Jimmie Sue said, running her arm through mine.

"I've completely got myself out of that business. I've gone off here with Red. He's my knight in shining armor."

"Cousin," Eustace said to me, "I'm guessing I'm short that four bits, and she's what got your armor polished."

"Afraid so," I said.

"No—you did what I told you to do, and I'm glad you did it."

"He's glad, too," Jimmie Sue said. "Aren't you, hon?"

I nodded.

"I used to fuck his grandfather," she said.

I winced, and Shorty laughed a deep chuckle that made my pride hurt.

"Is not your grandfather the one who was a preacher?"

"Don't go and try and make him feel bad," Jimmie Sue said. "Like I was telling him, Jesus forgives, and he's bound to understand a fella has to get his pipes cleaned from time to time."

"I am in total agreement," Shorty said.

"Does that hog bite?" Jimmie Sue asked, as Hog had always been her main point of interest.

"Yes ma'am," Eustace said. "And really hard. He wanted to, he could tear your leg off, though he'd have to work on it a bit and pull some."

"You ought to comb that muddy mess out of his hair," she said.

"I don't think he'd like that," Eustace said.

"All right, then," Shorty said. "Where is this Fatty bastard?"

I told him.

Eustace put the sack on the ground and leaned the four-gauge against the side of the livery. About that time the liveryman came out wearing overalls and no shirt. His work boots had a coating of horse manure and hay on the bottom so thick it stuck out on the sides and at the toes and heel. He was fat and bald and squinted behind some thick glasses. One lens was cracked, and the earpieces had string tied to the ends so that the glasses were bound to his head. He was carrying a horseshoe hammer.

"I thought I heard you two," he said to Eustace and Shorty. "Are these friends of yours?" said the liveryman, and then his eyes nestled on Hog. "What's that hog doing there?"

"We include the hog in our organization, such as it is," Shorty said. "Have you met our secretary?" He motioned at Jimmie Sue. "What is your name?"

She said it.

"The hog is our troubleshooter," Shorty said.

"Say he is?" the liveryman said. "Does he bite?"

"A common question," said Shorty. "And the answer is yes, he does."

"Hard," said Eustace.

The liveryman lifted the hammer slightly.

"Do not appear threatening," said Shorty. "Hog has a hair-trigger temper."

I glanced at Hog. He didn't seem all that angry to me. He seemed distracted by a fly on his nose.

Before the liveryman could process this information about Hog, Jimmie Sue looked at me, said, "Shorty talks funny. Is that because he's a midget?"

"I don't think so," I said. "I don't think that comes with being a midget."

"I can hear you, you know," Shorty said. "I am standing right here. And let me assure you there are midgets who talk in the same backwoods, ignorant manner that you do, but I am not one of them."

"You know a lot of midgets?" she said.

"None currently," Shorty said.

"Then you don't know," she said. "They may all talk like assholes."

"I knew several in the past," Shorty said. "Come to think of, some of them did talk like assholes."

"Who cares?" Eustace said.

"Well, I don't know what the hell you're talking about," said the liveryman, "any of you, but your horses are all fed and watered. Did you find your friend?"

"No," Shorty said. "Not yet. We are still looking for him."

"Well, he was the only fat guy came in on a horse with a nicked shoe, and I've fixed that for him. You tell him that, you see him."

"Sure," Shorty said.

"And the borrowed horse?" I said, looking directly at Shorty.

Eustace and Shorty looked askance.

"Borrowed horse?" the liveryman said.

"The spare horse," I said, correcting myself. "Sorry. Slip of the tongue."

"I bought him," said the liveryman.

"That's how I got this bag of goods," Eustace said. "And there's money left over."

"I give a fair price when it's a fair horse," said the liveryman. He seemed proud of himself. Like a rooster that's just dismounted a hen.

"I assure you," said Shorty, "that if anyone should ask, or if it should come up, we will make sure you are known for just that virtue."

"Why, thank you, midget," said the liveryman, and I saw one of Shorty's eyes twitch.

He calmed himself, though, said to the liveryman, "I would like to ask that you maintain our horses awhile longer, a service we will pay for, of course."

"Of course you will," said the liveryman.

"We have a bit of business to attend to," said Shorty. "Something that we thought might arise and now has."

"You take care of your business," said the liveryman. "Come back and get them when you're ready. You got the money, I got your horses. By the way, you want to sell that hog? He would hang comfortably in my smokehouse."

"Anything dead hangs comfortably," Shorty said. "But he is not for sale, as he is not owned."

"Then he's a free agent, so to speak," said the liveryman.

"Free, but under our protection, as we are under his," said Shorty.

"You're an odd congregation," said the liveryman.

"I suppose it is all in perspective," said Shorty. "We will return for our horses."

The liveryman went back inside, and we walked off down the street in the direction of the whorehouse.

Shorty said, "We thought we might have to leave and find the old trail if you didn't come across your man. But now that you have, we can find him, have a nice talk, and have some better idea where we are going."

We came to the whorehouse and stopped in the street and looked at it.

"Where in there is he?" Eustace said.

I explained as best I could where the room was, and what the boots looked like that identified him.

"He's in there with Katy," Jimmie Sue said. "She's got a little gun she keeps just under the bed, on a little stool there. So if you're going inside you might want to keep that in mind. And you might want to keep Steve in mind, too. He's near the door with a .410."

"I think our best course of action would be to wait him out," Shorty said. He turned and looked across the street at the old abandoned house there. "We can go there and wait, and when he comes out, we can take him."

"What about me?" Jimmie Sue said.

"What about you?" Shorty said. "When we get this done, you go back to either whoring or moving along. You are not our concern."

"He finds out I told where he was, he'll kill me," Jimmie Sue said. "Either him or his cousin Katy. She's mean as a snake. Fact is, I'm taking a chance standing here. Someone in there will see me, and then I'm in for it. Pretty soon, they're going to figure out I'm gone, and Steve don't like his whores taking a mind of their own."

"That still is not our concern," Shorty said.

"Yes, it is," I said. "I promised her protection."

"She is a whore," Shorty said. "She was merely looking for a way out of a mess she was in, and you were it. Just because you lowered your rope in her well does not make you her protector."

Jimmie Sue let go of my arm, which she had continued to clutch on our walk to the whorehouse.

"I'll slap your face," Jimmie Sue said to Shorty. "Even if I have to dig a hole to stand in so I don't have to bend over."

"Oh, that is clever," Shorty said. "You try and slap my face, you will wake up with your arm up your nose. I can promise you that."

"I said I'd help her, and I plan to do just that," I said. "And you aren't going to slap anyone."

Shorty turned his head and looked at me. Eustace laid his hand on Shorty's shoulder, said, "You asked me if I thought he had sand, and I said he did. You said he didn't. What now, Shorty?"

"I suppose there is a trace of sand in him," Shorty said. "But there may be just enough there to cover him in a grave."

"Well, it's all right for the moment," Eustace said. "Let my cousin Jack have his girl. She ain't in the way right now."

"She will be," Shorty said. "Come on, we do not need to be seen staring at the whorehouse anyway. Let us move along."

"Yeah," Eustace said. "They're gonna wonder what a big nigger, a midget, a kid, a whore, and a nasty hog are considering out here."

As Eustace and Shorty went away, Jimmie Sue said, "Midgets are not very friendly."

"I don't know if that goes all around, or just with this midget," I said. "But my personal experience is the same as yours."

We went across the street to the abandoned house. It was without doors or glass in the windows, and the floorboards had rotted. The roof had holes in it, and rain had come inside. Oddly, there was a table and chairs and a stained settee still inside, and we perched on those. There was a back room with a door, but we didn't go in there.

"What about that dead boy?" I said.

"We left a very clear note with details where his body might be found, and we slipped it under the door of the sheriff's office," Shorty said.

I wasn't so sure that was true, and my look told them that. Eustace said, "That's truth, boy. That's what we did. Shorty wrote it, and I slipped it under the crack of the door, stealthy as an Indian."

It still sounded suspicious.

"I'm hungry," Jimmie Sue said. "I had a long night and busy morning. I could use something to eat."

"We did not make our menu out with you in mind," Shorty said.

"Oh, hell, Shorty," Eustace said. "Quit being such a jackass. We got plenty, and we need something, one way or the other, we'll get more."

Shorty hesitated.

"You got what you got in that bag from selling what Eustace calls a borrowed horse," I said. "It's not like it's out of your personal poke."

"I was the one that borrowed the horse," Eustace said.

"You sold a borrowed horse?" Jimmie Sue said.

I looked at her, and then she got it, said, "Oh. I see."

Shorty gave in. When we finished eating some tinned meat, we had a pull on a canteen from the tow sack, and then we sat and waited. Me and Jimmie Sue and Eustace sat in chairs at the rickety table, Shorty on the settee. Jimmie Sue said she had some jokes, and she told two, but nobody got them and nobody laughed. Shorty said, "You only got part of the joke, dear. They are supposed to have a punch line."

"It was funny when I heard it," she said. "And maybe there was more to it. I thought I was a good joke teller."

"I am going to say you are not," Shorty said.

"I didn't know it would matter that much," she said. "I was trying to help pass the time."

"Perhaps," Shorty said. "But what you have done is tie an anvil to the feet of time, causing it to drag itself about in circles."

The joke telling stopped. Jimmie Sue pouted for a while,

but not for long. She seemed to be too positive for a lot of ill feelings for herself or anyone else. She rubbed my knee while we sat, and I had to move her hand because it got me thinking about something besides Fatty. She smiled at me, but finally gave it up. I couldn't decide if she felt real affection for me or was playing a ruse to stay clear of the whorehouse. Right then, I didn't care. I liked being with her, even if it was sitting in chairs in an old rotten house, and even if my insides were boiling over from all this waiting and my fear for my sister's condition kept pushing at my every thought.

So we sat there, intently watching across the street through the missing front door, waiting on Fatty. Except Shorty. Shorty wasn't watching anything. He had stretched out on the settee and gone to sleep, snoring gently.

"It might be a good idea to smother that little shit in his sleep," Jimmie Sue said.

"You just got to get to know him for a while," Eustace said. "Then you'll really hate him."

Eustace and I laughed. Jimmie Sue smiled, let her breath out, said, "Steve is coming out."

We all leaned forward to see the pimp come out without his shotgun, spit off the side of the porch, stretch, and go back inside.

"Does he do that often?" Eustace asked. "Come outside like that?"

"I have no idea," Jimmie Sue said. "Usually I have business other than when Steve is going to spit or stretch or take a leak."

"All right," Eustace said. "I was just trying to time him."

"No help here," Jimmie Sue said.

Eustace nestled back in the chair, and with a sound like a

rifle shot, the chair collapsed out from under him, landing his big butt on the floor.

Shorty was startled awake. He came up with the revolver in his fist. When he realized what had happened, he burst out laughing, and so did the rest of us, even Eustace, when he got over being embarrassed.

As Eustace was getting up, Jimmie Sue said, “There he is. That’s Fatty.”

We all looked. Shorty stood up on the settee to look out one of the windows.

It was him, all right. He was on the porch, and there was a woman with her arm around him, giving him a kiss on the cheek. She was kind of plump, but not fat, and she had hair dark as midnight. I suppose if she was tubbed down in hot water and there was plenty of soap used, you might say she was attractive if there was no one around to compare her to and it was a little dark.

“They’re cousins,” Jimmie Sue said.

“Me and Jack are cousins,” Eustace said. “We don’t kiss.”

“Are you cousins?” Jimmie Sue said. “Really?”

“Maybe,” I said.

“He don’t kiss me and I don’t kiss him,” Eustace said. Then: “But I want to.”

We all looked at Eustace, and he laughed.

“Not so loud, you clutch of morons,” Shorty said.

We had all moved to the doorway to see Fatty walking down the street. He had left his kissing cousin, Katy, on the porch. She went inside and closed the door.

Shorty said, “We need to follow him before he gets too public.”

* * *

It didn't happen quick, and it didn't go down easy.

Fatty got ahead of us and went into the saloon. I couldn't go in because he knew me, and Eustace couldn't because colored weren't allowed. Shorty would draw too much attention, and Jimmie Sue didn't care to have it announced she was out running around on her own, lest it bring Steve into play. Hog was neutral and of no help.

"We could talk to the sheriff," I said.

"We could," Eustace said, "but we won't. To get money, we have to bring him in ourselves. We point him out, that ain't the same. The sheriff keeps the money, or at least half of it. I think that's how it works."

"I believe you are correct," said Shorty. "My suggestion is we cross into that bit of woods there and keep our eyes on the saloon, wait for Fatty to leave."

"He could be in there all day," Jimmie Sue said.

"It has to close sometime," I said.

"It don't," she said. "It's open round the clock."

"And I can't just sit around," I said. "Lula is out there with those men, and no telling what all has been done to her. I'll go in and get him if I have to. I don't give a bird crap if he recognizes me or not."

"He might make short work of you," Shorty said. "Or you might accidentally kill him, though that is less likely. What is more likely is that you will be found somewhere out back of one of these establishments with a knife in your ass. If you die and you still have the land papers on you and I can learn to forge your name, things might work out. I do not wish to take that chance, however. So do not damage our plans."

"You call what we've been doing planned?" I said.

"I admit our tactics have been flexible," Shorty said. "But there is indeed a plan buried in our actions somewhere."

"Well, then," Eustace said. "That narrows it down. We got to go in the saloon and get him. We got to go in and be out before they can figure I'm black and you're short and so on."

"An unlikely variation on our highly variable plan," Shorty said.

Right then I looked down the alley between the livery and the saloon and saw Fatty out back, practically waddling off toward an outdoor convenience, tugging his hat down tight over his head as he went.

"There he is," I said.

"Betrayed by his natural need to piss or shit," Shorty said.

Fatty went inside the outhouse and closed the door.

"Ain't no need in all of us going," Eustace said. "Y'all go on back to the shack, and I'll fetch him."

Before anyone could respond yes or no, Eustace was crossing the street, carrying his four-gauge, Hog following.

"I would not want to be that fat man," said Shorty.

"Aren't we supposed to go to the shack?" I said.

"We are," said Shorty. "But frankly, I like to watch Eustace work."

Eustace walked briskly through the alley and came to the outhouse. Hog sat down, waiting, as if this was something he had gone through before.

Eustace swung the shotgun, used the butt of it to hit that door as hard as a buffalo stampede. The door flew back off its hinges, and there was Fatty, squatting on the drop hole. Eustace grabbed him by the front of his shirt and jerked him out of the toilet, Fatty's bare ass flashing in the last of the day's sunlight. Fatty's shirt ripped partly away in Eustace's hands.

Fatty yelled out, "Get away from me, you crazy nigger," and then the stock of that shotgun caught Fatty upside the head and he was out.

Eustace picked up Fatty and slung him over his shoulder like he was a bit of wet wash, and came carrying him across the street, Fatty's bare ass shining to the world. Let me tell you, Fatty was a big one, and for anyone to do what Eustace done, it was a feat not too unlike that of Hercules.

Hog ran out in front of them, ran ahead of them like an escort.

6

Oddly enough, no one seemed to notice a big black man carrying a fat white man with his ass hanging out and a large wild hog in tow.

Eustace crossed the road, toted Fatty to the shack across from the whorehouse, hauled him into the back room, and dumped him on the floor. He pulled one of the chairs from the front room in there and boosted Fatty into it. Shorty tied Fatty to it with four bandannas that Eustace pulled out of his pocket. Hog sat and watched Shorty tie Fatty down. He was well focused on what we were doing, as if he were learning to tie knots.

Shorty pulled out a handkerchief, which he let us know contained a goodly portion of his snot, and stuck it in Fatty's mouth. Fatty still had his pants partway down, and he didn't have any shorts on underneath, so it wasn't a pretty sight. And though I knew Jimmie Sue had seen such things on a regular basis, I asked if she'd leave the room, and she did.

Shorty slapped Fatty a little, trying to bring him around, but he didn't snap to. Shorty said, "You hit him hard, Eustace."

"I thought it a damn good idea at the time."

"Well, you may have moved his brain around to the point that he thinks he ought to be walking ass-backwards everywhere he goes."

"It was a solid lick," Eustace said. "Now, wait a minute, look there. He's coming around."

"Watch that he don't kick at you," I said. "He has blades in the toes of his boots."

"He can't kick shit with his feet tied," Eustace said.

"I just wanted you to know those blades are there," I said.

Fatty moaned, tried to spit out the handkerchief, but Shorty poked it in deeper. He said, "Listen here, fat ass. I am going to remove the handkerchief, but if you call out, I will have Eustace here hit you again with the butt of his shotgun."

Eustace grinned and held up the shotgun to show how possible that threat was.

"Now, if you believe in your little black heart that you can stay quiet, I will yank out the handkerchief. Just nod if you agree. You can shake your head no as well, but when you do you will get the shotgun stock between the eyes."

Fatty nodded, and Shorty removed the handkerchief. Fatty focused on me for the first time. He was still ugly, his mouth sucked in due to lack of teeth. He spoke in a way that sounded as if he were trying to eat his words. "You, Red. What you doing here?"

"What do you think?" I said. "I'm looking for my sister."

"Well, she's done been spoiled, you know," he said.

"She's not an apple," I said. "She is not spoiled."

"Call it how you like," Fatty said. "She's been plowed pretty good."

That went all over me, but I gathered myself. "I still want her back."

"One thing for her," said Fatty. "She's good and broke in by now."

"Eustace," said Shorty.

Eustace stepped forward, popped Fatty between the eyes with the shotgun butt. "What the hell?" Fatty said. "That hurt."

"No shit," Eustace said.

"That was a well-contained strike," Shorty said. "Am I right, Eustace?"

"If you mean I held back a good bit, I reckon so," Eustace said.

"That is precisely what I meant."

"All right, then," Eustace said. "That's right."

Fatty lifted his head, said to me, "Where'd you get this sawed-off piece of shit and the nigger?"

"We came by mail," Shorty said. "From the Sears and Roebuck. We have our photos in the back. You can order us. I come mad, and so does Eustace. The whore may or may not be listed."

"I know her," Fatty said. "She thinks she's too good to fuck me."

"Actually, I can see how that might be a common conclusion among women, and that somehow explains why it is necessary for a cousin to take mercy on you," Shorty said. "Here is the situation. I am going to ask you a series of simple questions, and in between questions, I am going to pistol-whip you. My thought is that when I finish it will be difficult for your hat to fit. Even if you answer the questions I am going to pistol-whip you. The reason for this is simple. It is to help you understand that I intend to pistol-whip you even more severely if I do not get answers. I may ask Eustace here to see if he can make your brains leak out your nose if you should in any way hesitate to lay out what we need to know."

"I get a beating I talk and one if I don't," Fatty said. "That don't make no sense."

"You will receive a beating, as you call it, that is true," Shorty said. "But that is merely to show you we mean business."

"What if I just take it on faith that you mean business?" Fatty said.

"I am not much on faith, to tell it true," Shorty said. "But I think if you take a beating and know it will be worse and more constant if you hesitate to lay out the facts we want to know, you might be more inclined to give us what would like revealed more quickly. When you answer directly, and if I believe you—this will, of course, be my judgment call—I stop hitting you with my pistol. Do you have any teeth left in your mouth?"

"What?" Fatty said.

Shorty said, "I believe you heard me." Shorty took off his coat and pulled out his pistol and held it down by the side of his leg. "I will not repeat the question."

"A few," said Fatty, and from the look on his face it was obvious he was confused as to Shorty's line of questioning. So was I.

"Which side are they on?" Shorty asked.

"Both sides," Fatty said.

"Exactly where?"

I could see Fatty was growing even more nervous.

"Why do you want to know?" said Fatty.

That's when Shorty's pistol fanned alongside Fatty's head with a smacking sound.

"Goddamn," Fatty said, jerking his head aside.

"Do you really need to do that?" I said.

"Listen to that boy," Fatty said. "He's got some of God's mercy in him."

"True, he does," Shorty said. "I do not."

Shorty slammed the barrel of the gun down on Fatty's parts, which were laid out on the chair like a stumpy sausage and two potatoes. Fatty screamed, his head nodded forward, and a bit of whatever he had been drinking in the saloon came out and splashed on the floor.

Hog, finding this all too much, got up and left the room and, for that matter, left the shack.

"Even a hog won't taste your leavings," said Eustace. "And I've seen him eat shit."

"Shorty," I said. "For the love of God."

Shorty turned to me. "Jack. You be about your business, and I will be about mine."

"I don't have any business," I said, though I won't go on and lie. I liked that Shorty had given me a chance to leave the room. It was all I could do not to tremble. I hadn't considered the possibility of anything like this. I had seen myself at the head of a noble rescue, assisted by a capable tracker and a bounty hunter. Somehow it hadn't occurred to me the meanness it all might sprout. I wasn't at the head of anything, and the tracker was someone who lost the trail, and the bounty hunter was an angry midget with a revolver. I didn't like it, and I wanted to stop it, but I determined myself to remain steadfast for Lula's sake.

"Find some business," Shorty said, "and close the door on your way out. Fatty, try not to yell real loud. Louder you yell, the worse it will go for you."

"You little bastard," Fatty said, but there wasn't any real enthusiasm in it, and he was already bringing his voice down a few notches.

I went out and closed the door, my hand trembling on the knob. I glanced at Jimmie Sue. She was sitting on the couch looking at me like a wild animal with her foot in a trap.

"What are they doing in there?"

"Remember when I said they meant to interrogate him and that meant they were going to pistol-whip the shit out of him?"

She nodded.

"That's the sum of it," I said. "And I believe Fatty is about to lose some teeth."

"He has some?" she said, and at that very moment we heard Fatty let out with a scream.

"I think that was one or two of the ones left," I said.

"Take it and like it and be quiet about it," I heard Shorty say on the other side of the door. "You talk when I ask a question. Not any other time."

Then came Fatty's voice, his lips sucking into what I was sure was now a bloody mouth. "Then ask a goddamn question."

I said to Jimmie Sue, "Why don't you and me go outside careful-like, away from this?"

"I don't mind hearing it," she said. "It don't bother me."

"Yeah, well," I said, "it bothers me."

I looked out the door and saw the whorehouse door was still open, but it wasn't open so wide I felt I could be easily seen. I went on out, started around the side of the old house.

Jimmie Sue caught up with me.

"I'll come with you anyway," she said.

Behind the house I could still hear the pistol hitting Fatty, and I could hear him grunt, trying to keep the pain inside, trying not to yell.

"You're kind of softhearted, ain't you, Jack?" Jimmie Sue said.

"Reckon so," I said.

"For me, I guess it depends," Jimmie Sue said. "My father was a preacher, which is why I sort of took to your old grandpa."

"I don't want to hear about it," I said.

"Ah, it ain't nothing," she said.

"It's something to me."

We sat on a big stump near where the woods were broke up from tree chopping and burning. I thought about how large that tree had been and how little it had been to the men who cut it down and took its years and sawed them up and put them on a fire. Not for warmth or lumber in this case, just for space. We seemed to always be needing space. Lumbermen wanted certain trees and they didn't care about the others, and those just went to hell in sawdust and smoke.

I knew right then, if it wasn't for my sister being out there with those men, I'd have just gone and walked on out of there and been done with the whole lot of them, including Jimmie Sue. But those men did have her. And they had done things to her. The thought made me sick, small like she was, and afraid, and with no one there to help her. I couldn't hardly stand the thought. But I had to.

"Hear that?" Jimmie Sue said. "They're really beating the hell out of him."

"I hear it," I said.

"Sorry," she said. "It's just I'm thinking about your sister and it brings to mind what was done to me, and how I come to be sitting right here with you, having met you in a whorehouse. You think I grew up thinking I'd like to be a whore? That fat bastard groaning and such is music to my ears. I remember the first time I had men on me. It wasn't by choice, and they worked me over good. Steve told me after he picked me up at the depot how special I was, and then I ended up here. He had a bunch of men take me and have their way. He said they was 'breaking me in.' "

"Horrible," was all I could say.

"Yeah. It wasn't something I'd wish on anyone. And now that I know some of the same kind of men have had their way with your sister, I don't feel the least bit bad for that porky son of a bitch. They find out where she is, then it was all worth it."

"I suppose," I said. "I guess I have to think that way."

"Ain't no other way to think, Jack. You either want her back or you don't."

"I want her back," I said.

"She ain't gonna be just like she was. You know that."

"I reckon she can get over it. If you did, I reckon she can."

Jimmie Sue lifted her head and looked at me. Her eyes narrowed, and she looked much older all of a sudden. "Who said I got over it?"

7

Even out there we could hear what was going on inside the shack, and I was thinking it could be heard across the street, but this was probably just because the whole thing was something I had my mind directed to.

After a while things went silent, and Eustace come from alongside the shack to where we were. He squatted down on his haunches, took out some makings, and rolled a cigarette. It was the first I had seen him do that. He spilled tobacco ever which way, and Jimmie Sue got up, said, “Give me that.”

She took the makings from him and rolled a quick cigarette, poked it at his mouth. He bit down on it. She said, “Now there.”

Eustace found a match in his shirt pocket, struck it along the side of his pants, and lit his cigarette, the light of the match wavering a little as he did. The wind shifted and picked up, and I could smell the ash from the chopped and burnt-down woods behind me.

“He tell you anything?” I said.

"He said plenty," Eustace said. "He wasn't gonna talk at first, but he come around. There was a nail in there, sticking out of an old board, and Shorty laid that on his goober and drove it through it with the butt of his pistol. I thought before that Fatty wasn't gonna talk, but when that happened the fat bastard sang like a goddamn songbird so as to get that nail pulled out."

"It wouldn't have taken me that long," I said. "I'd seen Shorty pick up that board with a nail in it, I'd have started talking. It wouldn't have taken any time at all for me."

"Me, neither," Eustace said. "I figure if you're gonna take one for not talking, and it's gonna stop when you talk, talk right up front and avoid as much pain as possible, because truth is you're gonna talk, even if you tell a lie. It was hard for him to get that nail out, by the way. He caught up the head of it on his pistol, the trigger guard, and got it hooked enough to pull out. The pulling seemed to me worse than the going in, but I reckon you can't go around the rest of your life with a chair nailed to your pecker."

"You would always have a place to sit," Jimmie Sue said.

"That's right," Eustace said, grinning around his cigarette. "You would."

"You said he talked," I said.

"Yeah," Eustace said. "Sang like a goddamn bird."

"How do you know he ain't lying?" Jimmie Sue said.

"Don't," Eustace said. "From my experience a fella will lie when you torture him if he thinks it'll get him out of it, and he'll tell the truth, too. I think he told the truth. We got some directions. Fatty said the rest of them, with your sister, are heading over into the main of the Big Thicket, as he put it. Over there beyond Livingston, down in the brambles and the high-ass pines. It's a badlands there, down in them deep, dark woods. There's lots of colored who have run off there to trap and live, and there's lots of outlaws, too. I knew some colored that left here to go there, and I ain't never seen them since. Law don't like to go in there, cause lot of time they do, they don't come back. That's where we got to go if you want your sister back, and there ain't nothing else for it. You sure it's worth it to you?"

"It is," I said. "You sound like it's not to you."

"Not my sister," Eustace said.

"What about the deed I got for you?"

"I think about that, and it holds me up some, but that's some bad place down in the Thicket, so I got to linger on the idea a little," Eustace said.

I was surprised. I thought I could see him wavering, and I figured the best thing to keep him at it was not only to remind him of the deed but to step on his pride a little.

"You scared?" I said.

"Ain't you?" he said. "Being scared, even if you go ahead and do a thing, is what keeps you alive. You ain't scared, it's because you're too stupid to know what's down in them woods. I know. There's folks was raised there that ain't never been out. I heard all about them. How they can live off the land, climb a tree, and pull a bear out of it. How they're all fucking one another down there—family members, men and women, dogs and squirrels, and for all I know fish and birds. So, yeah, I'm scared enough cause I got sense enough to be. Only time I ain't scared of nothing is when I'm drunk. Then you got to be scared of me. Sober I know which end of my ass to wipe and which end to feed. And I know when to be scared."

"Sounds like wild fairy tales to me," I said. "Like them kind Shorty was talking about."

"Well, it ain't," Eustace said. "Most of it, anyway."

"He's right, you know," Jimmie Sue said.

"How would you know?" I said.

"Cause now and again there is some that leave them woods, and I suppose you might call them the sophisticated ones. They come into town here, trade skins and such for dollars, get drunk as skunks, then they like to come to the pleasure house across the street. I know what they are and what they're like from my own experience. They're the ones want you to strip down naked but wear your shoes, bend over the dresser, and yodel while they do it. They bring their own axle grease to loosen up your asshole. They like me to call them daddy or brother while they do it, or they like to howl and bark like dogs when they're at it. They always end up blacking your eye or busting your lip, and when they leave, the room stinks like something dead, cause that's how they smell. From the way I look at things, that's how they act—like they're something dead that just won't lay down. They ain't just mean, Jack; they're something wrong in the world."

I wasn't much for Grandpa's sayings right then, but I thought of one and said it: "There's a new world coming, and those that live the lives of men won't live in the world of God."

"Yeah," Jimmie Sue said. "I always hear about that new world coming—from your grandpa, for one. But when he got through riding me and I looked out the window, the new world hadn't come. It looked just like the old one to me."

"Well, now," Eustace said. "I got to go back to it, like it or not. I might need to pick up the shotgun again."

He dropped the cigarette, stood up, put his heel to it, and started back around the side of the house.

When he was gone, I said to Jimmie Sue, "What you said

about those folks from the Big Thicket—you were exaggerating some, weren't you?"

"I was pulling back on the reins, you want to know the truth," she said. "I didn't want to scare you any more than you already are."

"I didn't say I was scared."

"You don't have to say it."

"I'll do all right," I said. "But you, you don't have to go. There isn't any real reason for you to be in this."

"Not like I got anywhere else to go but with you," she said. "I like you, part of the reason. I won't tell you I won't run off at some point, but I got to at least start off in that direction. I know I promised you some ass and such, and I'm not saying you can't have it, but I'm saying you may not have it for long. I may decide to become an independent contractor in my profession. Who knows? Closer we get to those backwoods, the more I might want to set sail, so to speak."

I nodded. "All right, then."

There was nothing more I could say. But the idea of Jimmie Sue with other men in the future—it was bad enough in the past—made me hurt all over and in places that seemed outside of me.

"I better go inside there and make sure they don't kill him," I said.

"It won't be a big loss if they do," she said.

"It will be to me if I just let them do it."

I went back inside the shack, leaving Jimmie Sue sitting there on that old stump at the edge of what had been a forest.

8

When I came inside the shack the door to the back room was open, and I could see Fatty in there. He was still tied to the chair and asleep. Which is a nice way of saying he was unconscious. He was bloody, too. The place stank of sweat and piss and shit. Shorty wasn't kidding about what would happen when he gave someone a pistol-whipping.

The whole thing made me ill and caused me to feel sick to my stomach. Not only that it had happened, but that I had let it. Shorty was sitting on the couch taking a rest, rubbing his shoulder with one small hand. Eustace was in a chair, and his face was bathed in sweat.

Shorty said, "My arm is tired. I should have traded hands more."

Eustace grunted.

Hog had returned and was lying on the floor. He grunted, too.

"We have been discussing the possibility of going over to the sheriff's office so that he might take Fatty here, and perhaps receive a reward," Shorty said. "We can do that or we can shoot him in the head first, then take him over. Either way, we get the reward."

"We've talked about this," I said.

"Killing him has its merits," Shorty said. "First off, I do not like him much, a feeling I assure you from his end is mutual. And while we are talking, Jack, I admit to you that Eustace and I did not leave a note for the sheriff about the boy's body."

"We up and lied about that," Eustace said.

"Why?" I said.

"Sometimes it's just our way," Eustace said.

"Well, your way isn't so good, as I see it."

"As he sees it," Shorty said, glancing at Eustace.

"Look here," I said. "You do within reason what you got to do so I can get Lula back, but you don't need to kill him. It's not that far a hike to the sheriff's office. What I don't understand is why you lied to me about the note."

"We didn't think we ought to get the sheriff mixed up in this just yet," Eustace said. "It didn't seem—what was that big-ass word you had, Shorty?"

"Prudent," Shorty said.

"Yeah, Prudence," Eustace said.

"No," Shorty said. "Prudent . . . oh, hell. Never mind. It was not a good idea."

"Why not?" I said.

"We didn't want to take the chance the sheriff would see us," Eustace said. "He knows us some."

"And to know us is to love us," Shorty said.

"You mean he hates you," I said.

"Naw," Eustace said. "We're friends. He used to bounty-hunt some. Then he got married and got respectable and needed a job. He ended up sheriff. Fortunately for him his wife ran off. So he's got it pretty good. But thing is, being a bounty hunter and taking bounty money dies hard. He knows Shorty's handwriting, and if he knows we're on the hunt he might just stick his nose into our business."

"My handwriting is fine and distinct," Shorty said. "I am proud of it and cannot bring myself to purposely print or write cursive poorly. I learned my penmanship from my friend Walter the Midget, who had a very fine education. But how he became educated is of no interest to you, I presume."

I felt he was laying that out there as a trap, so that I might feign interest and he could tell me the complete story about how he had acquired good handwriting. So I took a dodge. "Look," I said. "We got to take him to the sheriff. That's all there is to it. We're going to do some of this my way or not at all."

"And if we were to choose to abandon you?" Shorty said.

"Then you can go back to your little telescope, and you, Eustace, can go back to digging graves or digging burnt folks up and putting them on doorsteps," I said. "We'll do this my way or no way at all."

Shorty looked at Eustace. Eustace smiled. "Well, now," he said. "I like to see a little rooster grow up some."

"Very well, then," Shorty said. "I suggest we find something to wipe Fatty down and haul him over to see the sheriff."

I went over to the livery and borrowed a bucket of water and some rags and told the liveryman I wanted to have a wash-down. He said the bucket was old and so were the rags and I could keep them. I hauled it all over to the shack, doing it in as sneaky a way as I could manage.

I brought the stuff inside the shack, where I found Jimmie

Sue had joined Shorty and Eustace. I set the bucket down, and they asked if, as the woman of the bunch, Jimmie Sue would do the honors of cleaning Fatty up. She told them they could go do something to themselves that I had never heard of before, and then Shorty turned to Eustace for the job, and Eustace didn't want it, either. That left me or Shorty.

It turned out to be me.

I went in there with my water and rags and set the bucket beside Fatty's chair. I stood for a moment looking at him, holding the rags. I took a deep breath and put the rags on the floor. Fatty was unconscious, and my first thought was I wanted to take a gun and shoot him, and my second thought was that was too easy. I wanted to make him suffer. I wanted to shoot him in the feet and then the knees and then the elbows and then the groin and then the neck. I wanted him to die slowly. I wanted to shoot him and take my time between shots. I thought first I would wake him, and then I would start shooting, and with each shot I would say my sister's name. I could imagine him and her and what he might have done to her, and what the others might have done, and I felt a rising in my stomach. I didn't want those thoughts in my head, but they had already roosted there.

Dampening a rag, I touched it to Fatty's face, over his eye, where he had taken a good blow. It was a deep cut and bloody. I touched it, and he groaned. I was reminded of a dog I had found all cut up once. I don't know how he got that way, but it looked as if someone had been at work on him with a knife. I had picked the dog up and taken it home and put it in the shed out back. I got water and rags just like this, and I had gone out there and cleaned him up. The dog was so hurt it didn't move. Fatty was the same. So hurt he didn't move. I liked the dog better than Fatty, so Fatty became the dog in my mind. I touched the wet rag to all the spots on his face and the sides of his head where it was bleeding through his hair. I cleaned him in places I didn't want to clean him. It took a lot of time because there was a lot of blood, but just like the dog, he was a healer. He didn't keep leaking. He had already started to dry up.

After I had wiped Fatty down he came awake. I expected a stream of bad language and such, but he didn't say a word. I think he had been trained by Shorty that the pistol might come out at any moment, and for the least little reason, so it was best to watch in silence, yet the glare in his eyes was sharp as a knife. There was no gratitude for cleaning him up. I remembered then that after I had cleaned the dog and treated its wounds with medicine, I fed it, holding its head so it could eat. The dog finished eating, gained its strength, and bit me on the hand. When I pulled back from the bite, the dog that had been near death just a short time before jumped up and darted out through the open door of the shed. Still, I had felt good about myself then. I was my mother's good boy, the one who had cleaned up and fed the wounded dog and endured its bite with understanding, but considering I was the reason Fatty was where he was and in the condition he was in, it wasn't a feeling I could cling to now with as much enthusiasm.

I had Eustace come in and help me untie him and get him out of the chair. Fatty was damn easy to handle, being as weak as a broom straw in a high wind. I gave him the damp rags and had him wipe his ass and throw the rags in the corner of the room, and then I had him pull up his pants. I picked up the three bloodied teeth he had spat on the floor, wrapped them in one of the bandannas, and gave them to him. I don't know why I did that, but I did. Fatty took them and clutched them in his hand, not even knowing what they were. I don't think right then he knew who he was. He put the teeth in his pocket.

Finally, with me on one side of him and Eustace on the other, we hauled him out of there. Jimmie Sue, Shorty, and Hog followed. We hitched his lard over to the sheriff's office, a few people staring but no one seeming to care one way or another, and managed him through the door.

The sheriff was in one of the two cells lying on a cot, and when we came in and shut the front door to his office, it woke him up. He sat up quickly and looked at us. He was a lanky fellow with a face made for being most fondly remembered from a distance. He had one leaky hay-fever eye and a nose that flagged to one side and a mouth outlined by deep scars. He had an ear missing. His hair was oily and was parted on one side and flapped over his bald head. There was a kind of pink, gnarled scabbing in spots on the side of his face and the top of his head, but another look told me it wasn't scabbing at all but burnt-over skin that had ribbed up in places.

He studied us—not only Fatty, Shorty, Eustace, Jimmie Sue, and me but also Hog.

"Is that the same old hog you had, Eustace?" he said. "Or did you eat that one and get another?"

"Same one," Eustace said, "though there's still a chance he might get eat up, I get hungry enough."

"And I see you still got your midget," the sheriff said.

"That is funny," Shorty said.

"Why I said it," said the sheriff. He came out of the cell then, wandered over and sat in a chair behind his desk. On the desk was a half bottle of whiskey and a greasy plate with a biscuit lying on it. Behind him on the wall was a telephone. Actually, it was the first I'd ever seen, but I knew what it was, having seen photographs of them in the Sears and Roebuck. His battered and dirty hat was on the end of one of the chair arms, and he took it and put it on. It improved his looks due to the shading of his face. "That there fellow that's all beat up, I don't reckon he's a friend."

"Oh, he and I are extremely close," said Shorty. "If you prop him against the wall and lift me up, I will give him a kiss on the cheek."

"Ha," said the sheriff, and then his eyes rested on Jimmie Sue.

"Jimmie Sue," he said. "How's your cat?"

"Resting comfortably in the fork of a tree," she said.

"I been thinking about coming over and seeing her sometime," he said. "I'd like to pet it a bit."

"Thing is, Winton," Jimmie Sue said, "she's not as available for petting as she once was."

I had no idea what they were talking about at first, but it came to me gradually, and I could feel my face redden.

"That's a shame," the sheriff said.

"I've retired," Jimmie Sue said. "You'll have to look for another kitty."

Perfect, I thought. Not only me and Grandpa, but the one-eared sheriff has been in the same fork of the tree where I'd nestled earlier that day.

The sheriff gave Jimmie Sue a little grin, nodded at Fatty, who was wobbling. "What's his story?"

"It's a whole dime novel," Eustace said, then turned to me and nodded.

I told the sheriff all about it. Just as I finished up, Fatty, who had begun to bleed from a number of spots, fell down and lay on his side.

"Get him up and lay him on the floor in there," the sheriff said. "I'm not for having blood all over my cot. And he stinks something awful."

"Yeah," Eustace said. "He do at that. But some of that stink, just to be fair, is Hog."

Me and Eustace dragged Fatty into the cell and closed the door. The sheriff tossed Eustace the keys and Eustace locked Fatty inside and tossed the keys back to the sheriff.

"I seen him around before," the sheriff said. "But what call have you got to say he's the desperado you're looking for? You said you didn't see the robbery, now, didn't you, boy?"

"It's him," I said. "And if he didn't rob the bank, he was in on the kidnapping. I was there when that happened. I told you that."

"So you did," said the sheriff.

"I seen the robbery," Eustace said. "I seen him ride out of town to beat the band and shots buzzing at him like bees, and him buzzing some back at folk. It was him, all right."

"Well, now," the sheriff said. "Well, now."

A back door opened and a colored man came in carrying a bucket of water in one hand, a mop in the other. He was a lanky fellow and had a white spot on his forehead that started just above his right eye and ran wide and up into his hairline.

The sheriff looked at him, said, "Spot, you going to have to come back later. I got folks here and a prisoner."

"You don't want the cell swabbed out?" Spot asked.

"I didn't say that. I said I got company."

"I see 'em," Spot said. "It ain't gonna take but a minute." He had already come in by now and let the door, that he had been keeping open with his butt, close behind him. He glanced at the cell where Fatty lay on the floor. "I can mop around him," he said.

"Goddamn it," the sheriff said. "I run this office or you?"

"I run this here mop."

"Shit, mop on then."

There were some chairs along the wall, across from the sheriff's desk, and Shorty climbed up in one and sat down, his short legs jutting out. I took a chair beside Jimmie Sue. Eustace sat on the corner of the sheriff's desk, and Hog lay on the floor. Spot started cleaning. All progress stopped while he slopped that bucket and mopped, making what looked to me more of a mess than a cleaning, but he stayed at it. He may not have been good, but he was determined. We lifted our feet, and he mopped beneath us. When he came to Hog, the beast looked up and snorted. Spot mopped a wide space around him. Then he had the sheriff put his feet on the desk, and he mopped under there. Spot said, "Y'all keep your feet up till it dries."

"Spot, for God's sake," the sheriff said.

"God likes a clean room same as the next fella," Spot said. We all kept our feet up while Spot took the keys off the desk and walked across his fresh-mopped floor, making wet footprints. "Don't y'all worry none about that," he said. "I'll mop myself out when I finish in the cell."

He unlocked the cell, went inside. We stayed silent, watched him mop around Fatty and under the cot, then he nudged the slop bucket a little with the mop. I could hear water moving inside it; there was good possibility it would be filled with piss and turds. I feared he'd knock it over, but he didn't. He just pushed it aside and mopped where it was, hooked the mop against it, slid it back in place. He mopped his way out, going back over his footprints, slinging the wet mop strands a little, hitting Fatty on the shoulder. He closed the cell door, locked it, started mopping again, working his way backwards, wiping out his footprints until he come to the back door. When he got there he tossed the keys on the sheriff's desk and bumped his butt against the door so that it came open. He went out, and the door closed. We could hear him splashing the water out of the bucket on the ground.

"He thinks he owns this goddamn place," the sheriff said.

"You want your trash carried out this week, and that chamber pot full of what I figure is your shit," said a voice from behind the door, "you better treat me a little more special."

"Goddamn nigger has ears like a coyote," the sheriff said.

"You can be sure of that," came Spot's voice again. The sheriff sat silent, and after a while he got up and went to the back door and peeked out. "He's gone," he said. He looked at Eustace. "I didn't mean nothing by that nigger remark."

"Hell, I know that," Eustace said. "We been in enough tight spots together for me to know that. You don't got to explain yourself. What you got to do is give us our reward money."

The sheriff turned crafty. You could see that craftiness light on him like a bird. His mouth twisted, and he showed his teeth, and even with his face like it was that smile lit him up and gave him a friendly look. The kind of friendly that makes you put a hand on your wallet.

"You know we got to fill out papers, send them in, and wait," the sheriff said.

"Sooner they are filled out," Shorty said, "the sooner the proper items will be in the mail and we can await reasonable return. Though we will have to leave for a while and come back through for it."

The sheriff nodded at Fatty in the cell. "How'd he manage to get all marked up like that?"

"He resisted while we had him tied securely to a chair and beat him with a pistol," Shorty said.

"And a shotgun stock," Eustace said.

That made the sheriff laugh.

"We told him to stay put," said Eustace, "but he kept falling out of the chair. And he was tied to it."

"Uh-huh," said the sheriff. "I seen him around before, but I ain't got no paper on him."

"He robbed the bank just the other day," Eustace said. "It's gonna take a while for the bulletin to show up. Wouldn't surprise me none, though, to find out there's already some kind of paper on him. What we'd like to do is get those reward papers filled out, then we can be on our merry way. When we come back you might have some merry money waiting for us."

"You're going after them others Red told me about?" the sheriff said.

"My name is Jack," I said.

"What I said. Red."

I gave up after that.

"That is our plan," Shorty said. "Track them down, bring them back. One way or the other. File claims on them, receive the reward money. Simple, really."

"Y'all get killed, don't come back," said the sheriff. "I got them papers sent in, then who is that money going to? Maybe I should wait till you come back with the others before we mark up the forms."

"We will come back," Shorty said. "And if we do not, we can make someone out as the beneficiary."

"Would he be someone we know?" the sheriff said.

"It could very well be someone in this room," Shorty said.

The sheriff considered on this for a moment by leaning back in his chair and looking at a large, dark water spot on the ceiling. The ceiling sagged there, and pretty soon a good rain was going to break it through. It was right over his desk. It was like that sword of Damocles you hear about, and one day it was going to fall. Well, the sheriff sat there for some time looking at that water spot, and pretty soon all of us, except Hog, who had drifted off to sleep, were looking at that spot as if waiting for it to take on the shape of Jesus.

Finally the sheriff got up, went to the telephone. He took a little cone off of a hook, took hold of a crank jutting out of it, and went to work squirreling it around. He'd come up on the toes of his boots each time he took the crank high, and then settle on his heels as the crank come down. Finally he quit cranking and started yelling at somebody in the phone as if they were standing across the street and he was in his doorway.

After a moment he listened, and then said, "Uh-huh. Uh-huh. No goddamn shit. We'll, I'll be set on fire, and in fact I have been before." He laughed at his own joke, said a few more uh-huhs, and hung up. He went back to his desk. "I called the doctor's office over in Hinge Gate. Only one I know there has a phone. He said the bank was robbed."

"Now, ain't that a surprise?" Eustace said. "We done told you that."

"I got some descriptions of the robbers, and that there fella does seem to fit the description of one of them, except they didn't mention all them bruises and red marks."

The sheriff grinned when he said that.

"So are we going to receive the financial reward or not?" Shorty said.

The sheriff dug around in his desk drawer and came up with some papers. Shorty dropped out of his chair, waddled over to the desk, and began filling them out with a feather pen that he dipped into a little bottle of ink that the sheriff had taken out of a drawer and placed on his desk.

"They have a thing now called a fountain pen," Shorty said. "You should get you one."

"Naw," the sheriff said. "I'm all right. I don't like change. That phone and the two or three places it connects around here are too much. Besides, I was thinking you fellas, and the young lady with the cat in the tree, are heading out after them others pretty quick, and since I'm thinking about going with you, I don't need to fill out the papers."

Shorty stopped writing while the sheriff's words sank in. "Wait a moment. You are not a bounty hunter anymore, Winton. Why would you be going?"

"I'm a goddamn sheriff," he said. "You might need someone along like me."

"If you were to go with us," Shorty said, "might your prisoner in there starve to death?"

"Ha," the sheriff said. "I got me a deputy. He's out getting me and him lunch right now. There won't be enough to share, by the way. We just got enough for ourselves."

"Ain't nobody asking for none," Eustace said.

"Problem solved," the sheriff said.

"Look here, Winton," Shorty said. "You do not have jurisdiction where we are going."

"Oh, I don't think it really matters, do you?" the sheriff said.

"I believe that is how the law works," Shorty said. "You might want to read it sometime, as it is the sound basis for your job."

"It gets in the way of my arrests," the sheriff said. "I like to think for myself, not let the law get all mixed up in it."

"That is our liberty, not yours," Shorty said. "You have an obligation to the law. We do not."

"I think I can take that liberty, I want to," said the sheriff. "I was thinking I could ride along, and we could split the money five ways. I say five because I assume Hog is not receiving a share. Four is already a good bite into it, so how would one more hurt? That way no one makes much, but we all make something."

"The girl is not receiving one red penny," Shorty said. "She is merely along for decoration, and as a sometime saddle mount for the kid."

"Hey," said Jimmie Sue.

"You don't have no call to talk to her like that," I said.

"Perhaps not," said Shorty. "But that is exactly how I am talking, is it not?"

Feeling Jimmie Sue had been insulted, I stood up. Jimmie Sue nabbed my pants leg with her thumb and forefinger and tugged. I paid it no mind. I said, "I've had just about enough of you, sir. First you have been rude to me and insulted my religion, and now you have insulted Jimmie Sue, who has been most kind to me."

"For four bits," Shorty said.

"That's enough of that," I said.

"To get it straight," Eustace said, "that was my four bits."

"Listen here, kid," Shorty said. "If you think it has come time for you to kick the midget around the room, I assure you

I will climb you like a chipmuk, land on your head like a ton of fat bricks, and drop you all the way to the bottom of hell. But if you feel the bear is in you, come ahead."

I clenched and unclenched my fists.

Jimmie Sue, as if he had insulted someone other than her, and then me for taking up for her, said, "What's a chipmunk?"

Eustace said to me, "I think we should stay on friendly terms, cousin, and the best way for that to happen is for you to sit your ass down before Shorty tunnels up your butt and comes out your ear."

I didn't like it, but the truth was, they were all I had. Besides, looking at Shorty, I saw that he was indeed ready to climb me. I had seen him about that business earlier with the chicken fighter and wanted no part of it. Still, I felt that to sit down and say nothing in front of Jimmie Sue might scar me in her eyes. I was about to say something smart when Jimmie Sue tugged at my pants again, said, "You want to find your sister, don't you?"

I looked at her, nodded, and sat down.

She whispered in my ear. "What's a chipmunk?"

"Kind of like a squirrel, I think. They got them out west, I figure. It really matters to you?"

"I like to be up on things," she said.

"Well, then," the sheriff said. "Now that it's been determined that the girl don't get a bite out of things and the boy has sat down, you can count me in, can't you?"

"I hate all you sons a bitches," came Fatty's voice.

We looked over at him. He had gotten up and was sitting on the cot.

"You shut up in there," the sheriff said. "Or I'll wash your mouth out with soap."

"I heard what you said about someone robbing a bank," Fatty said. "But it wasn't me."

"Oh, yeah, it was," Eustace said.

Fatty didn't argue. He just sat on the cot with his head hung.

About that time the front door opened and a man with a clean white hat sitting high on his head came in. He was wearing a gun slung low on his hip and tied down with cord against his leg. The holster tipped forward a little, and the butt of the gun was oversized for good gripping. The man himself had a fresh-scrubbed, pink face marked with shaving nicks. He had stuck bits of brown paper to them to soak up the blood. He was wide-eyed and had plenty of straw-blond hair poking out from under his hat. He was a little chubby, and his feet seemed small in his boots. They kind of sloshed when he walked.

He saw Fatty behind the cage, sitting on the cot. He closed the door and went over there. "Why, look at him," he said. "He looks like he's been dragged through a patch of prickly pears."

"Go fuck yourself," Fatty said.

"Who is that in there?" said the young man.

"That there is a bank robber, a kidnapper, and probably a rapist," said the sheriff. Then to us, he said, "This here, gentlemen, is my deputy, Harlis."

Harlis turned around and looked at us, said, "You got a big hog lying on the floor there."

"You noticed that, did you?" said the sheriff. "Stay away from him. Don't let his snoozing mislead you. He'll take right away to your nut sack."

"I wasn't gonna pet him," Harlis said.

"You do, you might just draw back a nub," Eustace said.

Deputy Harlis had already turned his attention back to Fatty. "You're behind bars, ain't you?"

"This is one smart fella, now, ain't he?" Fatty said.

"Nothing gets by him," the sheriff said. "There ain't a fly he don't notice."

"You're a fat one, ain't you?" said Deputy Harlis.

"Like you're some kind of stretched-out rag," Fatty said.

"I'm big-boned," Deputy Harlis said. "All my family are big-boned."

"I think what it is," Fatty says, "is you and your whole damn family, right down to your hound-dog-fucking grandma, are fat like me."

"Give me them keys," Deputy Harlis said. "I'm gonna whop him some."

"Forget it," the sheriff said.

"You ever watch your old hound dog mount your grandma?" Fatty said. "You ever do that?"

"I'm gonna find something and hit you with it," Deputy Harlis said. He drew his pistol quick-like. But not as quick as the sheriff picked the biscuit from his plate and threw it, hitting Deputy Harlis on his right cheek.

When that biscuit struck, it sounded like when Papa used to take a hammer to a cow's skull at slaughter time. Deputy Harlis stumbled, looked at the sheriff. "Damn, Winton. That hurt. You could have broke something."

"With a goddamn biscuit?" the sheriff said.

"Café cooks them up hard from the start," Deputy Harlis said, holstering his gun. "They sit awhile they might as well be a rock."

"You'll live," said the sheriff. "You're gonna be in charge here for a spell, as I'm gonna be leaving, and you will not pistol-whip or hurt the prisoner unless I say so. He's already had a good thrashing as it is."

"Oh, hell," Shorty said. "There it is. Winton is definitely going with us."

"That's right," the sheriff said. "Just to see things are done right."

"Oh," said Shorty. "That is a relief."

Deputy Harlis had finally fixed his eyeballs on Shorty, and as he looked at him, his mouth slowly came open. "I thought you was some kid sitting there."

"That there," the sheriff said, "is what you call a bona fide goddamn midget, Harlis, you fucking ignoramus. Why the hell would I have a kid sitting in a chair there? This ain't no barber shop. Damn, boy. I think Fatty might be right about that hound dog, only it wasn't your grandma, it was your mama, and you are the result."

Eustace said, "Tell you what, Winton. Just so we know, why don't you toss a stick and see if he fetches?"

9

Now, Shorty didn't agree to let Sheriff Winton go right away, no matter if Winton said he was, but I was beginning to see the handwriting on the wall. Shorty was wearing down. I think it was because the sheriff was suggesting the papers for our reward might get misplaced, or someone else might get the credit for bringing Fatty in. Someone like the sheriff, which I figured would take some hard believing on the part of anyone who knew him, as I had him figured for quite the layabout.

I am going to add right here that I would be well proved wrong on this, but right then there wasn't much to see in him other than the fact he looked like he'd been through a fire and someone tried to put it out with a dull hatchet.

Finally Shorty gave in. As I said, I think it had to do with him thinking he might not get anything without the sheriff's proper help, but also I could tell they were actually right smart friends and trusted one another, at least as far as they could throw each other. I figured the sheriff might be able to throw Shorty pretty far, by the way. And there was Eustace, who wouldn't easily be thrown if he cooperated and there was plenty of assistance. He was friends with that old burnt-up sheriff, too.

Pretty soon they were discussing how many there were that we were after, and then Sheriff Winton afforded there were probably a damn sight more of them that needed arresting for bounty than we were looking for. He said the whole woods was full of them, thick as seed ticks, and they had done all manner of crimes, and if we just shot them as we come to them, we could have a regular nest of dead folks that would generate a passel of dollars. He thought we might need a couple to three pack horses to tote them out.

I said, "Sheriff, there's a dead boy in a ditch that's maybe part eaten by Hog, and he needs a proper burial."

"Oh, yeah," Shorty said. "The young one here has been agitated to a remarkable degree ever since we found the dead boy, and he cannot quite get into his head that the boy will get no deader."

The part about the dead boy had been left out of my story previously, but now Shorty explained it. When he was finished, the sheriff said, "Now, that does present a problem, but I figure I can get someone to go out there and see if they can find him and box him up and bury him with the understanding he might have to be dug up and buried again, once it's figured who he belongs to."

"He needs digging up," Eustace said, "I can do that for a fee. I ain't got time to go get him and put him down, though."

"We'll find someone," the sheriff said.

"Does that please you?" Shorty asked me.

"Once I know for a fact it'll be done," I said, "I'll be covered with contentment."

* * *

After the papers were filled out, coffee was made, but no matter how hard I tried to get them into a mode of haste, nothing came of it. I said, "We should move on. Time is wasting and my sister is with them, and maybe not doing well."

"If they've already gotten the cherry from the box," said the sheriff, "then she is as well off as she is going to be."

"What the heck does that mean?" I said.

"If they've been at her," the sheriff said, "then they've had their fun, and if they don't want her anymore she'll be found dead as that boy back there you said Hog was nosing at. But if they liked her well enough and she didn't scratch out no one's eye, then they probably kept her. Which means she's alive and with them."

"They could change their minds," I said. "They could decide to kill her now or tomorrow, so we ought to get."

"Since you got information where they're going, we got just as much of a chance of finding her tomorrow as today."

"She's gonna do laundry," Fatty said.

He was standing up now, looking through the bars.

"Laundry?" I said.

"We first had an old woman done it," he said. "Someone's mother that we passed around between washings, but one night she run off, so we got this part-Indian gal, but she tried to stick Cut Throat with a butcher knife, and he stove her head in with a stick of firewood. That caused the laundry to pile up. He don't like doing laundry, likes to have a woman do it. You better hope, son, your sister knows how to do laundry, cause if she don't, once they get her to the Thicket, she ain't gonna last any longer than it takes for a tear to dry."

"Don't pay him no mind," Eustace said. "He was so smart

and knew everything, he wouldn't be in that goddamn jail having been pistol-whipped by a midget. Now, you think on that."

The sheriff made plans with Harlis to see someone was sent for the boy's body, then he said he was going to throw some things together and off we could go. A short while later Eustace took the dead chickens out of his saddlebag and fed them to Hog, who gobbled them up as easily as a toothless man might eat a wet biscuit.

"I didn't want them to waste, and I figured he's hungry as us," Eustace said. "I was going to fry them up for us tonight, but I reckon in all this heat they might be on the spoiled side. I had an uncle ate a chicken that had gone a little ripe, and he said he had a fever and felt like he was trying to shit an anvil for a week. A hog, though, if there's enough gravy on it, can eat an anvil. Chickens don't need no gravy."

We watched Hog eat and cough feathers while Shorty and the others finished getting their stuff together—all but Jimmie Sue, who stood with us and watched the eating of the chickens.

"He likes them with the feathers on?" she asked.

"He likes them in tar with a stick up their butt," Eustace said. "He don't have a picky bone in his body about food, though he doesn't much care for the smell of fresh-cut hay, which I can't ponder a reason to. It causes him to move on. I think it makes his nose stuffy."

When Hog finished, he made a coughing noise, then spat up some chicken bones and feathers and something that didn't look like anything we had seen him eat. That coughing up of his meal seemed to be our signal, and we mounted up and set out. The deputy had said he would like to go, too, but Shorty threatened to kill him, and Harlis appeared to believe him. I know I did.

What we were trying to do was cut a trail that would get us where Fatty said his comrades were, and I kept wondering if he was telling it true or if we were on a wild goose chase. Shorty felt certain he and his pistol and the butt of Eustace's shotgun had helped Fatty be accurate in his directions, but I was still unconvinced.

We went along until night came, and by then we were deep down the trail that led through the woods and was supposed to be a shortcut. I was heartened a bit when Sheriff Winton said he knew the path and claimed he had a pretty good idea where Fatty was talking about. He said it was a place where a lot of the bad and the unwashed gathered, as if the sheriff himself were any example of fine grooming. I made sure I didn't ride behind him, because when I did, and there was a wind blowing back at me, I got about what I figured to be a few months' body stink, some rancid hair oil, and some onion-stink breath, not to mention the pack horse he was tagging behind him was about the foulest-stinking creature I have ever encountered, way it cut wind and dropped turds. Compared to them, Hog's stench was even refreshing.

I looked over at Jimmie Sue, and she was fanning herself. I couldn't help but wonder how she had dealt with him as a customer. Later I would ask when we took a stop for the horses to blow, and she'd say she put a lot of smell-pretty on him, which I reckon was some kind of perfume.

But at this time we rode up past him, found position near Eustace and Shorty, placing us upwind of the stink. Still, it didn't improve my spirits all that much. By the time night come falling in through the timber I was about as low as I had been since Lula was stolen away and Grandpa was killed. Fact was, I felt so low I could have crawled under a peanut hull and called it home.

We stopped now and then to make water in the bushes—or, as I said earlier, to let the horses blow, but mostly we rode on. We went along a little ways even after night, cause the trail was clear and there was some moonlight and the stars were as bright as candles. But finally we stopped and put together a rough camp. It was hot weather, even at night, but we made a rope line for the horses, built a fire and heated up some beans with weevils in it, and, disgusting as it was, for a few moments with hot food in my belly, I felt better about things. We sat around the fire and I amused myself by pushing a small log I had chopped up for firewood into the flames. When I did this the fire would crackle and there would be a few sparks, but nothing serious enough to catch the woods on fire. There were lots of fireflies out, and they glowed their tails all around us. Once I looked over at Shorty, and he had a halo of the things around his hat. The minute I looked and saw them, it was like they were embarrassed about it and flew off.

While we sat the weather cooled a might, and a wind kicked up. It had a smell about it that was mixed with water and pine needles and forest dirt. It wasn't a bad smell. It made me think of when me and Lula was kids and we'd dig in the dirt together looking for fishing worms. I could close my eyes and picture us out back of the house near the woods, digging with a shovel or a garden trowel. She would have loved being here in front of the fire, thinking her strange thoughts about the woods and what was in it. Everything to her was a mystery.

I took off my boots and laid out my blanket and crawled under another and let my head rest on my saddle. Jimmie Sue pulled her dress over her head right in front of everyone, kicked off her shoes, and got under the blanket with me. The men didn't hesitate to turn their heads and look, and I could even hear them breathing heavy. Jimmie Sue wanted to snuggle up, but I wouldn't have it, not with them others watching. Finally she said, "Suit your ownself," and turned her butt into me and went to sleep. After about five minutes, Hog come along and nestled on the other side of me, squeezing me up like a sandwich.

Eustace said, "Me and Hog used to be right smart buddies till you came along."

"That so," I said.

"That's so, but you know," Eustace said and laughed, "I don't miss his smelly self none."

"Hog does stink," Jimmie Sue said, then went silent. After a short spell I could hear her breathing evenly in sleep. Eustace took first watch with his four-gauge, up on a rise between some trees overlooking the trail we had come down, near the tied-out horses.

I eventually drifted off and dreamed. It was one of those dreams that seems to make a lot of sense when you're having it, but talking about it now, it seems pretty silly and not worth mentioning. When I come out of it, it was still night, and I rolled over and glanced out and seen that Shorty was awake and sitting by the fire, leaning toward it, reading a book. The way the fire popped and waved, it made Shorty's shadow throw up against the trees, and it was much larger than Shorty.

I watched for a little while, and then weariness took me over and when I awoke it was to Jimmie Sue's shoe in my ribs.

"They done gone on ahead," she said.

"What?" I said, sitting up. Jimmie Sue was dressed, wearing some loose pants and a man's old blue shirt. She had her regular shoes on.

"Where'd you get those clothes?"

"Winton gave them to me. He brought them along in his saddlebag for me. Thought I'd be more comfortable. I am. He said they belonged to some fella got shot and got buried, but not in these pants. They don't smell the way Winton does. They're pretty clean."

"That stands to reason," I said.

"That they don't smell?"

"No—that whoever owned those pants didn't get buried in them. You're wearing them."

"Yeah. Winton said that dead fella, his parents put a nice new suit on him that was bought with two pair of pants, and these was left over. Somehow Winton ended up with them after the funeral. And though all that is just as interesting as it can be, Jack, I thought you might be more interested in knowing everyone, including Hog, has gone on without us."

"Damn them," I said.

"They ain't left us for good," Jimmie Sue said, "just gone on ahead. I know how they're going. Eustace said he figured you needed a sound rest, since you hadn't really had a good one in the last day or so."

"He did, did he?"

"You saying you wasn't tired?"

"I'm feeling all right," I said.

"That why didn't you want to ride me last night?"

"No spurs."

"That's funny, Jack. Right firmly hilarious. All them men

done seen what I got, or someone who's got something similar. It wouldn't have been no big surprise to them."

"Yeah, but I'm not all that anxious for them to see what I got."

"I thought we was gonna have fun," she said.

"This isn't a holiday," I said.

"We got to go somewhere and it takes a while, we might as well make the best of it. I mean, I could try and tell funny stories, but as you've seen I ain't as funny as I thought. But I know I'm good at the other, so that seems the right choice, don't you think?"

While she was talking, I had shook out my boots in case a scorpion had crawled up in them. I put them on, rolled up my bedroll, and went to saddling my horse. Jimmie Sue had hers saddled. She said, "Don't expect no breakfast in bed or me in your bed if you ain't willing to do your manly duties."

"I have duties now?"

"Ain't we kind of together?"

"Kind of. Yeah."

"Then you act like it."

There was really nothing to say. It was like she was a bottle of something with fizz that had been shook up and uncorked, and she wasn't going to stop talking until her bottle run out.

We got on horseback and Jimmie Sue reached in her saddlebags and pulled out a couple of biscuits. She gave me one. She said, "You ought to kind of suck around it before you bite, cause you might lose some teeth. Woman at the café makes them."

"One of the biscuits that the sheriff hit Harlis with?"

"Yep," she said. "And maybe the same batch. Winton gave me some this morning."

We started out then, sucking on our biscuits, following the trail, going the way Jimmie Sue said to go. I never could do more than get my biscuit to flake a little, and the flake lay in my mouth for a long time like a metal shaving before it was gooey enough to be swallowed.

10

The morning was hot as a rabid dog in an overcoat. The way I fit in that saddle made me chafe and burn, had me wanting to cinch up my manhood so it wouldn't rub. About noon we stopped and let the horses blow and had another one of them biscuits, which was enough work for an hour and gave you the impression you had eaten more than you had, because they lay in your stomach pretty much like a stone.

When we got to where we felt the horses were rested and we had them grained, we took them down to a little creek to drink, but just a little, so they wouldn't bloat up with all that grain in them. After we done that, we was coming up a hill leading them when we heard a large bit of cussing and the Lord's name being taken in vain pretty frequent. At the top of the road we seen a colored fella riding from the direction we had come on the back of a big mule. He was riding fast, bouncing the way a mule will bounce you, which was what was making him cuss. I recognized him right off because of that pale place on his forehead. It was the swamper from the jail. Spot.

He raised a hand when he seen us. As he got up close, he stopped and slid off the mule, which didn't have a saddle and had to have been rough riding. He said, "I come looking for the sheriff."

"They done gone on ahead of us," Jimmie Sue said. "What you all het up about?"

"It's about Harlis," he said.

"Someone get a better lick on him with a biscuit?" Jimmie Sue said.

"He's done been shot in the belly this time," said Spot. "And it's a lot worse than a biscuit."

"I'll say," Jimmie Sue said.

"It was that damn whore," Spot said. "No offense, lady."

"I'm taking a little," Jimmie Sue said. "But go on."

"I come to the jail to pour out the slop jar, you know, and I had to have the cell opened, and Harlis come there with his gun and the key and opened it up. I went in and got it. I wasn't but just outside the cell when that whore come in smiling, one they call Katy, and she said, 'I come to see my cousin.'

"Well, now, Harlis, he says, 'Why don't you come to see me? I ain't got no cousins to talk at.' I don't know them was his exact words, but I think it's in the corral more or less, cause I wasn't paying all that much attention. I put the slop jar by the door, went to do some other work I had to do in there, and about that time Katy pulled out a little pistol from her purse and said something like, 'Don't bother locking up. Just let him on out or I'll shoot a hole in your gut.'

"Now, then, I was looking toward the back door, thinking maybe I could run out of there fast-like, but she waved the barrel of that gun at me, said, 'Get over there, nigger.' I knew she meant me, so I went over and stood by the wall near the cell where she was pointing. Harlis had done closed the cell back, and he said wasn't no way he was going to open that cell, so she shot him. He caught a blue whistler in the stomach, sat down against the bars of the cell, and pissed himself. He wasn't dead, but he sure wasn't happy. He was moaning and taking on something terrible. Then Katy pointed the gun at me, said, 'You want one, nigger?' She meaning me—"

"We got that," Jimmie Sue said.

"—so I said, 'No, thank you,' and she says to me, 'Now, you pick up them keys and let him out.' I couldn't have picked up them keys any faster than had they been a gold coin. I opened the cell door and let him out. He come out smiling, and he says to me, 'Go over and get that there slop jar,' and I did. I brought it to him and he dumped it on Harlis's head, and then went to forcing it down over his noggin. Harlis was screaming and trying to get away, but there wasn't no doing it.

"That jar is one of them wide-mouth ones like the sheriff likes cause he can rest his butt comfortable on it, and so in time it got forced over Harlis's head, though it split a little as he done it. It made a big mess. By the time he got that done, Harlis was bled good, and his fire had done blown out; he was just ashes on the other side, so to speak. I don't know if he drowned in that stuff or the stomach shot got him, but one was as good as the other in the long run. It was right then I had a thought if I didn't run for it I was going to be dead next, so I broke and made like a rabbit, hit that back door so hard it come off the hinges, and me and it went out into the back there. A bullet come past me like it had to meet someone downtown and was late, and gave me a hot kiss on the ear as it passed. I went over the little ridge back there, and there was people peeking out of their houses and the like, but nobody was moving in the direction of the jail. Next thing I know I seen the fat man and that woman on horses, which she had brought with her saddled and ready to go, no doubt, and they was riding fast along the street. I seen that Fatty had a rifle in his hand, one he had taken from the office there, and then they was gone."

"How'd you get ahead of them?" Jimmie Sue said.

"They didn't come this way," Spot said.

"Then Fatty lied to Shorty," I said.

"I don't know about that," Spot said. "I don't know where they're going, and I don't know where the sheriff's going, but I know the way y'all come; you wasn't hard to follow. I figure if Fatty knows where the sheriff is going, he might be taking a shortcut. I would. I wouldn't want to face up to Sheriff Winton, Shorty, and Eustace square and on the level. And there's the hog and all. I was Fatty and that whore, I'd be getting up ahead of them and waiting to bushwhack their asses."

"Or he isn't going where we think," I said. "It could be he lied to Shorty all along."

"He probably told it true when Shorty was giving him the pistol," Jimmie Sue said, "but he didn't mention that quicker way to get there. That was his ace in the hole."

Spot nodded. "That's the way I see it. I come to warn the sheriff and tell him about Harlis, on account of he's been good to me mostly, and I'm thinking I can make a tip on this. I think one is due, don't you?"

"I don't know about nothing like that," I said.

"I think you earned one," Jimmie Sue said. "When I worked my job at the house back in town, if I bootblacked your boots, I did it to seem like it was out of the goodness of my heart, but actually I was hoping for some extra money. I didn't always get it, I'll tell you, and it was a disappointment when I didn't, me sort of counting on it and all. So I'll know how you feel if you don't get any."

"That didn't never cross my mind, about not getting anything for it," Spot said.

"Well, I can tell you now there's plenty of bootblacking I've done to get nothing but dirty fingers for. So you got to brace yourself for the possibility."

"Jimmie Sue, for the love of God, let all that go," I said. "What about Harlis? What was done with him? He isn't still in the jailhouse dead with turds on him, is he?"

"I told folks at the saloon nearest the jail what happened, so I guess they done dragged him out and wiped him off and are getting him ready for the ground," Spot said. "I'm sort of hoping they clean up after the place, too, cause that part of the job I'm not looking forward to, especially if I don't get back there for some days."

"Why wouldn't you get back sooner?" I said. "We can carry the message."

"I'll tote it myself," he said.

"There's nothing to tote," I said.

"Except the words in my mouth, and that's the way I want it," he said, and looked at me with his head turned to the side. "Besides, I ain't having as good a time as you might suspect back in town."

"We got to catch up with the sheriff, then," I said. "And right away."

11

We caught up with them pretty soon, because they had stopped to eat something themselves, and they were just about to mount again when we rode up. Hog wasn't with them, but I figured he wasn't far away.

We dismounted, and Spot told them what he told us.

"That goddamn Harlis," said Sheriff Winton. "I knew he was going to end up deader than a post. It was writ all over him. It's like there never was a fella more inclined to catch a bullet or a severe beating than Harlis. You took that son of a bitch's brain and put it in an empty ink bottle and shook it, it would sound like a round of shot in a boxcar. Only reason he worked for me was he didn't take much money and was too simple-headed to know he might could get shot, so I guess some of it's my fault. That's what I get for giving him a job when he didn't have the head for it."

"He was dumb," Spot said. "But what I done told you, that's news you needed to know, ain't it?"

"Reckon so," said Winton, who was, I could tell, still collecting all this information and trying to sort it.

"You didn't have that news," Spot said, "you wouldn't know that fat ass and his cousin is gonna go a short way and maybe cut you off somewhere and bushwhack you. Or get all the way to the Thicket and warn the others."

"You know a lot about my business, don't you?" Winton said.

"The boy and the whore here told me," Spot said.

"Some of that's true," I said.

"I pick a little up by listening at the back door to the jail," Spot said. "And that's where I got most of it. I heard what these fellas told you about the fat man, and it all sort of fitted together for me. I think it's real important that you know about it, don't you? What I know, I mean, about Fatty escaping."

"Yeah," Winton said. "It is, but now you done told me."

Winton stood there looking at Spot, who was standing there looking at him the way a dog will if it thinks you're going to drop something on the floor it might can eat.

"He wants a tip," Jimmie Sue said.

"A tip?" said the sheriff.

"It's a polite kind of thing to do," Spot said.

"My tip to you," said the sheriff, "is next time you got some news for me, you need to know up front you ain't getting shit for it. And don't be listening at my back door no more."

"Then you ain't gonna get no new news, you think like that, now, are you?" said Spot.

"I reckon not," Sheriff Winton said.

Spot looked as if his old mama had just told him he was uglier than the yard dog.

"That ain't no way to treat him," said Jimmie Sue. "Now, you give him something."

"I ain't got nothing for him."

"You can promise him something and mean it," she said.

Winton studied Spot, as if looking for a weakness. "How about I fix you up with some biscuits for your ride back, Spot. How about that?"

"You're yanking my pecker, ain't you?" Spot said.

"No, I ain't. I got the biscuits right here."

"I don't want no damn biscuits. No one can eat them biscuits, less'n you want to knock a bad tooth out. I was thinking of something more solid."

"What could be more solid than them biscuits?" Winton said.

Spot fixed an eye on the sheriff. "Some money would be nice."

"It would be," said the sheriff, "if a fella had any. Ain't you one of them that's about doing something out of the goodness of your heart, just because it's good and you don't need any other reason?"

"No," Spot said. "That ain't me."

I glanced at Eustace and Shorty. They were listening to it all carefully.

"Damn," said the sheriff. "I don't got to give you nothing. But I'll tell you what. I don't get killed, and we make some money out of this deal, all them bounties, I'll give you a tip then."

"How much?"

"I don't know. A dollar?"

"Five dollars."

"That's a lot of money, Spot," said Winton.

"That's why I want it," Spot said.

"You are a nuisance. All right, then. Five."

"It's a deal?" asked Spot.

Sheriff Winton stuck out his hand. He and Spot shook on it. "Deal," Winton said.

"I'm gonna just ride along," said Spot, "so maybe I can keep you from getting killed and make sure I get my five dollars."

"What if you get killed?" Winton said.

"Then I won't need no five dollars, now, will I?" Spot said. "You'll come out ahead, not owing me nothing."

"He's got you there," Eustace said.

"Spot," Shorty said, "if I am ever in the need of someone to do bargaining for me, would it be all right if I came to you to be my representative?"

"I don't know what that is," Spot said. "But I reckon it'll be all right with me."

12

Near nightfall Hog showed up. There were vines all twisted up around his legs and snout, and he was muddy and slimy. I reckoned he had found a creek somewhere to snuggle up in during the hot of the day, and when it cooled he had come out and tracked us.

Like I was saying, it was near night, but there was still some light, it being mostly red like a plum on account of the sun was sinking low beyond the trees, and it was just about then, when the last of the light was dying out, that we come upon a trading post setting off the side of the road in some cleared timber. It was right where the road forked, one side not being much of a road, really, but more a path through the timber.

We were still a good ways back from the trading post, but not so much we couldn't get a good look at it. There were stumps all about, the remains of what had been used to build the place, and a few of them were smoking from fires having been set on them to burn them out.

The trading post had been put together in a hurry, and

stupidly, with green logs, and it leaned a might. The logs weren't all barked-off, and some were cut longer than they needed to be and jutted out here and there. The door was set low down, like it was made that way for someone not much taller than Shorty. The door was fixed to the wall with leather straps for hinges, and you opened it by pulling on a thong of leather. There were animal hides hanging off nails along the outside walls, and there was this right nice seat-swing on the porch, hanging from chains. The wind made the swing move and the chains creak.

I thought we might get some food and drink there, so I was eager to get inside. Before we did, Shorty threw up his hand. "We may prefer to be cautious."

"That was my thought," Winton said.

Winton noted there was a remuda of horses out back of the cabin. He said, "Why don't you drop off that mule, Spot, go back there, and check for the horses them two rode out of town on. I figure this may be the fork they took, as it brings us to the same place. They might not be as far ahead of us as they hoped, or most likely Fatty got to thinking about having a drink. He's the kind of fella that would like a drink over common sense. I know. I'm a bit that way myself."

Spot slid off the mule's back, handed me up the reins, then walked on back and looked at the run of horses. He come back pretty quick, said, "They're both back there. It's the same horses."

"You're sure?" Winton asked.

"There's a pinto that the whore was riding, and that bony palomino the fat man was riding."

My heart started pounding. I was thinking the whole mess could end here, and that Lula could be returned to the bosom of her family, which in the immediate sense, due to a series of recent events, was me and some aunt we didn't know in Kansas.

"All right, then," Winton said. "I figure we can go inside and see how the curtains hang, if you fellas are ready."

"I was born ready," said Shorty. "But I think we need more of a plan than that. I would suggest that I and Eustace—and we will take the boy here in case there is someone else he can identify from the ferry incident—go inside and see if we can stir some activity. My recommendation is we do not make a direct attempt to arrest if they should pull weapons, but do immediately what is necessary."

I assumed that to be a long-about way of saying they were going to kill them.

"They don't have to be killed, do they?" I asked.

"They themselves will be responsible for our determination on the matter," Shorty said.

"That means he's going to shoot them, doesn't it?" I said to Eustace.

"It might work out that way," Eustace said. "It sure could."

"Rest of you stay out here," Shorty said. "Winton, I recommend strongly that you move to the rear, in case someone comes out. But I would stay down low in consideration that Eustace could come out that way and cut down on an escapee with the shotgun. That shot does not care who is in its path. The whore can do as she pleases."

"That's right nice of you," Jimmie Sue said.

"Spot," Shorty said. "You do as you please as well."

"That's what I was thinking," Spot said. "I ain't got no gun anyway, and I ain't strong enough to throw this mule at them."

"Then you are as set as you are going to be," Shorty said.

Eustace swung off his horse, pulled the shotgun out of a loop on the side of the saddle, got a fistful of shells from the saddlebag, and stuck them in his pants pocket. He patted the pad on the vest at his shoulder, as if to assure it everything would be all right, but more likely to assure himself he was padded up good for the stock of the four-gauge. The mouth of that gun looked like a hole to hell.

I got down off my horse, and Eustace pulled a pistol out of one of the saddlebags and gave it to me. It was one I hadn't seen before. It was an old converted .44, and heavy as a plow.

Shorty used his ladder to climb down, unholstered his Colt, which seemed extremely large in his little hands, said, "Winton, if you should prefer, take my Sharps there when you go out back, and if anyone should make a run for it, and you got the sight for it in this light, nail him with it. But again, watch for Eustace and that four-gauge."

"I can do that," Sheriff Winton said, and dismounted.

"Just make sure you do not shoot a midget or a big colored man coming out the back, because that will be us," Shorty said. "And there is the boy, of course."

"Thanks for remembering me," I said.

"Let me give you a tip," said Shorty. "The pistol you are holding is not modern and requires that you thumb back the hammer. I thought it best that those of us with training have the best guns so that we can fire shots off quickly."

"Seems to me, as someone untrained, I should have one of the better guns."

"Well," said Shorty. "You will not have the better gun, and that is the finish of it. You can find a place to hole up with the whore and Spot if you prefer."

I shook my head. "I'm going in. Lula might be in there, and I'd like to try and make sure no one shoots her, including us."

"All right, then," Eustace said. "That long end is what you point at them."

"I am past humor," I said.

"Everything is humorous," said Shorty, "except your own death. But other people will laugh."

Now, I will not lie to you. I was hoping with all my heart that Lula was in there and safe. I was so scared I could feel my feet wiggling in my boots like a snake trying to crawl out of a slick-sided hole. I didn't know what to expect, and I believe I had thought this would be more simple than it was turning out to be. I had figured we'd surprise them and say, "Throw up your hands, you're all under arrest," and we'd tie them up and lead them back to town. I was having my doubts now, and sick to my stomach to think I might actually have to draw a bead on someone and shoot him. Or end up shot up myself, thrown in a ditch out back of the place for the ants to eat.

The sheriff got the Sharps, and Jimmie Sue wheedled him out of his pistol, and they started out back. Spot said he had to pee, then he disappeared into the bushes with his mule. The three of us, and Hog, started down toward the trading post.

When we pulled on the leather sling and the door swung back, a stink come with it full of bean farts and sweat and something sweet as honey, and that honey smell just made it all the worse. There were three or four lanterns lit up, and they gave about as much light as the damned get in the grave. As we come in, I saw to the left there were four people at a little table playing cards, sitting on stools of different heights. There was a plate of cornbread between them and a bottle of syrup. I could see that good because they had a lantern sitting right next to the plate. I searched their faces, but none of them were Nigger Pete or Cut Throat. They were all white men, but none looked familiar. They all looked as if they had been rode hard and put up wet. They were all staring at Eustace and Hog, as if they were one of a kind.

Back of the counter was a man who appeared out of place, due to being clean and having his hair cut close and his face shaved to a nice pink lantern-lit glow. There was a lantern on either end of the bar he was behind, and the bar was a warped plank over some old barrels. Behind him, on the wall, were three shelves with assorted items on them, mostly bottled goods that I took to be whiskey or beers, a couple of Dr Peppers and Coca-Colas, and a few bottles with colored liquid in them that could have been hair tonic or sarsaparilla. There was another table to our right, but there wasn't but one man sitting at it, and he was back in the shadows and I couldn't make out his face, but one thing was sure, wasn't no one in there Fatty, the whore Katy, Cut Throat, or Nigger Pete.

I stayed on the right side, near the single man at the table. Shorty was in the middle, and Eustace was on the left. Eustace had that shotgun cradled in his arms like a baby. The man behind the counter said, "We don't serve colored, and you can't bring that hog in here."

"That a fact," Eustace said, and walked up to the plank, his head turned more toward the men at the table, who had now given up their cards to stare at us. "Give me a bottle of whiskey."

"I said—" the bartender said, but Eustace cut him off.

"I know what you said," Eustace said. "But trying to avoid a bit of unpleasantness, as my short friend here would call it, I say give me a bottle and I'll pay for it, and nothing angry will happen. As for the hog, I didn't bring him. He come on his own. But he don't want nothing. Let me be sure. You want anything, Hog?"

Hog looked up at Eustace, but I don't think it'll be any big revelation to say Hog didn't ask for anything.

"Nah, like I thought," Eustace said. "He don't want nothing. He's done ate and don't drink after four. It's his digestion."

The bartender studied Eustace, then leaned over the plank and looked down at Shorty. "What the hell's that?"

"That," said Eustace, "is what we call a midget. That is a short man with a big pistol."

"And a big dick," said Shorty.

"That's something I don't care to figure on," Eustace said. "But I want to point out to you, Mr. Bartender, that pistol he's got is easy for him to level under the plank there so that he can lay down a shot on your balls."

"It's in the holster," said the bartender.

"It can come out," said Eustace.

The bartender looked at me. "What's he for?"

"To hold the midget up if I get tired."

"Why you got a midget with you?" asked the bartender. I heard Shorty sigh.

"Why, that's my son," said Eustace. "I noticed he come out white, which means my wife is going to have some explaining. And you know what I think, Mr. Bartender Man?"

"What's that?"

"I think if I was a fella called Nigger Pete, you'd let him have a drink."

"I don't know no Nigger Pete."

"Then you may be better off than you think. Now put that whiskey on the plank before I go back there and get it."

"Niggers and pigs both have a smell about them," said one of the men at the table. He was a squatty fella with a beak of a nose and a mustache that looked like someone had painted it there with charcoal.

"Now, that ain't mine or Hog's stink," Eustace said. "What you're smelling there is a thick wipe of shit just under your nose."

The man at the table stirred, but a touch from the fella next to him stayed him on his stool.

Eustace smiled at him, then looked away.

The bartender glanced to both sides of the room, perhaps for help, but no one was moving. I glanced at the back of the place, to the left of the plank, and there was curtain over a doorway. I thought I heard someone move back there. I laid my hand on the pistol I had stuck in my belt.

Seeing there was no assistance forthcoming, the bartender put the bottle on the plank and said, "Just this once."

"Unless I come back," said Eustace. "Then it'll be twice."

The bartender said, "Give me six bits."

"Six bits?" Eustace said. "This better be the stuff the angels drink. Get me two glasses. Make that three. Give the kid a Dr Pepper."

Eustace hoisted Shorty up so he could sit on the plank. Shorty took six bits from out of his clothes and dropped it on the plank. The bartender opened the Dr Pepper and a bottle of whiskey and put them on the plank. He set down two glasses. One for Shorty, one for Eustace. Eustace slid the glass to Shorty, said, "Pass it on."

I remembered then that Eustace avoided drink. I didn't

pour any of the Dr Pepper, and when the bartender put the whiskey bottle in front of Shorty, Shorty just looked at it.

I turned to look at the man at the table. He was watching me like a chicken watches a bread crumb. Hog was watching him like he was an acorn.

Shorty poured himself a drink. I didn't move.

"Just sip it to be polite," Shorty said.

I didn't pour any. I just picked up the bottle and took a swig. I don't remember tasting it.

"Here is our situation," said Shorty. "We are looking for some people. We are looking for a man called Cut Throat, and one called Fatty, and a man called Nigger Pete. Do you know them?"

"I heard tell of them," said the bartender.

"Okay," said Shorty. "So we are that far along in our investigation. Let us be more direct and more precise. Have you seen them as of late?"

"I can't say I have," said the bartender.

"Here is a thing that should be explained before we continue our conversation. If you say you have not seen them, and we should deduce that you have, well, there could be considerable unpleasantness. Do you understand?"

"See?" said Eustace. "I told you he'd call it unpleasantness."

"You think that concerns me?" said the bartender.

"It should," said Shorty.

"Why, I shit turds bigger than you," the bartender said, and one of the men at the card table let out with a single loud laugh. It was the one with the mustache like a charcoal stain. He seemed to be the bravest one there.

Shorty looked toward the table. "You might best have a chicken bone hung in your throat I hear that again."

The man moved slightly, turning himself on his stool so that he was facing us. I glanced at the single man at the table on my right. His hand was resting on his pistol. A single drop of sweat went into my right eye, and I wiped it away quickly with my sleeve.

"Now," said Shorty. "Here is what I am thinking. I am thinking that a big fat man who has been severely pistol-whipped by a midget—that would be me—and a whore who is his cousin but has no considerations about the men she diddles, are back there behind the curtain, listening, and armed with a stolen rifle from the sheriff we have with us outside. And I am also reasonably certain that you are lying to me, and to my good friends here, and this is about to go very bad."

"For you," said the bartender. He put one hand behind his back.

"If your hand comes back into view, and it is holding anything other than what you might have dug from your butt crack, I will shoot a hole in you."

"I don't believe you got no sheriff outside," said another of the men at the card table. He was the man who had held charcoal mustache back. He was bony and looked as if his face had once been filled with thorns. He had on a greasy hat, and he pushed it back with one hand so as to see us all better.

"Your belief is in error," said Shorty.

"We ain't even got a sheriff around these parts," another man at the table said. He leaned forward, and I could see his face now. It was just a face under a hat, nothing memorable.

"He is not from here," said Shorty. "He is from No Enterprise."

"He's out of his place, then," said the man. "He ain't got no call to do nothing here."

Shorty nodded. "He does not indeed, if he were worried about legalities and had not turned bounty hunter. And I should also mention that me and the colored gentleman here are also bounty hunters. The kid is looking for his sister, Lula. And if you have seen a young woman who seems to be moving about against her will with any of the aforementioned folks, or with anyone who might be associated with them, you could create considerable goodwill by revealing that information."

"You talk like you're one of them cranked-up phonographs," said the man to my right. "You just go on and on." He, too, had leaned forward now, and his fingers had wrapped around his pistol handle. There was little light over there, but I could sure see his hand and that pistol, as he was sitting slightly to the side of his table. He was a little guy with an old face.

"So can I assume that no assistance will be forthcoming from any of you in this room?" Shorty said.

No one answered. Shortly let the silence rest. He drank his drink. He said, "Any of you who would like to be left in one piece, you might want to skedaddle, and not out the back door, as the sheriff has my Sharps fifty and he will blow a hole in you if you go that way."

"There ain't no sheriff," said the man who had barked a laugh. "And if you are bounty hunters, ain't none of you but the nigger look worth his salt, and he ain't but one man."

"You are all of one mind and in agreement, then?" said Shorty. "You plan to protect the hardened criminal in the back room at the cost of your lives?"

"I ain't got nothing for him," said one of them at the card table, the one who had said nothing up until that point. He got up and left through the front door.

"That explains a lot," said Shorty. "And now our situation is properly laid out."

No sooner had those words come out of Shorty's mouth than the bartender pulled a pistol out from behind him, out of his belt, and Shorty pulled that big Colt fast and swung it around with one hand and shot. I kind of saw the bartender's head jerk and his brains splatter, but mostly I had my eye on the man to my right, who stood up and fired. A bullet went by me close enough it sounded like a freight train passing. I tugged my pistol, but it hung up in my belt. The man fired another shot, and I got my pistol out, barely remembered to cock it, and fired. I missed. The man fired again and missed. I couldn't see how he could, close as we were to one another, but he had missed three times and I had missed once. Hog got him. He went under the table, knocking it over, biting a chunk out of the man's leg, then another, and this time he hung on. The man went back against the wall and started hitting Hog with the pistol. If it bothered Hog I couldn't note it. I cocked and fired again, and this time I hit him, and he went back against the wall and dropped his pistol and said, "Shit," and then Hog went to work on him. The man screamed a lot, and Hog grunted a lot and squealed a few times, but not in pain. Hog was feeling pleasurable.

I turned and looked at the three men at the table. They hadn't moved. It's like they had been flies stuck in molasses.

"Now, keep it like that," said Eustace, speaking to them.

The curtain at the back parted. A rifle barrel poked through. Shorty fired at it. The shot sent the rifle winding, and we heard running in the room and a back door being thrown open, and then there was a scuttling sound and the roar of that big Sharps .50, and then it was followed by a couple of snaps from a pistol.

A woman's voice, Katy, I'm sure, yelled out, "Shit on a goose," and then went silent.

Shorty leaped down off the plank and strode over to the man I had shot. Hog had him by the ankle now and was jerking his head from side to side, causing the man to knock over chairs and the table, and he was banging the man's head against the wall when he slung him back. Shorty said, "Hog, that will be enough."

Hog let him go, reluctantly. It was easy to see the man was bad off. He had gotten hold of his gun again, but he didn't look strong enough to lift it, bleeding from hog bites and a pistol shot as he was. I could see now that Hog had got him in the face, too, and had chewed off an ear and part of his nose. The only career he had left was working in the circus.

He looked up at Shorty, wheezing as he did. He acted as if he would like to lift the pistol, but it was just too much for him. He quit trying. He kept wheezing and looking at Shorty. Shorty shot him between the eyes. It was quick and it was cold-blooded. I felt light-headed.

Eustace had darted through the curtains and into the back room while I held my pistol on the men at the table, the hammer cocked and ready. Shorty joined me with his gun pointed at them.

"Nice night, is it not?" Shorty said.

Eustace came back carrying the rifle Shorty had shot out of the hands of someone back there; I had a pretty good idea who. "Back door is open, but I ain't going out of it. I figure Winton has reloaded the Sharps by now and I wouldn't want him or Jimmie Sue to mistake me for someone I ain't."

"Absolutely," Shorty said.

We all started moving toward the front door. Eustace said,

"If any of you men are wanted, we don't know of it, and the sheriff doesn't have papers on you. But you want to talk about where you think the men we're looking for have gone, though we have a pretty good idea from Fatty himself, we are all ears. Or you can just sit there with your thumbs up your asses and stay out of the way."

"I ain't never even liked the idea of no midget," said charcoal mustache. "Let alone having one in my sight."

"Now is your time to eliminate one of my ilk," Shorty said. "If you think you are tall enough."

The man didn't move. He seemed to have quickly decided midgets were just fine with him. We went out the front door. My ears were ringing.

"You didn't need to kill the man I shot," I said.

"I thought I did," Shorty said.

"You didn't need to," I said.

"Need and want sometimes do not mix well," said Shorty. "He was bit up good, and your bullet had caught him in the lungs. He was not going to make it. I did him a favor."

We were talking softly as we backed off the porch and out into what would pass for the yard. There were a number of large stumps out there, and we just stood between them for a while, waiting to see if the sheriff or Jimmie Sue would come around.

13

It was one of them things that looked like it was over, but it wasn't. There's a thing about men that is both special and foolish, and that's pride; I reckon those men at the card table had been overwhelmed with it. They come out then, and I even seen the man who had decided he didn't want any part of it coming out of the dark, off to the left of the trading post, coming back to set right what I guess he considered cowardice on his part and what I considered common sense.

The men on the porch lined up straight across with their handguns drawn. The other man come up on the porch, stood just to the side of the swing, opposite them other three.

"You do not need to do this," Shorty said. He sounded calm, like he was just reminding someone to button up their fly.

"I reckon we do," said the man with the charcoal mustache. "I reckon we can't have a midget and a nigger and a pissant kid come into a place where we play cards and kill our bartender and whoever that was at the other table. He throwed down with us, so we got to see him as one of us."

"I saw him that way," said Shorty.

"It's just something we can't let lay," said the man with the thorn-poked face.

"I understand your position," said Shorty.

Shorty was still holding his pistol, but he put it in its holster. What the hell was he doing?

Then a man on the porch moved. I don't even remember which one, and it may have been more than one. When it happened, Eustace swung that shotgun up and let fire with one of the barrels. The men on the porch went away, as if yanked by an invisible hand. The door behind them blew apart in a shatter of splinters and sawdust. The shotgun rode up so high it appeared Eustace had to snatch it down after it was fired. The man at the swing fired his pistol, and Eustace's hat went sailing. Eustace swung the gun around. The man had already been hit by the wide spread of the shotgun, but when that barrel turned directly on him, even with nothing more than moonlight to see by, I saw his eyes go wide and his mouth fall open. He fired a shot. He didn't hit anyone. I don't think he came close.

Eustace cut down with the other barrel and the man came apart and the swing swung up high and slammed against the wall. One of the chains came off one end of it and it dropped down on the porch with a thud.

We stood there a moment, our heads ringing. The sheriff came around on the right of the trading post then. He said, "Don't nobody shoot me."

When he got around where we could see him good, he said,

"That fat bastard pulled the whore in front of him, and I got her, not him. He run to his horse and rode off."

"That is unfortunate," said Shorty.

"How is Katy?" I said.

"Well, she's alive, but I knocked a hell of a hole in her. Shot went through her, and Fatty took a piece of it, but not so much he couldn't spring like a frog onto that pinto Katy had been riding. He rode out of here wearing nothing but long johns."

Shorty walked up on the porch, and I followed him. He lit a match and held it up. There were some pieces of clothes and dripping meat splattered against the wall. It looked like someone had given the side of the trading post a thin coat of barn red then thrown some guts against it. Shorty's match went dead. He stepped over to where the other man had stood. He lit another match by striking it on the trading-post wall. He held the match and took a look. I gagged a little.

Shorty moved the match along what looked to be a ragged pair of pants that had most of a leg in them. He come to the broken-down swing with the match and stopped.

"Here is one of his balls," Shorty said. "His hat is here. And something nasty in it. I think it is part of his head, but it could be most anything."

I stumbled off the porch and over to one of the stumps, sat on it, bent over, and threw up.

"That's all right, kid," said Eustace. "Killing folks is messy."

Out back, Jimmie Sue was on the ground and she had lifted up Katy's head and had it draped over her knee. When we come up Katy was gasping for air the way a fish out of water will. I noticed she had around her neck the chain with the star on it that belonged to Lula. I knew where she had got that, and though it could have meant Lula was dead as last spring, somehow it made me think of her and feel confident she was alive. There was no reasoning behind that kind of thinking, of course, but the thought run over me and made me warm inside like hot cider.

"She have anything to say?" the sheriff said, looking down at Katy.

"She called Fatty a bastard and a lousy fuck," Jimmie Sue said.

"I will take her word on both," said the sheriff.

I went over and bent down and took Katy's hand. I said, "You have any family you want notified?"

Katy slowly and painfully turned her head and looked at me and smiled, then coughed blood that sprayed all over the front of my shirt; and that was all for her.

Sheriff Winton lit a match and leaned over and held it close to Katy. The match was a flat light in her dead eyes. He said, "I got her right there under the heart. I'm surprised she lasted that long. She had a pistol drawn, so I guess she had it coming, but it was Fatty I was aiming for, and he pulled her in front of him. That's only the third woman I ever shot in the line of duty, or nearabouts."

"That necklace," I said. "That belongs to my sister, Lula. I reckon Fatty gave it to her."

"That would be like him," Jimmie Sue said. "He wouldn't buy nothing he could steal." Jimmie Sue stood up. The moonlight lit up the wet blood on the knee of her pants, made it look like a greasy spot. "I didn't like her, but I hate to see her go like that. As for Fatty, I think I shot him once, maybe twice while he was running."

"He's got a piece of that Sharps and Jimmie Sue's shots

in him, then," said the sheriff. "I know that fifty went right through her and into him. It had to have."

"It would be wise, then, to pursue," said Shorty. "Even in the dark. Since with those wounds he may be slowed down. Which way did he make his exit?"

Jimmie Sue turned and pointed.

14

As the necklace belonged to Lula, I didn't hesitate to take it off Katy and put it in my pocket. My plan was to return it to her when we found her, and with a bit of fanfare and a smile. I imagined our reunion in all manner of ways, but it was always a happy one, with us back together and her glad to be home. I hoped I wasn't fooling myself. I had thought she was pretty silly about a lot of things, but right then I hoped she was still a girl that could look up at the sky and name a star for herself.

It was decided me and Jimmie Sue and Spot would stay at the trading post and bury Katy and the others while Shorty, Eustace, and Sheriff Winton went in pursuit of Fatty. I was not fond of the plan, never liking any idea that might separate me from Shorty and Eustace and give them the chance to strike on out on their own. My little bit of land in my pocket, so to speak, might have been less of an inducement than it once was because they had outlaws they could claim bounty on, and they might prefer that than having to deal with me. I had yet to completely accept them in my camp, and I felt it was the same for them.

Before they left, the sheriff looked around at what was left of the dead, thinking maybe he might recognize somebody, but unless he had a poster with a drawn picture or a photograph of a man's left nut and some guts, there wasn't much there to recognize them by.

Inside the trading post he determined that the bartender was someone he had seen and that the man had done some time, but he didn't know of anything new on him that might claim a reward. The man I had shot and Hog had chewed on wasn't much to look at, neither. Hog had snuck on in there while we were dealing with Katy out back and had gone to work on the face, getting at the softer parts. Winton talked firm to Hog about getting off the man, but Hog didn't pay him no mind. Jimmie Sue come in and petted Hog a little behind the ears, got him distracted, and then me and Winton grabbed the fellow by the boots and pulled him to the middle of the floor and got one of the lamps and set it down by him.

"This fella could be my son and I wouldn't know him, not the way he's chewed up," Winton said.

After we had our look, the ones leaving after Fatty took some fresh horses from the remuda out back, left the mule and pack horse, and rode on into the night. As I said, I didn't like the idea, but I'll tell you truer than the rising of the sun, I was tuckered out and felt strange and was glad to stay there. My ears still rang, and those dead men were still moving about in my head. I kept thinking about how I had shot that man and he had gone down and Hog had got him. I thought of those men on the porch, how when that four-gauge went off it had knocked them right out of their clothes and into blood-sodden pieces.

We went back inside the trading post and set about relighting some of the lanterns. When the door got knocked off the hinges by the shotgun blast, I swear to you it caused a wind that had blown a couple of the lanterns out, so we needed more light. We went about cleaning the place up so as to give what was left of those men and Katy a Christian burial. There were shovels in the ragtag storage room, along with all manner of goods, and after we had Katy down, I said some words over her I had heard Grandpa say at Mama and Papa's funeral. We buried the bartender and the partly hog-eaten body of the man I had shot side by side. The rest of those boys were kind of guesswork. Scraping a little here, a little there, trying to decide what was part of a man and what might have been part of one of them animal hides that had been on the wall.

We finally just scraped up what we could and put it in a barrel and buried the barrel. I will admit I didn't have a lot to say over the grave, but I did say something. I figured even the worst among us deserved a few good words. I said a thing or two about how they must have loved their mamas or a dog and maybe even believed in Jesus. I finished with, "Dust to dust and such," and we went on about our business, me feeling that in spite of my insincere best wishes, the bunch of them had done gathered up in a wad and gone straight to hell.

When that was all finished, we went back to the storage room and found some food back there—jerked salt pork, beans and flour, and some lard and a few eggs in a box. There was a stove back there and wood for it, and I lit a fire, and before long we had some lard melting in a frying pan. Though I could smell the lard was on the edge of rancid, it wasn't close enough to scare me. I asked Jimmie Sue if she would cook, and she said she might be a woman but she wasn't a cook, and she had done told me that. I managed to warm up the salt pork and beans and made some pan-fried cornbread in another pan. It's an easy thing to make if you know what you're doing, but if you don't you just get these hot, fried pieces of corn that taste a little like what I imagine cat mess to taste like if it's dried up good and salted. I got a bowl and cracked some eggs in it, and none of them was rotten. I put in some cornmeal, and since I didn't have any milk, which would have been preferred, I used some water I heated on the stove. You heat it, and it mixes in with the cornmeal better. I spooned a bit of lard into the bowl, the hot water helping it break down. There was plenty of cornmeal in sacks, and I used several cups of it and mixed it real smoothe while the water was still hot and spread it out thick on a long pan that I put in the oven when it was good and heated. When the cornbread started to get firm from the heat, I slid that tray out by using a rag, then I slicked the top with more of the lard. When that was done, and the salt pork and beans were simmering, I added some salt and pepper to that, seasoned it all up.

It wasn't bad. It would have been better with some dandelion greens, but I didn't want them so much I was willing to go out in the dark and look for them.

We ate till we were full as ticks, then we found some cured bear and deer skins and made ourselves pallets. It occurred to me before we lay down that we had to close and bolt the back door, and since there wasn't any front door, and one of the two windows that was on the front porch was blown out, it also occurred to me we ought to post a guard at the curtain in case someone came into the place looking for supplies, or someone who was friends with what was left of those men in the holes out back come sniffing around.

But it didn't work out that way. We got to preparing pallets and talked about posting a guard, but none of us hopped to it. I found a shirt in the trading-post goods that allowed me to get rid of the one with bloodstains, and the next thing I knew we were all asleep. I didn't know another thing until morning and there was another toe of a boot in my ribs.

It was Shorty. I sat up quick, said, "Did you get him?"

"We did not," Shorty said. He had found some of my leftover cornbread in the warmer, as had the others. They'd poured up some molasses in a bowl, made a fire in the stove, sat the bowl next to it so the molasses would loosen up. They had a coffeepot on the burner hole. They poured coffee in cups and dipped the cornbread in it and sometimes the molasses while standing there looking at us. They had to have been there a while already, but we were so tired we hadn't noticed.

"Fatty gave our Natty Bumppo here the slip," Shorty said.

Eustace listened to all this while he poured from the coffeepot into the bowl of molasses. I knew lots of people liked a bit of coffee in syrup to warm it and make it run so they could sop with cornbread, but I have never cared for it myself. Molasses is too sweet and makes my head hurt when I eat it, and mixing coffee with it didn't ever appeal to me.

"What?" Jimmie Sue said, having come awake. It was like she had joined a house party about the time everyone would have been putting up the fiddle and looking for their hats.

"He means Eustace didn't track him," I said.

"Oh, he tracked him for a while," Shorty said, turning to look at Eustace.

"Don't start in on me, you little turd," Eustace said.

"He was bleeding all over the countryside," Shorty said. "He was dripping out his life force. He was leaving us a path to follow, and at some point he took to the woods and Eustace lost him. We were still looking when the day broke, but nope, there were no more blood spots, so Eustace's ability to pursue had gone the way of last year's south-flying ducks."

"I know them sons a bitches go south," Eustace said.

"Yes," said Shorty. "You are correct. You are acquainted with the set and absolute pattern of ducks, but when it comes to tracking, unless the juice of your prey is lying on the ground he can give you the slip."

"In all fairness," said Winton, "it was a good track. When we got down in the creek bed, well, any blood there had gone in the water and had washed along pretty quick. He might be dead a few miles up from where we quit."

"Why did you quit?" I said.

"Because we thought we should come back for you," Shorty said.

"That ain't entirely the truth," Winton said. "Fatty seemed to be heading off a way we didn't want to go, a way that wasn't toward the Big Thicket. He might have been purposely leading us astray, though I think he was unlikely in the frame of mind to do much of anything but get away from us, in any direction he could go. I still think Shorty's information about them others being down there around Livingston, in the Thicket, is good. We needed to come back here for the other horses, and it occurred to us dead men don't need theirs, and we might can sell or trade their rigs and mounts for something on down the road."

"Shorty don't know shit from wild honey," Eustace said, the

words coming out of him like vomit. "He's the sort wouldn't know the difference between the two even if he was a bee."

Spot had awakened now. He sat up on his bearskin, said, "Is that coffee I smell?"

This distracted the argument, and we ate breakfast, drank our coffee, and gradually the mood shifted. With our bellies full, and with the failed pursuers full of hot coffee, things mellowed considerably.

We packed supplies we figured we needed, got all the horses and made a line of them to follow the ones we were riding, and started out. We had also collected all the guns the men had used and stuffed saddlebags with them. A tow sack had a bunch more guns we had found in the back room—a twelve-gauge pump shotgun, an old Winchester, and a bunch of single-shot squirrel rifles, .22 in caliber. The idea was to sell some of them, keep the rest. I was beginning to get used to breaking the law. Besides, I had a sheriff with me and he was doing it, so I will admit to you, sadly, that I was comforted in my criminal activity.

Riding along, Hog kept running off in the brush and startling birds. I thought of when I was younger and Papa would take me out to shoot quail and doves and the like.

What I remembered wasn't the pleasantness of those days, me with Papa, but of a time I shot a bird with a single-shot shotgun and how when it fell it had a wing broke off and its beak was open and it was trying to suck in air. I thought it was a good shot, but when I got up closer, the way that bird looked, the pain and confusion in its eyes, and that beak open like that, well, I felt sick, plumb sick to the bone. I stood over that bird looking down, and when Papa came up, I said, "You think we could repair its wing and nurse it back to health?"

He picked up the bird and twisted its neck so that it popped and the bird went still. "Nope," he said. "He ain't going to get his wing fixed and he ain't going to have his health improved."

This was true. We ate him that night along with several others we had killed. I know those men weren't nothing like that bird. We darn sure didn't plan to eat them. So it wasn't like we were out hunting food. I told myself we did what we had to do, them having guns and an attitude to kill us. But the feeling I had about it was like with that bird, only deeper and sadder and more troubling. I kept seeing Katy, the way her mouth was open, and how that blood came out of it, and her eyes, all pained and confused the way that bird's had been. I didn't feel too good about anything right then, even if she had been protecting one of the men who stole my sister from me. I knew that I had in that moment, back at the trading post, crossed some kind of dark divide. No matter what my intent in doing so was, it had done something to me that hurt worse than a beating. I felt farther from Jesus and closer to Satan than I had ever felt before. It was a feeling that made my old fears about jacking off in the outhouse less important. My thinking God was watching me work my weenie over a woman in drawers in the Sears and Roebuck didn't hold a candle to helping kill a man and watching his life being sucked out, and then having a hog eat chunks out of him.

It must have been around three in the afternoon, way the sun was riding, when we come across that pinto Fatty had escaped on. It was wandering out in the road, and it was limping. Spot got down off his mule and took a look. He said, "The sweat on it is well dried. It's got a broke foot. Reckon it stepped off in a rabbit hole. It ain't gonna fix."

He took one of the rifles we had borrowed from the trading

post, loaded it up, walked the horse off in the woods a piece, and after a while we heard a shot. Spot come back.

"That was one fine hoss," Spot said. "I hated doing that."

"This means Fatty is around here somewhere, don't it?" I said.

"It means that or it means he ain't nowhere around here, and the horse stumbled and throwed him and he ain't got up, or he did get up and has wandered off somewhere," Eustace said. "And with the sweat dried on the horse, it means he's had time to move on a bit. I'm going to take a look around, see if I can pick up some sign."

Eustace dismounted and tied his horse to a scrub tree.

"Good luck with that looking around," Shorty said.

"Go fuck yourself," Eustace said, and went into the woods.

"He is looking for a note in a bottle from Fatty," Shorty said. "Something along the lines of I am about two miles from here, on the left of a big oak tree, leaning against a dirt mound, and I am dead."

"Cut him some slack," Winton said. "He's doing all right. He followed Fatty in the night better than any of us could."

"Yes," said Shorty, "but none of us are supposed to be a tracker. Besides, if I do not ride him, he will become complacent."

"We wouldn't want none of that complacent shit," Jimmie Sue said.

We got off and joined Spot on the ground and let the horses blow. It wasn't more than twenty minutes later that Eustace come out of the woods. His dark face looked ashen as he come up on us.

"There's a woman down there," he said. "An old woman and an old man and what I figure must have been their grandchild, a boy. They're all dead, and the woman has had her dress hiked up and her undergarments pulled off."

"Ah, shit," Winton said.

"He must have hijacked them this morning, was hiding out there in the woods waiting for someone to come along the road so he could get a horse he could use. But way it looks, what he came across was that man and woman and child in one of those motorcars. That's what the tracks show. No horse, but tires. He probably came out of the woods acting like he needed help, killed the man and boy, dragged them off in the woods, and it looks like the woman helped him. Had to, I figure. Now, that would be a thing, wouldn't it? And then he raped her and shot her in the head and took the motorcar and the old man's pants and boots."

"That means he has covered quite a patch of ground, then," Shorty said. "We have to conclude, however, that if he is in a motorcar, he will continue the straight path, the machine not otherwise being able to travel the same route as a horse or a man on foot. And he is wounded. We have that on our side. Though if he was able to kill and rape, maybe he is not as bad off as we first assumed."

"Or he is one bear for recovery," Jimmie Sue said. "Oh, that poor family. A thing like that."

"We aren't going anywhere this time," I said. "Not without us burying those poor people first. For all I know that boy we left had had his bones scattered from East Texas to Nebraska. We will bury these three, and make note of where so their kinfolks can come pluck them out and bury them where they please."

"You are not one for practicality," Shorty said. "Even when it is your sister we are trying to rescue."

"I've noted we pause when you like," I said. "I love Lula, and I want her back, but I have gone far from my Christian training as it is. I won't go farther."

"You think burying those unfortunate people is going to make up for killing a murderer?" Shorty said. "Could that be your thinking?"

"It might be," I said.

"The problem, kid," Shorty said, "is there is no one on either side of the fence keeping measurements about what you do. God is an idea, and the devil is us."

"Leave him be, Shorty," Winton said. "We'll bury them. We got a fold-out shovel in our goods, and I'll do the digging. I have to. Like the boy, I'm not for leaving those poor people lying out there in the woods, that woman with her drawers pulled off and her womanhood exposed. The man in his drawers. I won't do it."

"You are quite the goddamn gentleman, are you not?" Shorty said to Winton.

"We can take turns with that shovel," Spot said, and went to pull it out of the packing on one of the horses.

That was the end of Shorty making protests. We went and found them. It was a brutal sight. Yet somehow it soothed me some to think we were about burying these poor innocents, giving them proper respect, and that the ones we had killed were not innocent at all, even if they weren't the ones who had directly taken Lula. They had no love for womanhood, those men, protecting Fatty and the location of his comrades the way they had. And I had no love for them.

Jimmie Sue collected the woman's underthings and pulled them back on her, and when the grave was deep—and it took work, there being so many roots up there in the woods—

I took hold of the woman's feet and Spot took her head. I saw then that she was old and worn and had gray hair. She had lived life this long without dying, and her husband had somehow come by the money to buy a motorcar, and it, and their hospitality for a traveler in need, had gotten them killed, nothing more. We put her in the hole and went after the other two. The boy, about nine, I reckoned, had a hole in his forehead from where he was shot, and his eyes and mouth were held in a manner that made me think he had died during a moment of amusement. The old man had taken one in the heart. I never noted the old woman's wound, and didn't care to check it out. We lowered them all into that cold, common grave as gently as we could manage.

After that we mounted up and started out, our string of horses tagging along behind us.

15

Horses can gallop. Motorcars roll along at a steady rate. The thing is, though, motorcars don't have to eat and drink and rest, long as there's gasoline. So the car already had a lead, though even I could see from the tire marks in the road that Fatty was driving all over the place. He had nearly run off the road and into the trees a half dozen times. I was hopeful that would be how it turned out, and we'd find Fatty wrecked beside the road with some of that car stuck in his chest.

I was riding along between Jimmie Sue and Winton. Winton said, "You look pretty sad, kid."

"I think you're aware they have my sister," I said. "I got a right to be sad."

"So you do, but it seems to me a kind of mood has settled down on you, and I was hoping to cheer you up a little."

"I don't understand you people," I said. "We killed men back there, and you're riding along like it's something just comes every morning with breakfast."

"They pulled on us," Winton said.

"Yep, they did," I said. "I'm not denying that. But killing a man ought to mean something, even if you have to do it."

"It means we didn't get killed," Winton said. "And after that, I quit measuring it."

"Still," I said.

"They were protecting Fatty, were they not?" Winton said.

"But they were still men, and we killed them. I never shot anyone before."

"First time or two I did it, I felt a might weak-kneed, too," Winton said. "But that was on account as to both times I thought it might have been me got shot. It does get a lot easier to do, though, after a time or two. But I tell you, boy, they were bad men. Why, I reckon they weren't so blowed up from Eustace's four-gauge I might even have found out there were arrest papers on them somewhere. Even if that isn't the case, you can bet they are just the type would have stolen your sister theirselves. And let me tell you something. Those men at that trading post, that's a place for criminal activity. It didn't cater to good folks."

"Are we good folks?" I asked.

"Well, now," Winton said. "If you could lay out who we are on a board side by side with them that was killed, and we took a measurement of the good and the bad in each, and long was bad and short was good, our size might be longer than we'd like but a lot shorter than theirs. Life isn't just black or white, here or there; it's got some mud in it, and we're some of the mud."

"That doesn't really cheer me up," I said.

"Not everything is cheery," Winton said.

"You said you were trying to cheer me up," I said.

"All right, I did," he said. "But you want to do this, and

you say it matters to you to get your sister back, you got to be willing to accept what it takes. So maybe I'm not so goddamn cheery after all. I'm missing an ear and I look like I been rolling around in a campfire, and that kind of takes some of my cheer, even when I say it don't."

"I just don't know it takes murder."

"Self-defense. The three of you tried to walk out after the initial dustup, but they came out on the porch after you, didn't they?"

"They did," I said. "But we initiated it."

"And you knew Fatty was in the back room, didn't you?"

"I did," I said.

"Then you did what you had to do, and they'd have done to you what you done to them had they had the chance. To me it's clear. End of story. I'll leave you to recollect on events," Winton said, and rode on ahead of me and Jimmie Sue to join the others.

"He's right, you know," Jimmie Sue said. "Just a year ago I kept thinking this ain't fair, the way things have turned out for me. Then it come to me clean as spring rain. Life is just what it is, and it ain't fair at all."

"Can't we make it fair?"

"You can try, but all that other unfairness keeps seeping in."

It was near the last of the day when we come upon the motorcar. It was in the yard of a farmhouse. The farmhouse was small but neat, and there were flowers in a bed around the front of the house, and out back was a little red barn, and the door was wide open on it. It was a nice house to be out here in the wilds, and it made me sick before I knew what was what, just knowing someone had worked their way into the Thicket to build and live and make a life of it, clearing trees and planting flowers. But that stolen motorcar parked in the yard didn't bode well.

We rode up and dismounted, left the horses with Spot, spread out, except Winton. He went up to the door. The door was open. He knocked and called out, but didn't anyone come to answer.

He pushed the door open with his foot and pulled his revolver and went inside. Shorty and Eustace rushed on up there, and I took the back. After a moment I heard Winton call out. "Come on in. Jimmie Sue, you might want to stay out."

Jimmie Sue didn't stay out. We all ended up going inside. There was an old man dead by the fireplace. He had been dead a while, because his blood was hard-dried on his head and the floor. There was a table with food on it and a big pan in the center of the table with cornbread crumbs. I could tell from how light-colored it looked it hadn't been good cornbread.

"I reckon Fatty run out of petrol," Winton said. "So he come here and took whatever he wanted, maybe even had a dinner with the old man, then killed him. That's how it looks. Fella was hospitable, and then Fatty thanked him with a bullet. I figure one of the other things he wanted besides food was a horse. I bet that's why the barn door's open."

Sure enough, the barn was empty, but Eustace found tracks. There was some blood on the ground, too.

"His wound is still open," Eustace said. "Or he's broke it open again. One or the other. But there wasn't any horse in here."

"Now that he is bleeding," Shorty said, "perhaps you will be able to pursue him without losing him."

"Shorty," Eustace said, "you are close to the end of all that. Quit on it now."

Shorty must have heard something in Eustace's voice that

told him enough was enough, because it went against his nature to quit on something once he got started. But he gave up on that trail of talk and went silent, though I figured it pained him about as bad as a knife in the ribs.

Back at the house we had to pull the old man off the floor. It sounded like someone ripping a newspaper when we pulled him up. That blood was so hard it had glued him there. We toted him into the room with the bed and put him on it and pulled a blanket over him. Winton wrote out a note telling who he was and what he had found, and who we was on the trail of, and that he was an officer of the law. He stuck that on the outside of the front door with a pocketknife. When we were all outside, I went over and looked in the car. There was a picnic basket in there, and it was empty. I figured that's where the man and woman and child had been going when Fatty waylaid them—on a picnic. Or maybe they had finished. Whichever, either them or Fatty had eaten what was in the basket, and all that was left was a crumb-covered cloth napkin and some broken dishes.

We left out of there and headed on down the road where Fatty had gone. After a while Eustace determined Fatty had wandered off the main road and taken to the woods. That's the way we went, and it was a hard go. We come across a piece of Fatty's long-john shirt that had been caught up on a thorn, and it was bloody. I couldn't see how a man that big and beat up with a pistol—and shot up, too—could kill all them others and keep going and not fall over dead, or at least not be so weak he couldn't move. But he was moving on at a steady clip and making us move on after him. I didn't know about the others in our party, but I knew I was tired, and I could tell from looking at Jimmie Sue she was feeling weary.

It finally came down to stopping because Winton and Eustace thought the horses were failing. I was about to the point where I couldn't go on, and I was glad those horses were tuckered out. I had told myself from the first that no matter what, I would push on night and day, tirelessly, but what I didn't reckon on was getting tired. I had the idea, too, that Eustace was tracked out, and that he could only go so far on the trail in the dark. If Shorty thought the same, and I'm sure he did, he didn't mention it.

There was a clear patch in the woods, and there looked to have been a lightning strike there, and a plot of land had burnt out. The trees were skinny and dead, but the fire had been some time ago. Most of the char had given way to a field of grass between fire-stripped trees. We stopped and took care of the horses, stretched a rope between two scraggly persimmon trees that were somehow alive after the fire, if not real healthy, and tied the horses to the rope. It was as if we were down in a hole with all these big trees on the edge of our patch, and in the night, with the shadows and all, they were like a wall that went all around us.

We built a small fire for cooking, because we didn't need it for any other purpose. It was a bright night and warm. We cooked and ate and laid out our bedrolls with a plan to leave at first light. Hog wandered off in the woods and found a place to lie down on the pine needles, which I was glad for, since I didn't want to share my bed with him.

Jimmie Sue had made her bed below what was left of the fire, and some of my religious zeal, which had once held me strong, was starting to rust around the edges. On that night it pretty much could be said it completely collapsed. When I thought everyone was asleep, I got up and crept over to where she was and lifted up the blankets and got under there with her. I nuzzled her ear with my lips, and she come to slowly, said, "Ain't Jesus going to be mad?"

"Don't say that," I said. "It puts me off a mite."

"I reckon Jesus can forgive if he wants to," she said. "And if he don't, then he ain't near the forgiver he's made out to be."

"Now you got to bring up Jesus?" I said.

"You bring him up when he suits you," she said.

"So he suits you now?"

"I'm just saying I can't imagine a man, even Jesus, not liking to take his pleasure from time to time. I also like to have my faith when I want it. That way it works. If I think about it too hard I know it's a lie, but if I just squint at it I'm okay."

"I don't know," I said.

"Oh, shut up and kiss me," she said. "And may Jesus give you strength."

She rolled over then, and we kissed. Her breath was a little stale, and I figured mine was, too. But after we got to smacking I didn't notice anymore. Pretty soon we were shedding our clothes under her blankets. We went at it until the moon had gone down and it was near morning. I had just thought I was tired, but had certainly found some energy for that, though I was reluctant to give credit to Jesus. Jimmie Sue went straight to sleep, but I was all heated up still, and ended up pushing back the covers enough to let the air cool my naked chest. In that moment, no matter that we were on the trail in search of my sister, I felt as good as I had felt in memory. The Sabine River was never really blue, always a muddy brown, but in my mind it was blue then, and the grass was always green, even in winter, and the wind was cool, the earth was rich and firm, and all the world was full of light. It was a wonderful feeling. I lay there and enjoyed it, even as it was eased away from me and memory of why I was on the trail flooded back over me and wilted my mind's grass and hardened the ground and turned my light to shadow.

When that happened, and I came back to myself, I saw that Shorty was on the other side of the fire, not thirty feet from us, sitting on his bedroll. He had moved it there without us hearing or noticing. He had a book in his hand, was wearing his glasses, and was leaning toward the fire for light.

I pulled on my shirt and put my pants on under the blankets, got up, and went around in my bare feet to squat next to him. "You could have cleared your throat," I said.

"I could have banged a pan and sang a couple of songs, but I did not want to distract you from your business."

"You didn't have to watch," I said.

"There was nothing to see but covers going up and down. I sat here to read my book."

"You read a book while that was going on?" I said.

"Well, I will admit that now and then I took a glance in case the covers had fallen, but my greatest fear was seeing your naked ass instead of hers."

"I guess I wasn't near as sneaky as I thought," I said.

"You two sounded like two pigs going at corn in a trough. Do not tell Hog I said that, as I believe he views himself as fastidious."

I looked down the hill where the others slept. They seemed to be tucked in tight and unaware of what was going on. I could even see Hog's pale shape out there in the pines. He looked snug.

"I feel guilty now that I done it."

"Did you feel guilty when you were doing it?"

"Not in the least, but I was caught up in doing it."

"There are many things you can get caught up in doing that you should not do and should be ashamed of, but believe me, a woman is something to enjoy completely, so there is no need to feel guilt. She is no one's wife, and she is willing, and it does not say in the Bible that Thou Shalt Have No Pussy. Not that I care what it says."

I let all that settle on me and then changed the subject. "What're you reading that can hold your attention that well?"

"Twain's book on travel again. It makes me want to follow the equator. It makes me want to do anything but what I do. The drawback is money. I had money I could travel and I could buy women and I could have fine food and all the things that would be to my enjoyment. I am not saying I deserve it more than others, but I am saying I probably would like it more than others."

I laughed a little. "Someday you may go."

Shorty shook his head. "I do not think so. You know what I was thinking? I was thinking someday soon I will die on a trail like this one, or I will die at home, or on that hill where I place my telescope, and though none is any worse than any other place, if I had my pick, I would die on a great ship somewhere at sea, on the way to some foreign port, and if not that, then by the telescope, and maybe, when I think about it, that would actually be the best. I have picked my own star. It is mine. Others may have picked it, but I have claimed it for myself and will allow no others to have it. When it is visible I find it in the sky at night, and it is like a shiny eye looking directly at me. It is not God. It is not a star. It is my own self looking back at me."

"You sound like my sister," I said. "She found a star for herself."

"Really?" Shorty said. It was a rare moment in that he showed true surprise.

"Yeah."

"She sounds extraordinary."

"We just thought she was odd," I said.

"Those who see like you, see those who are sane as blind," he said.

"I'm sane."

"You are in the world, but are not part of it. Therefore, you are not sane."

"You think highly of yourself, don't you?"

"I do. I have to. I see everything from low down. It is a different way of looking at the world. Look here, kid. I do not think I act better than other men. Like the worst of them, I have killed and wasted. I helped wipe the buffalo into nearly nothing. I have killed men and been paid for the deed. But I know who I am and I know what this world is, and in spite of what you say, you are set to do the same things I have done and call it something different. You keep waving a flag of righteousness, and you talk around it, but in your own way you are as ruined as I am."

"Nonesense," I said. "You get all this because you and my sister picked out a star?"

"You should pick one of your own," he said.

"I'm sorry I mentioned it," I said. "It's just that like you, she is peculiar, but of a better heart, I can assure you of that."

"I will not quarrel with that. I wish I could go backwards and do it all again, and different. But I cannot. I just hope Lula can see her star. I hope during this troubling time she can look up and see it and feel that it is herself, and that if she should leave her shell she can imagine that star making her part of the halo of the world."

"That sounds like religion," I said.

"It sounds like one of the lies we tell ourselves to get by," Shorty said. "But the difference in me and you is I know it is a lie."

He put the book in his lap and studied me for a moment. "Where would you like to go if there were no restrictions?"

"What?"

"If you could do anything in the world, go anywhere in the world, where or what would it be?"

"I don't know," I said. "It's not something that can happen, so why think about it?"

"Take a moment. Where? What?"

"Had my druthers," I said, "I'd just soon go back to my farm and maybe have a wife and some kids and raise some crops. I don't know it's such a bad life, and it's seeming better to me all the time."

"But if we find your men and rescue your sister, you will not have any land."

"You said what I'd druther. I figure me and Lula can make the best of it."

"What about Jimmie Sue?" he asked.

"I think maybe she's had too many adventures to settle down," I said.

"That is a polite way to express it," he said. "But maybe she has had so many she wants to. We are not all the same, and trying to define us is like trying to determine which way a frog will jump."

"Toward water," I said.

Shorty smiled. He looked amazingly warm in that moment, like a kindly uncle about to offer you a piece of fruit. "You are so definite, kid. Seldom right, but always certain."

I didn't respond. I didn't want to feed the tiger. The fire crackled. We watched it. I said, "I was wondering about Sheriff Winton. How'd his face get like that?"

Shorty placed the book on the ground and kept studying the fire. "He has not always been a sheriff. He was a bounty hunter. But before he was a bounty hunter, he tried to settle a ranch out in North Texas, which to my mind is a part of Texas they could fill in with rubble and barn-floor scrapings and it would be improved. It was then home to the Comanche, or what was left of them. Truthfully, their home was more broadly spaced than that. It is more fair to say that North Texas was one of their haunts. They moved about hunting buffalo. Nomads is what they were. This was near the end of things for them, but they did not know that yet. Or perhaps they did and were not ready to accept it. People rarely accept something even when it is looking them in the eye. And that is the way it should be. Nothing was on their side. White men were coming in droves with better weapons. The buffalo, which were the Comanche's general store, were almost gone. But still, the Comanche were formidable.

"Settlers kept coming and the Comanche pushed back. They pushed back hard. I was tracking a bounty up that way. I had known Winton before. We had hunted buffalo ourselves, for the hides. It was a purely nasty and smelly business, and to be honest, I could not do it now. I could not shoot those buffalo as I did then. I have come to think it is man that should be shot and animals to be left alone. But I did it. I skinned them and left their meat to rot on the prairies. I sometimes took meat for myself, or a buffalo tongue, which when prepared right is tasty, but mostly they rotted. It was too much for me. I quit the work and moved on.

"Winton stayed in the North Texas country. He met a gal. She was, between you and me, as ugly as sin and as contrary as a rattlesnake. She was so damn ugly she would have to sneak up on a biscuit and force it to be eaten with the point of a gun. She was long-faced and skinny and thin of nose—so much, in fact, it could have been removed and used as a sewing needle. She had lips like the stitches on a deerskin coat. But he loved her and they had a child. I had heard tell of that, his having become a father.

"I was passing that way in pursuit of a bounty, which I had lost track of and never did find. That is one of a few that got away from me. But got away he did, and to my knowledge was never arrested. His name was James Plant and I was after him for the murder of a storekeeper. It was said he killed that man because of something said to his niece or some such. I do not remember. Many thought he was innocent of anything besides killing a skunk. But it did not matter to me. He was money on the hoof, and I went after him. As I said, he got away. I have heard over the years that he moved up north and made good of himself, and has been in no other trouble, but I cannot verify any of that information. What I can verify is what happened to Winton.

"I come to his place of the evening, and I yelled out from a distance who I was, and Winton came outside and greeted me and let me in. His wife—and this was the first time I had met her, though I knew much about her from Winton—looked at me like I was some sort of weed. The child, who was three or so, was amazed at my size and saw me as a playmate. I was forced into games of piggybacking her and sitting on the floor and playing all manner of competition with cards and checkers, none of which she truly knew how to play. I must say that I enjoyed it in spite of myself. The little girl was charming. She did not judge me at all. She was merely impressed with my smallness, my uniqueness. I ended up staying a few days, and it was not long that Winton's old lady, Sarah was her name, came to accept me as well. And I came to like her. I think she was eyeing me with a bit of curiosity, as to what it might be like to have me mount her. That may sound as if I think a lot of myself, but I assure you that was the impression I got, and I do think a lot of myself. I also knew one thing for a fact. Sarah had once upon a time been a sporting girl, which did not surprise me. Winton was not the sort that would meet a future wife at the opera. But I, of course, was not interested. Had she been willing and not Winton's wife, then I could have got past that face, which was like a hatchet to the soul. But that is what eyelids are for, to shield you from sights hard to bear. However, nothing happened between me and her. What happened was much worse.

"You see, come early morning that little girl got up and went outside, because there was a new calf she wanted to see, and before it was good light, the Comanche had pulled the sneak. They were right up on that house and had already cut the throat of the hogs and cattle and had even arrowed the dog from a distance, so there was not a bark of warning. They were planning on stealing the horses, and that is when the little girl slipped outside, and they nabbed her. They did not get their hand over her mouth in time, and she screamed.

"Sarah, as a mother will do, if she is worth her salt, sprang to her feet and was out the door before we could grab a gun, and then we heard her scream, too. By the time we were outside with the rifles, all we could see were the Comanche riding off, Sarah slung over a saddle, and the little girl out of sight, but we could hear her caterwauling. She was yelling, "Papa, Papa," over and over. It was the sort of thing that could tear your heart out and boil it.

"Now, they had killed all the livestock except the horses, but when they nabbed the child and Sarah and we come out with guns, they made for the distance. It was not because they were afraid but because they had already punished Winton for trying to live on their land and raise livestock. The horses they had meant to steal, but it ended up that they only scattered them. It took us over an hour to rustle up a couple of the horses, get them saddled, and get ourselves dressed. Mind you, we chased those cayuses all over the plains in our bare feet and underwear, toting a rifle.

"So we were mounted and armed, and we set out after them. A Comanche is an unpredictable bird is what he is. Sometimes he will take a woman and make her part of the tribe, but that is generally for the younger ones that can be raised as a Comanche. Sometimes disease or war parties of other tribes, sometimes even other branches of the Comanche, can steal or kill their women. Sometimes, to make sure there are more of their tribe, they steal women to have children. When it gets right down to it, the Comanche are a mixed group of Indians—lots of white blood and other Indian blood, and colored, and so on. What makes a Comanche is less about blood than how he lives. Considering on the fact that they would often do that sort of thing, take whites to be part of their tribe, I tried to keep a hopeful mind-set. It was something I could say to Winton, who was almost in a state of wildness akin to a rabid raccoon. This would work against him."

Shorty turned and looked in the direction of where Winton lay sleeping.

"I knew it could quite easily go in the other direction. That they could take a whim to do just the opposite. A Comanche can be vengeful one second and give you food and a buffalo robe the next, though they are not quick to give away a horse. Horses are their survival. They are great horsemen.

"An Apache prefers to be on foot. The Apache see a horse as a tool. They will ride on until it is tired, and then they will ride it some more. If it falls over they will build a fire up against it to make it stand back up until it can stand no longer, and then they will eat it. The Comanche are not like that. They talk to horses. On the ground the Comanche are a bowlegged ugliness, but on horseback, it is as if they and the horse are one, a centaur.

"I have strayed from my story and how Winton came to look the way he does. It was anger and love that got the better of him, and already being skeptical of love, from that day on I avoided it even more than before, as it can lead one into foolishness.

"We followed them. It was a hard go. From the tracks, Winton determined we were closing in on them. The Comanche must have determined a similar thing, for they did a bit of business to slow us down. We were so close we could hear the baby crying in the distance. A plaintive wail if there ever was one, and it grew in sound as we went, and before long it was a caterwauling."

It was here that Shorty hesitated in his story. The night seemed tight around us, like we had been dunked inside a bag. I felt a little dizzy. I had been holding my breath.

Shorty let his own breath out as if it were his last, and that hard look on his face turned soft in the firelight.

"There were some brush areas that we came to. There were thorns on some of the brush. Big thorns, like nails. We could see where something had been dragged through the brush. Then we found bits of the baby's clothes that had been ripped off by the brush, and we saw then something shiny in the sunlight, white as snow streaked with wet clay. It was neither snow nor clay. They had sharpened one of the limbs of the brush, and the baby was on that sharp stick. They had stuck her through the belly, and that, of course, had been what all the horrible screeching had been about. They had dragged her by rope through the thorns before they stuck her, and impaled the poor darling in such a way the child could not wiggle off. If it had, it wouldn't have mattered. The wound was horrid enough to insure its death."

"The monsters," I said.

"They are humans," said Shorty. "So therefore your word is accurate."

"Human?" I said. "There is nothing human about something like that."

"I have known of men to rape and murder Indians with the easy understanding that they are not quite human. I am sure that Eustace can tell you unpleasant and accurate stories about how colored are treated by white men, so I will not defend either white man, Indian, or colored against their basic nature. I hate them all evenly, including myself. No use expecting more from humans than they are capable of. I guess I should not hate them all, as it is akin to hating water for being wet or dust for being dry. But I do nonetheless, and sometimes with a certain pride."

Shorty paused, pulled himself back to his story.

"The obvious thing is, the child slowed us down. We removed it from the sharpened stick. There was no more crying by that time, though the baby was alive. We made a shade of a horse blanket by throwing it over a brush, and laid the child under it. Did what we could for it, which was essentially nothing. The child died near nightfall, never having really come around, having bled out, even though we stuffed the wound with leaves and some handkerchiefs. It was like trying to mop up the Gulf of Mexico with a jar of cotton balls. We dug a place with our hands under the blanket and put the child down there. We took the blanket and put it back on the horse. Then we rode after them. It was night, and I attempted to encourage Winton to wait, but he would have none of it. In our haste my horse hit a chuck hole, fell, broke its leg, and I had to cut its throat to keep things as silent as we could.

"Winton would not let me ride double, fearing it would slow down his progress, so he went ahead. It was not like here, with all the trees. It was mostly a stretch of clear land with occasional brush. Winton foolishly went ahead, and I went after him, carrying my rifle and wearing my sidearm. I, of course, soon lost sight of him. I rested very little. Stopping now and again, catching a few minutes of sleep here and there, but mostly I walked and walked until my feet hurt and there were blisters on my heels the size of boiled eggs.

"Finally the light came and I could easily see the tracks of Winton's horse mingled among the tracks of the Comanche ponies. Winton should have known he was being led into a trap, but he was too blind with anger. They were making it easy for us to follow, and a little later on I saw they were adding to Winton's anger. His tracks led to a draw that dipped down into the land, and there was a stream running there, so small and weak of flow it was more like the run from a snotty nose than a real stream. The draw itself was enough to grab some shade, though, and I walked down in it, and leaned against a cool wall to escape the rising heat of the day and to rest my weary self. I took off my boots and laid my heels in the little bit of water for perhaps an hour. I judged it by the sun. I carried my boots with me and walked barefoot down the stream to cool my heels and to give my feet a rest from the boots. I came upon a hollow at one side of the draw, and in that indentation I saw naked feet, and the rest of whoever was in there was in the shade. I took a look, and it was Winton's wife, or what was left of her. I knew she had been raped to death, as her legs were spread and her sex was bloody. Her nose and lips had been cut off and her mouth was stuffed with dirt. They had raped her and tortured her, and then killed her by stuffing her mouth and throat with dirt so she could not breathe. They had most likely held her feet while they stuffed her mouth, and I could tell from looking around, seeing horse tracks, the tracks of Indian feet, and the booted feet of Winton, that he, too, had found her. Felt he was close enough to her attackers he did not bother to bury her, feeling that he would come back to take care of the body later. I knew his thinking under the circumstances, and it was not good thinking. Those he had wanted to rescue were lost, and it would have been better to have shored up the body inside the hollow and to have collapsed the dirt on top of it. At least until he could go back and find a wagon and come for both the woman and the child. But his anger had overtaken him and made him as blind and savage as the Comanche.

"I put on my boots and plodded ahead, knowing full well

I should not. My fondness for Winton kept me going, even though I knew that he cheated in cards and that he had hornswoggled me out of several bounties in my time, and had lied to me on frequent occasions, and had even spoken badly to me when he was drunk. But he was a boon companion otherwise, and I could at least always depend on him to be himself. I followed the stream until it trickled out into a spread and finally into nothing. It was really more of a runoff from recent rain I had not experienced, which accounted for its slimness. I would have known that sooner had I been thinking. I had, however, fortified myself by drinking from the stream, had found a lizard and bit its head off and sucked out its guts and had managed not to puke it. So I was not as weak as I might have been, which, considering what I was to discover, was a good thing.

"I think the Comanche thought Winton was the only one tracking them, had no idea I, too, was in pursuit. They had been purposely slow about drawing him in, and it had worked. By midday it was hot enough to sweat a Gila monster to death, and I was exhausted from walking and carrying the Sharps. I saw ahead a dark shape on the plain, and near it I saw other dark shapes. There were all manner of buffalo bones about, scattered in all the directions of the compass. In that spot there had been a mass slaughter of buffalo and a piling of bones. I got down on my belly and began to crawl. I crawled until I came upon one of the mounds of bones, a couple of big buffalo skulls among them. I laid up behind one of the skulls, eased an eye over it, saw that a pole had been put up right there in the prairie; and then I saw it was not a pole at all. It was an old scrub tree that had grown out there in the midst of nowhere by its lonesome, as if its sole purpose was to provide a stake for Winton. He was tied there, and there was a fire built of dried dung and sticks, or some such thing as the Comanche are able to do. They find sustenance and all their needs where no one else can find enough in the way of wood to pick their teeth. There were six Comanche, and I decided then and there they were the bulk of the war party, their number matching the horse tracks. The horses themselves were hobbled nearby, and all the Comanche were taking part in working on poor Winton, who by this time had begun to scream. They had removed burning sticks from the fire and were applying them to his face, and they were cutting him with knives, sawing off one of his ears. They were working on his ear when I placed the very Sharps I carry today, the one Winton used himself the other night, on top of the buffalo skull and took a bead. My first inclination was to kill Winton himself, to spare him the torture, and then it would be up to me to try and kill the Comanche or run them off before I myself could be killed. But when I looked down the barrel, I decided Winton was not too far along for rescue, so I beaded up on one of the Comanche, who at that very moment was slowly bringing a fiery stick toward Winton's eye. I made that one my focus, and though it was nowhere near the dynamic shot that Billy Dixon made on a Comanche, it was a good shot. Of course, their delight and preoccupation with what they were doing, and not thinking anyone else was in pursuit, had allowed me to come quite close with less effort than would have normally been needed.

"I usually aim for the body, as it is a surer and larger target, but I caught this buck in the head—exploded it with that Sharps round as if it were a ripe squash. Now, I do not know if it is the way my memory works, or if it is the true event, but that Comanche's head seemed to come completely off, and the body turn in my direction of its own accord, without a head, before collapsing. By that time, I had already without looking or thinking about it slipped another round into the rifle and was taking aim. I potted another one of the Comanche braves before the rest of them could decide to shit or go blind; got him in the back. That left four, and as is the practical nature of the Comanche, they bolted for their horses to make a run for it, possibly thinking those two accurate shots in rapid succession meant they were being pursued by a larger posse. By the time it takes to blink hard twice, the rest of them were on horseback, trying to make a break for it. Also in Comanche tradition, they were attempting to lead along the now-spare horses they had stolen as well as those belonging to their dead comrades. That gave me another shot, and I fired. I did not know for sure if I had hit one of them, but the rear-line Comanche dropped the guide rope on the stolen horses and lit out. They were gone before I could reload, having gathered their wits about them.

"When I was sure they were gone and not just trying to trick me, I went and cut Winton down and laid him out under that tree, which provided no shade at all. I then went and caught up two of the horses. Winton was not up for much, as you might suppose, so I took a little bag off one of the dead Comanche, found some awful mess of seeds and such in it, and gave it to Winton to eat, to build up his strength. I tore off some of the Indian's clothing to make bandages for Winton's head and put dirt on the burns to quell some of the pain. I tell you, with one ear cut off and bleeding, and burned up good and raw, you would have thought that at this point Winton would have been a quitter. But he was not. He got to his feet after a short rest and we took to the horses and he insisted on going after them, though he no longer had a rifle, only a knife we had taken off one of the Comanche dead.

"We went on ahead, though, and before long we come upon a dead Comanche they had laid out and covered with a blanket, being practical about the matter. My shot had been a good one after all. Winton took to the body like a butcher. I had to walk off and find a place to be alone while he carved it up, yelling and cussing it all the while, as if it might hear him.

"When he was done with his butchery, we went after them. After two days passed we had to give it up. They had by this time taken to all their Indian tricks and melted away, perhaps into Palo Duro Canyon. Thing is, we never saw them again, not even a track of them. We started back, and by this time we had both grown weak. Except for me shooting a rabbit with the Sharps, tearing it up a might, we didn't have anything to eat for the next couple of days heading back home. The horses lived on what grass was growing, and a bit of trapped water here and there. When we arrived back at Winton's homestead we rested up a couple days, then we went out and found the bodies of his family and brought them back and buried them under a large oak tree, Winton's place being the only spot around with ample greenery and water. We stayed on another day and put some supplies together, and after Winton visited the graves, we burned down the cabin because that is what he wanted, and we rode off, and that is how Winton got his scars."

16

By bright morning we were well back at it. As we went, Eustace looking for sign, I glanced over at Winton with his scars, thought about the story Shorty told me. I remembered what Winton told me, too, about killing. Considering his past I supposed it made sense he might have a different picture of it than I had. It also begin to come down on me why he had wanted to go on this hunt. It wasn't just the money but the chance to save someone where before he hadn't. That was as clear to me as the sun in the sky.

I thought about what Shorty had said about humans all being pretty much of the same nature. I couldn't get it out of my mind, and couldn't place God's grace in there and make it work.

I was also thinking on thoughts that were more practical, like we were in country far less open than what Shorty and Winton had been in when chasing the Indians. It was easier to hide here, and Fatty was, in his own way, as dangerous as any Comanche. He was just mean as a snake for no other reason than it pleased him; all those men he had been with were like that, and I wondered then what made a man that way. I didn't come up with any answers.

Where we were riding was a rolling hill country full of trees, and there was no good sure path to take. I was fearful one of the horses would find a hole to step into, or get snakebit, or some such thing. The tracking seemed good, though, and Eustace was leading us along at a right smart pace. We hadn't heard a peep out of Shorty about Eustace's lack of tracking skills, but this may have been due to the fact that Eustace had lost his sense of humor on the matter.

We startled some birds and deer as we went, and every time a bird flushed or a deer leaped, I nearly messed myself thinking it was Fatty with a rifle. Each time the birds flushed, Hog dashed off in the bushes after them as if he might sprout wings and fly up to bite them.

Winding along on a narrow trail, a deer path, really, we rode mostly in single file. Jimmie Sue was right ahead of me when she turned and said, "It don't appear like Fatty is trying to be careful. Maybe he don't know we're still after him. Eustace seems to be following him easy enough."

Shorty, riding ahead of her, said without turning to look back, "Or he is bringing us where he wants us to go."

I thought then of the Comanche and how they had led Winton into an ambush; all my fears about Fatty with a rifle came back, though they were appeased a might when Shorty said, "The benefit we have is I believe Fatty is trying to make his escape, perhaps find someplace to lick his wounds, which I would think are considerable. No one can say he is not a tough one, though. He took a pistol-whipping, got shot full of holes, has bled all over East Texas, killed folks along the way, run an automobile out of gas, and is still making time."

Eustace said he figured Fatty was well ahead of us, but it was most likely a good idea to serve ourselves a supper of the things we had brought along and not even think about shooting. We determined a small fire to heat our supper was of no importance, as with all the trees and what distance Fatty had gained it wouldn't serve as any warning. We were also careful not to use dry leaves or damp wood, as both would give off with too much smoke.

Eustace reckoned we might come upon Fatty the next day, him having fallen off his stolen horse, bled out, and died. I liked the sound of that, and I hoped for it. It made me feel as if that was a choice of God and not a bullet from one of our guns or a scatter from Eustace's cannon.

That night me and Jimmie Sue didn't go about the business of the night before, though this time I made no secret of us lying together, even if it was only in fitful slumber with an occasional touching of her on my part to make sure she was still there. I found her somewhat overwarm beneath our blankets, but it was comforting to have her there just the same, so I stood it just fine.

Eustace took the first watch, and then Shorty, and then Winton. It was supposed to be my turn thereafter, and then Spot's. Jimmie Sue was ruled out, her being a woman, but it occurred to me she would have done right well at it, being of sound mind and a certain determination. She had shot at Fatty back at the trading post, so it stood to reason she was no shrinking violet. Nonetheless, the others weren't for it.

Way it worked out, though, was the first three watched and never woke me or Spot. I don't know if it was them being polite, or if they feared I'd be inadequate and that Spot, during the night, might decide to go home.

When I awoke the next morning, it was to the others preparing their horses. Hog was sitting on his haunches, watching as if he were a supervisor of some sort. Jimmie Sue was already up as well, along with Spot. I was the last to rise. I thought to say something about it, but the truth was, much as I wanted to find my sister, I had begun to feel powerfully tuckered out. Like down in my bones there were weights of some sort, and the weights were dragging me deep into the ground and I didn't have the gumption to climb out. I felt older than I was and meaner than I wanted to be.

The country grew rough enough we were not always able to ride, and had to lead the horses through the forest, traveling the way Fatty had gone, the way Eustace was tracking. I stole a number of sidelong glances at Jimmie Sue, and the more I looked at her the prettier she got. She was in the rough, so to speak. Anything that might have passed for makeup had long since vanished. Her hair was tied back and bound with a black ribbon, and the tail of her bound hair flapped against her back in such a way as to excite me. I was uncertain what it was that caused this. It was just hair, but there you have it; it was making me yearn to be with her again, to hold her—and, of course, I had discovered the pleasure of what my grandfather used to refer to as carnal company.

That thought, when it came to me, was heavy as a brick-built disaster. To think I had shared Jimmie Sue with Grandpa, as well as the sheriff, was not a fine thought. Soon my attraction to her developed a limp, so to speak. But even with that knowledge in my head, I pretty soon pushed it aside, began to think it was me she had left with, none of the others, and that meant something. Again, this was not practical thinking, and one thing I have learned about women by now is they have a tendency to wound your logic. I propped it up by thinking she could have abandoned me at any time, gone her own way, instead of sticking to a hard trail and possible danger.

I began to wonder if she was with me to stay, and if I could pin any hope to her, or would her old profession draw her back. I couldn't at first see the reasoning behind such a thing, her wanting to go back to such, but when I thought about Mama and what little I remembered of Grandma, it was mostly about them washing up and cleaning up, feeding and caring for men. In her own way, that was what Jimmie Sue was already doing, but on her own terms and for a price. It gave me mixed feelings. I didn't know which side of the predicament to land on. There was actually something appealing about a woman that was willing to tote her own water and speak her own mind, and she certainly had me drawn up tight like a fish with a hook buried deep in the gills.

All this musing was stepped on when about high noon we came upon Fatty's stolen black horse. It was lying on its side, up a slight rise, in a clutch of pines. It was alive, but its leg was broke, and it was breathing heavy and near done in.

We were leading our horses at the time, letting them blow, when we come upon the dying horse. Eustace handed me his reins and went over and looked at the animal. Even from where I stood, next to Jimmie Sue, I could see there was dried blood on the horse's saddle. Fatty hadn't taken it with him, though the saddlebags were gone. I figured he had food in them, or weapons, and that's why he wanted them, and it wouldn't be smart to try and lug a saddle, even if it was a good one.

Eustace squatted down and petted the horse gently on the head, said something soothing. Hog came over for a look, but Eustace asked him to go on, but polite-like. Hog went off into the bushes in that kind of mad way he had of doing things from time to time.

Shorty walked over with his knife and cut the horse's throat, the way he told me he cut that horse's throat the time he was on the trail of the Comanche. The poor horse quit tossing its head pretty fast, bled out, and died. It was getting so every time I turned around I was seeing something hurt or dying, and if I wasn't seeing it, I was hearing about it.

"It stepped in a hole right here," said Eustace, "and that bastard didn't have enough decency to put the beast down. I don't like him for sure now. That's two horses he's rode out."

"I suppose he reckoned a shot would give us notice," Winton said.

"He could have gone on and cut its throat," Eustace said. "He could have done that."

"It's all about him," Jimmie Sue said. "He was always like that. You'd have thought when he come to the pleasure house he would have known he was ugly as a pile of horse shit, but he always acted like he was the best-looking dude that ever oiled his hair and come down from New York City. It was like he looked in a mirror and saw someone else."

"Well," Spot said. "That was some mirror he had."

Eustace moved to another squatting position next to the dead animal, studied the dried blood on the saddle. He said, "This here blood means the horse must have fell some hours ago. That blood is Fatty's cause it's dry. It dried fast in this heat, so he's ahead of us, but not by all that much."

Standing up, Eustace looked about, found something that interested him. He said, "He's gone off to the west there. He's walking with a limp, but damn if he ain't walking."

"He must be near run out of juice, way he's been bleeding," Spot said.

Eustace shook his head. "I don't think he's been bleeding the whole time. I think he got it all plugged up, but when the horse fell, it started him leaking again. Still, he's got some kind of sand in him to be able to keep going like that."

Eustace disappeared into a thick of trees. He wasn't gone long, though, and when he come back, he said, "I think what ought to happen is I should follow him and see I can catch up with him. We all go, then we got to worry about the whole line of us, but I can go on foot and maybe spot him. I might be able to put him down."

"You should take my long gun," Shorty said.

"Nah," Eustace said. "I'm gonna get up close to him with the shotgun, see I can get his attention."

"I'm walking with you," Winton said. "It's all right to keep it a small hunting party, but you ought to have some backup. Ole Fatty seems to have more wit about him than I would have suspected. Like a wounded bobcat, he could turn on you—could be laying for you someplace and lead you into it. It might be better if there's at least two of us."

"All right, then," Eustace said, "but come on and let's get to cracking."

They put together a few supplies in some saddlebags and Winton threw them over his shoulder. He had a Winchester he had taken from the trading post, and of course Eustace was carrying his cannon and had a pistol stuck in his right front pants pocket. I had seen once that that pocket was lined with leather. His other pants pocket was filled with shells for the shotgun. He was still wearing his vest, and he had his hat pulled low down and tight, which is the way he pulled it when he felt like doing serious business.

"Way I observe it," said Shorty, "is you two follow the trail as swiftly as you might, and we will attempt to follow your trail, though I am not a tracker, as you know, and have never claimed to be."

"But I am, right?" Eustace said.

"You are less likely to get lost," Shorty said. "That much I will give you."

Eustace smiled, reached out, and touched Shorty on his hatted head like he was a little boy. "I get killed, you can have any of my dung you find along the way while you're following. I wanted you to know that."

They shook hands, then Eustace grinned at the rest of us. Winton waved, and they were off, leaving us there holding the horses.

When they were out of sight, Shorty said, "What we need to do is give them lead time, so that we will not be behind them sounding like a herd of cattle. We will give them two hours and then go after them, leading the horses. When the terrain is appropriate, we will mount and continue our pursuit. That will help us catch up and give them time to put the sneak on Fatty."

To kill our two hours and allow Eustace and Winton to make their way quietly ahead, we stopped and made a fire and cooked some white beans and salt pork in a little pot. I made up some simple makings with cornmeal and water and stuck it all together with a bit of the lard. It wasn't a real good way to make cornbread—even fried bread—as an egg mixed into the batter would have been better. While it was cooking, Hog showed up and watched me doing the frying. I got some cornmeal and tore up a paper sack we had, put it on the ground, and poured him some of the cornmeal on it. He ate the cornmeal, and he ate the brown paper sack, too. I might as well have just poured it in the dirt.

After we finished eating, we heated up some coffee, drank that, then put the fire out. Shorty took out his pocket watch and looked at it.

While he did, Spot said, "I ain't heard no shooting."

"Nor have I," said Shorty. "But it is unlikely they have had time to catch up with him, and it is also possible that he has given them the slip. It occurs to me that if he has, he may be circling back on us."

That had not occurred to me, but now I took notice of my surroundings and laid my hand on the pistol I had in my belt. I thought that if I had to pull it again, I would be sure the sight didn't snag.

"You think he even knows where we are?" Jimmie Sue said.

"Unlikely," Shorty said. "I think his nose is forward and his ears are laid back, and he is trying to find some sort of sanctuary. If his wound is bad enough, that may be his only thought. It may be that his planned sanctuary is not where we intend to go, but he is still our best bet. If that fails, then we know where the Big Thicket is at its fullest, and we will go there and nose about. There is always a way. That said, I suggest we not become too casual and depend too much on Eustace's tracking skills."

"You don't never cut that man no slack on that, do you?" Spot said.

"You have not been lost with him as many times as I have," Shorty said.

It might seem strange to you that just after me telling you how alert I was for Fatty, I grew tired again and sat down with my back against a tree, but that's how it was. One minute I was full of piss and vinegar, and the next I was as empty as a drunk's glass.

I had my hat pulled down over my eyes, was drifting in and out, when I thought I heard two sharp snaps, followed by a third, like someone stepping on a twig—one, two . . . and three. But it didn't seem close. It was a sound in the distance. I lifted my head and pushed back my hat to see if anyone else had noticed, but everyone seemed to be relaxed and unaware of any sounds. I considered on it awhile, decided I had day-dozed and dreamed it. Hog had come over to sleep by me, and as I lay back against the tree, he lifted his head and rested it across my knee. I put my hand on top of his hard noggin, closed my eyes, drifted out again.

When Shorty felt we had waited long enough, he roused us, and we started leading the horses in the direction Eustace and Winton had gone. They had made a trail so obvious even I could follow it. We traveled through the trees for a while, then come to a logging road that had been hacked through the middle of the forest. There were stumps of trees everywhere, but there was a wide patch of road cut through it with the stumps dynamited out. Any resemblance to the natural greenery of what had been there before was purely accidental. There were hardwood trees piled up and burning, and all the pines had been toted off to make lumber. Even the birds didn't sing.

Along the wide-cut road we went, and finally we came upon a pile of metal milk cans and some bushel baskets of overturned sweet potatoes and a dead dog. It was a medium-sized black dog, and it lay among the sweet potatoes and the milk cans, some of which had the lids knocked off of them, milk spilling out in such a way to mix with the blood of the dog—for it appeared to have been shot—and a pile of dried-out sweet potatoes.

By this time we were riding our horses, leading the others, but for this bit of business we got down to look. Spot pointed at the road, said, "I ain't no Daniel Boone, but them there are fairly fresh wagon tracks."

Now, I couldn't much tell fresh tracks from those made last week, but Spot seemed sure, so I decided to believe him. So did Shorty. He got off his horse and bent down in the road and looked and stood up and glanced around and nodded.

We got down off our horses then, looked around for anything that might explain the situation.

Shorty pointed at the ground, said, "The wagon came through here not long ago, and here you can see tracks of men walking. There are more tracks, coming later, because they are even fresher. One of those tracks is Eustace's, which makes the other Winton's. I know Eustace's tracks by the turn of his boot heels, which are worn on both sides. Eustace tends to distribute his weight to the sides of his feet, and one heel is always slightly more worn than the other."

"I thought you weren't a tracker," I said.

"I am not," Shorty said. "But that much I learned from Eustace. That much he knows."

"He's right," said Spot. "Them tracks there come up later. I ain't no real tracker, either, but I can follow a deer some, and I can make out this."

Jimmie Sue said, "You know, that milk might not be spoiled, and I'm hankering for some. Shall I open a can?"

We agreed she should, as there were still a few with the lids tight on them. I helped set up one, and she unscrewed with Spot's help. The milk smelled like it was still good, but it had grown warm. We got our cups out of our bags and went to dipping milk. I reckon I had three cups before Shorty said we should all stop, as milk didn't mix well with the stomach in hot weather, especially riding a horse.

Jimmie Sue had paused to pick a few of the better sweet potatoes up and shove those in her saddlebags. About then, Spot, a cup of milk almost to his lips, said, "Oh, hell. Looky there, will you?"

He lowered the cup and pointed.

We looked, saw there was a leg and a bare foot sticking out over a log. Going over there to see, we found fastened to that leg a whole man. He was a white fella, about forty, I reckoned, and his hat had twisted so that his face was down in it and the hat was pressed to the ground. He was as dead as the dog. Hog had been off in the woods a spell, but now he came out and came over for a look. Shorty said, "No, Hog. Leave him be. Go eat the dog."

Hog left the man alone, and he didn't bother the dog, either. I figure he had been scrounging for acorns and roots and was full as a tick.

"He has been shot in the head," Shorty said. "Now I see what has happened. Fatty came down this way without a horse, and, as providence would have it, along came a man and a dog in a wagon hauling milk and potatoes to market. Fatty ambushed the man and the dog, probably because the dog tried to bite him or barked at him, or he saw him as a threat. Then he tossed all their goods out the back of the wagon so that it might roll faster. When that was done, he took off down the road. Along came Winton and our own tracking legend, Eustace, and now he and Winton are on foot and in hot pursuit of a wagon drawn briskly by horses."

It was then that it came clear to me that those three snaps I had heard had been three shots, and they had been those meant for this man and his dog, and a third that was probably a miss.

We mounted up, followed their tracks, and I didn't mention burying anybody. What I wanted was to catch up with the murdering bastard. I had never known anyone like that, who would kill for any reason whatsoever and who was as hard on livestock and dogs as he was on people, not to mention how rough he was on cans of milk and bushels of sweet potatoes.

17

We rode along at a brisk trot, but not a run. Shorty was certain that we would soon come upon Eustace and Winton following the trail Fatty had left.

Jimmie Sue and Spot had fallen behind a bit, riding beside one another, and for some odd reason the sweet potatoes had led to an argument between them on how to prepare them best for a meal. Jimmie Sue held out on butter and sugar placed in a split tater and baked, while Spot was certain it was best to place few fork holes in a tater, let it cook, split it when done, then add the sugar and butter. There was also an argument on frying sweet potatoes that had something to do with floating them a bit in milk first, but it was a conversation, though as important to them as interpreting scripture, I not only couldn't follow, but wasn't interested in. This is why I ended up beside Shorty.

In a brief time we ceased to trot the horses and let them walk so as not to wear them down too soon in the day, as it was already growing warm and would soon be sticky as molasses in an armpit.

I said, "I don't know about women. I don't know about Jimmie Sue."

"You mention this in a quest for advice?" Shorty said.

"I suppose."

"You know I am not one to be large on love, or any component of it, though I admit I am not entirely immune."

"So you've been in love?"

"In lust," he said. "As a younger man I had a hard time separating the two, love and lust, as both involved fucking. There is supposed to be a difference, however, and I suppose I was in what I thought was love then. Now I know the need for someone is usually some weakness of self."

"You can't believe that," I said.

"I can, Jack, and I do. But there was Cherry Wilson. She was a whore, like Jimmie Sue, and like her, she was comely. I think she had considerable feelings for me as well. The problem was the public. The idea of walking the street with a man who when you held his hand gave the appearance of a mother and small child was too much for her. Once, when we had sex from the rear, I had to stand on a footstool to get my position. It made me feel foolish and made her feel even more so. It was a doomed relationship from the start. She would have loved to stay with me, I think. On a personal level, in the darkness of a room, my size was not a consideration, but there was no street time for our romance; there were just too many people to see us. I think she would have rather been seen with a known murderer with one eye and a limp than with a midget.

"We parted from one another, and I was a mess for some time after that. Went on a drunk and bought whores. I am ashamed to say I was mean to them. I took up a job, like a normal person. I became a shopkeeper in central Texas. An ugly place, I assure you. It is the very bunghole of Texas. My store was built along a road that I was sure would supply much traffic. It did not. The traffic had chosen to use a different road that wound past a rail station. I could not give away a keg of flour if I had it tied on the back of a free donkey. It was like my store sold cow turds. Not enough people dropped in to make business matter, though I did have a number of nonbuyers who liked to come by and sit on the porch and talk politics, as if any of them had ever voted or even knew how. They liked to argue religion as well, which usually boiled down to controversy over being baptized by submersion or sprinkling, a distinction that seemed to be without matter or purpose to me. There were plenty who came to see me as well, though they were not eager to buy anything. It was as if I were still in the circus.

"I reached my fill of being an object of display, and on a dark Wednesday I made this point clear to a man who insisted that he was going to pull my clothes off and make me wear a dress and dance. He had brought the dress with him. It was a nice dress, bright red, but not to my liking. Had it been fine and come with a free pair of shoes, I can tell you emphatically I was neither prepared to have my pants pulled off nor wear a dress. He mistook my size for easy submission, and I shot him in the balls and he died.

"The law was inclined to believe it had been something of an overreaction, and that it would have been much simpler had I let him pull my pants off and put me in a dress. I continued to maintain my disagreement with this. I ended up with a drunken lawyer that was being paid by the court and did not give a hoot if I was hanged, castrated, or given a tea party while wearing that dress and those shoes. He once joked to me that it sounded funny and he would have liked to see it. Underestimation of my abilities led me to leap high and swing a hard right. That played a significant part in my escape, for that is what I did, and for years I thought I might be caught up with. Later, I learned the courthouse had burned and so had records of my arrest. The trading post had been taken over by the relatives of the man who wanted me to wear a dress, and it seemed they felt that was adequate compensation, as he was not that popular, even among his kin. Many of them, it turned out, had been forced to wear dresses, and it was known among the community, if not to me, that the man whose balls I deflated had liked to dress up himself, and that he had a particular penchant for women's underthings, especially girdles. Even if my records had not burned, it seemed clear that by this time they were ready to let me slide rather than fall down on the side of a swinging dick in a red gingham whore dress. So here I am today. Without true love or a trading post, but not wearing a dress and little shoes, either."

I was digesting all this when up ahead we saw Eustace and Winton sitting by the side of the road with a young colored boy. He looked to be about thirteen or fourteen, but when we come riding up on him I saw he was a little older, but still a boy, small of height and thin. He held a hand to his head, and his mouth hung open, showing his teeth.

Eustace looked up as we were coming, lifted a hand. When were alongside them we got down off our horses, except for Jimmie Sue, and walked over for a look. Hog went over, too, and at first the boy was frightened by him, but Eustace calmed him down. After a moment the boy was petting Hog.

"Fatty done it," Eustace said. "We come down out of the woods, found a dead man and dog, some overturned milk. There were wagon tracks, so it was easy to figure what happened. Fatty. We took on after him. But with all the stuff dumped off the wagon, he was traveling light and making good time."

"We seen all that," I said.

"We come on down the road and found this boy sitting here, holding his head," Winton said.

"He was hired to load the milk and potatoes and was on his way to market in Livingston," Eustace said.

"Let him tell it," Shorty said.

"I done told it," the colored boy said. "I was riding in the back of the wagon with the goods. Mr. Druskin and his dog, Butch, was in the buck seat driving the mules. I mean Mr. Druskin. The dog didn't know how."

"That's disappointing," Jimmie Sue said.

"Yeah," Spot said. "I would have liked that. A dog driving a wagon."

"Would you two shut up?" Shorty said.

The boy took up his story again. "This fat white guy come out of the woods on us. He was carrying a rifle and he looked rough and red-faced, like he had been boiled and was ready to be buttered. He opened up right away. He shot the dog first, then Mr. Druskin. I jumped off that wagon, took to running like a rabbit. He shot at me and cut a bullet alongside my head, right here."

He took his bloody hand down. There was a light groove over his ear and along the back of his head where it had plowed through his woolly hair like a middle buster through burnt grass.

"I went in the woods and hid out. I must have stayed there an hour or so, then snuck back and seen Mr. Druskin and his dog dead, like I figured. All that milk and taters was tossed off, and the wagon was gone. I don't see how that man could have gone on, way he looked. It was easy to tell at just a glance he was hurting bad. But he took the wagon and drove the horses on. I followed—not so I could catch up with him but because I figured he wouldn't be coming back my way, and if he did, I'd catch sight on him and could run like a rabbit again. Then I got dizzy and realized I'd been creased. I sat down beside the road, and these two fellas come up. I done told them what I told you. This hog ain't gonna bite me, is he?"

"Just don't move sudden," Eustace said.

"We got an extra horse, you want it," Winton said.

"I could sure appreciate a ride," the colored boy said.

"It's a horse ain't no one gonna need anymore," Winton said. "So you take it and ride it. It ain't got a bridle or saddle, but I reckon you can make a bridle and some reins with a bit of rope. I think we got some rope."

"I'd appreciate that considerably," the colored boy said.

"How far is Livingston?" Shorty asked.

"It ain't that much on down the road," the colored boy said.

"All right, then," said Eustace. "I guess that's the direction we got to go, and it might not be good to be in too big a hurry. Maybe it's best we catch Fatty where he's holed up with the rest. That way we'll have all the snakes in one pile."

"Yeah," Winton said. "But one snake is easy enough to kill with a hoe, but a bunch of them at one time might prove harder to reckon with."

"When we get to Livingston," Shorty said, "Jimmie Sue

might want to find a place to stay until we are through, or they are through with us."

"I think not," she said. She had never gotten off her horse and was still sitting up there looking down on us. "I've come this damn far, I don't intend to quit coming."

"It's not your fight," I said.

"You and me are together, ain't we?" she said.

"I guess so," I said.

"Well, now, you need to quit guessing and go to knowing."

Right then every doubt I had ever had grew wings and flapped out of my head and out of sight into the sky of my thoughts. It felt good to say, "We are."

"Then that there settles it," Jimmie Sue said. "We'll all go down to see them rascals together. I kind of like the idea of seeing those men shot up. I wouldn't mind doing some of the shooting."

A couple of those doubtful birds that had flown away flew back out of that sky and back into my head, and I thought perhaps I could hear a few wings of the others beating my way.

"You and me are friends, ain't we?" Winton said to Jimmie Sue. I figured him having had experience with her, he wanted to see which side of the chart he was marked on.

"You were one of the good ones," she said.

"I'd rather not hear it," I said.

"Oh, let it go," Jimmie Sue said. "I've given up everyone else for you, and you're gonna have to start thinking of me different, if you can. If you can't, then you and me don't need to hook together anyhow. You give that some thought, Jack. Give it some serious thought. I got strong feelings for you, but they can be dampened. A girl like me hasn't that much furniture to move around."

"What about you, Spot?" Shorty asked. "What is your current position on matters?"

"I'm just here to see I get my five dollars," he said. "I ain't in on no gunplay, knife play, or fistfights. So I guess I'm still thinking on things and haven't come up with nothing solid yet."

"Fair enough," Shorty said. "But you might have to make a decision on the run."

We gave the colored boy a horse without ever learning his name, and he decided he wasn't going to Livingston after all, and rode back the way he had come. We started out again, mounted, Hog trotting along with us, Jimmie Sue riding alongside me, and me giving thought to what she had said.

The wagon we were following had a groove in one of its wheels, and it made a clear mark that set it apart from other tracks on the red clay road, but when the road hardened out in places the track disappeared from time to time. Mostly, though, the road was like a red pepper, as it had dried out in the heat and gone soft. When the wind blew it picked up the dried red clay and blew it about, getting in the nose and eyes and seasoning us all over with a fine red mist. Jimmie Sue commented that it matched my hair.

We weren't as close to Livingston as we thought, but by the end of the day, when the sun was going down, we come to it, all of us tired and heavily dust-colored. It wasn't much of a town, but it was more of one than where we had come from, and better organized. Shorty said it was the sort of place all the fun had been sucked out of by too many churches being built. I was a little more comfortable there, though I had to admit that No Enterprise had given me a taste of sin that I hadn't found all that disagreeable. To some extent I find sin like coffee. When I was young and had my first taste of it I found it bitter and nasty, but later on I learned to like it by putting a little milk in it, and then I learned to like it black. Sin is like that. You sweeten it a little with lies, and then you get so you can take it straight. I just didn't want to do it all the way. I wanted to keep a little milk in it. And then there was the fact it was getting harder and harder to see what Jimmie Sue and I were doing as sin.

By the time we rode on into Livingston, I began to feel like I had been turned inside out, salted, and given to dogs to eat. I could hardly hang on to my horse. We stopped at a livery, and Winton went inside and had a talk with the liveryman, and when he come out he had arranged for us to stay in a little shed out back that was floored with hay and had an ample amount of horse manure in it. We was given pitchforks and a big scoop shovel, and we cleaned it out. I guess that was part of our pay for being able to put up there. It took a shorter time than you can imagine, as we was all anxious to get it done. When it was scraped clean, Winton got a wheelbarrow and brought some hay from the main livery and spread it on the floor, then I took a turn and went and got some of it. We did this trip several times, taking turns—even Jimmie Sue, who insisted—and before long the damp dirt floor was spread over with hay and it smelled clean and it was dry.

The liveryman had taken our horses and unsaddled them and put them to grain and water, and we spread our bedrolls in the shed and laid out to sleep. Jimmie Sue rolled up with me, and we hugged one another gently, and I remember putting my face against hers and knowing then that I had grown used to her smell, which was nice, even though she hadn't taken a bath since we left the whorehouse. She was sweet-smelling by nature, and her natural perfume blended nicely with the smell of the hay.

But I'm starting to sound like some kind of lovesick coyote, which I was, so I'll move on. We slept, and it was a good, deep sleep. The best I had had since we left the farm to go to Kansas and it hadn't worked out.

It was night when I woke up. Everyone else was asleep but Shorty. The shed door was open, and he was sitting on an overturned bucket in the moonlight smoking a cigar. He had the Twain book in his lap. I could smell the tobacco burning, and he turned to look at me. He always seemed to know if you or anything else was stirring. I didn't say anything or make a gesture. I just rolled up tight with Jimmie Sue again and went back to sleep.

The heat woke me up. I guess that was why me and Jimmie Sue had come apart in the night. She was lying on her back with her eyes closed and her mouth open and I could hear her breathing. Everyone else had started to stir. I didn't see Spot. Shorty was still at the doorway, though he had changed positions on the bucket.

I sat up, and since me and Jimmie Sue were at the back of the shed, I pushed my spine up against the wall. Without my asking, Winton, who was pulling on his boots, said, "Spot's done gone over to get us some grub from the café. I still got some biscuits in my saddlebags, but I tried to bite into one this morning and couldn't do it. They've grown solid. I was gonna soak it in some water, but then I figured I had enough money to go us all breakfast, though after this I think we'll have to eat grass. I ain't got but a dime left now, and I'm saving that for some kind of emergency."

Eustace was also pulling on his boots. He said, "If you ain't come to an emergency yet, I ain't sure you're gonna recognize one when you do."

Winton grinned at him.

Spot come back later carrying two metal buckets. They had their tops covered over with thin white towels. Inside the shed he took the towels off, and in one of the buckets was a stack of sweet-smelling biscuits, fluffy as clouds, flaky as dandruff. Underneath them was another towel, and underneath that we found a pile of sausages. The smell that came from them was so strong and good it darn near floated me up to the ceiling of that little shed, though I might add that wouldn't have been to any great height. It was tight in there.

Hog ended up eating some of the old cornmeal I had left over. I put it out for him before we ate. I figured a biscuit might have been all right for him, but we were too greedy to share them with a porker, and I thought giving him a sausage was just somehow wrong. He ate quickly, before we had our meal even sorted out.

The other bucket had a pot of coffee in it and some thick, hard cups. We ate our breakfast and drank our coffee with the enthusiasm of a hog in a corn patch. When we finished our meal and the coffee was down to the last drop, Winton went to see about the horses.

When he came back all he had was a horse apiece. He had sold them spares from the trading post to pay for our stay and filled his pockets with the leftover money.

Checking our supplies, we found we had plenty of ammunition for our weapons, and Shorty made sure we were all strapped up with knives, some of which we already had and some of which we were able to buy at the general store, though Winton gave up the money with the same reluctance a banker gives up a dollar he knows isn't actually his.

Next thing we done was wait outside in the street while Winton and Shorty went into the saloon for a while. It turned out our wait was to be a long while, and we ended up tying the horses outside to a hitching post that stuck up in front of the saloon and had big metal rings fastened to it. We sat on the sidewalk boards and waited. Jimmie Sue sat by me and looped her arm through mine and rested her head on my shoulder and slept some more. One thing I was to learn about that girl was she liked her sleep and went at it with the dedication one might have to a job.

While she was sleeping I watched some horses with riders come along the street, and I seen a bunch of motorcars as well. There was some kind of altercation when a motorcar made a horse jump and threw the rider off. The man in the machine stopped and got out. He and the rider got in each other's faces and gave me a full education in foul language. As a Christian, I hate to admit it, but I tucked away a few of those words for later use, and there was one so foul I made a pact with myself to only use it inside my head.

Hog, during all this, lay at our feet snoring, or, rather, snorting. He was a big one, I'll tell you that. Folks kept coming by to take a look, and one man offered to buy him from us and pay us to help scald-pot him and butcher him out, but we turned him down. Hog never stirred. Like Jimmie Sue, he enjoyed his sleep, and we could have cut his throat and sold him and he'd have never known it. I said as much to Eustace.

"He wouldn't sleep like that he didn't trust us," he said. "He's more on the scout usually. I think he really likes you and Jimmie Sue."

After what seemed like an hour or so, Winton and Shorty come out of the saloon. Winton was weaving like a sailor riding the deck in a storm, and he nearly fell off the boardwalk—and would have if little Shorty hadn't grabbed him and shown himself to be far stronger than would be expected.

"I thought y'all done moved in," Eustace said.

"We were at the task of acquiring information," Shorty said. "And during the process, Winton thought it was polite to buy drinks and drink some himself."

"Some?" Spot said. "It's like he's a fish and done tried to drink the ocean."

"Yes," said Shorty. "But this ocean was at least a hundred proof."

Winton, still sitting on the boardwalk, leaned over and threw up in the street.

"There goes that fine breakfast," Shorty said. I was near Shorty, and though he was not drunk, I could smell that he had taken in a bit of the ocean as well. "What we learned is that this band of men we are looking for could be near the Indian reservation. On out a little farther, but near. They have their own camp there, in the deep woods, and it is likely that there will be more than just Cut Throat and Nigger Pete, just as we expected. But it seems possible that there is quite a large number. Fact is, what we know is not a whole lot more than what we already knew."

"What do we do, then?" I asked.

"First thing we do is see how many of us here are sticking. I know Eustace and Winton and I are in, and I can assume you will be, Jack, as you are the initiator of all this. Jimmie Sue has indicated that she plans to stay with us, so I suppose that only leaves Spot. Now you have to decide how close to us you want to be, Spot, and how much that five dollars is actually worth."

"Could I get shot up?" Spot asked. He had been sitting on the boardwalk whittling on a stick that he had been carrying with him for just such an occasion. He had the new knife from the general store to try out, and that's what he was doing. He didn't look up when he asked his question.

"It could turn sour," Shorty said.

"Meaning I could get myself shot," Spot said.

"Correct," Shorty said.

"I don't want to get shot none, but I don't want to go back to swamping out rooms and tossing out chamber pots. I'm thinking I'd just like to take my money for giving the information I gave, then I can go on to whatever. I don't see no reason to get killed. I've already been in more tight situations than I would prefer."

"You ain't getting shit," Winton said. He had recovered considerably after throwing up his breakfast, and was holding his head.

"You said you would pay me," Spot said.

"I didn't mean it," Winton said.

"He will pay you," Shorty said. "But the truth is, we need all the money we have until we are through with our mission. We may need more food and ammunition. You can wait here until we get back and see if we collect some bounty. It could take some time, but the sheriff here will pay out. Papers are on them all over East Texas."

Spot studied on that suggestion. "I think I better go with you. I wait, you might get killed, and I wouldn't know for sure you was dead, and here I'd be looking for another chamber pot to empty. I could starve."

"If we do not get killed," Shorty said, "you will get your five dollars."

"I bet you could pay me now," Spot said.

"We could," said Shorty. "But we will not. As I said, we may need that money."

"All right, then," Spot said. "I'll come, but I'm staying out of the thick of it if I can. I might wait up in the trees somewhere."

"That is agreeable," Shorty said.

"We met a gimpy fella in there says he knows a little about where they might be," Winton said, "and he'll come by later to talk to us at the stable. He didn't want to be seen talking much in the saloon, not knowing who might see him. He feared word might get back to Cut Throat. He seemed awful scared of him. Oh, damn. I feel just godawful."

"You're still drunk," Eustace said. "I wish I was."

"The hell you do," Shorty said.

Later turned out to be late afternoon. The fella that come by was a little man, though not as short as Shorty, of course. He had a face that was like a sack full of burdens. He came to meet us in our shed. He limped hard when he walked, and he had a woman with him. She had a good build and wore black and had a veil pulled down from a dress hat she wore, and it covered her face. It wasn't a regular kind of veil, more of a cloth, really. There was a slit cut in it for her eyes.

The man came in and sat down on the floor. Shorty got a bucket and brought it over for the woman to sit on. The rest of us sat around near her, Jimmie Sue the closest. Eustace sweet-talked Hog into staying over in the corner. A hog likes a corner. They'll usually just do their business there, like it's their own outhouse, and keep the rest of the pen clean as possible. Hog didn't have no pen, but he had crapped in the corner of the hay and I had only just cleaned it out and put fresh down when the little man and the woman showed up.

The man said, "I figured I ought to tell you what you're up against, least you think what you're dealing with is a garden party."

"We do not think that," Shorty said.

"All right," said the little man.

"I do not remember your name," Shorty said.

"I didn't give it none, but it's Efrem."

"All right, Efrem," Shorty said. "I understand you want us to know what a bad gentleman Cut Throat is, but what we want to know is where he is hiding."

Winton, who was still getting over his drunk, said, "And I want to know what she's doing here and how come she's wearing that mask."

Efrem nodded. "Let me tell you this before you get into it. I can't pinpoint where he is, I can only point you in the general direction."

"We have that much information," I said.

"Less general than what you've got," Efrem said. "Or at least I think so. But I couldn't point you in any direction without telling you about Cut Throat Bill. We got a farm about two miles out, and one day about two years back, we looked up and seen these men coming along. There was three of them. They rode up to the farm and asked if they could water their horses and get a drink for themselves out of the well. Now, we wasn't against that, and they watered the horses and drank, and my sister here, Ella, offered to cook them up some food. I think she was kind of sweet on one of them who was young and a good-enough-looking fella. Would you agree with that, Ella?"

Ella nodded.

"So they stayed for supper and got fed, and then they wanted some liquor, and we didn't have any. They said they figured we did, for medicinal purposes. But we didn't. We ain't drinkers. Well, one of them, the fat one, the one they called Fatty, he got up and went outside and he come back with a little bottle. They had some with them, but they had hoped to drink our whiskey. But there wasn't none. They had been polite about it all, but the way it was going I was getting nervous. The more they drank, louder they got and the rowdier they got, and then the young one, he said he had some cards he'd like to show. He pulled them out of his shirt pocket. They was all cards with pictures of naked women on them. When I seen what they was, I said, 'Why don't you put them up? My sister is here.' Well, now, that just made the young one laugh, and by then, Ella, she wasn't so fond of him. He said something about how she might like to look at the cards, and I said I wouldn't want her to do that. Suddenly he stood up and grabbed an ax by the fireplace I kept there for kindling and chopped down on my foot. That's why I limp. He cut off my toes, plumb off. I fell over, and I won't lie to you, I passed out. When I come to they had Ella's clothes pulled off of her . . . It's okay, Ella."

Ella had turned her head to the side so as not to look at us.

"We got to tell these folks so they know what they're getting into. They had her clothes off . . . and they had their way with her, and the young one, he kept saying while the others was at it that he ought to have gone first and been the one to . . . well, to open her up."

"We get the idea," Eustace said.

"I don't like talking about any of this, and in front of a colored fella it's even harder," said Efrem.

"I can go outside," Eustace said.

"No," Shorty said. "He cannot. What white ears can hear, so can black ears. The color does not change the listening."

Efrem nodded. "I suppose that's true. Well, I tried to get a rifle I had hung over the mantel, but I couldn't move good because of my foot, and they caught me, and Cut Throat, who had already had his turn with Ella, come over and dragged my foot into the fireplace. We had fired it up to cook the beans, and he put my foot in it and damn near burnt it off, and that fat man sat on my head while he did it. I didn't pass out that time, but I wished I had. Thing was, I was a pure coward for a while after that. I couldn't do nothing and wouldn't. The young one complained so much about not being first, Cut Throat told him he couldn't put the cherry back in her so he ought to do what he could with the box it come in. I'm sorry, Ella. But that's what he said."

"You can quit," Shorty said.

"I can, and I will," Efrem said, "but Ella wanted me to tell you. I think she wants to get it off her chest."

"Go on, then," I said.

Jimmie Sue moved over by Ella and sat her butt on the hay by the bucket and quietly took Ella's hand. Ella let her have it.

"The young one pulled Ella in the back room, and the others sat in there with me by the fireplace and drank out of that bottle. Cut Throat Bill, who when we first met that day just called himself Bill, said when he was young his mother had told him she didn't want him in the first place and had decided to get rid of him. The other one, the fat one, said, 'I thought it was your father.' Cut Throat said, 'Depends on which day I'm telling it.' My guess was it was something he was telling that was mostly true, and as he started talking, I knew then who he was. He had a reputation, and I hadn't really thought too much about that scar around his neck, thought maybe it was an accident. Didn't want to think it was anything else. I heard it was a robber done it to him when he was a boy. I read about him in the dime novels, and I think that's where I got that. But he said he got his throat cut slow and they all thought he was going to die, but he didn't. He said it was powerful painful. At that time, way my foot hurt, the way I lay there not able to move or speak, I had some idea what he meant. He said, 'You know, it was a strange thing, cause it didn't hurt at first at all.' Said it stung a little after the fact, and then he got weak cause he was losing blood, but he survived it cause he got the wound bound and his mother hadn't cut deep enough with the straight razor. Then he said, 'You know, it wasn't my mother. It was a demon done it. A demon that wanted my soul. And you know what? He got it.'

"That's when he just quit talking, reached in his pocket, and got out a razor and come over quick and grabbed my burnt and chopped foot and just started sawing pieces of meat off of it. I was so weak, and it happened so fast, I couldn't do nothing about it. It was over before I knew it happened, but I tell you, a moment later I was damn sure it had happened, because the pain on that foot was something fierce. I passed out again. I don't know why he didn't kill me, but right in the middle of it, right before I passed out, he got up and went in the bedroom. I didn't know nothing after that, but when I come to they was gone. The front door was open, and the place had been thrown about. My rifle was gone, and so were some odds and ends, and later I found out that the money we had saved in a milk jar under the bed had been taken as well as some we had hid up in a rafter. I woke up and I couldn't walk. I crawled to where Cut Throat Bill had thrown the hatchet in the floor, and I got that and made my way crawling to the back room. Now, I don't know what had happened or why. But the young man was there, and he was on the bed, facedown, but his face was turned sideways toward me and his eyes were open and his blood was soaked into the bedclothes. He had his pants pulled down to his ankles. I didn't see Ella. I was still on the floor, and I reached up and dragged him off the bed, and he fell on his back and I seen then his throat was cut; fact was, his head was darn near cut off. Bill had got mad at him for whatever reason and had come up on him and cut his throat. While I was there looking at him, I heard something, and looked under the bed . . . there was Ella. She opened her mouth, and I seen right off that her tongue had been cut out."

"Jesus," Winton said.

"Ella?" Efrem said.

Ella took hold of the bottom of her mask and lifted it. I could tell she had been a real looker in the past, but now her mouth had been cut on both sides so that there was a thick scar that ran up from the corners of it to under each ear. She opened her mouth, and there remained just a bit of her tongue; it wiggled like a little fish tail. I thought then about what Shorty had said about humans being pretty much the same—Indians, whites, what have you. I didn't mean to, but I looked at Winton and what had been done to him, and then back at her. I wished then that I wasn't a man at all but a hawk, something with some kind of integrity about what it killed, that did it for food or survival, not for sport or revenge or to satisfy something rotten inside.

Ella closed her mouth and quickly pulled down the mask. I was glad she did.

"He ain't just a bad man with a gun and a razor," Efrem said. "He's something wicked. I don't know which story is true about how his throat got cut, and he may not even know, but I tell you this: he's a thing you don't want to mess with. You want to leave that be. I tell you this hoping you won't. I'm hoping you'll go after him and do him in, make him pay for whatever you want him to pay for, cause that will be for us, too. But I couldn't just send you and not let you know how he is and how it could turn out, and not in your favor."

"With that understood," Shorty said, "we are set on a true course to find him, no matter what."

"Where is he?" Eustace said.

"What I can tell you is he's southwest and in the Thicket," Efrem said. "He's got a place not many miles from a sawmill. You go down the main road out, and you come to that sawmill, and you aren't far. More than that I can't tell you. I only know that through hearsay."

"Then you don't really know much at all," Winton said. "I think you always wanted us to go after him. You wanted to fire us up with that story. You haven't given us any kind of directions that help a bit. You ain't told us a damn thing we didn't already know."

"All right," Efrem said. "I suppose that is true. They ruined our lives. I can't hardly even work. I got to grow a small patch of vegetables and raise a few chickens. Ella here, she ain't never gonna marry. There ain't a thing for her and me but just living till we die. Yeah, we want you to get him."

"You didn't need to convince me," I said. "He has my sister."

"Oh, my goodness," said Efrem.

"No need to say it," I said. "I got to believe she's all right."

"I suppose it's possible," Efrem said. "Cut Throat ain't got no balance. I don't think he knows what he plans to do from moment to moment. Man's law don't mean nothing to him, and he's got no fear of it."

"I got to trust in God and believe she's all right," I said.

"Don't you think I prayed that night when Cut Throat come in our house? Don't you think I prayed after he chopped on my foot and put it in the fire, sliced meat off of it like it was a roast? Don't you think I did that? Don't you think I did when Ella was in that room with them? Don't you think that?"

"I suppose so," I said.

"Ain't no suppose to it," Efrem said. "I did. And I guess I could say thank God for sparing Ella. But then I got to wonder what he had against us in the first place. We was raised up good, and every time the church door opened, we was there. But I'll tell you, boy. I ain't been back since, neither of us, and I don't never plan to go again."

I didn't have anything to say in return.

"I hope your sister is fine," Efrem said. "I do. She could be. Like I said, Cut Throat, he hasn't got any balance about him. You never know what he's gonna do. That young fella got crossways with him, and I think he thought on that and decided to take care of him. And then he did what he did to Ella. Why that, I don't know. Why anything he does, I don't know."

We all sat around silent for a while after that.

When the silence got too heavy, Efrem stood, said, "I guess I did get you folks to listen to me dishonestly. Don't know how to tell you where they are. Just wanted you to know what happened to us. You want to find him, and I want you to. I can't do nothing about it myself, and if I could, I don't know I would. They scared me so bad I'm fearful if a bird's shadow falls over me."

"It ain't nothing to be ashamed of," Winton said. "I get some fear myself from time to time when the night comes. And I got some problems with the mirror, in more ways than one."

Efrem held out his hand to help his sister off the bucket, but Jimmie Sue was already up and helping her. She hung on to Ella's arm until they were outside the shed, and she walked with her on out into the street.

As we watched Efrem and Ella go, saw Jimmie Sue coming back toward us, Winton said, "I want that Cut Throat son of a bitch bad. Real bad."

Eustace's voice was deep, like he was bringing it from a well in a bucket. He said, "Me, too."

Shorty stood short and silent, the last part being unlike him.

We rode outside of town and stopped near a clearing. Shorty had us dismount, then laid us out some guns on a horse blanket. We already had weapons, but he collected them, and then placed them and the ammunition out with the others so we could see what was what. The only thing that didn't get collected and redistributed was Eustace's shotgun. Wasn't anyone else could shoot it comfortably without having the stock take out a tooth. I wasn't sure why he was doing this, but I didn't squawk. I was long past trying to figure out Shorty's mind.

Shorty got back his Sharps and a big Colt pistol and a small pistol, which he stuck in his boot. Eustace was given a little revolver to go with his cannon. Winton had an automatic we had taken from the trading post.

I was given an old navy .36 with shells, all of which had been taken from the trading post. Jimmie Sue was handed a Winchester. They gave Spot a just-in-case gun, an iffy-looking pistol that broke open in the middle. It fired five shots, if I remember correctly. I have never cared much for guns, and don't take to them like some folks do, and don't always remember their details. A gun is a tool, but I never learned to love one as much as a rake or a hoe.

After we got to riding along, I expressed just that opinion to Shorty, who, along with Spot, was riding closest to me right then. I told him I was glad to have a gun like a comfort pillow, but I didn't know if I was good enough with it to be put in the forefront.

"I'm willing to stand there," I said. "Just saying I don't know how much good I'll be when it comes to the nut-cutting."

"Might I remind you that you have already used a gun and did quite well?"

"That was mostly an accident. I missed until I didn't."

"Then you better work close. Listen here. You have proved brave as any man I have been with in a tight spot. You did what you had to do and did not make like a rabbit."

"I don't like guns, and I don't like killing," I said.

"A gun makes me feel taller. As a man ages a gun's machinery becomes more important than the machinery of the flesh. You can fix or replace an old gun, but an old man cannot be fixed. That said, it is best not to learn to love guns, because they damn sure do not love you back."

"I shot a crow once was pecking on a shack I was in," Spot said. "It woke me up, and I was mad at it."

I was kind of startled when he spoke up. I had forgotten about Spot riding close to us. I turned in the saddle, said, "What?"

"I shot that sucker," Spot said. "And then I seen there was another crow nearby. I was gonna shoot it, too, but saw how it was fluttering from limb to limb, all upset, and once it dived down near that dead crow for a look, then up. Figured it was the mate to the one I killed. I thought about it some, then went on and shot the other on account I didn't want it to be alone."

18

I haven't done much of a job explaining how we thought we could be on Fatty's trail. Even the peculiarities of the wagon wheel were now lost in the traffic marks on the road. Efrem had pretty much given us hoot-and-holler directions, some guesses, and a might-be. All he had told us that was solid was that some said they stayed beyond a sawmill back in the woods. But the Big Thicket is a lot of woods. And for that matter, there are a lot of sawmills gnawing through the country like rats through cotton.

Pretty soon we come upon one of those sawmills, and, stopping near it, we watched the colored workers hack small limbs off logs with axes and take the big limbs off with a gasoline-driven saw that whined like a cooped-up child.

The man running the sawmill was a little white fellow. He was standing out front of a little shack built by the road. Even from a distance we saw what you would expect of an old sawmill man. He was missing some fingers. Two on his left hand, and on his right his forefinger and little finger were nubbed and yellowed at the tips. He seemed nervous, like he was expecting important news from far away.

Me and Shorty went over to see him, leaving our people on the other side of the road. When we got up to where he was, standing by the shack, watching some colored men haul lumber into the sawmill camp, he turned and looked at us.

He let out a laugh, looked at Shorty, said, "I thought my eyes was fooling me on account of I had me a little nip about an hour ago. I was thinking you was an ugly child, and this boy here was your father, but I can see now he's too young for that and you're too old to be any child."

"Very observant," said Shorty.

"One minute," said the man. He ducked into the shed and came out with a bottle of whiskey. He opened and swigged it and recapped it and slipped it in his back pocket. This might be part of an explanation as to why he was missing fingers.

I told the man about the wagon and Fatty, but without details as to why we were looking for him. I said we'd heard there might be a camp of some fellas living off in the woods near a sawmill, and Fatty might be with them.

The man scratched his head, said, "I don't know about no camp, but I seen your man, I'm pretty damn sure." He looked at Shorty and grinned. "You do any flips?"

"I beg your pardon?" said Shorty.

"You know, somersaults."

"Why in hell would I do flips?"

"I thought midgets did flips and stuff like that. I seen one in a circus once that rode a dog."

Shorty was turning red in the face. I said, "He doesn't do flips. But this fat man you seen in a wagon. He's someone we're trying to catch up with."

"Why would that be?" said the man. "You ain't said yet. I'm going to be giving out words on him, I'm thinking that's something I ought to know." He turned his head to the side a little, as if he suspected an untruth he might have to dodge, but it turned out he was the sort of person that knew how to embrace a lie with enthusiasm—and the bigger the lie, the more he wanted to hold it close to him.

I found this out when I said, "That fat fellow is this midget's manager, and he run off with money he owes him that Shorty was collecting for his midget wife to have her foot fixed."

"Her foot?" said the man. "What's wrong with it?"

"They aren't sure," I said. "But she's got to have it broke and set for a while, but even then she'll still have to wear some kind of special shoe so she can walk."

The man looked down at Shorty. "He stole your little-shoe money?"

Shorty nodded. "Yes, sir. He did. All of it."

"He took some of Shorty's clothes, too," I said. "I think he's planning on letting his monkey wear them."

"He has a monkey?" said the man.

"Two," I said.

"Aren't they pretty small?"

"My clothes?" said Shorty. "Or the monkeys?"

"The monkeys," said the man.

"Why, yes, they commonly are," said Shorty, getting into the spirit. "But these are some big monkeys, out of the jungles of Brazil. They are nearly my size and are known to be carnivorous."

"What?" said the man.

"They eat meat," said Shorty. "They could easily wear my

pants and shirts, and perhaps even my little boots, and eat you, too."

"That's a terrible thing for him to have done, taking your duds like that," said the man. "And planning on giving them to man-eating monkeys."

"My sentiments exactly," Shorty said. He dropped his eyes and let his lips droop and tremble a bit, like no sadder short man existed on earth.

"Well, he come through here. I was right here when he passed. If'n it's the man you're talking about. But I didn't see no monkeys."

"They wouldn't be with him," I said.

"No, sir," said Shorty. "They have been packed away somewhere and he is bringing the clothes to them. Once he has them suited up again, I think he is going to take them on the road. They have a little act, see. I was once part of that act, but we had a falling-out over my little wife, bless her heart. One of the monkeys bit her left pinkie finger off."

The man held up his left hand, then his right. "Least it was just one. Where is your wife?" He started looking around, as if we might present her to him.

"Back at the circus," Shorty said. "She does not travel well. Her little foot and all. My wife and I had been saving up for some time to have that foot fixed and booted out. But now we are without funds for either the surgical repair or the footwear."

The sawmill man nodded, took a swig of his whiskey. I thought I saw his eyes glisten for a moment. "Well, this fella was fat, all right, and he looked the worse for wear. White-faced and leaning forward a bit, like he had a bellyache."

"That sounds like him," I said.

"He come through going pretty fast, and working them old mules that was pulling the wagons harder than I think you ought to work mule or nigger. I don't work my niggers too hard. I try and keep them and the mules on the same level of work, you see. Steady but not abusive."

"That is mighty white of you," said Shorty.

"I see there's a nigger with you," said the man. "I got an opening he wants a job. It pays about half what a white man gets, and I'm the only one around here pays his niggers that good."

"No, actually," Shorty said. "He works for us. He is from the circus."

"He's too big to do flips, ain't he?" said the man.

"Yes," Shorty said. "Yes, he is. He cleans up and serves part of the time as a lion tamer."

"I guess a fella that would know a lion would be a nigger. And if they get eaten there's always another one out there that will need the work."

"They are very easy to replace," Shorty said.

"That big hog part of the circus, too?"

"He walks the high wire," Shorty said.

"That hog?"

"He is quite agile," Shorty said.

"If I was to string up a rope between some trees, could he walk it?"

"No," Shorty said. "He has to have a very taut wire, and he does not work without a net."

"Why's that?"

"Because he does not want to fall and strike the ground."

"Oh, yeah. I can see that. I know I'd want a net. Course, you ain't getting me up any higher than a footstool."

"About this fat thief," I said. "We would love to get that money back and buy that shoe."

"The monkeys can keep the clothes," Shorty said.

Turned out that fellow knew what everyone else knew. That there was a gang of ruffians down in the woods somewhere, and that a fellow named Cut Throat might be among them. We were of course playing it that Fatty was taking our money and joining in with them, and that they all planned to go into the circus business together financed by the money for Shorty's wife's little shoe.

"I tell you this," said the man. "I've heard about Cut Throat. I think I may have seen him come by, though I ain't sure it was. One of the niggers said it was. This fella, whoever he was, always had a mess of men with him, ten or twelve. And if he's down there and half of what I've heard about him is true, you might want to tell that midget woman she's just gonna be a cripple and that's all there is to it. Or you got to start back saving up your money again to buy that shoe."

"We'll keep that in mind," I said.

The exact place they were staying he didn't know, but he knew it was off to the southwest. He was about as helpful as spinning a bottle in the dirt and following where the mouth of it pointed. But at least he had seen our man Fatty.

As we turned and made our way back to our group, the sawmill man called out, "Hope that midget gal's foot gets fixed and you can afford the shoe, little fella. I'd give you something toward it, but I got to pay the niggers."

We accounted how this was understandable and wandered back to our posse.

Eustace, who had been eyeing us from a distance, said, "How'd it go? What was that about a shoe?"

"We told him you were a lion tamer," Shorty said.

"What?" Eustace said.

"You heard me," Shorty said. "And there was much to-do about man-eating monkeys and a shoe for a crippled midget woman."

"What the hell?" Jimmie Sue said.

"Your young man started it," Shorty said to Jimmie Sue. "And to tell you the truth, he was pretty magnificent. Course, it helped the man was half drunk and nearly all stupid. That said, we know only that Fatty came by and was seen. That wraps up our information."

Spot, I noticed, had suddenly turned toward inner thoughts. After a moment, he said, "Are there man-eating monkeys?"

"Of course," Shorty said.

We were well down the road by the time the heat of the day had burnt out and a bit of cool darkness had slipped in and the road and trees seemed to become as one with the shadows and the birds quit singing and began to coo in the darkness.

19

After riding a fair piece we found a narrow path cut in the woods and decided we ought to go down it and find a place to camp where we were out of main view. We couldn't make the path out very well at first, but our eyes adjusted to it better after we had been among the thicker trees for a while, and then the woods broke wide where more trees had been chopped down and sawed, most likely by the colored men from the sawmill some miles back.

We rode on through the clearing until we came to where the woods were wild again, and we nestled up within the pines and hardwoods for cover. We figured ourselves safe enough there, and it wasn't any time at all until we had the horses fed and watered and hobbled. We were too tired to eat and pretty much just fell out. I lay out in the open on my bedroll with Jimmie Sue, and Hog came and lay down by us.

I was nearly asleep when Jimmie Sue put her arm across my chest and brought her mouth close to my ear. "I wanted to grow up to be a princess, but instead I'm a whore. How did that come to be?"

"I guess you took a wrong turn."

"No doubt about that."

"I wanted to be a farmer and I've come to be a killer."

"We both missed our turn, didn't we?"

I put my arm under her neck and pulled her to me. "You're a princess to me, Jimmie Sue, no matter what turn you took. You asked what I wanted back there on the road, or words to that effect. And I got the answer. I want you."

"Tonight or forever?"

"I don't want you tonight, actually," I said. "I'm so tired I can't even take my pants off."

"That does mean something."

"How's that?"

"That you say you want me even with your pants on."

"Yeah. I guess so," I said. If Jimmie Sue said anything after that I didn't hear her, because I fell fast asleep.

I awoke in the middle of the night with a burning thirst and saw Spot was awake, sitting on the ground just outside the thick of the pines, between a jagged stump and a burnt spot where a stump might have once been. There were also some places where the stumps had been dynamited out.

I looked around and seen then that everyone else but Eustace was still rolled up in their bedrolls and the horses were quiet, and no one had swooped in on us to cut throats. I could hear Hog snoring next to Jimmie Sue. He may have been good in a fight and dangerous, but he wasn't much of a watchdog.

Now, as I said, I had been tuckered out in a serious way, but when I woke up I felt refreshed and a little eager. I felt good about Jimmie Sue. I watched her sleep for a few minutes. Her face was smooth when she slept and she looked even younger and less worn down and more pretty than usual. In sleep she was the princess she wanted to be.

My good feelings only lasted a moment, and then I started thinking about Lula. I thought of her dressed in an old rough shirt, men's overalls, and clodhopper boots, lying on her stomach looking at dewdrops on a blade of grass. When I came to get her, to call her for chores or to come in to breakfast, without taking her eyes off that blade of dew-dotted grass she would say, "Jack, all those little drops of water on the grass. If you were small enough, a little, little fish, that drop would be the same to you as an ocean." Being neither small enough nor a fish, I couldn't understand what it was Lula was getting at. Right then all I could think about was her, where she was now and what was being done to her, or had been done to her, and I felt a boiling sickness inside of me and it was all I could do not to scream.

I slipped out from under the stuffy blanket without waking Jimmie Sue, picked up my pistol, stuck it in my belt, trudged over to where Spot was, and sat down by him. He had built a small fire and was cooking up some coffee. He had the weapon that had been given him lying nearby.

"You know how to use that?" I asked him. I was talking softly, cause I didn't want to stir the others.

"I'm gonna reckon you don't mean the coffeepot but the gun," he said.

"Either one," I said. "I've had enough bad coffee this trip."

"The gun I'm no real good at and don't plan to use it. As for coffee, Shorty likes it too black, Eustace likes it too watery, Jimmie Sue don't drink enough to matter, and the sheriff don't care one way or another. So I got to make it how I like it."

"What about me?" I asked.

"I ain't considered on you much," he said.

"Thanks," I said.

"I mean I can't get no handle on you. I can't figure your ways."

"What on earth do you mean?"

"I mean I know your sister has been toted off, but I'm wondering what you think you'll be getting back."

"My sister," I said.

"Someone who looks like your sister," he said.

"You can't know that. I'm tired of hearing that from everyone. You can't know a thing like that."

"I guess not," he said. "But my Grandpa Weeden, he told me in slave days he got sold from his mother and father. Actually they sold his father off early on, when he was a runt, and then he got sold a few years after. He reckoned he was ten, but he wasn't entirely sure. Wasn't much paid for him, and the man bought him didn't really need him, but bought him because he wanted to separate the piglet from the sow, so to speak. Grandpa Weeden said he figured that's how it was and why it was, cause on the farm he saw how much this fella liked to pull a piglet away from a sow hog, how much he liked to hear that pig screech and that mama hog carry on. He liked that so much, he would get him a board and whip on that old mama hog. Then he'd throw that pig up in the air, over the slats in the pen, and let it fall down in the mud. He thought that was funny. My Grandpa Weeden said that was how he figured the man saw him, as a piglet he could buy cheap and take away from the sow and he'd just wean it and never think about where it come from."

"If you're talking about my sister being weaned, I'm sure she'll remember where she come from and how things were."

"That's the problem I'm talking about. She'll remember, all right, same as Grandpa Weeden, but there's just some places you can't go back to, and the remembering of them makes it worse."

The coffee water was boiling. I went to my saddlebag, got my tin cup out of it, and brought it back. Spot had his own cup, and he poured us some of his makings. It was good and dark, but not too bitter or too weak. It had a taste that was akin to the way it smelled, which ain't always the case with coffee.

I looked around, noticed Eustace hadn't come back. I said, "Where's Eustace?"

"I don't know exactly, but I seen him wander down there into the woods. I think he had a bottle with him, and I figured him pretty drunk on account of he had that drunk way of walking, like one foot was on high ground and the other one hurt."

"He's not supposed to drink," I said.

"You go tell him that," Spot said.

I shook my head. "Not me."

"Listen here," Spot said. "I'm gonna put a bite of beans to heat in a pan. You watch them while I go relieve myself in the woods. Only thing you got to do is stir them now and again, and don't let them scald."

"All right," I said.

He got the beans ready, gave me a big spoon, and went away into the woods. It was less dark now because it was near morning. Light was seeping in near the bottoms of the trees. There was one spot where it was golden and the light appeared to jump a little. I was watching that when Shorty came up.

"You have more beans?" he said.

"No," I said. "You got to ask Spot if he does. He'll be back in a moment. He's taking care of his toilet."

"Where is Eustace?" Shorty said.

"Spot says he thinks he has a bottle. Saw him wander off this morning, into the woods there."

"Damn. Got it in town is my guess. I thought I smelled liquor on his breath last night. He probably had a nip, woke in the night and had another, went off in the woods to finish it. That, my friend, is not a good thing. But I will deal with him . . . Jack, I will say this just once. What I said about true love. Maybe I am wrong. I watch how you look at Jimmie Sue and how she looks at you, and I have to say it seems more than lust."

"I think we are going to marry," I said.

"That might be carrying it too far, but I wish you luck and prosperity. Even if, when this is over, Eustace and I will own all your land."

Shorty grinned, stuck out his hand, and we shook. "Good luck to you, Jack," he said.

"Thanks," I said. "Considering your feelings on love and marriage, I got to take that as sincere."

"Right now it is sincere," he said, still holding on to my hand. "Ask me how I feel tomorrow."

He let go of my hand. I said, "I hate to spoil a good moment, but I have to go make water. Watch the beans, will you?"

"In love, but practical," Shorty said.

I gave him the spoon.

Like a moth, I started to where the sun glowed most. I walked on out until I was well in the woods, because I had more in mind than a watering. I got my pants down without dropping my pistol in the dirt, leaned against a tree, and took a mess right there. I wiped on some leaves, being careful not to gather up any poison ivy leaves in the process.

I finished my toilet, pulled up my pants, turned to look toward the brightening of the sun. That glow I had seen was still there. It seemed to be hanging between the trees even as the light grew bright. I walked toward it, sniffing the air, because now I could smell smoke. I could hear, too, a kind of crying. I pulled my pistol and went along quietly, using a deer trail so as to make less noise. The light I had been watching grew brighter, and it jumped a little. The smell of smoke was thicker, and there were thin snakes of it floating in the air. I knew then that it wasn't the light of rising morning I had seen but a big fire. The crying was still going on. My gun hand trembled. I could hear voices, laughing, and a kind of snorting sound.

I ducked low and crept along until I come to where I could hear the voices better and I could see the fire, if not its source. It was rising up high over a hill that was covered in brush and dropped off out of sight. I eased up to the brush, hunkered down behind it, and peeked through.

20

Below me there was a great fire built in a clear spot, and the logs had collapsed and flames were licking the last of them; most were already burnt into embers and ashes. Sunlight was breaking clean and heavy, and I was able to see better what was down there, though it all had a rosy haze about it from the fire and the rising sun. It made the dew on the bushes sparkle like tiny jewels.

The woods were cut open wide, and there was a small cabin. It was cruder than the trading post. It was flat-roofed and didn't have a chimney, but there was a metal stovepipe poking up out of it, and the smoke coming from it was black and greasy-looking. I guessed that was the cook fire, and the fire out front of the place had been where people had gathered and had light to see by. Considering the weather, it would have been a hot evening.

More peculiar was a black bear with a thick logging rope tied around its hind leg, the other end bound to a tree. I reckon the bear had about twenty feet of rope to go out on.

The bear wasn't anywhere near the fire or the cabin. It just sat still and snorted from time to time.

There was a crude log corral out back with horses in it. I counted them. There were twelve. That didn't mean there were twelve people, of course, as there could have been spare mounts, but it didn't mean there were only twelve, either, if you considered every horse had a rider and that some might have been riding double and there was a wagon without mules or horses pulled up in the yard. Starting out to the side and running alongside the cabin there was a narrow dirt road that ran into the clearing. It was a logging road, and fresh. I bet just a month before it had been nothing more than a critter trail, but now it was wide as a wagon and winding onto land that looked to have been cut down with Satan's own scythe.

But none of this held my attention as much as something else. Cut Throat and Nigger Pete had Spot down close to the fire, just out of reach of the bear. They had stripped Spot's clothes off and had been at his chest with a stick of burning wood. In fact, Cut Throat still held the stick in his hand. He was chewing tobacco and saying something to Spot I couldn't understand, and now and then he'd spit tobacco on him. Spot couldn't do anything back, because Cut Throat was sitting on his legs and Nigger Pete had hold of Spot's arms and had the back of Spot's head against his knee.

There were some other people down there, too, and they wandered up for a look at Spot, then wandered away. It was as if they had seen something curious, like a fly stuck in a jar of honey, and then grown tired of it. They meandered about the place, spitting and drinking from jugs and peeing off to the side of the house. One skinny, shirtless man, wearing overalls with one strap loose off a shoulder, was near the bear. He looked as if his nose had been borrowed from someone bigger, and he was the only one I seen wasn't wearing a gun. He was making dirt clods and throwing them at the helpless bear. When the first clod hit, the bear stood up and waved its paws and growled. The man laughed and threw more clods.

In that moment Spot looked up, his mouth open, crying heavily, and I can't honestly tell you I know he seen me for sure, but he was looking my way, and for an instant I think his eyes widened because I think he saw my face between a split in the brush, and for a moment his face softened, as if he thought I might be there to help him. He could have called out for me, but he didn't, and I don't know if that's because he didn't actually see me and I just thought he did, or was being brave and not wanting me to get caught, too, or if he just didn't have the juice left in him to make any noise. But I do know this. If he did think I was there to help him, I wasn't. Oh, I wanted to. But I couldn't. I just couldn't.

I was just a boy with a gun I didn't really know how to use, and down below was all of them, those monsters, and maybe I'm putting too fine an explanation on it, and not mentioning well enough just how scared I was, but the bottom of the creek is that I didn't do anything about it because I was afraid to. That ain't really an excuse, but it's all the one I got.

Spot turned his face away from me and looked slightly to the side in a manner that seemed to say I quit on this entire thing we call life. I just quit. That's when Cut Throat, having had all the fun he wanted, put down the burning stick and pulled a razor from inside that dead man's suit of clothes he was wearing, opened it, and very slowly, with the skill and precision of a barber shaving a pesky eyebrow hair, leaned forward and cut a deep wound in Spot's forehead. The blood didn't spray. There was just a line of a mark from the razor, and then in the now-bright sunlight that had risen above the tree line, the cut turned red and Cut Throat moved. Nigger Pete, as if he'd had the practice, tilted Spot's head back and the blood sprayed and Nigger Pete cackled like a hen that had just laid an egg.

Cut Throat stood, and Nigger Pete lifted Spot up so that his feet didn't touch the ground. Spot tilted his head to one side and closed his eyes and let his arms hang loose at his sides. Nigger Pete lifted him even higher and moved him toward the bear. The bear didn't seem interested. The man with the clods was still there, and now he knew how it was, and that caused him to giggle and get busy with leaning over and grabbing dirt, making and throwing clods at the bear that was now riled and had taken to standing on its hind legs. Cut Throat came in front of Spot, and the razor moved again, and then Cut Throat stepped aside. This time the cut struck Spot's throat, and there was the same queer delay, the red line, and then a spray of blood that went wide and far and splattered on the bear's face and beaded in its fur, the sun making the beads look like wet rubies.

The bear seemed reluctant at first, but the blood was hot and the bear was hungry. The bear came forward, and Pete pushed Spot toward it, causing him to fall face-first in front of the bear. I like to think Spot was already dead when the bear went at him. Except for being grabbed by the back of the head by the bear and shook like a rag and flung aside, there was never another move out of Spot that made me think he suffered.

A couple of men that had been wandering around in the yard, peeing and just strolling about, came over to watch the bear work. One of them nudged Spot with his foot, spoke up. "Now there's a little nigger done gone to heaven."

I felt in that moment as if I had come unstuck from life and that I was somewhere outside the real world, in some insane place where common decency and the laws of men were just silly things, like lace pants on a donkey. My eyes turned wet. My bowels went loose. I didn't know if I should move or stay still, and was uncertain I could do either. Then a hand came down on my shoulder.

"Stay quiet," said Shorty's voice.

I turned, saw Shorty behind me on his knees with his Sharps, starting to move backwards. I eased back with him until we were maybe twenty feet from where we had been, hunkered down under a wide elm. When we spoke our faces were as close as lovers and our voices were as light as the beating of a gnat's wings.

"Cut Throat," I said. "He . . ."

"I saw."

"I didn't do a thing."

"There was not nothing you could do. Nothing I could do. Spot saw us both, Jack. I was looking just over your shoulder."

"I didn't know you were there," I said. "I didn't do a thing."

"Was not anything you could do. Spot said not a word. He died game."

"I haven't any consolation in that," I said.

"I think he did."

Shorty got me by the sleeve and pulled me away, deeper down the trail and out of sight of the cabin. My legs wouldn't hold me after that, and I just sat down in the middle of the trail. The world was blurry.

Shorty hunkered down by me.

"He might have give us up," I said, "and we just don't know it yet. You don't know he didn't." I said that because I wanted him to have given us up. I wanted not to think he just looked at me and I looked back and didn't say a word and he stood brave and I sat coward.

"I believe not. They do not act like men that are worried or even mildly concerned about anyone else being about. I think he gave them a lie about himself and they took it."

"He just wandered off to shit, went too far, and they got him and hurt him and fed him to a bear," I said. "One moment he's cooking beans to eat, the next thing is he's being eaten."

"That is about the size of it," Shorty said.

I felt boneless, as if I might come apart and trickle away into a hole in the ground.

"What do we do?" I said.

"Gather our posse and surprise them. To be more precise, we shoot the hell out of them before they know we are coming. Eustace, however, may be a problem. I went looking for him and did not find him, and that is the way he gets when he drinks. He wanders and hides until it takes him over. When it does he is a wild animal. We should sober him up. We need his shotgun. How many did you make out down there?"

"Six wandering about, counting Cut Throat and Pete, but the horses and the smoke coming up from the cabin make me think there are more inside."

"Did you see your sister?"

I shook my head.

"She may be inside the cabin," Shorty said.

I nodded. "I can't believe what they done to Spot."

"Believe it, son. Come on, let us find the others."

We had gone back but a short piece down the path when we come across Eustace, drunk as a beaver at the bottom of a whiskey barrel and making enough tromping noise to arouse Cut Throat's men. He had the shotgun in one hand and the liquor bottle in the other.

"Hey," Eustace said when he saw us. "I been drinking."

"I can see that," Shorty said. "Eustace, I am going to need you to get quieter and become sober quickly, because we have come upon them."

"Who?"

"The killers and kidnappers," Shorty said.

"Oh, oh yeah, those fellas," Eustace said. He burped, lifted the bottle, which was a big one, and took a chug from it. It was nearly empty. When he lowered it, he looked around, said, "Have you noticed how many pine cones there are? I saw some under an oak tree. Why is that?"

"They roll with the wind," Shorty said. "It is a simple mystery. Now, listen to me, Eustace. Please. We will need to prepare a strategy."

"A what?"

"Prepare a plan to take care of the kidnappers."

"Hell, I got a goddamn plan," Eustace said. "Go down there and shoot their dicks off. Which way are they?"

"They have killed Spot," Shorty said.

"Spot?"

"He came out here to do what nature demands, must have heard them, or one of them walked up on him. Whatever, they got him and they killed him in a bad way."

Eustace looked at me as if this needed to be agreed on. I nodded.

"Little Spot? That can't be. He wasn't doing nothing to nobody. He wasn't bigger than a bump on a log. He was just riding with us. He ain't in on this."

"Nonetheless," Shorty said. "He is dead by their hands."

Eustace started to cry. Shorty grabbed him by the hand with the bottle in it.

"Come on, Eustace. We need to go back to our camp and get Winton."

Eustace ignored him, started walking in the direction of Cut Throat's camp.

"Dog fuckers," Eustace said.

"No," Shorty said, taking a firm grip on Eustace's arm. "No."

Eustace started trying to sling his arm free, but Shorty clung to it.

"What are you?" Eustace said. "A tick?"

"We need Winton and Hog, maybe Jimmie Sue," Shorty said. "We need all our guns."

Eustace was starting to get loud, and though we were some space from Cut Throat and his men, it wasn't so much it didn't worry me.

Eustace started swinging his arm, and Shorty swung with it, like he was tied to it. Then Eustace snapped his arm a little, and Shorty came free of it and rolled up under a pine tree, losing his hat and his rifle.

I ran and grabbed Eustace's legs and tried to take him down, but he wasn't going anywhere. Shorty was up now. He ran behind him, jumped up, and grabbed the back of Eustace's shirt and pulled him backwards. Between the two of us we took him down on his back. He dropped the shotgun but clung tight to the bottle of whiskey.

It was a short-lived victory. Eustace took a deep breath, sat up, and flung us both away from him, knocking me down the trail a ways, sending Shorty to roll back under that same pine tree.

"Damn it," said Shorty, picking up his hat and sticking it on his head again.

Shorty grabbed up a large stick, ran up behind Eustace while he was trying to stand, and hit him in the back of the head as hard as he could. Eustace was on one knee when he took the hit. He didn't budge, just turned and looked at Shorty.

"Shit," Shorty said.

Eustace rose up and loomed over Shorty like a mountain. The look on his face made me think he was about to take hold of Shorty and mash him like an accordion. Then, without the least bit of warning, Eustace toppled over on his back, somehow managing to keep that whiskey bottle in his fist. He lay there and didn't move.

Me and Shorty eased over to him. Eustace had both eyes closed. He opened them suddenly, making me jump. He said, "They got Spot?"

"Yes," Shorty said. "They finished him off."

Eustace sat up. He lifted the bottle to his lips and started swigging what little was left. A moment later he tossed the empty bottle aside and got up. He went over and picked up his shotgun, though it took him a couple of tries.

"You have to take it easy," Shorty said. "You are drunk as a skunk."

Eustace said, "I'm going to kill someone. I got lots of shells in my pocket. Some of them I'm going to kill twice."

I started to say something. Shorty said, "It is no use. He has got some of his sense about him, but not much of it is common sense. You go on back and get Winton and Jimmie Sue. Me and him will go down there and see what we can roust."

"No," I said. "I'm going with you."

"I am past arguing," Shorty said. "I cannot leave him, and we need the others."

It was decided for us. Eustace was already staggering down the trail toward the cabin. Shorty grabbed his Sharps and went after him, and I went after the both of them. There was part of me that figured I was walking right into the mouth of death, but I remembered those men back at the trading post, especially the one that had walked off and then come back and joined the others. They were trying to fix something about themselves, too. It didn't turn out too well for them, but now I understood.

There was a bit of good fortune, though. Eustace didn't sober up, but I think Shorty telling him Spot was dead brought him around a little, curbed his drunkenness. He stopped his shambling and started walking quietly and carefully, and before we got near the place overlooking the cabin, we all took to whispering.

Eustace ducked down with me and Shorty, and we worked ourselves up behind the brush on the hill and looked down on things. The light had gotten brighter. The same men were there to be seen, and another I hadn't seen before, a stubby guy with a raw patch on his forehead that looked as if someone had tried to scalp him but had been unable to finish the job, came out of the cabin and stretched and spat on the ground and looked at the sky to figure the nature of the day. He walked over and looked at the bear gnawing on what was left of Spot's body. He said something to the big-nose guy, who had returned to tease the bear. The bear wasn't paying any attention. It was chewing on Spot. The stubby man eased forward, got hold of Spot's foot when the bear wasn't looking, and yanked the corpse back and out of the bear's reach. The bear came at him, but the rope held it and caused it to fall. Stubby laughed. It was the kind of laugh a mean child might make seeing a friend trip and fall. The bear was pawing out at the body, but it couldn't reach it and instead scratched at the dirt.

I turned my head away and looked at Eustace.

"Poor little guy," Eustace said. He was careful to keep his voice down, but squatted there on his heels behind the brush he looked as if he might topple over any moment. There were tears in his eyes.

It grew more lively down below, so I turned back to look. That man with the big nose, who had been throwing clods at the bear, got him a long stick out of the fire and came over with it. The man who had pulled Spot away from the bear went over and leaned on a sapling to watch. Suddenly he seemed tired and looked to be getting over a drunk. He said, "Go on and stick him, Skinny."

The stick Skinny had was red on the end with heat. He started poking at the bear with it. The angered bear rushed to the end of its rope, trying to claw Skinny, but the little man, fast as a rat, would dart back out of the way, laughing, pulling the stick back with him. Now and again he glanced around at his comrades to make sure they were watching him, and then he would go at the bear again, poking him with that hot stick. I could smell the bear's fur being scorched from up there on the hill. The poor old bear looked tired and ready to fall over. It was thin and weak, pieces of Spot probably the only thing it had eaten in a while.

The man with the stick said, "You ain't so bad, now, are you, you dumb bear?"

Right then Fatty came out of the cabin. I couldn't believe it. He was still standing. He had on a blood-spotted white union shirt, too-small black pants that were unfastened at the waist and held up by a belt. He wasn't wearing shoes. He had on a gun belt and holster with a revolver in it, and a smaller gun was poked into the pants belt against his belly. He looked somewhat feeble, but considering all he had gone through he was surprisingly of sound nature.

After a time, another man came out; that cabin must have been stuffed tight as a full-grown hog in a tow sack. This man I hadn't seen before. He was tall and dark-skinned and had black hair that was going thin at the crown. He was wearing red long johns and an ugly face. He had on a gun belt with a pistol in it. It looked kind of funny, him in his drawers wearing that gun.

Eustace, all of a sudden, quit squatting and just sat down, kind of loud, but with that man down there yelling at the bear and the men starting to talk among themselves, he wasn't heard. Eustace sat there with his eyes closed, breathing evenly.

Shorty came close to my ear, said, "I will cause a disturbance, and I expect you to take advantage of it. Do not do a thing until I give you that disturbance."

"What about Eustace?"

"When I give you the signal, you poke Eustace, gently, and watch your head, because he might take it off with a fist. Poke him and say, 'Go down and get them.' "

"Will that work?"

"I do not know, but that is what I would try."

I didn't find this idea all that stimulating, but I didn't argue about it. All I could think about was what they had done to Spot and wonder if Lula was in the cabin. I said, "When you start this disturbance, and I tell Eustace to go down and get them, what am I to do?"

"Do you still want to take them prisoner?"

"No," I said.

"Then we are going to kill every last one of them," Shorty said. "If Eustace does wake up and goes down with you, I advise you stay out of the path of that shotgun. The blast from it does not sort friend from foe."

"You got to watch for Lula," I said.

"I know that. We need to kill everyone outside the cabin before they can get inside and hole up. And at the same time we have to keep in mind that there may be others inside with guns."

Shorty glanced down at the man tormenting the bear. "I cannot abide an animal abuser," he said. "Nor do I like the idea of our dead comrade lying down there without his pants and his head chewed on. It is time."

Shorty crept off then, crawling on his belly, dragging the Sharps along. He went low and quietly down the side of the hill on the left side, toward the big oak that the bear was tied to. The man with the stick was still poking at the unfortunate bear, cackling and giggling as if there couldn't be anything funnier.

"How you like that, you hairy old fart?" Skinny said, and turned and wiggled his ass at the bear. "You sure would like some of my ass, wouldn't you? What you get for killing my hunting dogs, you nasty piece of shit."

Eustace opened his eyes a little, his mouth, too, and then he closed them. I thought: Perfect. He will be as useless as tits on a boar hog.

Although I had a good view of Shorty as he crawled, he was at an angle and behind enough brush those down below couldn't see him. He inched down the side of the hill and shimmied up even with the tree. He stood up behind it, leaned the Sharps against its trunk, pulled out his knife, and cut the rope where it was tied. The bear didn't know it was free right away, but Skinny had gotten bolder and was running at the bear, stopping just short of where the rope would reach, poking at it with the stick, which by now had lost its heat, and this time the bear was able to swat it out of his hand. That didn't discourage Skinny. He began to prance at the bear, then prance back, teasing him, tucking his hands up under his pits and flapping his elbows like chicken wings. It was clear to see he thought he was entertaining, and was getting laughs from the others, who had now turned their attention on him.

He danced in another time, and the bear lunged forward, and then, as the man danced out, doing the chicken wings with his arms again, he came to the knowledge that the bear was still coming and the rope wasn't holding him back anymore and that an angry black bear can move fast on all fours.

When he realized it, he said, "Shit," and that was the last thing he said, cause that bear did three things at once. It came up on its hind legs, growled loud, and struck out with its paw. It caught Skinny upside the head and sent him reeling like an acrobat. He tumbled along the ground for a goodly distance and then flopped limply into the fire. His hair caught ablaze and his head did, too.

Cut Throat, who was near the front door, leaning against the cabin wall, hooted out loud. Nigger Pete, who was nearby, started laughing himself, along with the others, including Fatty, who had to hold his wounded stomach when he did. Their dead pal's demise was funnier than a puppet show until the bear came running toward them, dragging that rope. Their guns came out and they started firing, but if they hit that bear once I couldn't tell it. That bear was the distraction Shorty had given us. I reached out and grabbed Eustace's knee, said, "Go on down the hill shooting."

Eustace opened his bloodshot eyes and looked at me, and I tell you, I saw something in those eyes I've never seen before or since, and I'm comfortable with that. I pointed down where all the laughing was going on.

Eustace, without one ounce of sneak about him, rose up, plowed through the brush, and started downhill, toting that four-gauge like it was Excalibur.

The noise of the bear, the laughter, and all those gunshots had brought everyone out of the cabin, including two men we hadn't seen before, both of them stout boys carrying pistols. They were undoubtedly twins, and mighty ugly twins at that.

Eustace was halfway down the hill when he started up a hooting sound, like an owl trying to give birth to a watermelon-sized egg. I ran down there, too, going a little wide and to the right of Eustace. Out of the corner of my eye I saw Shorty coming out from behind the tree to the far left, where the bear had been tied.

Even with Eustace making that sound, and us in plain view, that bear still had their attention, as it had taken to running around out there in the yard in a confused and circular manner. The men were still firing at it with the same lack of success. The bear finally ran right through the middle of what I guess you could call the front yard, around the edge of the cabin, and galloped down the road fast as any horse, dragging that rope like it was a snake chasing it.

By this time we were on them. It was good we had gotten close, as Eustace had the shotgun and would need to be right on top of them, and, as I have said, my skills with a pistol are such that I might have been better trying to catch them individually and beat them to death with it. Shorty would be all right with his Sharps, though it was a slow loader compared to the pistols he carried.

Just as the bear made his exit and we were down on them, out the front door came Lula. She was wearing her same clothes, but they had gone ragged. Her fiery hair was bound up and had a pointed stick through it as a kind of twist-pin. She looked thin and haggard and a lot older than I remembered. Her looks wasn't something I could dwell on, though, because the ball had started.

21

Lula saw us about the time I saw her. She didn't seem to recognize me, but she realized I was toting a gun, and that led her to darting back inside the cabin. Fatty rushed inside with her.

The twins had moved to the side of the cabin to watch the bear's retreat and had just now figured we had shown up. They turned and started shooting at me at the same time I was shooting at them. Bullets were flying every which way, but after they fired six shots and I fired four, wasn't nobody hit on either side, though I felt a couple of bullets had come close enough to me that you might could have called us companions.

Now, I can't tell you all that Eustace done while I was trying to shoot one of those twins, but I heard his pistol popping, and when I glanced at him I saw he had the shotgun still in his left hand and had pulled his pistol and was shooting it at Cut Throat. I only seen two of his shots fire, because I had fallen down, a stray shot from either Cut Throat or Nigger Pete having gone low and clipped off my right boot heel. I fell on my ass, which was a good thing, because the next shot fired at me by Nigger Pete—who, I might add, was shooting crossways of Cut Throat—would have split my head open had that heel not gone out.

The two sin-ugly twins come running out at me then as I was firing from the ground my last two shots and missing with both of them. That's when Eustace dropped his pistol and wheeled the shotgun around on them, even as a shot from Cut Throat hit him in the shoulder. I heard the Sharps crack, and Nigger Pete went back against the outside cabin wall and made with a grunt. It seemed like a long time before Shorty made that shot, but you got to understand this was all happening fast, and frankly some of what I'm telling you I put together later, or realized in some part of my mind, but as you might expect, I was at that moment not concentrating on it.

Eustace's shotgun opened up, and those two twins danced a little in their spot as that bad buckshot tore through them. When the one closest to me turned, I saw his belly was gone and there was a hole the size of a baby's head in him. The other twin took some of the shot in the face. He screamed and grabbed at his chin.

I heard a noise behind me, a whooping sound, turned to see Winton on horseback come leaping out of the brush and down the hill, a revolver in either hand. He looked magnificent. I don't know if it was Nigger Pete or Cut Throat, but one of them shot him clean out of the saddle, mostly by accident, I figure, and then shot and killed the horse, which rolled over on Winton and then kept rolling.

I had snapped off all my shots, and so far I had managed to knock some bark off the rough logs of the cabin but had yet to draw any blood. I heard Shorty's Sharps snap and Nigger Pete yell something at him, but beyond that I was struggling to put shells from my gun belt into my pistol, me still lying on the ground as it were.

I got it loaded, but the ugly twin with part of his chin knocked off was still standing and was reloaded, too. He ran at me shooting, the bullets hitting around my head like raindrops. He got to where he wasn't fifteen feet away, yet he was still missing, not only because he was a bad shot like everyone else but Shorty, but because he was crazy over his brother getting blown away. By then he was right on me. I knew the only thing left for me were harp lessons and a set of wings, and that's when I heard Eustace cock back the mule-ear hammer on that four-gauge and cut down with it again. That twin went away in a spray of blood, the load in that barrel being a mite heavier than the previous and the shot managed from a closer position. My head rang like someone had mistaken it for a bell.

A little man who I hadn't seen before hopped out of the doorway with a pistol and fired. The shot knocked Eustace's hat off, and then a second shot hit Eustace, who acted like he had been stuck with a tack. I think the only reason he got hit at all was because he was a much bigger target than the rest of us, and though that may have also explained the horse, it didn't explain the bear. After the hopping man took that shot, he leaped inside the cabin again.

By this time I was loaded and Cut Throat had run into the cabin, damn near knocking the little hopping man down. Eustace was trying to get shells out of his pocket and load the shotgun. All of a sudden he sat down and then lay down; not like the shots had done him much harm but like the liquor had caught up with him.

I glanced at Nigger Pete, who was hunkered down and wounded, his back against the cabin wall. He was firing at Shorty but hadn't so much as landed a single shot. Shorty had the Sharps loaded again, fired, and hit Nigger Pete in the chest, a shot that would have killed a buffalo, but still Nigger Pete didn't die.

"You little bastard," Nigger Pete said, then stood bolt upright and started running at Shorty. Shorty dropped the Sharps and pulled his pistol and snapped off three shots. All three hit Nigger Pete because I could see the dust on his shirt powder up. This didn't drop him, but it made him turn and go for a run around the side of the cabin, moving fast enough to give that bear's pace a run for its money. Shorty started after him. I could hear him firing his revolver as he ran.

I sat myself up and fired at the hopping man in the doorway, snapping off shots as fast as I could. I missed time after time, and then he ducked back inside, out of sight. That's when a tall man wearing nothing but boots come charging out of the cabin right at me with a bowie knife. I guess he hadn't got the signal that this was a gunfight, and I had a sincere doubt this was his regular method of dress for such a ruckus, but when I fired at him, still sitting as I was, my chambers were empty.

Pulling myself to a crouch, I was going to try and ward him off with the pistol when out from the side, like some kind of white panther, came Jimmie Sue. She clung to that naked man's neck and yelled out, "Leave my man alone."

The naked man flung her off his back with a shrug, then come at me. That's when Hog come bolting from over the hill and leaped right at that naked man, seeming to fly. Hog hit him in the chest so hard it took his legs out from under him. The man tried to get up, but Hog got him by the leg and started shaking him about. Hog finally swung him loose, and before he could grab him again, the naked man stabbed out at Hog and caught him a good one behind the neck. Hog jerked away with a squeal, and in that instant, the naked man came at me again. I fought back, using my gun as a club. He cut at me at the same time I swung my pistol. My blow was just ahead of his knife, though, and I cracked him down the middle of the skull. Still, he cut me across the stomach.

I staggered back, holding my belly. Hog hit him again, right about the calf, coming at him like a cannon shot. It sent the naked man flying, and before he could recover, Hog dragged him off and out of sight into the woods, crashing him through the brush and him screaming like someone had run a weasel up his ass.

When my courage was up, I looked down at my wound. Amazingly, it wasn't bad. Missing the heel on my boot, I walked over to Jimmie Sue like a man with one foot in a ditch. She was crying. She went straight away to pulling up my shirt, expecting my guts to be hanging out. But it had only cut through my shirt and bit my skin a little bit. There was more blood than there was wound.

"Come on," Jimmie Sue said, and started dragging me away.

"I can't," I said.

"Come, come, come," she said, and pulled me over to Winton's dead horse, and jerked me down behind it with her. From there I could see where Winton had landed, and that the horse rolling over him had flattened his head and face considerably. Wasn't any doubt in my mind that he was dead as a post.

I handed Jimmie Sue my pistol because she didn't have one.

Later I would learn that when she heard the shots she had panicked and come running on foot, losing her weapon in the process. Hog had run after her. Anyway, I gave her the gun and the gun belt, pulled the Winchester from the saddle scabbard on the dead horse, laid the barrel over the dead critter, and pointed it at the door. I thought maybe I could hit something with a long gun, though that was mostly wishful thinking.

I could hear gunfire going on out back of the cabin. I could hear Nigger Pete cussing Shorty and Shorty cussing back. I lay there for a long moment, said to Jimmie Sue, "You stay here, or run for it would be better, but I got to go get Lula."

"You go in that cabin they'll shoot you to pieces," she said.

"I got to try. You know I got to try."

"Get Shorty first," she said. "I think Eustace is dead."

"No," I said. "He's drunk. But he's no good to me. He might as well be dead."

She pulled me to her and kissed me. I gave her the Winchester, too. I said, "You keep a bead on that doorway for me with that Winchester," then I took out my knife and, more easily than I would have expected, pried the heel of my other boot off so as to have even balance. I bounded up and made a run to the far left of the cabin, but in the process I stopped and picked up Eustace's shotgun and fished a handful of shells from his pocket.

Somewhere out back of the cabin, I heard Nigger Pete say clearly, "I been shot by a goddamn midget." He said this as if he just realized the other side was shooting real bullets, and then I heard a gun bang again. I kept running until I was at the side of the cabin, and I could look back there and see that Nigger Pete was sitting on a log, and he was hit bad. Blood was pouring out of him like rain out of barrel with holes in it. Shorty was standing ten feet away, snapping an empty pistol. Nigger Pete had a pistol in his hand, but he was having trouble lifting it. "Goddamn you, you turd of God," said Nigger Pete.

Shorty threw the pistol down and pulled the little gun out of his boot and started walking toward Nigger Pete. Nigger Pete finally got his pistol up, but by then Shorty had shot him in the head, causing him to fall back off the stump.

I took a deep breath and broke open the four-gauge, pushed the big loads into it, then looked to see if there was some kind of window on that side of the house. There wasn't. I began easing along the side wall of the cabin, holding the shotgun in front of me, realizing suddenly that this beast of a cannon might not only take out whatever bad guys were inside but might also kill Lula. I didn't have long to think on that matter, because I was halfway along the wall when the hopping man hopped out of the doorway with his pistol, said, "Aha," and Jimmie Sue shot him in the side of the head with the Winchester. He crumpled and started bleeding out.

"Aha," Jimmie Sue yelled out.

I glanced in her direction. She had her head raised up from behind the deceased horse. I nodded at her. She smiled and ducked down out of sight.

I was trying not to breathe heavy, but it was easier said than done. I was sure I sounded like I was a bellows trying to heat up a fire and that my heart sounded like I was banging on a drum, but something kept me moving toward that doorway. I could see that the hopping man had dropped his pistol and that it lay on my side of the doorway. I decided I ought to grab onto it so maybe I could manage to have something to shoot that might not take out the whole room, including my sister.

The thing against that, however, was my bad marksmanship. I decided on the pistol nonetheless.

My head was throbbing from all the firing, my ears ached so bad from all the gunfire I thought they might bleed, and the stench from the burning body of the bear tormentor was thick in the air, making the coffee in my stomach churn, and there was a taste in my mouth like spoiled buttermilk mixed with copper.

I got my mind back on my business, and just as I was at the doorway, reaching down to get the dead man's revolver, I heard Shorty yell out behind the cabin at Nigger Pete, "Are you not dead yet?" and there was another shot.

I figured that was a good time for me, since Shorty's voice and the shot might have put the ones in the cabin slightly off their game for a moment. I stepped through that doorway, the pistol in my right hand and the shotgun in my left.

22

I reckon they were waiting on me, but I think me actually stepping through that doorway bold as the devil took them a bit by surprise. The stubby fellow with the scalped head was standing right there, but he wasn't ready to act. His eyes went wide, like he had stepped on a snake, and he may have thought about lifting his weapon, but that was about as much thinking as he did. I poked the pistol in his chest and let a round fly. It killed him deader than a hammer.

Cut Throat grabbed Lula by the arm and dragged her out the open back door. I couldn't shoot at him for fear of hitting her. I hoped Shorty had him in his sights, but he didn't.

I was distracted for a moment, the wheels in my head turning in frustration, and as I was about to go out the back door after them, Fatty stood up from behind a pile of something or other and took a shot at me. I don't know if he had been storing up his courage or his strength while I stood there, but I had damn near forgotten all about him. His bad aim held. The bullet slammed into the cabin above the open door. I crouched down and fired the revolver wildly, two times. My luck was better than his. Fatty made a grunting sound and collapsed and lay on the dirt floor. It was dark enough in there that his shape was all I could make out, and now as I come nearer to him, my eyes getting used to the dark, I saw he was reaching for the pistol he had dropped. One thing you have to say for Fatty, he wasn't a quitter.

I tossed the pistol aside and lay down quick, right there on the floor, stretched out and leveled the shotgun against the dirt and stuffed the stock tight against my shoulder. Fatty had just reached his gun when I cocked back both mule ears on the shotgun. He looked up at me as he brought the pistol around, and I pulled both triggers. The world went red, then black, then white, and there were all these little dots moving around, and then Shorty was shaking me. I come to, my chin aching and my eye hurting like hell.

"You all right?" Shorty asked.

"Fatty?" I said.

"He is not so fat anymore," said Shorty.

I took a look. It was really messy over there. I hurt like hell, and that was because the shotgun had been too much for me. It had jammed my shoulder, and the stock had bucked and caught me under the chin, popped on up into my eye. The eye was swelling rapidly, but I could still see out of it.

"Cut Throat has Lula," I said.

"He has already taken horses and bridles, rode off with her, the both of them bareback. I was in the wrong spot when he came out, and by the time I saw them they were riding off."

Shorty stuck out his hand and pulled me up. He was strong

for a little man. Pain raged through me like all the fires of hell. "I'm going after him," I said.

Jimmie Sue had come in the front door, and she tossed the Winchester aside and run over to me, turned my face in her hands. "You shot?"

"Shotgun kicked," I said. "I got a small hole in my side, but it isn't leaking much. I got to go after Lula."

I stumbled outside, toward the corral. Jimmie Sue and Shorty came after me. The corral was open where Cut Throat had taken a couple of horses. Some of the other cayuses had run off, but there was a pony wandering nearby and still a couple in the open corral. Overcome with weakness, I leaned against one of the corral poles and took a breath. By the time I got some of my strength back, Jimmie Sue and Shorty had caught up a couple of the horses and bridled them, but didn't bother with finding saddles.

About that time I saw Hog come out of the woods, his snout a bright red from him having finished off the naked man. He looked happy for a hog. When he was up by Jimmie Sue, she reached down and petted him. There was a bit of blood on his neck where he had taken the knife, and there was some on his snout where he had been digging in his dinner, but otherwise he looked fine.

"Stay with Jimmie Sue, Hog," Shorty said. "You understand?"

I guess Hog did, because he sat down by her.

It was hard to do, my shoulder hurting like it did, but I pulled myself onto the paint, and with the two of us riding our mounts bareback we started out in the direction Cut Throat had to have gone. In front of us were miles of cleared timber. Cut Throat and Lula weren't even in sight.

* * *

We galloped down the wide wagon road side by side, leaning low to the necks of our horses, snot blowing back out of their nostrils and across our faces. Going along, the nature of the countryside changed. You could not only see the stumps, you could see where stumps had been set on fire and some had been blown out with dynamite, making small craters. I even saw that bear Shorty had cut loose. It was off to our right, back where the woods started up again. It was dragging that rope, heading out of the clearing and into the Thicket.

Way down the road there were two dark dots that looked like crickets, and the sun rose over them and threw their shadows long behind them. Because of the sun I had to squint, and when I did it seemed as if the crickets jumped, and when I opened them wide again I realized I was seeing Cut Throat and Lula on horses, and I got the impression, if not the true sight of it, that Cut Throat was slightly ahead and was leading Lula's horse. They weren't running full out, but they were moving briskly, and so were we. My guess is they were near a mile ahead of us and better mounted. Cut Throat had obviously taken the best horses.

I yelled out at Shorty, "Shorty, you got to take the shot."

He glanced at me, and I couldn't tell if he heard me or not, but I knew one thing for sure: we weren't going to catch up to them. Not on this day, not with our mounts.

I reined my horse to a stop and swung off its back. Shorty wheeled and rode back to me. He leaned forward on his horse and looked at me. "What in hell?"

"You have to take the shot," I said.

"What shot?"

"You know what shot I mean," I said. "It's clear enough here."

"They are a mile or more away."

Then what he had said came to him. He swung off the horse with the rifle, tumbling as he hit the ground. His horse bolted a little, but was too tired to run off. It just strayed off the road and started looking for grass among the stumps.

Shorty picked up the Sharps, which he had dropped, and ran forward until he came to a stump. He put one foot on the stump and looked at the riders.

He said, "It is much too far a shot, and the sun is in my face."

"Bullshit," I said. "Billy Dixon made that shot."

"So they say," Shorty said. "He did not have the sun in his eyes, though."

"You can make that shot."

"I am not positive Billy Dixon made that shot."

While he was talking he stretched out on the ground on his belly and laid the Sharps across the stump.

He sighted down it, said, "I think they have gone over a mile."

Sure enough, there wasn't much to see of them now; two specks like dust dots in the distance, and beyond them a line of green. If they got to the woods they would have plenty of places to hide, and there wouldn't even be a chance of a shot.

Shorty stuck his finger in his mouth then held it up, testing the wind. He said, "Do not say a word."

He stuck the Sharps stock tight against his shoulder and let out his breath, took in another one slowly, and kept sighting. He did this for what seemed a long time. Then he cocked back the hammer and cleared his throat. He readjusted himself and lifted the rifle higher. It was more like he was shooting at the sky than at them. I saw his body rise with a breath, and then the breath eased out, and when it did the shot came so quick as to make me jump. It seemed like a long time between the firing and the homing in of the metal pigeon, for it most certainly found its nest. It looked to me even from that distance that Cut Throat threw up his hands as if to praise Jesus, and at the same time the horse's feet collapsed under it. The horse went down, and Cut Throat rolled off of it and didn't move. The horse didn't move. Lula, having been freed of Cut Throat's grip on her horse's reins, rode on without stopping.

"The hell with Billy Dixon," I said.

Lula had ridden on without waiting and was out of sight altogether. We rode up on Cut Throat and his horse, cautiously, in case he was playing possum and it was the horse that had taken the shot.

I dropped off my horse and helped Shorty down, something I could see he resented. Examining Cut Throat, we saw that the shot had gone through his back, cutting him through the spine, about six inches above the ass. The shot had gone on forward and struck the horse in the back of its neck and traveled into the base of its brain, killing it as well as Cut Throat.

"I hate it for the horse," Shorty said. He looked at me, said, "I should also admit I was aiming for Cut Throat's head. The load had a lot more drop in it than I anticipated. Had he been another six to eight feet ahead of where my bullet found him, I would have missed."

"But you didn't," I said.

"Well, now," Shorty said, sitting down on a nearby stump, clinging to his horse's reins. "I am going to rest here while you find your sister. I think my horse is more blown out than yours."

I rode off then, looking for her. I rode for some distance, and after a time came upon her horse. It was sitting with its legs under it, its mouth open, bellowing air. It had worn out, crouched down, and quit. Lula was nowhere in sight.

I carried on, and finally I saw Lula walking up ahead. She was walking fast. I started calling to her, but either she didn't hear me or didn't care. She walked faster and faster, and finally she started running all out. She got tripped up as she went and fell down on her hands and knees.

Jumping off my horse, I yelled out, "Lula, are you all right? Stop. It's me."

I ran over to her. She turned and had a derringer in her hand. I guess she had picked it up and hid it in her clothes during the shootout. She shot me with it.

23

Damn it, Lula," I said. "You've shot your own brother." It was a solid shot to my knee, and it took the support out from under me. I dropped back and fell on my butt and cocked my knee up and cradled it with my hands.

She came over then, poked the derringer, which was a two-shooter, straight into my face. Her eyes looked like they were on fire. She cocked back the second hammer.

"I'm your brother, Lula. Jack."

Lula kept glaring down at me, the way a brat might before stepping on a bug. Then her face softened, seemed to slide around on the bone. She narrowed her eyes and licked her lips and her expression finally settled in one place. I guess my swollen eye and banged-up face and all the dirt I had acquired had changed my looks some. She tossed the derringer and dropped down and grabbed me and lifted my face and planted kisses on my forehead. I hugged her and kissed her tear-stained face, and then I, too, was crying. We cried like that for some time. Cried so much I forgot how bad my knee hurt. Remember what I told you about us Parkers? Once we let it out, we really let it out. So we opened the gates, crying and moaning and kissing each other on the head and cheeks, and just pretty much falling all apart.

Lula started saying, "Jack, Jack, Jack, Jack," over and over, as if she had just remembered my name.

It was a pretty long moment in time before I got up, and Lula had to help me. My knee hurt something awful. I looked up and saw Shorty was riding slowly toward us. He was leading Lula's horse, which had gotten some of its wind back.

Lula said, "A child on horseback?"

"A midget," I said. "But don't ask him to do circus tricks."

As we watched him ride closer, Lula, without looking at me, said, "I ain't as pure as I once was, Jack."

"Who is?" I said.

"All those men," she said. "They—"

"I have something for you."

I dug the necklace from my pocket and held it up for her to take. She looked at it, almost reached for it, said, "I can't, Jack. You got to keep it for now. I can't take it. A different girl wore that."

"You're just the same to me," I said, and slipped it over her head. Her expression changed slightly, but I couldn't quite figure it.

Shorty rode up and dropped off the horse.

"How'd you get up there without your rope ladder or a boost?" I said.

"With the assistance of a tall stump and considerable determination. So this is Lula."

"Shorty is the one that took the shot that put Cut Throat down," I said.

"And, unfortunately, his horse," Shorty said. Then to her: "You are a lovely sight, Miss Lula."

Lula had a weak smile for him. "I look much better cleaned up," she said.

"You look fine to me," Shorty said. "And just for the record, cleaned up I look pretty much the same."

Lula actually smiled. It seemed to be a smile borrowed from someone else; it didn't quite fit her face. But it was a smile. It melted like frost on a warm windowpane.

"I seem to have shot my own brother," she said.

When Jimmie Sue saw us, she ran out to meet me. Hog came loping out as well. I dropped off the horse, forgetting my wound to the knee, and collapsed. The knee was swollen up like a sausage stuffed too tight in a skin.

Hog got there first, nuzzled me like a dog. Jimmie Sue helped me to my feet. I took her in my arms and we kissed. Jimmie Sue had tears on her cheeks.

"I figured you had gone under," she said.

"No," I said. "I'm fine."

Lula swung off her horse, came around, and looked at Jimmie Sue.

"This here," I said to Lula, "is my fiancée, Jimmie Sue . . . what was the last name?"

"Forget it," Jimmie Sue said. "It's going to be the same as yours."

"That ugly beast right there," I said, "is Hog."

Jimmie Sue smiled at Lula. She said, "Come here, sister."

Lula did so, walking like she had two wooden legs. Jimmie Sue took hold of her and held her. Lula broke out crying again and damned if Jimmie Sue didn't cry with her. Pretty soon I was sniffling and had to walk off and leave them together so that I didn't turn into a blubbering fool again.

There isn't much left to say. Eustace wasn't dead, but he was shot up some. It had about as much effect on him as bug bites. When he was sober, he and Shorty loaded up bodies in the wagon, except for the burnt-up bear tormentor. Eustace got a bucket out of the cabin and made some scoops in the dirt with it and threw the dirt over the fire and the bear tormentor. It wasn't a very good job. Skinny's arm and hand were still sticking out, and one of his burnt-up feet. When Eustace finished his chore, his wounds began to bleed. One bullet had gone all the way through and hadn't hit anything vital, and the other didn't bury deep enough in him to cause any real harm. He was able to squeeze out the lead with nothing more than pressure from his thumb and forefinger.

Spot and Winton were put in the wagon, too, at the back of it, away from the riffraff. Shorty found blankets in the cabin and covered them, but not before Eustace found a pair of pants to pull on what was left of Spot. Nigger Pete wasn't where Shorty had left him. He hadn't been dead after all, and had crawled off in the woods a ways and died there. As his body was loaded in the wagon, Shorty called him a regular Rasputin, whatever that is.

I was sitting on a stump while the loading was going on. I could hardly walk. Lula cut my pants open to the knee to examine where she shot me. The derringer hadn't been much of a gun, fortunately for me, and Lula was able to heat up a knife and dig out the bullet. I near fainted a couple of times, but once it was out I felt considerably better and the swelling started going down right away.

It was late afternoon by the time Jimmie Sue came back

from our old camp with the horses and supplies we had left. The horses we chose to hook to the wagon belonged to Cut Throat and his gang and were obviously experienced with that sort of thing, and they pulled it well enough. I rode on the wagon seat with Jimmie Sue, and she drove the team. The others came along with the horses. Hog, of course, just trotted nearby as he always did, disappearing from time to time to do whatever it was he liked to do.

We picked up Cut Throat's body on the way out.

When it was all said and done and days had passed, there was some reward money out of Livingston and some out of No Enterprise—even some out of Hinge Gate, though there wasn't any kind of overlap. The government didn't play that way, and though those towns promised us payment, there was none forthcoming immediately. We ended up having to travel over to Tyler, which was the county seat, to get things straightened out on full payment. While we were there we saw lots and lots of motorcars, as if they had bred overnight like fly larvae and grown up to honk horns and run on gas; the world seemed to have changed in the short time we had been manhunting and chasing the bounty.

We did eventually get paid, and me, Shorty, Eustace, and Jimmie Sue shared the reward money. I signed over the land to Eustace and Shorty, like I promised, but that event went a direction I didn't expect.

Before I explain that, though, I will say we ended up putting Winton in a cemetery in No Enterprise. We paid for the burying, as none of the townspeople wanted to chip in. Spot was buried on Grandpa's old property, out under a nice spreading oak. We got both Winton and Spot a stone for their sites with their names on them, though we never did learn Spot's last name, because I wasn't sure if the Grandpa Weeden he mentioned was his mother's father or his father's father. I just had to have SPOT carved on the stone. We didn't even know when he was born; we only had a blank there and the date he was killed.

As for Grandpa, his body was never found, but we put him a stone next to Ma's and Pa's graves on my property and let that stand in his place, though I often dreamed of him down there at the bottom of the Sabine River, caught up in weeds and being nibbled on by catfish. Sad as I felt about that, I never did forget he had been one of Jimmie Sue's clients, and that he had spent a lifetime telling me how righteous he was. I didn't never put flowers on his grave, but Lula did. Then again, neither me nor Jimmie Sue ever told anyone our information about his whorehouse activities, and this is the first time I've mentioned it openly. I'm either tired of holding that secret or I just don't care anymore. Truth be told, I'm not sure which it is.

I was saying how I signed my property over to Eustace and Shorty, but I should add they wouldn't accept all of it, us all having grown tight together there at the end, having sealed a friendship on the day of the shootout with blood and gunpowder. They made it so I got a deed to Ma and Pa's old place, and they split Grandpa's between them, finding different ends of the property to build homes, which in time they did. Nice enough places, I might add, though Eustace's house smelled funny on account of Hog was always laying up in it. Shorty sold off his previous bit of land and house to a fellow from Oklahoma.

When I rebuilt on Ma and Pa's land, it wasn't where the old

house had been but in a place far from there. I always associated smallpox with where my folks were buried, and I didn't want anything to get planted there lest that old disease might come up from the ground to find me and finish off what it missed out on. We let that spot become a family cemetery, though at that point in time the only other ones we expected to be buried there were me and my sister and the woman who became my wife, Jimmie Sue.

It wasn't any time at all until oil was discovered on that land Eustace and Shorty had split up. Oil was found right on the line of their properties, and it led to some good humor among the two, and considering on how much money was brought in by that well I can see why they were amused. There was some chance there was more oil there, but that's the only well they let be drilled, because the both of them decided they'd rather keep the property rich in trees and farmland. Lot of folks found this odd.

Before the oil was discovered, another peculiar thing happened. Shorty took to visiting Lula at our new house, and in a few years they went into Hinge Gate, which of course by this time was well past any kind of smallpox, and got married by a judge at the courthouse. Shorty told me he married her not only because she was lovely and appealing and they got along and liked to talk about stars and dewdrops and such but also because she was more than willing to hold his hand no matter where they went. He was certainly a might older than her, but by this time she was full into her adulthood and had a mind of her own. I liked the way they looked at one another.

Eustace didn't marry; said he couldn't get along with anybody that had to stay with him all the time. That didn't keep him from coming to see us right regular, and we had a number of fine holidays with him and Shorty and Lula.

Hog aged out and died. Eustace himself died after falling off a wagon and having it roll back over him, breaking his neck. Some said he was drunk, but I don't believe it. I think he told it true when he said he would never take another drop. He was the richest colored man in our county. He left what he owned to Jimmie Sue and me, and that included his land and house, half of the oil well, and that old four-gauge and a fistful of loads. That made us rich as Midas overnight and gave us a formidable weapon, though after my experience with the four-gauge I never wanted to fire it again, and to date I haven't.

Shorty and Lula had a child named James, and he grew up to be normal height but looked just like his daddy. A handsome fellow, a fine nephew, I must say. I expect he'll grow up and be something special someday. As for all that travel Shorty talked about, except for a trip to a world's fair up north in a brand-new motorcar with Lula and his son, Shorty never went anywhere outside of East Texas again. He didn't seem to mind at all. The travel books got put away, and I never saw him reading them again. He built a tower on the highest part of his land, and at the top of that tower he put a telescope. Not the old one but a new one, a more powerful one. In bad weather he covered it with an oilcloth.

It was there some ten years later that Lula found him. His heart gave out; he died too young, though he wasn't any spring chicken. He was sitting in a tall chair, the telescope in front of him. He had been looking at the stars. I hope his eye had been on the lens when he passed on, and that his last sight was of Mars.

There's more to tell about Lula and her son, and how me and Jimmie Sue had children, a son named Lucas and a daughter named Lula, after my sister. But it doesn't fit here. I also want to say that all I've told you might not be the perfect truth, but it is the truth as I remember it. As Jimmie Sue says, you don't always remember it so much the way it was as how you thought it was.

Not long after Shorty died I got to considering on the adventure we had together, and how we saved Lula, and how her life turned out to be better for having met Shorty. I thought about that great and impossible shot he had made. It was a shot that had not only saved her from Cut Throat, it had brought Shorty and her together. One night, thinking on all this, I decided to take my new Ford motorcar and drive over to Shorty's telescope tower.

I came to the tower in the late dark, climbed the ladder up. Once at the peak, I sat in Shorty's special chair in front of his telescope. I sat there not moving for a while, then, careful not to budge his settings, I put my eye to the lens of his telescope and looked out at the velvet-black night sky that was riddled with stars; the view seemed to fall right through that scope and into my head.

I looked for a long time at the stars, thinking about Shorty and him telling me about reading a book about a man who spread his arms and went to Mars, or at least some part of him did. I thought it might be nice if that happened to Shorty. That his spirit had gone to Mars. Then I realized he didn't want that anymore. He was happy. And though he never did come to believe in God, I think he did come to believe in love.

I watched those stars and the blackness between them, and had a kind of funny thought. It was that my old idea of God and heaven, harps and angels, was too small for all that I was looking at, and that the black out there, the stars spotted on it, belonged to something bigger and harder to explain than God. I have to tell you that right then was the first time I felt I was truly part of something stranger and more wonderful than I had ever imagined.

It was a thought that didn't bother me at all.

Joe R. Lansdale is the author of more than a dozen novels, including *Edge of Dark Water, Vanilla Ride, Leather Maiden, Sunset and Sawdust,* and *Lost Echoes*. He has received the Edgar Award, the American Mystery Award, the British Fantasy Award, the Grinzane Cavour Prize for Literature, and nine Bram Stoker Awards. His novella *Bubba Ho-Tep* was made into a film starring Bruce Campbell and Ossie Davis and directed by Don Coscarelli. His short story "Incident on and off a Mountain Road" was also made into a film; it stars Bree Turner and was directed by Don Coscarelli for Showtime. Lansdale lives with his wife in Nacogdoches, Texas.